DESCRIPTION OF A STRUGGLE

DESCRIPTION OF A STRUGGLE

The Vintage Book of
Contemporary Eastern European Writing

EDITED BY
MICHAEL MARCH

VINTAGE BOOKS
A Division of Random House, Inc.
New York

FIRST VINTAGE BOOKS EDITION, DECEMBER 1994

This collection and preface copyright © 1994 by Michael March
Introduction copyright © 1994 by Ivan Klíma

All rights reserved under International and Pan-American Copyright
Conventions. Published in the United States by Vintage Books, a
division of Random House, Inc., New York. This collection was
originally published in hardcover in Great Britain by Picador, a division
of Pan Macmillan Publishers Limited, London, as *Description of a
Struggle: The Picador Book of Contemporary East European Prose*, in 1994.

Library of Congress Cataloging-in-Publication Data

Description of a struggle : the Vintage book of contemporary Eastern
European writing / edited by Michael March. — 1st Vintage books ed.
p.   cm.
"Vintage original"—CIP info.
Also published under title: Description of a struggle, the Picador book of
contemporary East European prose.
ISBN 0-679-74514-9
1. East European prose literature—Translations into English.
I. March, Michael, 1946-
PN849.EP2D47   1994
891.8'08—dc20   94-27166
CIP

Manufactured in the United States of America

10   9   8   7   6   5   4   3   2

FOR MY PARENTS

Contents

Contents

Contents

Contents

Contents

Contents

Contents

Contents

RUSSIA

Editor's Acknowledgements

I am grateful to the translators, for sharing their poetry.

I especially wish to thank James Naughton, Michael Molnar and Jarosław Anders for their friendship.

Dušan Puvačić guided former Yugoslavia. Vallery Tchukov delivered Bulgaria.

Ivan Klíma listened, and gave us his *voice*.

As for the writers: 'You broke my will, but what a thrill.' Shades of Nietzsche in Memphis.

Michael March
London,
December, 1993

Preface

The Czech philosopher Jan Patočka said, 'It is morality that defines man.' But man has been ill-defined for a long time. Marx stood Hegel on his head: 'They know, yet they do.' In the wake lies Eastern Europe, which has appeared as a lost continent for over forty years.

Eastern Europe has its attractions. It gives us none of the affirmations so eagerly sought by politicians. Its literature remains *unhealthy*, despite the fall of the Berlin Wall. As Dostoevsky mused: 'Only those burdened with a common affliction understand each other.'

I stole the title *Description of a Struggle* from Kafka, who wrote: 'The thing that pleases me the most about the short story is that I have got rid of it.' I wished to preserve his sense of *timing*, his black-hole metaphysics in an anthology that clearly shares his weapons. I have tried to capture the delinquency of authors whose interior designs inevitably landscaped the times.

I have gathered what I have *heard*. Forty-three resident authors were chosen from the territories of Eastern Europe, whose once smug borders now resemble collapsed lungs. For those who wish to debate the location of Eastern Europe, turn to the *New York Review of Books*. For those who think that communism is dead, locate and consult Danilo Kiš, who will object.

'The roads that do not promise their destination are the loved roads.'

Michael March

INTRODUCTION

Writing from the Empire behind the Wall

Description of a Struggle is, of course, a title borrowed from Franz Kafka, from a man who, if he had somehow not died prematurely and then survived the Nazi slaughter, would have found himself behind the Iron Curtain, behind an impenetrable wall of bricks or electrified wires, in a world which people began to call (how this Central European would have been amazed) Eastern Europe.

I opened Kafka's text, which I last read a quarter of a century ago, and was struck by a sentence I had marked at the time. It says: 'You're incapable of loving, only fear excites you.' Like many of his other statements, this one, doubtless, stems from harsh introspection but, like many of his words, it seems to capture brilliantly the moral climate of today. We are in danger of being excited solely by struggles to the death, by stories of dreadful bloodshed.

This anthology comes from a world habitually called Eastern Europe, though it would be more precise to call it the Soviet realm, the Empire of Stalinist tyranny, the Empire of great illusions, of broken dreams for a better world. For me, it is the Empire behind the Wall. Reagan called it the Evil Empire, which might make one conclude it was the Empire of a single, basic struggle. For in few other places did the struggle between impersonal power and the individual, between tyranny and the desire for a worthwhile life, assume such visible form as here, where fear became a daily companion, where tragedies were played out with bloodshed.

Describing the 'basic struggle' in its most visible form had a great lure for many writers: in Solzhenitsyn this theme turned into an almost elemental conflict between good and evil. I allow myself to say this, because I, too, was attracted by this idea for a while. I remember working on my novel *Judge on Trial*. It was a time when I was often called for interrogation (more humiliating than cruel), when I suffered a house-search lasting several hours (again, more humiliating than thorough). The political situation seemed hopeless. Power, including media control, was in the hands of men installed by Moscow. Lies and pretence dominated public life, as in all Soviet-bloc countries. There was virtually no opening for voices of criticism or disagreement. I felt the need to embody this situation in my novel, to express my disgust with the system, which I viewed as a dumbly arrogant force of destruction. After I had written the novel, I was summoned for interrogation again. It was in a grey room, impersonal like all such rooms from Vladivostok to Sofia to East Berlin (long after Stalin's death and official condemnation, his portrait would often hang in such rooms), and I was told that I had written an anti-state document, and if I tried to disseminate it, charges would be laid. I managed to smuggle the manuscript to Switzerland. A year later, a translation was published in West Germany, while copies of the work circulated at home. No charges were brought, indeed they never even mentioned the novel again, life went on unchanged. As time passed, I realized I had to rework the novel. I had been trapped by my theme, enthralled by a loveless world, ruled by malice, knavery and fear, where the struggle for human values happened only on the most obvious level. Once we are fascinated by our adversary, even if only to reveal him, we draw him into our own world, we give him undue respect. After all, even in this so-called Evil Empire, people achieved self-fulfilment, simply by refusing to admit this evil into their scale of values. I realized I had succumbed to that age-old simplification, which sees everything dualistically, as a clash between good and evil, the powers of God and Satan. But writers, I was increasingly convinced, should reach under the surface of things, their picture of the world should embrace more than the vision of politics.

Nevertheless, the bipolarity of a world divided between two superpowers reinforced and made this view easier; in doing so, it closed off paths to a multi-dimensional view of human destiny.

Once in the early eighties, I was visited by a Canadian writer who was writing a play whose setting was to be either my country or one of its neighbours. He had a plot all worked out, in which courageous freedom fighters struggled desperately with the police. He wanted to hear about police brutality. I knew he would be glad to hear how I was tortured under interrogation, or at least beaten up. He wanted me to confirm his expectations, but I wouldn't, and he left disappointed.

The Empire where I lived (where the writers of this anthology lived) was much more complex from the inside than it looked from without. Even the sufferings were quite different from those modelled from a distance by my Canadian colleague. Moreover, the Empire changed, with the character of the dictator or his local boss, changed as the Empire slowly disintegrated. Time blunted the brutality of the revolutionary era: the rule of fanatics, ready to murder in the name of an idea, was followed by the rule of bureaucrats (though often police bureaucrats), who established some kind of ground rules, which allowed most people to adapt and carry on with their lives.

It is interesting how even good writers succumbed to this simplified view, when they observed these goings-on from the outside. This anthology shows how writers 'inside' were generally resistant to a bipolar vision. Their world is not overrun by corrupt Party secretaries, members of the secret police, or unwavering dissidents: it is full of ordinary people, loving and hating each other, committing rape, suffering, dying, waging pointless wars; here (as everywhere) trees blossom in spring, sons love their mothers, husbands long for a mistress; here (as everywhere else in the world) there are rogues, saints, eccentrics and lunatics, but most people have their ordinary joys and worries, prepare weddings or pig-slaughterings, some get drunk, others have higher aspirations, seeing that even in situations outwardly lacking in liberty those who try may find a good deal of freedom, while others go through life as a witness observing the strange theatrical spectacle offered by an existence full of paradoxes. (People outside have often read about opponents who were put in mental homes. In one of the stories, readers will find such a place described as 'an ideal environment' characterized by 'peace and absence of fear'. Yes, this too is a way of expressing the paradox of life behind the Wall.)

These authors' fictional worlds are sometimes very physical – at other times metaphysical, real, fantastic, serious, grotesquely deformed, with occasionally a flash of apocalyptic vision. (Can anyone who reflects responsibly upon the future of civilization not see its fatal trends?) Their worlds are as rich and varied as the company of creators assembled in this anthology.

For Michael March has produced a unique anthology. This collection presents contemporary authors, many young, some well established, some familiar to me, others previously unknown. But all lived under the system of the Empire. In so far as there is a common bond, it is this experience of totalitarianism: the system forced people to live a lie, to profess what they did not believe, disallowing what they wanted to believe. Their suffering did not have to be physical, it did not have to be caused by hunger or a prison cell, just by the fact that day after day (without visible hope of change) people listened to defiled words, witnessed the falsifying of history and the present (the system's underhand efforts to divide the world and people), saw the awarding of privileges to the least capable, while the able and talented were rejected.

What was the lot of writers in this Empire? What was the attitude of rulers to writers? Although I shared for years the lot of a banned writer, I would not like to take a simplified view, especially in retrospect. It is true that the system took a crudely ideological view of art. Art was viewed as an instrument for educating and influencing 'the masses' (one of its favourite terms), a means of propagating its own ideas. Its attitude to the artist was manipulative, insensitive, often cynical. In the worst times, opponents of this view were killed or imprisoned, later they were 'merely' banned. On the other hand, the ideology which the system (at least initially) believed in, was an odd mixture of nineteenth-century rationalism and romanticism, incorporating something of that century's attitude to artists. As a result, the rulers tended to exaggerate the importance of the written word, they accorded great respect to the person of the artist, and felt a need to possess their own recognized figures. At a time when the celebrity of pop singers and tennis stars had long since eclipsed that of famous writers in the West, the ideologues dreamed of finding, or even creating, then decorating with titles, their own Tolstoy or Dostoevsky, or at least a Turgenev, for which they were willing not only to use violence, but also to lavish wealth and favours upon their chosen ones.

What about the attitude of artists to the regime? It, too, passed through a complex evolution. The illusions about a rationally planned society, in which poverty would vanish, and the arts would become vital to the broadest masses, were shared by numerous artists (indeed, still are shared by many intellectuals). Only the repeated shocks, show trials, firing squads, and the bitter experiences of censorship, which steered artists towards reflecting life not as they saw it, but life as the rulers of the Empire wished to see it, finally led to disillusionment and an ever-growing chasm between artists and political power. At the same time, it is undeniable that the system often retreated and made compromises. Many outstanding works of literature saw the light of day in this fashion.

As the gulf between the arts and political power widened, artists, especially writers, began to enjoy growing favour with the public; on publication days long queues would form in front of bookshops from the early hours, banned writers' books often circulated in hundreds of typewritten copies. Here, too, people often speak of the extra-literary function of literature beyond the Wall. Literature did frequently take on the functions of journalism or politics. This was not because it dealt with political themes – it was simply that in situations where civil or basic rights are suppressed, many forms of expression become political: unconventional language, a love story with no ideological message, historical writing with heroes other than those officially recognized, a critical picture of the ailments of civilization or moral problems which the regime refuses to recognize, for it insists that everything which somehow complicates life is a throw-back to the old era.

Asked once why Kafka was banned in his own country, I replied: 'Because he was too genuine.' My answer was taken as a joke, but it was meant seriously: anything genuine threatens a world built on deceit, in the Empire behind the Wall it became political discourse. Right until the end, regimes continued to react vitriolically to any such 'political discourse', persecuting and victimizing obstinate artists, putting them in mental hospitals or prisons, but mainly just sidelining them, forcing them to adopt another livelihood. This frequently subjected writers to experiences they would never have had in a free society.

Deep experiences do not make a great writer, but I am convinced that great literature seldom arises without it. Even pure fantasy needs to draw on real life, otherwise it is lifeless and forced. I have often thought that what this Empire deprived us of in terms of freedom, it returned to us in the form of experience.

I am not suggesting that such experiences create a wall between the writers of this anthology and its Western readers. On the contrary. The anthology not only demolishes the language barrier, opening up unknown spaces of 'little' and little-known literatures, presenting new talents, it also bears convincing witness to the fact that we live in a single world with similar problems, albeit some of them may have taken on sharper edges behind the Wall and so exhibit truths which might otherwise elude us. Nevertheless, the real struggle, be it between good and evil, life in truth or life as a lie, life as universal order or being in nothingness, takes place as Kafka saw it: within every one of us. That is the struggle which truly fascinates a writer.

Ivan Klíma

Translated from the Czech by James Naughton

Serbia, Croatia, Slovenia

Bora Ćosić

Russians By Trade

In 1936 Ivan Ponomaryov, a bandleader, went berserk and murdered four members of his band, and then hanged himself. The same year Yasha Sevitsky, an unemployed engineer, built a stove that would burn worthless, useless stuff – that is, shit. The Russian Cossack general Pavlichenko, in utter defeat, fled from the Soviets into our country, on a horse, and gave lectures about it all; the horse died later. At about the same time Lidia Przhevalska, for whom another horse was named, from the nature study course, fell under a streetcar, because her nerves were frayed. All these events happened in our country, and yet they were carried out by foreigners, members of the émigré community – Russians. Grandpa protested: 'They're all we need!' We had two names for all the bugs around the house: the black ones we called 'Krauts', and the yellowish ones 'Rooskies'; the Krauts were always bigger.

I had friends named Rudika Froehlich, David Uziel, Isaac Abinum, and so on, but there were other ones, too, like Nikita Gelin, Lonya Bondarenko and Igor Chernevsky; this last one wore glasses. Nikita Gelin had a woman's blouse that buttoned on the side. At his house we drank tea out of a saucer; Mum said: 'Heaven forbid!' but I thought it was great. I called Nikita by his name; everybody else called him 'Roosky goose!' My friend Igor Chernevsky showed me a notebook; in it someone had written: 'I might kill myself!' I asked: 'Is that out of a novel?' He said: 'No, it's out of here!' and pointed to his heart. Then he asked me: 'Haven't you ever thought of killing yourself?' I answered: 'Never!' My friend Igor Chernevsky walked along the ledge outside the sixth floor with his arms outstretched. His mum fainted. Voja Bloša admitted: 'I wouldn't dare!' Lonya Bondarenko's mum wore big hats, frightful brooches, and dresses that were really gaudy; Grandpa said: 'She'll

3

poke somebody's eyes out with those pins!' My aunts admired her style, but still they declared: 'A dog wouldn't have anywhere to bite her!' Lonya Bondarenko's mum suffered from a great shortage of money; all the same, she smoked through a long cigarette holder and was always saying: 'Ooo-oo-oh-h!' which was the best Russian word of all. My aunts asked her: 'Is it possible we might some day see the famous and handsome Nijinsky who dances *Swan Lake* and is crazy?' Lonya's mum only smiled, sadly, and immediately started explaining how to make butter by shaking spoiled milk. We marvelled at all this, but Mum later said: 'If she just weren't so vain, and besides, she never takes a bath!' My aunts objected: 'Russians are very fine people, like Mr D. M. Kuzmichov and his sons, the tea merchants.' Dad got carried home by a baggage porter and put down on the couch; he mumbled something and smiled, gently. Grandpa declared: 'He's dead drunk!' but Mum put it differently: 'He's drunk as a Russian!' My aunts asked: 'When are we going to hear Olga Yanchevetska the Russian café singer perform with a flower in her hand?' Mum replied: 'We don't need anybody else hanging out at those joints!' She was referring to my dad, of course, which everybody understood right away. My uncle explained: 'I know Miss Yanchevetska-Azbukin personally, and also a lot of girls she teaches who sing excellently in Russian even though they're from our country!' My aunts told him: 'Nobody can keep up with you!' My uncle brought home a little book called *Zosya, the Pretty Russian Girl*; it had a lot of drawings that were excellent but absolutely forbidden. My friend Isaac Abinum stated: 'I think Russian women know how to take their clothes off better than anybody in the world!' There was another forbidden book: *The USSR in Words and Pictures*, which showed a big tank going over a little Finnish house; my aunts kept this book behind the stove; because of this the tank was a little yellowed. Then Lonya Bondarenko's mum offered to make us a lampshade, an amazing gadget for lighting up an area very cheaply. Grandpa concluded: 'That's so you don't see how dirty their place is, since it's half dark!' While the film *The Mannerheim Line* was being shown, an usher came out holding a flashlight and said: 'Don't anybody shout "Long live the Russians!" or you'll get arrested right away!' In the same film, when

Finland was being liberated by big Russian tanks all the Russians were in white lab coats and were very large, but the Finns were quite small. Of all the Russians in that film the one I liked best was Joseph Stalin, who was always smoothing down his moustache as if he had just eaten. I thought everybody in Russia had a moustache and ate food that was rich and greasy. Stalin also smoothed down his moustache during the best newsreel in artificial colour, with Mr Ribbentrop, a German general who came to Moscow to shake hands with all the Russians. Grandpa warned me: 'I'm not going to let you watch that nonsense!'

Then Lonya Bondarenko's mum tried to plant a love in us for raising flowers, which we didn't need then. She also showed us a thick book called *Vegetable and Flower Gardening* by L. Muratov, which said: 'The blossoms are blue. They blossom in June!' Right away my aunts said: 'That's a poem!' My mum said: 'What I care about is having spinach and leeks to feed my child – forget about your chrysanthemums!' Lonya Bondarenko's mum found a picture in the book entitled 'Pearl Leeks' and pointed it out, but my mum stuck to her opinion. Lonya's mum finally said: '*Nichevo!*' and it ended there.

Right at that time my aunts learned to perform two Russian songs, to a guitar: 'Those Green Eyes of Yours' and 'East and West Are Red', both sung while crying. Grandpa asked them: 'You have a pain somewhere?' The way I understood it all Russian singing signified some ailment, like a cold or maybe worse. Every time Mum told the depressing story of the Russian countess who was seduced by the cavalry junior sergeant and jumped in front of a train, she would say: 'Life is sad, especially for women, Russian women!' Undoubtedly this was out of some book, too. My uncle asked: 'Then why do you throw Mrs Bondarenko out when the woman wants to show you how to crochet?' Mum replied: 'What's it to you?' Afterwards she told him: 'You want to catch some Russian disease!' but nothing like that happened. Voja Bloša only asked me: 'If you know Russian, then what does "*Davaj spičku da zakurim*" mean?' We could have asked Igor Chernevsky about this, but we didn't. Igor went on hovering up there in the air, going along the ledge like he was sleepwalking. I realized that every Russian's life was full of dangers but was utterly unthinkable without them. Lonya Bondarenko's mum confirmed this over and over again by sighing a lot in the presence of my uncle, whose hair was always smoothly combed. Lonya's mum came to see us many times and forever offered to do us some favour or other, but my mum usually turned her down. Lonya's mum offered to make something useful out of silk, but mostly she watched my uncle, who would be reading a book. My uncle kept interrupting his reading and saying something inaudible to Lonya's mum: afterwards Lonya's mum would run to the door and stand by the wall, breathing heavily. I noticed that Russian women would usually run out, stand outside the door and breathe, very heavily. At one time it appeared that our whole life depended on the Russians who lived in our neighbourhood and knew about everything. I am referring to their reports on various appliances and flowers, and also this thing about the breathing.

All the Russians had famous names; some of them were made up. In our neighbourhood there were four would-be daughters of Nicholas the Second, who had been sawed in half, and twenty-seven countesses. Their names all ended in 'ov' or 'ski'; they knitted shawls and crocheted and things like that for a living. Lonya Bondarenko's uncle could multiply any two numbers together from memory; his name was Lebedev but nobody believed him. Lebedev worked at a bank, while Nikita Gelin's dad was the best one at making artificial letters out of lead at a print shop. We used the Russian word *kvalifikovani* for all of them; this got on my mum's nerves most of all because she didn't think it was a real word. At that time I thought being a Russian was some sort of trade, one of the most important ones. In any case, the Russians were similar to my dad, my uncle and everybody else except that they wore glasses, kept looking at the sky, and pretended they were sad. Russian people and our people were very similar in their drinking, swearing and their particular love of one sex, the female one. The Russian language was similar to ours, only it was stretched out in some places. Russians talked the same as our people do, only when they're drunk. All this was very exciting for us, especially my aunts. They kept complaining: 'Why weren't we born Russian?' Mum tried to explain to them: 'Right now you wouldn't have any bread to eat!' They replied: 'So what!' This was when Lonya Bondarenko's mum taught my uncle how to write the old Russian letter 'ъ', with a little hook. She admitted: 'It doesn't exist now!' I concluded from this that when Russians talk they use letters that don't exist, and that none of us except my uncle knew what they were.

In 1937 the would-be countess Yevdokia Krutinska asked us to sign a paper she needed in order to get a job with a steamship company. Dad signed it, but the countess still didn't get the job. She stayed at home and took care of nineteen cats, and then would come to visit us with thread and hairs all over her coat. Grandpa protested: 'Just so I don't find a cat hair in my soup!' In 1942 the countess brushed off her coat, put a swastika on her hat and announced: 'We are occupiers, too!' Grandpa recalled Ribbentrop, who shook hands in Moscow, and asked: 'Is this because of him?' but nobody answered him. In 1942 Mum nevertheless said, in a hushed voice: 'God bless the Russians and their cavalry!' My uncle asked: 'What? After all your talk about how Mrs Bondarenko hangs her laundry in her room and never changes clothes?' Mum replied: 'You're lucky you don't understand!' I noticed that the Russians suddenly became great in spite of the fact they dried their laundry in their room, on a string.

Lonya Bondarenko's mum kept on coming to visit us, but didn't offer to do much. My aunts looked into her eyes and complained: 'If only we could be that sad!' Mum tried to explain: 'That's because the poor wretch doesn't have a husband!' Grandpa told them: 'You always have to be nonsensical!' Lonya Bondarenko's mum really did keep looking mournfully at one spot, nobody knew what for. Dad claimed: 'I've heard that every Russian drinks like a pig and then cries like a baby!' Mum said: 'They've probably got some reason to!' My aunts said: 'It's because nobody understands them!' Lonya Bondarenko's mum would often start telling something, then change her mind and stop. Grandpa said: 'They all keep wanting one thing and another, and that's how they spend their lives!' I also noticed that Russians would do something and later regret they'd done it. That's the way it was with my friend Igor Chernevsky, and with Nikita Gelin – the one at whose place we drank tea out of saucers – and with Lonya Bondarenko's mum, who was so nervous. Grandpa warned: 'Each nation has some direction it's going, but them – God forbid!' Even before then some students had told us: 'All people are brothers, but the Russians are our biggest brothers!' Grandpa said: 'How can that be?' I asked: 'Is it because of those tanks that knock down a Finnish tree in that film?' The students advised me: 'Forget that now!' My uncle said: 'That's right, we saw that at the Casino Theatre, where they had tables!' The students said, almost severely: 'We'll still be one of their republics – the best one, too!' Mum concluded: 'The poor masses!' Mum herself noticed everyone was constantly talking about sad things in Russian life and our own. So she announced: 'I'd just like to know what I'm going to die of and be able to see it like in a glass!' Grandpa answered her: 'And that's enough?' Later, Mum said: 'I envy anybody that falls asleep and never knew he was alive!' She thought that by doing this she was sharing the serious mental illnesses our Russian neighbours had, but this wasn't so. My aunts constantly kept trying to cheer up Lonya Bondarenko's mum, but then they remembered such bad things out of novels, that were also Russian, that they themselves began to cry. Mum finally took pity on Mrs Bondarenko and asked: 'Could your brother show my son a little mathematics? He's stupid as a horse in it!' Lonya's mum gave a short answer: *'Da!'*

When Lebedev, who was once a refined gentleman from the field of banking, arrived at our place, Grandpa commented: 'What can he know if his elbows are worn through?' My aunts said: 'They're all that way!' Lebedev started trying to explain the secret of the square of the hypotenuse to me, but he gave up right away and started singing: 'Ah, Woe Is Me!' Everybody hummed along with him, almost inaudibly. Dad's heart melted and he said: 'There's a good one!' My dad never drank more alcohol than when he heard Mr Lebedev the mathematician sing 'Ah, Woe Is Me!' So the work on mathematical science stopped, completely. Grandpa agreed with this. He said: 'Who cares how much three workers drink in six days if they drink five bottles of beer apiece, and other stupid things?' I myself noticed that arithmetic problems take the worst examples from human life, except in the end they draw a line under it all and add it all up.

Later, Lebedev got his sister to show us a ballet figure she had learned from Madame Nina Kirsanova, the queen of this art. Lonya Bondarenko's mum lifted one leg up very high, way up in the air. She looked like a compass opened up wide; it was as if this were also in honour of mathematics, that very neglected science. Everybody was dumbfounded. Lebedev said: '*Nu, yot!*' and pushed his glasses into place.

This story ends in October of '44. We went down to the street to see the Russian tank crews who were smiling from the turrets of their big iron machines as they went by. The soldiers on the tanks were eating bread and jam – black plum jam – and their ears were all smeared with it. People looked at the friendly faces of the tank-men from Kuibyshev smeared up with jam, and also at the would-be countess Yevdokia Krutinska, who was up on this machine, too. The countess had replaced her swastika with a very large hammer and sickle; Grandpa said: 'There's that woman again!' It was then that Lieutenant Miron Stepanovich Timiryazev, aided by vodka, the highly valued Russian drink, walked the whole length of Queen Natalia Street on his hands. Dad immediately announced: 'He's my man!' Dad and Timiryazev sat and sat at the table, a very long time; the Russian kept telling Dad: 'You are my friend, my friend are you!' Later he vomited a lot into his sleeve, so it wouldn't be noticed. Here's how it sounded: 'Bwah!'

Then Lonya Bondarenko's mum started staring at the many people who were going past our building, both the ones on the tanks and the other ordinary ones, with the rifles over their shoulders. Lonya's mum took off her hat and lay down in front of the biggest tank; no one riding on it noticed a thing. My mum later asked my uncle, crying: 'I didn't even know her name!' My uncle replied: 'Neither did I!' This all confirmed that every Russian remembers everything he ever did in his life and then later, at the end, adds one more thing to it, like a punishment of some sort. Russian women, especially.

Translated from the Serbian by Ann Bigelow

Drago Jančar

Repetition

In May 1945, in the hills of Slovenia, a military unit missed the destination the commander had marked on the map the night before in the light of a torch, and after a night's march found themselves above an unknown village. The glimmer of early morning light penetrated through the branches and trunks of trees, blinding the men of the night. They stopped without being ordered to and with an instinctive feeling, stemming from years of fighting, hid behind trees and bushes. Spring sunlight poured over the warm landscape beneath them, and their eyes wandered upwards, hungrily swallowing the glittering of the distant snow-covered mountains over which they were bound. Their tired eyes moved away from the painful glare, drifted into the valley and stopped on the gentle slope above the forest. There, a white church tower was sticking from a rounded grass belly. As they moved closer, they suddenly perceived a village below, with houses pressed to the hill, gathered around the church. And they discerned an unusual, mysterious sight.

On the shingled roof of one of the houses a flame was blazing. There was hardly any smoke, as if the light wood of the house had caught fire only a moment before. They could hear dry crackling, and the warm air above the fire shimmered in the clear morning light. It seemed that the fire would jump on to the neighbouring house any minute, and yet, apart from the dry crackle of the fire, no sound drifted from the village, no cry, scream, mooing of cattle, howling of dogs, no human or animal sound at all. Next to a house at the end of the village, on the road leading to the valley, stood a loaded cart. The two horses which were supposed to pull it lay motionless on the ground. As if somebody had wanted to harness them to take the load to the valley, but changed their mind at the last moment and killed them right in front of the cart. Slaughtered pigs had been thrown on the cart, white sucklings lay like swans among the big ones whose dead meat hung over the edges, and above them trembled the black-brown feathers of slaughtered poultry. The cow must have been killed last. Its huge belly lay by the cart; the head was hidden below, as if it had climbed between the wheels in agony; the belly looked like an inflated yellowish balloon, and its legs were tiredly kicking into the air. The men stood up, forgetting their usual prudence, and stared in surprise at the silent scene below, the scene in which no living soul had appeared so far. One by one they looked down questioningly and at the bearded face of their commander, who still could not decide whether to retreat into the forest or descend into the village. He took a few steps forward down the slope, and then suddenly threw himself on the ground, pressed his face to the wet grass and a split second later his men quickly lay down behind him, although they did not see what he had seen. The arms rattled with a metal sound for a moment, and then everything went silent again.

The commander thought he could discern human bodies lying around the houses.

For a long time they stayed like that, glued to the damp spring soil, listening intently to the crackle of the fire taking hold of the lower storey of the house; smoke started slowly coming from the inside. Then the commander crawled back. Together with his men he moved to the forest and stationed them along its edge, ready to fight or withdraw; he sent two men to look around. Like worms they squirmed down the slope without pausing for a moment. The others held their breath when they saw them rise and in a crouching run disappear behind a barn. A few more tense moments passed. Then they saw one waving his machine gun and they heard his incoherent screaming. All stirred at once and, weapons in hands, started moving towards the silent village, which in the morning sunlight appeared even quieter because of the crackling of the fire. The scene awaiting them was even more mysterious. Incomprehensible and horrible, a dreadful sight even for soldiers used to all kinds of terror.

The bodies lying around the houses were corpses.

It could not have been long since these people had been killed, since

11

some were dead, others were dying, and their limbs in their final convulsions testified that not much time had passed since the fight had ended. And clues on the battlefield suggested it could not have been a fair fight.

It was not a battlefield, no fight had taken place there. All the indications the unknown killers had left behind pointed to the fact that these people had been surprised, and that the slaughter had happened very early in the morning, quite possibly at dawn, when some were still asleep or lying in their beds, while others had started doing their morning chores in kitchens or stables. The corpses were half dressed, as if they had been dragged out of bed a moment before. A half-naked woman was wrapped in a crumpled blood-soaked sheet. An old man lay in the door of the stable, clutching in his dead bony fingers the handle of a fork he had obviously used to protect himself. The attacker was better skilled: he had cut his throat. By another corpse lay a dish full of polenta, still steaming. Somebody had tried to climb a barn; he was left hanging between the bars with a smashed skull. This was not an armed confrontation, not a single shot was fired, everything was done with blades and blunt objects, most of the bloody work was carried out with knives. It seemed that the silent slaughter had taken place a very short time before. The army, which instead of reaching a previously defined destination had happened on this scene of human death by mistake, had not heard any shooting, although they had been very near; these most terrible things probably happened just as they were crawling through the forest towards the light, probably an hour before, when they had been resting in a basin behind the village for a while.

In a small square in front of the church which thus far had been hidden from their eyes they saw ten corpses of young men, obviously selected for systematic execution, a bloody ritual sacrifice. The boys lay next to each other; probably all the boys in the village. Throats had been slit and blood was pouring from the wounds into vessels of different size and shape, overflowing with coagulating blood, which must have been collected from the houses by the bloody visitors, or else the boys had had to bring them along. It seemed designed by farmers with their peasant imagination. In this part of the world this is how they slaughter pigs: they place a vessel under their throats so that the blood is not wasted. The act pointed to the anger or revenge of the slaughterers, who had wanted to humiliate their victims even in death, and probably leave a message of slaughter; the air was heavy with the smell of blood and intoxicated lust. And yet, despite the dreadful sight, nothing was clear. Nothing implied what had caused the recent homicide, no one was left alive to tell the story. And it was not clear which of the armies that had traversed these Slovene hills in this month of May could have done it; there were no military signs, not a cap, not even a button torn from the sleeve of the executioners by a victim in agony, nothing at all. There was a broken bottle next to the corpses, reeking of spirits. Not a very enlightening clue. The cartload alone testified that they had wanted to take away food: the slaughtered pigs and poultry, the cow lying with a swollen belly by the cart, its head beneath it, the cow they could not or did not have time to load. All this led to the assumption that they had planned to cook it in a huge military cauldron, and that the slaughterers were a larger unit of an unknown army. They had left in a hurry; at the last moment they had killed even the horses intended for pulling the cart, slit their throats wide. The reason for such a hasty departure was probably the arrival of the unit confronted with the deadly scene; outlying sentries had probably spotted them. Then there had been a sudden instruction. The commander of the slaughtering army changed his mind after the work had been done, and left the dead animals behind in order not to slow down their immediate departure. War abounds in coincidences, motives triggering killing are always unpredictable, commands brisk and paradoxical. The chaos reigning in the hills of Slovenia in those days, in the hills where armies advanced and retreated, was unpredictable, full of sudden incentives followed by brisk decisions. And actions leaving questions, some remaining unanswered for ever. Therefore there was no reliable answer to any of the questions the soldiers asked themselves. In any case, they soon stopped asking questions altogether. *Although they did not know what had happened they were tempted by the spoils: they simply granted themselves the right of victors and set to work.* Even before the commander gave permission they searched the houses for things they could take. These things were of no use to the villagers; watches, which the troops liked most, do not tick for the dead, do not show the departing time.

And yet, not everybody was dead. A soldier taking a clock off the wall in a dark room of a village house suddenly heard a hiss. When he raised his eyes he beheld a pair of glittering eyes in semi-darkness, and a moment later a cat, ravaged by fear, jumped into his face. The screaming mad beast then ran into the wall, into the doorpost, jumped over a couple of corpses in the street and disappeared behind the houses. And where the cat had disappeared another living being emerged. An old, heavy horse in the meadow behind the church. It had a harness on, as if they had wanted to use it but it had fled, or else they had forgotten it. When the bearded soldiers tried to approach it, the clumsy old horse with big sad eyes suddenly became agile. It reared so that the men stepped back, and then it turned and cantered towards the edge of the forest. There it stopped, turned its head and looked at the village, at the house now almost completely eaten by flames.

Near the burning house which they dared not approach, two soldiers finally came across a living Christian soul. Two, in fact, but one was by all appearances already passing to the world beyond. A bloody trail led from the street into the house, as if somebody had dragged a heavy bloody load. When they entered the house, they momentarily forgot about the trail. With skilled hands they threw things around to find anything useful before the fire destroyed it. But a second later they stopped dead. They heard movements on the upper storey and, when they listened more closely, human moans. The dark red traces they had noticed outside led up the wooden staircase. The stairs squeaked under their boots and they heard another moan, of pain or fear of the coming steps. One of the soldiers carefully clamped a hand grenade between his teeth. At that moment a young woman emerged at the top of the stairs, dressed in a white cotton gown in which she had gone to bed the night before, just when the commander was marking the destination on the map in the light of a torch. She stopped for a moment, looked at them with terrified eyes, and then disappeared inside. They rushed after her.

By her bed, slightly leaning on it, lay a young man covered in blood. He had a white cloth at his throat, which had turned red. He was still alive, just, since his eyelids opened and closed with difficulty; and he was dead, but not quite, since only the white eyeballs showed under his eyelids, the pupils disappearing into the eye sockets. And the young woman, who must have been beautiful when her hair was not disordered, her teeth clenched and her eyes delirious, stepped in front to defend him. She had dragged him from the row of the young men's corpses with slit throats up here to protect him, to give him back his departing life. She was muttering fierce incomprehensible, words, blurred groaning sounds. The two soldiers stepped back; they did not want to harm her. They listened to her groaning with surprise, for the sound was like the crying of the mad cat. They stood facing each other for a few moments. Two armed, bearded, dead tired soldiers from the forest and a young woman, with that morning in her eyes, in hopeless defence of the dying young man, who was perhaps her lover.

This scene irresistibly brings to mind the beginning of Heliodorus' *Aethiopica*. Furthermore, from the very beginning the scene looked as if it was meant to be repeated. The repetition of a human situation which Heliodorus described in refined Greek in the third century AD: from the hills above the mouth of the Nile, men dressed like brigands descended. They watched the shore carefully, and their eyes rested on the glittering surface of the sea. Then they beheld an unusual sight. A loaded ship was tied to the shore, sinking deep with her burden, not a living soul could be seen on her deck or the shore. And the shore was covered in corpses. *It could not have been long since these people had been killed, since some were dead, others were dying, and their limbs in their final convulsions testified that not much time had passed since the fight had ended. And clues on the battlefield suggested it could not have been a fair fight.* The Egyptian brigands stared at the scene, which looked as though it had been left behind by an evil spirit: wine and blood, feast and slaughter, drinking and killing, offerings of wine and human sacrifice. All they could see were the defeated; the victors had disappeared. *Although they did not know what had happened they were tempted by the spoils: they granted themselves the right of victors and set to work.* When they approached the ship and the corpses, they saw a new, even more mysterious sight. An incredibly beautiful young woman was sitting on a rock. 'Deep sorrow poured over her face,' says Heliodorus, 'but pride and nobility radiated from her body.' Before her lay a handsome young man covered in wounds. The girl, a laurel wreath on her head, rested her right elbow on her left leg and put her face in her hands. Her head held high she looked at the wounded boy. The image was later called 'classical pietà'. At first the brigands were scared by the almost godly scene, and then they decided to take the girl with them and let the young man die. At that moment the girl pointed a sword at herself and threatened to kill herself if the men did not take them both. The commander decided to save them. And so in *Aethiopica* a new life started for the wounded Teagenes and beautiful Hariklea, and in the long story we read their exciting life brought to them by the gods. The author considered the act of the brigands' commander 'worthy of praise'. 'A noble sight and a glimpse at beauty,' he says, 'must soften even the hard heart of a brigand and defeat brute force.' And the reader gradually discovers God's economy in their story as it is said word for word in the original.

God's economy in our story, which in many elements restates the opening scene in *Aethiopica* and happened in May 1945 in the hills of Slovenia, unfolds in a different way. From the scene which stayed alive in the memory of one of the two soldiers and which he described many years later, it quickly proceeds towards its dénouement. No laurel wreath, no face in the palms, nobody noticed the nobility which would soften the hard heart of an armed man. A godly scene was not possible so many years later. Where in *Aethiopica* the story begins and takes its heroes into a new life, our story ends. The month is May, the year of our Lord is the merciless 1945.

So they stood facing each other for a few moments. Then the soldiers grabbed the girl, who muttered incomprehensible groans, kicked and bit, wet with tears and the boy's blood; they grabbed her, tore her away from him and pulled her to the square in front of the church. When they told the commander that somebody was still alive he ordered them to bring him too. He could not be carried so they dragged him by the legs and arms, his head and slit throat on the ground. They dragged him along the same trail, exactly to the place where he had lain among the corpses of his fellow villagers. His eyes rolled, he groaned through his cut throat, so that the cloth reddened with new blood; he whimpered hoarsely and gurgled, as if he had realized where he was, saved a moment before, and now again among the lost. The girl, who a moment before was rigid with sadness, pulled away from the two soldiers with incredible force and threw herself towards him, on to the dead. Suddenly there was a knife in her hand. She hugged the dangling head of the young man with her left hand, pressed it to her bosom, and brandished the knife at the two soldiers trying to step closer and in front of the commander's eyes undo what they had done in a moment of thoughtlessness. The commander waved his hand, gesturing to leave her alone. Then he stepped forward. He leaned over her and quietly whispered, 'We won't hurt you, we don't want to do you any harm.' When she had calmed down a little, it became clear in her delirious eyes that she had understood the words, but not their meaning. The commander moved even closer. Who was here, who had done this, he wanted to know. She shook her head and groaned. She pointed to the soldiers standing around. She pointed at him. 'She's mute,' one of the men gathered around her said; in war a new scene emerges every moment. And if there was an art historian among the soldiers, the narrator did not know it, he could not but think of the strange, distorted version of a modern pietà from May 1945. 'She's not mute,' said the commander, 'she's gone mad.' The man whose face the cat had scratched quickly added: 'They are all mad here, even the cats.' And the soldiers laughed loudly, to chase away the eeriness of her eyes and her finger pointed at them. 'Where did they go?' The commander shaped the question with his lips, 'Just tell us where they went. There?' He pointed to the valley. 'Or up?' He pointed to the hill. She never uttered another sound. She dropped the hand with the knife, and leaned over the boy's face so that she covered it with her long fair hair. A silent picture of deepest sorrow, no irresistible beauty, just sorrow. One of the soldiers, the one who told the story, turned away, feeling something gathering in his throat; apparently it happens even to soldiers. They were all silent. Somebody said: 'We're not getting anywhere.' The commander said, 'It's true, we're not getting anywhere.'

He stood up. He stepped towards the stairs of the church where his bag and machine-gun lay. He sat down and spread the map on his lap. While looking for their missed destination he outlined a new itinerary and briskly gave orders. The soldiers scattered around the village and started loading the cart with provisions for the long journey across the mountains glittering in the snow and strong morning sun. They harnessed the horse – they had finally managed to catch it. The cart was too heavy and the horse too old, so they had to push with their shoulders before it moved. The cart ran over the neck of the cow with its rear wheel, so that it rocked danger-ously. Then it moved quickly, since the road led downhill, towards the valley. The commander stepped after the cart, but, when they had left the village behind, suddenly stopped. He turned back towards the houses gathered around the church, towards the spiralling smoke coming from the ruin. He scratched his stubbled face and stared ahead for a moment. Then he waved and one of the soldiers came running to him. The commander nodded towards the square. They could clearly see it from there, with its silent, mad witness. The girl in the white gown still held the boy's head in her lap. The commander's gesture implied that something had happened in God's economy of this story which did not lead to a repetition but to the final end of something which had started there at an early hour, nobody knew how or why.

The horse with sad eyes slowly pulled the load along the road, easily now, because the slope gently descended. A soldier was running back and up. The knife he pulled from his belt glittered in the sun. Its reflection drifted towards the snowy mountains over which they were bound, and silently disappeared. The commander looked at the map. He did not want them to be lost again.

Translated from the Slovene by Lili Potpara

Slavenka Drakulić

The Balkan Express

Early Sunday morning a mist hovered over the Vienna streets like whipped cream, but the sunshine piercing the lead-grey clouds promised a beautiful autumn day, a day for leafing through magazines at the Museum Kaffe, for taking a leisurely walk along the Prater park and enjoying an easy family lunch. Then perhaps a movie or the theatre – several films were premièring.

But when I entered the Südbahnhof, the South Station, the milky Viennese world redolent with café au lait, fresh rolls and butter or apple strudel and the neat life of the ordinary Viennese citizens was far behind me. As soon as I stepped into the building I found myself in another world; a group of men cursed someone's mother in Serbian, their greasy, sodden words tumbling to the floor by their feet, and a familiar slightly sour odour, a mixture of urine, beer and plastic-covered seats in second-class rail compartments, wafted through the stale air of the station. Here in the heart of Vienna I felt as if I were already on territory occupied by another sort of people, a people now second-class. Not only because they had come from a poor socialist country, at least not any more. Now they were second-class because they had come from a country collapsing under the ravages of war. War is what made them distinct from the sleepy Viennese, war was turning these people into ghosts of the past – ghosts whom the Viennese are trying hard to ignore. They'd rather forget the past, they cannot believe that history is repeating itself, that such a thing is possible: bloodshed in the Balkans, TV images of burning buildings and beheaded corpses, a stench of fear spreading from the south and east through the streets, a stench brought here by refugees. War is like a brand on the brows of Serbs who curse Croat mothers, but it is also a brand on the faces of Croats leaving a country where all they had is gone. The first are

19

branded by hatred, the second by the horror that here in Vienna no one really understands them. Every day more and more refugees arrive from Croatia. Vienna is beginning to feel the pressure from the Südbahnhof and is getting worried. Tormented by days spent in bomb shelters, by their arduous journey and the destruction they have left behind, the exiles are disembarking – those who have the courage and the money to come so far – stepping first into the vast hall of the warehouse-like station. From there they continue out into the street, but once in the street they stop and stare at the fortress-like buildings, at the bolted doors and the doormen. They stand there staring at this metropolis, this outpost of Western Europe, helplessly looking on as Europe turns its back on them indifferently behind the safety of closed doors. The exiles feel a new fear now: Europe is the enemy, the cold, rational, polite and fortified enemy who still believes that the war in Croatia is far away, that it can be banished from sight, that the madness and death will stop across the border.

But it's too late. The madness will find its way, and with it, death. Standing on the platform of the Karlsplatz subway, I could hardly believe I was still in the same city: here at the very nerve centre of the city, in the trams, shops, in *Kneipen*, German is seldom heard. Instead everyone seems to speak Croatian or Serbian (in the meantime, the language has changed its name too), the languages of people at war. One hundred thousand Yugoslavs are now living in Vienna, or so I've heard. And seventy thousand of them are Serbs. In a small park near Margaretenstrasse I came across a carving on a wooden table that read 'This is Serbia'. Further along, on a main street, I saw the graffiti 'Red Chetniks', but also 'Fuck the Red Chetniks' scrawled over it. War creeps out of the cheap apartments near the Gürtel and claims its victims.

I am one of a very few passengers, maybe twenty, heading southeast on a train to Zagreb. I've just visited my daughter who, after staying some time in Canada with her father, has come to live in Vienna. There are three of us in the compartment. The train is already well on its way, but we have not yet spoken to one another. The only sound is the rattling of the steel wheels, the rhythmic pulse of a long journey. We are wrapped in a strange, tense silence. All three of us are from the same collapsing country (betrayed by the tell-tale 'Excuse me, is this seat taken?' 'No, it's free'), but we feel none of the usual camaraderie of travel when passengers talk or share snacks and newspapers to pass the time. Indeed, it seems as if we are afraid to exchange words which might trap us in that small compartment where our knees are so close they almost touch. If we speak up, our languages will disclose who is a Croat and who a Serb, which of us is the enemy. And even if we are all Croats (or Serbs) we might disagree on the war and yet there is no other topic we could talk about. Not even the landscape because even the landscape is not innocent any more. Slovenia has put real border posts along the border with Croatia and has a different currency. This lends another tint to the Slovenian hills, the colour of sadness. Or bitterness. Or anger. If we three strike up a conversation about the green woods passing us by, someone might sigh and say, 'Only yesterday this was my country too.' Perhaps then the other two would start in about independence and how the Slovenes were clever while the Croats were not, while the Serbs, those bastards . . .

The war would be there, in our words, in meaningful glances, and in the faces reflecting our anxiety and nausea. In that moment the madness we are travelling towards might become so alive among us that we wouldn't be able perhaps to hold it back. What if one of us is a Serb? What if he says a couple of ordinary, innocent words? Would we pretend to be civilized or would we start to attack him? What if the hypothetical Serb among us keeps silent because he is not really to blame? Are there people in this war, members of the aggressor nation, who are not to blame? Or maybe he doesn't want to hurt our feelings, thinking that we might have family or friends in Vukovar, Osijek, Šibenik, Dubrovnik, those cities under the heaviest fire? Judging from our silence, growing more and more impenetrable as we approach the Croatian border, I know that we are more than mere strangers – surly, unfamiliar, fellow passengers – just as one cannot be a mere bank clerk. In war one loses all possibility of choice. But for all that, I think the unbearable silence between us that verges on a scream is a good sign, a sign of our unwillingness to accept the war, our desire to distance ourselves and spare each other, if possible.

So we do not talk to each other. The man on my left stares out of the window, the woman opposite sleeps with her mouth half open. From time to time she wakes up and looks around, confused; then she closes her eyes again, thinking that this is the best she can do, close her eyes and pretend the world doesn't exist. I pick up a newspaper, risking recognition – one betrays oneself by the newspapers one reads – but my fellow travellers choose not to see it. At the Südbahnhof newspaper stand there were no papers from Croatia, only *Borba*, one of the daily papers published in Serbia. As I leaf through the pages I come across a description of an atrocity of war, supposedly committed by the Ustashe – the Croatian Army – which freezes the blood in my veins. When you are forced to accept war as a fact, death becomes something you have to reckon with, a harsh reality that mangles your life even if it leaves you physically unharmed. But the kind of death I met with on the second page of the *Borba* paper was by no means common and therefore acceptable in its inevitability: . . . *and we looked down the well in the back yard. We pulled up the bucket – it was full of testicles, about 300 in all.* An image as if fabricated to manufacture horror. A long line of men, hundreds of them, someone's hands, a lightning swift jab of a knife, then blood, a jet of thick dark blood cooling on someone's hands, on clothing, on the ground. Were the men alive when it happened, I wondered, never questioning whether the report was true. The question of truth, or any other question for that matter, pales next to the swirling pictures, the whirlpool of pictures that sucks me in, choking me. At that moment, whatever the truth, I can imagine nothing but the bucket full of testicles, slit throats, bodies with gory holes where hearts had been, gouged eyes – death as sheer madness. As I rest my forehead on the cold windowpane I notice that there is still a little light outside, and other scenes are flitting by, scenes of peaceful tranquillity. I don't believe in tranquillity any more. It is just a thin crust of ice over a deadly treacherous river. I know I am travelling towards a darkness that has the power, in a single sentence in a newspaper, to shatter in me the capacity to distinguish real from unreal, possible from impossible. Hardly anything seems strange or dreadful now – not dismembered bodies, not autopsy reports from

Croatian doctors claiming that the victims were forced by Serbians to eat their own eyes before they were killed.

Only on the train heading southeast, on that sad 'Balkan Express', did I understand what it means to report bestialities as the most ordinary facts. The gruesome pictures are giving birth to a gruesome reality; a man who, as he reads a newspaper, forms in his mind a picture of the testicles being drawn up from the well will be prepared to do the same tomorrow, closing the circle of death.

I fold the paper. I don't need it for any further 'information'. Now I'm ready for what awaits me upon my return. I have crossed the internal border of the warring country long before I've crossed the border outside, and my journey with the two other silent passengers, the newspaper and the seed of madness growing in each of us is close to its end. Late that night at home in Zagreb I watch the news on television. The anchor man announces that seven people have been slaughtered in a Slavonian village. I watch him as he utters the word 'slaughtered' as if it were the most commonplace word in the world. He doesn't flinch, he doesn't stop, the word slips easily from his lips. The chill that emanates from the words feels cold on my throat, like the blade of a knife. Only then do I know that I've come home, that my journey has ended here in front of the TV screen, plunged in a thick, clotted darkness, a darkness that reminds me of blood.

Translated from the Croatian by Maja Šoljan

David Albahari

The Pope

When Mendosa crosses himself in front of the television camera on his way off the playing field, the Pope sits bolt upright, excited. He looks around, but the cardinals are sleeping peacefully in their easy chairs. Mendosa vanishes from the screen, for a moment the Pope feels again the burden of solitude, but then the game continues and he succumbs to the inarticulate passions of soccer.

The Pope loves to talk with soldiers. They tell him about faraway places where he has never been. 'I would love to be a soldier,' thinks the Pope as he stops before troops standing in rows. The soldiers have arrived from far away. They are grimy, caked with sweat and blood. Some can hardly stand, some doze, leaning on their lances. 'Soldier,' the Pope addresses a lanky soldier and notices the youthful hairs on his upper lip, 'can you tell me what Jerusalem looks like?' The soldier tries to puff out his chest and the Pope notices how his muscles are trembling from strain and exhaustion. 'When I got there,' the soldier says, 'all I saw was ashes.'

In strolling along long corridors, the Pope first notices the symmetry of repetition. When he lifts his head, he sees arabesques, the meaning of which he cannot fathom. 'Why should everything have meaning?' wonders the Pope in a whisper, then he quickly bites his tongue and darts glances in all directions. These days even the walls have ears.

The Pope wakes early. The window is open, the air fresh, the sky blue. He gets up, tripping on his long night shirt, and notices a bird on the windowsill. The Pope goes back to the night table, but nothing is left of last night's sandwich. 'Bird,' says the Pope to the bird, 'will you wait while I send someone for a little bread?' The bird does not reply. 'Or would you prefer grains – wheat or millet?' The bird keeps quiet. The Pope lifts the receiver and calls the central warehouse. A sleepy voice says, 'Hello?' 'Is there any millet in the warehouse?' asks the Pope. 'Who's asking?' asks the voice. 'Forget it,' says the Pope and puts the receiver back down.

For ages he didn't know there were mirrors, then one day he was taken to a room where the countless smooth surfaces bounced back reflections of his face. For a moment the Pope could imagine a world full of popes and he clucked his tongue in delight. Then he called in a handyman and asked him to take all the mirrors down. He kept only one, in the attic, unknown to all.

If there is one thing he hates, it is mornings. Every time he wakes up, it seems, he finds his night shirt has twisted all the way up to his chin. 'I would rather sleep in pyjamas,' says the Pope and angrily stamps his foot. The cardinals exchange glances. 'And I've had it with this night cap,' howls the Pope and flings the cap from his head. The cap drops on to lined silk slippers, a gift from the Turkish ambassador. 'Our regulations do not permit it.' A cardinal finally dares to speak. Regulations, thinks the Pope, damnation – I should have stayed an ordinary village priest.

The Pope writes poems. A journalist asks him, 'In your case might one speak, indeed, of divine inspiration?' The Pope has read *Faust* and he knows where this question is leading. So he does not respond. 'Any other questions?' says the cardinal who is the Pope's press attaché, the Pope feels beads of sweat on his forehead like the touch of someone's icy hand.

*

Morning meetings, official noon luncheons, afternoon preparations for the next day; only in the evening (before and after Vespers) has the Pope a bit of time to himself. He sits by a window and gazes into the sky. Of all he sees he likes the clouds best. Each cloud is shaped differently. Some look like familiar things, other like things soon to be invented, yet others suggest distant worlds, and some dissolve as the Pope watches. Footsteps, heard from the depths of the palace, belong to a young monk who brings the Pope his chamber pot. The Pope would gladly speak with the young man, but the monk cut off his own tongue so that he could pledge all his thoughts to God. What nonsense, thinks the Pope. The monk sets the pot behind the door, covers it with a richly embroidered cloth, bows and leaves.

The Pope is alone. Nothing interests him. He has leafed through the Holy Gospels but could not find a single passage he did not already know by heart. He could call someone on the phone, but whom? He used to entertain himself by dialling numbers on the phone at random and then he'd giggle into his sleeve when some irate (male or female) voice barked: 'Hello! Hello? Who's there?' But the Pope feels that he has outgrown such petty diversions. Now he'd rather imagine a world in which there are at least two popes. He'd have someone else to play dominoes or chess with. Imagine if there were three! Cards! The Pope goes over to the desk, flicks on his computer and enters the question: 'When will the next Ecumenical Council be held?' The computer replies: 'The year 2012.' The Pope types: 'But I won't be alive then.' 'You won't,' replies the computer, 'but the Pope will.'

Is this my true face? muses the Pope, leaning over the sink. It is difficult to discern the precise state of affairs on the rippled water surface, but the Pope does think that he has bushy eyebrows, long lashes and blue eyes. The Pope scoops up water and splashes his face. When the water surface is still again, when he can see himself in it, he is certain his eyes are black.

*

The Pope strolls around the yard. The yard is surrounded by a high wall. Every time he reaches the wall the Pope listens. He can hear nothing. No sound comes from beyond the wall. Perhaps there is nothing out there, thinks the Pope, maybe I am alone in the world? Apples and pears drop behind his back: ripe fruit falls on to the mown lawn. 'Hey,' shouts the Pope, 'is anyone there?' Silence, silence, nothing but silence.

In the middle of a sermon, once, at a moment of tranquil solemnity, as the Pope was raising an index finger to make his closing sentence emphatic, one of the faithful rose and in a resounding voice asked, 'How can the Pope know the truth about family life? Who has a wife and children? Him or us?' Since the question was not addressed directly to the Pope, the Pope – like everyone else – looked around, but no one tried to respond. Maybe I might suggest an answer, thought the Pope, but then he noticed his uplifted index finger. Never had he seen his finger so illuminated! This is a divine sign, thought the Pope. With unconcealed anticipation he twisted his neck to peer up into the dome. But it was dark up there, so very dark up there, and the Pope was afraid of the dark. He brought his index finger to his face, cautiously: as if brandishing a torch, and then he fainted.

The Pope is certain that life has no beginning and no end. It simply changes features: today we are this, tomorrow, that. The Pope, of course, cannot explain how or why the number of people keeps growing. Has the quantity of lives remained the same, finding outlet in a larger number of human beings? Does this mean that people are becoming more numerous thanks to the extinction of certain animal species? Maybe I was once a dodo? muses the Pope. He pictures himself on one of the Indian Ocean islands, and sees the Spanish or the Dutch conquistadors as they come to him with a grin and an unsheathed sword. Do not approach me, he warns them, I am the Pope! But the Spaniard is quick, experienced: he knows, like the Dutchman, that the dodo is a stupid and helpless bird, endlessly naïve and gullible. Come, dodo, come, come, sing the conquerors. And then: the flash of the sword, the smell of blood, warm soup, a roasted drumstick, discarded innards thrown behind the pallisades which even dogs won't sniff.

The Pope kneels and talks with a six-year-old boy. They are in an orphanage at Saint Catherine's, or Isabela's, or Dominique's, or Genevieve's. So many immaculate women, thinks the Pope, in this, the worst of all worlds: nothing short of incredible! He makes a final stab at urging the little boy to talk, but the boy is intractable. The Pope knows what comes next: either the boy will start to cry, or stick out his tongue. His sweet, smooth, pink little tongue! The Pope, of course, would prefer the tongue, but one never can be sure with these rascals. The Pope gets up, resting in passing on the boy's shoulder (so small, so fragile) and takes the opportunity to tweak the child stealthily by his bright red ear. The Pope learned that trick in his younger years on the streets of V. and B. before they delivered him to the seminary. And so when he steps back and hears the child's howl (reminding him poignantly of the Inquisition), the Pope turns and shrugs helplessly. And one of the robust nuns tries to soothe the boy by saying, 'Don't cry, son, the Pope will visit us again.'

Am I a good man? wonders the Pope. He sits in a large, empty room in which all sounds are oddly amplified. When he moves his foot and his rheumatic knee cracks, all the saints seem to tumble from the walls. Maybe goodness is somehow related to staying still? The Pope pulls the silken cord: although he hears nothing he knows that in the depths of the Vatican a mechanism is set in motion which, a moment later, will appear at the door in the form of the young dumb monk with the chamber pot in his hands. 'This must be a mistake,' says the Pope. 'I summoned the cardinals, not you.' The monk shrugs, smiles and moves towards the door. 'But, no matter,' says the Pope, 'come here.' The monk comes over and the Pope takes him by the hand. 'Tell me,' says the Pope, 'am I a good man?' The monk's eyes fly open, he gropes for the right facial expression, and then he opens his mouth. The Pope first sees the stump of his tongue, strangely thick and lumpy, then he hears a voice which embodies all voices. Then the walls begin to crumble.

The Pope sits by a well. He feels chilly but no one thinks to bring him a mantle. I'll catch a cold here, thinks the Pope, and it may kill me. And still no one brings him a mantle. It will rain soon, then frost, then snow. At least I have enough water, thinks the Pope, and he leans his forehead on the stone well wall. 'If you have no fire, use ice': so said a proverb he read long ago in a manuscript from the secret chamber of the Vatican library. Another said: 'In order to return, first you must leave.' One is from Iceland, the other, Polynesia. The world is so big, thinks the Pope while the seams in the stone press into the refined skin of his forehead. If someone were to see me from some vast height, he thinks on, I would be no more than a miserable speck in the infinitude of God's garden: but who could see from such a distance? A moment later the first drop of rain falls on his neck. The Pope lifts his head to take a look at how far the clouds have come (perhaps someone has brought him an umbrella after all?), but instead of clouds he sees a huge eye on the blue dome of the sky.

The Pope is ninety-nine years old. He has long since stopped eating, sleeping and receiving visitors. He stares unswervingly at the velvet curtain behind which, he is convinced, God resides. He does not know where he has got this notion: why velvet and God seem associated: perhaps the particular rough smoothness of the fabric? Who knows? The Pope would gladly dismiss this with a wave of his hand, but he cannot move it. He continues to stare at the velvet curtain, longing for even the slightest trembling of its folds. God, however, remains silent, hesitating. The Pope recalls his life's most cherished moment: when he sat at a marble sweetshop table, still a boy, and they served him a large dish of ice cream. When the curtain finally does move, the Pope is not surprised when, instead of God, he sees a smiling waitress in a short skirt with dimples in her cheeks. Or is this, perhaps, God's countenance? It no longer matters, the Pope knows; he closes his eyes, sticks out his tongue and takes the last rites. With the drowsy aroma of vanilla.

Translated from the Serbian by Ellen Elias-Bursać

Poland

Piotr Szewc

Annihilation

What time is it? We cannot see the town hall clock from where we are, therefore we do not know. But for the Book of Day it has no meaning; it will be written by the clock, with what is happening and will happen according to its will.

What time is it? The counsellor looks at his watch.

The cab driver is right behind him. His horse snorts. The counsellor stops the cab with a motion of his hand. Where would you like to go, Mr Counsellor?

The moon is clearer now. Its glare is more distinct and reflected in cherry trees (which also reflect the street lamps lighting up here and there). The cherries – which no one has counted yet – are lamps and stars; several new stars, still barely visible, have just lit up. They have lit up for the benefit of the Eye of the Town, so it could look in between the rose petals. Let us part the branches and see the glow. We shall have a close look at the moon that tries to see itself in the petals like in a mirror.

(The day is coming to an end, so let there also be a bit of light that allows us to see its last moments. A bit of light for the closing Book of Day.)

The ducks in the park have hidden among the rushes. One cannot see the backs or spouts of fish, which may be showing above the surface of the water. Sparrows from the park have flown away – they have returned to their nests, or perhaps soared high, into the unfathomable space from which the meteor has fallen, they have risen to the stars, to the moon, in order to write new chapters of their own Books in its light. But we do not know. It does not have to be so.

A brown moth that had flown over our heads has dropped into the lake. Perhaps it was lured by the false light of the moon, the

33

reflections of stars, which are like lamps for the moth – it circles around them throughout the night. The moth still moves its wings in a disorderly way, more and more helplessly. Rings in the water disperse without a plan, the stars in the lake move. It does not last long: the moth grows motionless, perhaps it is still alive. The water is calm now. The glare is inert over the water.

Quiet gurgling. Every now and then a bubble floats to the surface, disappears. As if air was released through a hollow stem somewhere above the bottom. Rustling of insects. Crickets, perhaps. The air shivers. A long, painful voice of a bird from the island.

(Perhaps this voice indicates the beginning of the last chapter of the Book of Day.)

The policemen, Antoni Wrzosek and Tomasz Romanowicz, absent since the moment the meteor fell, return to the square. They have appeared near the mercer's store of Mr Hershe Blaum. One of them – is it Wrzosek or Romanowicz? they are of almost equal height, and therefore hard to tell from a distance, and we are unable to see Antoni's moustache – holds a branch with fruit – and yet again we are uncertain: are they sweet or bitter cherries? – which he must have picked on Ogrodowa or Mlynska Street. They pick the fruit and put it in their mouths. They lean on the wall of Mr Blaum's shed and look at the empty square. In front of them – a few lights. Lights in R.'s establishment, in several apartments. A train thunders. Far away.

'What's that? Sparks, as if someone sharpened a knife. Let's check it out.'

A brown cat looks sideways at the approaching policemen and nervously moves its tail. It would continue to shake the sun dust from its hair, but it finds a meeting undesirable. It lowers its head and disappears behind a store into the darkness of grass, the darkness of burdock.

'So that was a cat? And it seemed to me like some kind of light.' Antoni Wrzosek stops and looks into the stirring grass behind the store. He would have said something more, but he says nothing; the obscurity of sparks – or sun dust – shedding from the cat's hair forbids all commentary. And he does not notice the stones, still sparkled with light. This light will die out in a moment. Mr Tomasz

Romanowicz did not see the sparks, and does not see them now. If asked, he would not be able to tell what his partner, Wrzosek, is saying to him. He is too absorbed with his own thoughts to care about alleged sparks. Excessive vigilance.

The swinging door to R.'s establishment squeaks. A shaft of light from three lamps is cast on the square. It shows a shadow of a patron leaving the establishment. The shaft does not reach the two policemen, they remain unnoticed by the patron.

The accordion that each day plays Ukrainian melodies starts its concert. It will play for perhaps an hour. The policemen are used to it. The player is someone called Vasyl (What's his name, Antoni? I keep forgetting . . .) Czehyra. Let's go to Hrubieszowska Street. Five minutes of unhurried walk. That's where he is playing.

Again, the smell of rotting wood, wet planks, more intense than in the morning. The dying of houses, merchant's shacks, has its own time-honoured rhythm. They are alive. Still.

A new star. A small infinity. Barely visible. Who sees it?

A commotion of shadows and light in R.'s establishment. R. stands in the window shading his eyes from the light, he looks at the square and the policemen. (Why doesn't he stand in the door, or step outside?) And he lifts his eyes to confirm that stars are above the town, and it is time to close the establishment; this time – when there are many stars in the sky – is late for R.'s pub, and the customers should have left half or three-quarters of an hour ago. They have eaten what they had to eat, they have drunk what there was to drink. They talked, or rather kept silent together. Gentlemen, it is time to close. Please come tomorrow. Goodnight to all of you.

The two policemen approach Lwowska Street. (That's where we were in the morning, taking our first photographs.) Mr Antoni sticks the branch, its fruit all eaten now, behind the bar on the doors of a closed stall with soft drinks. The juices stop to assault the leaves, the mystery of the roots passed on to light. A cherrystone, spat out by Mr Romanowicz, falls to the pavement. The sand, the sun dust, sticks to it.

Now we can admire the beautiful moustache of Mr Antoni Wrzosek, who leans on the lamppost near the first house on

Lwowska Street. The sharp, white light coming from above allows us to see the stone, and notice that the stones have cooled off: they are grey, some of them light grey, quite unlike those that we saw at noon. They were white like the glare of the street lamps, hot, and dangerous. Mr Antoni Wrzosek, his hands in his pockets, his back resting against the lamppost, thinks about an explanation for the sparks – there were sparks, hard to deny, it was a light of some kind, very much like little sparks – which he saw not long ago in front of the northern wall of the square. And the large brown cat that disappeared in the grass, what did it have to do with this light . . . ? Mr Antoni Wrzosek's dark, neatly trimmed moustache ends between the corners of his mouth and his chin. The tips are roguishly twisted. The foam of the beer that he will drink tomorrow at the good R.'s will sit on them as on the rim of a glass.

Mr Tomasz Romanowicz has squatted in front of Wrzosek. He cleans his teeth with a wood splinter. Some of the lamps in Lwowska Street have been lit up. Mr Romanowicz looks into the empty street. The swing door of the pub opens and closes, squeaking silently, pushed and then released by the last customers leaving the establishment. Shafts of light move across the square like huge white wings – let us remember: the three lamps in the establishment are lit up, and one should also remember the fiery ball from the painting – they linger on houses and stores on the other side. Mr Antoni Wrzosek sees it all, because the light also falls on him, as it does on Romanowicz. In this light the shadows of customers grow to unnatural dimensions, only to disappear when the door is closed, and appear again when they are opened.

The accordion is playing, and the customers, dispersing in the square, try in vain to pick up Vasyl's melody.

R. blows out his lamps – the first one, then the second. When the third one is still burning, the eye of a herring notices some object left by a customer on a table; we do not know what it is, because the fiery ball and the third lamp give too little light to know for sure. Finally R. blows out the flame of the third lamp that stands on the counter near a jar of herrings, and he gropes in the dark for the knob of the kitchen door. He will still return to the square, in front of his pub, to close the shutters and to lock the door with a padlock. But this the eye of the herring will not see; it is dark, and the bay leaf is floating by it.

It is hard to say where the customers of R. intend to go, at least the few who have remained in the square – walking here and there and calling each other. We may look for the rest in the alleys, behind store walls, or maybe in Gminna Street. The Eye of the Town knows best.

The cab with the counsellor drives downhill, from Hrubieszowska Street, to stop in front of Miss Kazimiera's house. There is a dim light in Kazimiera's room indicating that Kazimiera is at home. The counsellor counts his fare, and bids the driver goodnight. Wet lilac branches, wet grass. The counsellor pushes away moist twigs that touch his temples. The dogs behind the brewery gate bark at the counsellor, who starts to climb the stairs. In the window above a curtain is moved, and for a moment we can see the face of Miss Kazimiera looking into the street. But the floor in the hall and the stairs are already squeaking as the counsellor walks upstairs.

The two policemen have left their place under the street lamp; they walk along Lwowska and pass Spadek. The cab is driving from Spadek into Lwowska, and Messrs Antoni Wrzosek and Tomasz Romanowicz must hasten their walk so as not to frighten the horses or to be run over by them. The driver bows to the policemen and turns towards the Old Town.

When the cab passed through the patch of light, the hair of the horses glistened.

'Perhaps the counsellor has paid Kazimiera a visit?' They could have asked the driver, but now it is too late.

'We'll see in a moment. Maybe the curtain has not been closed.' Mr Tomasz Romanowicz has stopped cleaning his teeth, and pitched the splinter away with a snap of his finger. 'Shall we go straight ahead, or turn into Listopadowa?'

'As you wish. We could turn into Listopadowa.'

Before the policemen have time to turn into Listopadowa, the cab stops in the square. Two of R.'s customers noisily climb inside and tell the driver to take them to a bar that does not close so early. When the horses start at a foot pace the two policemen are five steps away from Listopadowa.

Those five steps. That are. For us to hear, when the heels strike the pavement. For us to see. Five steps, five words in the Book. It passes. What passes? Does everything pass? To save. How can we save? For whom? Before it disappears for ever, tumbles into nonbeing, eternal forgetting. Five steps that have already transpired. Sparrows, pigeons have dispersed the smoke. Burned paper has landed on leaves, fallen among the grass. The sun at noon hanging at the top of the pear tree. A white butterfly flying above the pear tree. Before it is fulfilled. Sun dust raining on the town. A pair of people seen, or unseen. An empty Jewish cemetery. What can be saved? Before it is fulfilled.

Translated from the Polish by Jarosław Anders

Hanna Krall

Retina

1

The village is in a valley. A local postcard presents an immutable, undisturbed panorama. The dark green of wooded hills, light green patch of a meadow, red roofs over white houses, and a ribbon of blue in the middle – the river Murg. The river has its source in the nearby mountains and flows into the Rhine. The mountains belong to the Schwarzwald massif.

On one of the postcards the artist depicts a bench. It stands in the background under a tree – it is made of four wooden planks painted red. The planks look old and they might have come from the local sawmill. Perhaps they have been cut from timber shipped to the sawmill by French soldiers. As soon as they captured the village, they started shipping wood from the forests. (What did the French need these planks for? Tables? Coffins? A bridge? Bandstands?)

Stanisław W., whom the French and the Germans called Stani, came to the village straight from the camps. He worked in the sawmill. It is quite possible that he cut the planks for the red bench.

2

The French soldiers and their captain lived in a small house in the middle of the village. They took their meals in a former café. Gizela worked with a German family just above the café. She had exquisite credentials from a school run by Franciscan nuns: sewing, cooking, nursery care, baking (the local speciality, the famous Schwarzwald

39

cake, a unique composition of sponge cake, cherries, cherry liqueur, chocolate and cream), and immaculate manners. The graduates knew how to sit on the edge of a chair in the presence of a count, and how to listen to the countess's dispositions with lowered eyes. They had no difficulty finding positions with the best families, and when the world war was coming to an end, and when the best families were relocating from the front line they took their maids with them.

Gizela worked for a family fleeing from Düsseldorf. The family lived on the second floor, while the first floor was occupied by the café frequented by the French soldiers, and also by Stani.

Stani was tall, silent, and the best foxtrot dancer in the village. When Stani and Gizela went to a dance together for the first time, it turned out that the best foxtrot dancer among the women was a certain woman from Prussia. It is possible that she was in love with Stani, but she had three children and was waiting for her husband to return from the Eastern Front. Nothing serious, of course.

Stani and Gizela lived in one of the white houses under red slanted roofs. You can see it on the postcard. You can also see the spire of the church where Stani used to go with his Polish prayer book, and hotels for tourists. The tourists were not rich. The rich travelled to Switzerland. The visitors were people from the Ruhra mining district. In their shorts and handmade woollen socks they dutifully marched around the forests breathing deeply. They liked these forests – thank God. Because of them Gizela had something to do for the whole year.

Stani did not want to return to Poland. His mother was dead, and he had the impression he would not like the communists if he knew them. He also did not want to stay in Germany. They planned to go to Austria, but each time they packed their things they had to unpack again because Gizela was pregnant. They stayed in the village – thank God. What would she do in a strange country with four children and without Stani?

3

Stani was clean, diligent, and did not like to talk much. He told her neither about the war, nor about Poland, but sometimes he asked her things.

'Did you know about the concentration camps?'

'I did not.'

'And your father?'

'Mother did not allow us to talk about such things.'

Shortly before the end of the war she saw in Düsseldorf a group of people in striped uniforms. They were getting off a truck and were terribly thin. The pedestrians would throw them packs of cigarettes, which they stuffed with trembling hands under their shirts. Two men in black uniforms came running, their voices raised, whips in their hands. The crowd dispersed. She was surprised. She never imagined people could be so thin.

She told Stani about that incident. 'I thought they were from a regular prison. How could I know they were from a concentration camp?'

'That's good,' said Stani. 'That's good you did not know.'

'What is there that I should have known?' she asked.

'Nothing.'

'Why nothing? If you think I should have known something, why don't you tell me?'

She did not understand. Nor did their son, Stefan. When Stefan grew up, he asked her just the same question: 'Did you know about the concentration camps? And your father?'

Stani told them about two events: how they had to run around the barracks barefoot in the snow, and how they counted out: one, two, *three*, four, five, *six*, seven, eight, *nine*. The prisoners who were the threes, sixes and nines were to step out, and the counting resumed: one, two, *three*, four, five, *six*. Finally the threes, sixes and nines were marched out of the camp and the rest returned to work.

It was rumoured that the threes, sixes and nines were working at a *Bauer*'s in the village. Stani envied them. He dreamed about easier work and village food, and prayed to be a three, six or nine during the next count-off. His prayers were unanswered. After the war he learned that the threes, sixes and nines did not go a *Bauer*'s, but to their execution.

He told the story to Stefan when the boy grew up, but his son disapproved: 'He could have fought. Why didn't they defend themselves?'

One day Stefan said: 'Mother, I think I understand him now.'

It was many years after Stani's death, and Gizela was talking to Stefan through thick, bulletproof glass. The glass divided the room into two parts and was encased in heavy iron. The frame had two slots on both sides, through which one could hear a hollow, muffled voice. Sometimes the glass acted like a mirror and instead of the person on the other side one could see only one's own reflection. Stefan was talking in his muffled, hollow voice to the glass, to himself. 'Mother, I think I understand him now.'

'What do you understand?'

'Him. I have read . . .'

'What?' she repeated several times, but could not grasp the answer.

The warden beckoned that the visit was over.

4

Before the war Stanisław W. lived with his parents and siblings in Łódz. Their father was a weaver. They occupied an attic room – narrow, long, with a small window and a slanting attic wall . . . The room contained beds for seven, and, when the grandparents were still alive, nine people. Apart from the beds it had an iron stove with a pipe, a washing basin and two buckets – one for clean and one for dishwater. Potatoes were kept under one bed and coal under another. Also, there must have been some chairs, at least one, because when Mother returned from her smuggling trips shivering and wet Father would seat her in a chair and put a pan with burning denatured alcohol at her feet. The children gathered round and watched the flickering blue flame while Mother was sweating.

That room was remembered by Stanisław W.'s younger brother, the one who moved to a small town in the Western Lands after the war. He worked in a uranium mine which was closed after several years. When it was still in operation the town was a security zone. Strangers were not allowed in and soldiers checked identification papers on public buses. The brother's wife worked in a rug factory. These rugs were pretty, but the production was slashed and lay-offs began. There is still great demand, however, for wall hangings with the Black Madonna – size 120 by 90cm. The employees can get them for 170 thousand złotys while the market price reaches one million. They also tried to manufacture Our Lady of Ostra Brama, but the gold came out too pale – problems with the pigment. Recently something happened to Stani's younger brother's legs. Many people in the town have problems with their legs: their legs suddenly give in and people cannot stand. Some say it is from the dumps at the uranium mine, some say it is from Chernobyl, which hit the local mountains the hardest. Some say it is from vodka.

The younger brother was a child during the war and does not remember why Stanisław was taken to the camps.

First their father was taken and sent to work in Germany. Mother moved her children to a village and hid the oldest son in a haystack, but they found him anyway and sent him to work. In the autumn of 1940 their aunt came to visit and both their father and Stanisław were gone by then.

Next autumn their aunt was standing at the window and speaking quietly the names of those for whom mass should be said on All Saints' Day: 'For Father, for Mother, for my sister Czesława . . .' She shuddered: 'Why Czesława? Czesława is alive.' At this moment she saw her sister walking towards her in the middle of the road. She was as pretty and young as many years before . . . 'What is it that I see?' said the aunt and quickly opened the window, but the street was empty. A couple of days later she received a letter: 'Dear Aunt, please come. Our mother is dead and we are living in the streets.'

The younger brother knew where their mother was buried: section four, row five, grave nineteen. That's what the undertaker told the children to remember. They repeated in unison: 'Section four, row five . . .'

The mother of Stanisław W. was thirty-five when she died. She was returning from one of her smuggling trips. She stopped at her friend's and asked for tea. The friend went to the kitchen. When she returned, Stanisław's mother was lying on the floor. She looked more than thirty-five. A photograph shows a thin, hunched woman with gaunt face and sunken eyes. She is trying to smile to the camera but the smile looks more like a twitch deepening the lines around her mouth and her hollow cheeks.

She had a modest funeral on a chilly, cloudy day. A photograph shows a group of people around the fresh grave, a pile of dirt, painted coffin and the undertaker's cart.

Small, sad children huddle over the grave.

Behind them a tall boy stares at the coffin.

The boy is Stanisław W.

He was taken by the Germans during his mother's life, and yet he was at her funeral?

He mentioned something to Gizela about an escape. Perhaps he escaped to attend the funeral, and as a punishment he was sent to a concentration camp? But how did he learn that his mother was dead?

Perhaps he saw a young woman, as pretty as many years before, walking towards him in the middle of a road? But he could not have remembered his mother being young and pretty . . . More likely he saw that thin hunched woman with a twitch around her lips . . .

Stanisław's sister-in-law asks whether Stanisław met Gizela during the war. If he did, she could have been the reason for his imprisonment. When the sister-in-law was forced to work in Germany, she saw a Polish boy hanged in the city square for romancing with a German woman. All the Poles had been rounded up in the square and made to watch everything till the end . . . how the boy was pushing the rope away and crying to the hangman. Stanisław's sister-in-law does not know how to write it down in German, but it sounded something like this: *'Lass mich leben, lass*

mich leben . . .' So if Stanisław and Gizela met during the war . . .
But they didn't. They met at a dance after the war, when it turned
out that Stani was the best foxtrot dancer in the village, even if he
was quite needlessly dancing with the woman from Prussia. He
must have been sent to the camps for something else.

5

Stanisław W. was in three different camps, although it is not known
when and for how long. The Warsaw archive contains a register
from Dachau: small pink and yellow catalogue cards made by the
Polish prisoners after the camp had been liberated. Relying on their
own information and memory they have written down on each card
the prisoner's name, number, where he came from and where he
was sent. There are eighty cards with the name W., apart from
'Kowalski', the most popular Polish name. There are seven cards
with 'Stanisław W.'.

Stanisław W. from Bolimów was sent in by the Gestapo from
the camp of Flossenburg. Stanisław W. from Pieściorgów came
from the camp in Dzialdowo and was sent to Mauthausen. Stanisław
W. from Sierpc . . . Stanisław W. from Zielonka . . . Stanisław W.
from Anielin, Stanisław W. from Horbaczów . . . Stanisław W.
from Kutno came with a group transport and was sent over to the
camp in Natzweiler.

Stanisław W. from Kutno is the future husband of Gizela and
father of Stefan W. The camp number is also the same: 122962.

Stanisław W. died on 9 October 1953 in the Tübingen Clinic.
We learn from the death certificate that he was 180cm tall, weighed
69.7kg and suffered from a chronic kidney condition.

He was twenty-seven.

6

Gizela spent the last week in the clinic. On the last day a professor came, looked at Stani and ordered him to be moved to a separate room. Stani tried to console her. 'Tomorrow I'll be better, you'll see.' He was falling asleep, waking up. 'Tomorrow I'll be better . . .'

When she came to, she realized she was sitting at the table in her home clutching a small cardboard box with Stani's clothes and a small Polish prayer book, *We Sing the Lord*.

7

Dark green, light green, the ribbon of blue, the slanted roof of a hotel. Gizela washes the dishes and cleans the rooms. The flat roof of the laundry. Gizela folds and wraps men's shirts . . .

Walking in the local woods was the favourite occupation of the tourists. Throwing pine cones at the tourists was the favourite pastime of the local children. The school principal called Gizela for conferences: 'Your son throws cones at our tourists.'

'All children throw cones,' said Gizela. 'Why are you complaining only about my child?'

'Your daughter,' said the principal another time.

'Your son . . .'

'Your daughter . . .'

'It's because all the other fathers were heroes,' explains Stefan.

Gizela was hurt. Other children told beautiful, uplifting stories about heroes. Their fathers were shooting – usually on the Eastern Front. Their fathers were dying, yet fighting till the last drop of blood . . . And what could her children tell? That their father dreamed of being a *three*, or a *six*? Can a father who runs barefoot around the barracks and who prays for a happy number . . . Can such a father compete with heroes from the Eastern Front? Can the son of such a man evoke sympathy in the school principal?

(A certain woman from the village, who has her birthday on the same day as Stefan, each year sends him a postcard with greetings. In the postscript she always writes one and the same sentence: 'Were it not for that principal, you would have grown up an honest man.' Stefan already has over twenty such cards, all with the same sentence: 'Were it not for that principal . . .')

'Besides,' other mothers told their children, 'if his father was in the camps, there must have been a reason. Hitler was Hitler, but nobody was sent to the camps without a reason.'

After Stefan's second escape from school, Gizela turned for help to the psychologists from the Department of Youth Supervision. They advised her to send her son to a reformatory school. 'He'll get there sooner or later,' they said. 'But if you send him voluntarily it will be easier to get him out later on when he learns some sense.'

Stefan says he spent only one year in the reformatory school.

Stefan lives in an isolation cell in the best guarded part of the prison, known as Maximum Security Row.

He has been living there for twelve years.

After twelve years of loneliness the past begins to blur while space and time appear in a foreshortened perspective. The town where Gizela lives is six hundred kilometres away, and yet he thinks the town is nearby. He thinks he spent one year in the reformatory school, while a document in his files states clearly that it was six years.

8

The director of the reformatory school was a Protestant priest – a big man with a bloated face and heavy fists.

Each week he would grade his pupils in three categories: work, learning and behaviour. Six was the lowest, and one, the highest grade. If you got a six in any category you had to spend the weekend in an isolation cell with two wooden boards – one to sit on, and one to rest your head and shoulders on.

From time to time the inmates tried to escape, but they were quickly returned by the police. After each return they would tell about the goings-on in the world outside. One of the pupils, who ran to Frankfurt, told of students protesting about the methods used in reformatories. One girl had written a screenplay, and some people wanted to establish a reformatory with quite different methods.

The name of the screenwriter was Ulrike Meinhof, and the girl who called for different methods was Gudrun Ensslin.

9

After Stanisław's death, Gizela appealed to the authorities: her husband had died of kidney failure which was the result of his imprisonment in concentration camps. The four children of Stanisław W. were entitled to some help.

A lawyer advised Gizela W. to write to the Office of Compensations in Baden-Württemberg.

The office asked for the history of Stanisław W.'s illness.

The clinic was unable to establish whether the sickness of Stanisław W. was a result of his imprisonment. The examination of Stanisław's retina did not provide sufficient proof. The clinic requested an opinion from the Institute of Pathology.

The Institute of Pathology was unable to establish . . .

The lawyer appealed against the decision.

Gizela W. wrote a letter: 'Does the German state believe my children should rot to death . . . ? I am not a beggar, I am fighting for what I deserve . . .'

The lawyer was upset by the emotional tone of the letter.

The Office of Compensations rejected the appeal, because the deceased did not meet all the conditions stipulated in paragraphs 1 and 2, but it also suggested that he could possibly qualify under paragraph 167.

Eight years after Stanisław W.'s death the president of Köln informed Gizela: 'The Government of the Federal Republic of Germany has signed an agreement with the High Commissioner of the United Nations about a new regulation referring to cases of persecution based on nationality.'

Moreover, the president of Köln informed Mrs Gizela W., 'There is no evidence indicating that the deceased was persecuted because of race, religion, or ideology. He might have been persecuted because of his nationality ($167) . . . in which case, however, the compensation cannot be transferred to the surviving members of the family.'

10

During her first visits to the prison, Gizela was speaking to the bulletproof pane with slots on both sides:

'If your father were alive, he would certainly disapprove of all that. When the Americans liberated his camp they gave him a big stick and said: "C'mon man, get even." Do you know what your father said to them? "Sorry, gentlemen, but I am not cut out for that."'

After his mother's visits, Stefan conducted long conversations with his father. 'It wasn't even a machine gun,' he started. 'It was just a stick. And you didn't want to take it into your hands?'

He was not sure of his father's answer. 'I am not cut out for that,' is hardly a sufficient answer. Thus Stefan continued:

'You must have believed that the world would change after Dachau. Look at the fists of the director in my reformatory. Look at the two boards in the isolation cell. Look at me, sitting on one board and resting my head on the other. And don't forget Mother's face when she returned from the compensation officials. You didn't want the stick – it's your business, not mine. But please look at Mother's face.'

He addressed his father with growing impatience, as if there was a connection between the director's fists and the stick that Stanisław W. did not want to take in his hands. As if there was a connection between the stick, the people from the Office of Compensations and the solitary cell on Maximum Security Row.

11

According to the biographical note in his file, he spent several months as a seaman. For two weeks he worked as a ship's mechanic. Established contacts with leftist radicals. Took part in a demonstration at the Ministry of Justice. Sent his unemployment benefits to the prisoners' fund. Maintained contacts with persons involved in the preparation of the terrorist attack on the Embassy of the Federal Republic in Stockholm. Joined the RAF (Rote Armee Fraktion) and went underground.

From the file: RAF members rented a number of apartments in the area. Stole a yellow Mercedes and bought a white van. Obtained two Heckler und Koh rifles, one machine gun WZ 63 (made in Poland) with Makarov bullet cartridges, one Colt revolver . . .

At 5.30p.m. the blue Mercedes carrying director Hans Martin Schleyer and his driver approached, followed by a white Mercedes with three police officers. As they turned right the yellow Mercedes parked on the pavement cut in front. Dr Schleyer's driver started to brake. Assailants jumped out of the van and opened fire at the driver and the police officers. Dr Schleyer was pulled into the van unharmed and driven off in an unknown direction. The assault lasted two minutes. The driver and the three policemen died at the scene. Five shots were fired at the driver – one of them proved lethal. Twenty-three shots were fired at the first policeman, two of them lethal. Twenty-four shots were fired at the second policeman, three of them lethal. Twenty shots were fired at the third policeman, two of them lethal. One hundred shots altogether. All the lethal ones were fired with Makarov 9mm bullets. It happened in Köln on 5 September 1977.

Hans Martin Schleyer was the chairman of the Union of Employers in the Federal Republic. In return for his freedom the kidnappers demanded the release of ten imprisoned RAF terrorists including Andreas Baader and Gudrun Ensslin.

On 13 October four Arab terrorists hijacked a Lufthansa plane. They landed in Mogadishu and repeated the RAF demands.

On 17 October German commandos rescued the passengers and killed three terrorists. The captain of the plane was shot by the terrorists.

Several hours later the guards in Stammheim Prison found the corpses of RAF prisoners. Baader and Raspe died of gunshots. Gudrun Ensslin was hanging from the window frame. It was established that all committed suicide.

Two days later Dr Schleyer's body was found in the boot of an abandoned Audi 100.

Seven months later, in 1978, Stefan W. was arrested at Orly Airport for the kidnapping and murder of Hans Martin Schleyer.

The trial was held in 1980. Stefan W. refused to testify about the kidnapping and murder, though he volunteered his opinions on the actual goals of the German bourgeoisie, the tentacles of neo-colonialism in the Third World, and the war in Vietnam, which, in his opinion, revealed the true face of American imperialism. He was sentenced to life imprisonment.

12

Terrorists evoked general fear and hatred. There were rumours they were able to build and use a nuclear bomb. Polls showed a rapid increase in the number of people favouring restoration of capital punishment. Acid was thrown on the ten-year-old son of Gudrun Ensslin. The boy was playing; the acid was thrown by adults. His face was burned. He was taken to the United States where doctors made three successful skin transplants. The doctors had experience from treating soldiers burned with napalm in Vietnam. No cemetery wanted to bury the three from Stammheim. There were demands to have their bodies burned and ashes scattered or left on a garbage dump. Finally they were buried in Stuttgart at the personal request of the mayor. His name was Manfred Rommel and he was the son of Field Marshal Erwin Rommel – the 'desert fox' from Africa, and a participant in the plot against Hitler. He made the request because he was a Christian. Because he knew Gudrun from his childhood. Because many years ago, in Ulm, the parents of Gudrun Ensslin were living two houses from the Rommels.

Mr Ensslin was a pastor. After the war his daughters, Christiana and Gudrun, asked him the same question Stani asked Gizela W.

'Did you know?'

Unlike Gizela, the pastor knew. He knew Stauffenberg's conspirators. They were his parishioners. He knew the circumstances of Rommel's death in the local quarry.

The daughters blamed him for not condemning the crime. He should have done it publicly, from his pulpit, during a mass.

The pastor explained that Gestapo agents also attended masses.

'This is hardly a reason to keep quiet,' responded the daughters.

13

Christiana Ensslin cuts her hair short. She has dark, sunken eyes, a baggy sweater and she lives with a terrorist who spent sixteen years in prison and was pardoned by the president. She is a friend of a terrorist woman who is still in prison but will be pardoned soon. She spends only her nights in prison and during the day she makes costumes for a local production of *La Traviata*. When she is pardoned she will take vacations with a Swedish princess known as 'prisoners' angel'. Christiana Ensslin is active in the Women in Film Union. She is fighting for more funds for women producers. Most of all she would like to produce a film about Rosa Luxemburg's first day of freedom. It is 1918. Rosa leaves the Wrocław prison. She takes a train to Berlin, enters the editorial office, greets Leibknecht, sits down behind her desk and starts to write. She writes an article on the situation in Germany. Fine, but who is going to see that film? 'Me,' says the terrorist who spent sixteen years behind bars. 'Me,' says the terrorist who makes costumes for *La Traviata*. 'Me,' says Christiana, whose father has not condemned the crime. 'Me,' says Dr Ronge who interprets our Polish–German conversation. 'Me too,' I say out of pity for Christiana Ensslin.

14

Maximum Security Row was built specially for Stefan and his friends from the RAF. It is situated in the Northern Colony, at the very heart of Ossendorf Prison. There is no daylight in the cells. The walls have been made of materials which absorb smells and sounds. The keys do not jingle, digital locks do not grind, coffee brewed by Stefan W. does not smell. Stefan brought a thermos with hot water and jars to the visiting room. He poured Nesca and sugar from the jars, mixing carefully, slowly adding milk. He made cappuccino. The visiting room is a concrete cave decorated with prints. There is one of the equestrian statue of Peter the Great, one shows the inspection of guards on the Senators' Square, and one depicts the river Moyka in winter. They were placed there by Stefan's counsellor, who has a soft spot for St Petersburg.

Stefan was in a good mood. He has green-grey eyes like his father and a trusting smile. He shouted, *'Dzień dobry pani'*, which exhausted his knowledge of Polish, and switched into German. He said he was in Poland once, but only at the airport. When he and a friend entered the transfer zone, they noticed a most-wanted list with photos of the terrorists. Without difficulty they recognized their own faces. Luckily, no one paid any attention to the poster, or to them. After half an hour their flight was called. His second contact with Poland was through a Polish machine gun WZ 63. It was purchased abroad. A nice piece, handy, small, no bigger than a handgun. His friends liked it because it was so easy to conceal. Unfortunately it has one serious drawback: cartridges too short. It wouldn't stand a fighting chance against a comparable NATO weapon. Makarov cartridges fit only the Polish gun. The policemen and Schleyer's driver were shot with Makarov bullets. Stefan W. says that the driver should not have died. It was a mistake. Nor should the policemen have died, but no one knew there would be a police escort. Schleyer never travelled with guards. They started to keep an eye on him shortly before the kidnapping, after an attempt on a bank director. In short – a bungled job. 'On the other hand,' says Stefan W., 'if you pick up a gun, you should be prepared to kill somebody.'

Schleyer's kidnapping claimed many victims: Schleyer, his driver, three policemen, three hijackers, the captain of the plane, the prisoners in Stammheim . . . Yes, many victims, agrees Stefan W. But no one anticipated that the government would reject their demands. No one had the slightest idea. They knew capitalism was cruel, but to such an extent . . . ?

15

For the first time in sixteen years Stefan W. left Maximum Security Row and came to the general visiting room. It was a rather large room with two doors. One opened for the entering prisoners, the other for visitors. Each prisoner was accompanied by a guard, who carried a chart which he placed on the desk. At the desk, facing the room sat a woman supervisor. She was a plump brunette with gold earrings and a deep-cut top finished with black lace. She was wearing a skirt buttoned at the front. The lower buttons were undone and the skirt revealed her thighs. They were so thick that she could not keep her legs together. She sat with her legs slightly apart, in black patterned tights.

Apart from the supervisor's desk there were six tables with chairs. The prisoners entered first. They were mostly young men. They entered slowly, looking around and carrying plastic bags with dirty clothes. Then the visitors were admitted. They were women. They entered hastily, almost running, bumping into the chairs and throwing themselves into the men's arms. They were wearing long, loose skirts. They turned their backs on the room and immediately started chatting. They listened for a reply, burst out laughing, and resumed their tale.

Stefan W. explained the sources of RAF ideology, which derived from the urban guerrilla movements in Latin America. Contemporary imperialism feeds on exploitation of the Third World. The RAF supports the Third World and its liberation movements by striking right at the heart of imperialism. 'We attack the bastions of imperialism,' said Stefan W., 'military bases, banks . . .'

The women were moving from the chairs to the men's knees. Their long skirts reached down to the ground and protected them like screens. Their laughter turned into interrupted, muffled giggling.

'Mao said the working class in the imperialistic states is no longer a revolutionary force,' continued Stefan W. 'It also lives off the exploitation of the Third World. The new revolutionary forces of the world . . .'

The women were unbuttoning the men's clothes. The giggling slowly subsided.

'. . . are the people of the social margin. The homeless, the unemployed, former prisoners, youth from reformatory schools. They are the base of our struggle.'

The women started to sway on the men's knees – gently, like boats on calm water. Only Stefan W.'s voice could be heard in the visiting room in Ossendorf Prison.

'The rejected have to organize!'

'Factories to the workers!'

'When a capitalist calls the police, we respond with force!'

'"Violence is the midwife of the new world," said Marx. Freedom is just a matter of time.'

The supervisor gave a sign. The visit was over. The women started to button up their clothes and the clothes of their men. They adjusted their blouses and hair.

'Eastern Europe?' said Stefan W., much more quietly, thoughtfully. 'Well, Europe, one more failed experiment. The idea lives on, and millions still dwell in poverty.'

Guards appeared, taking the prisoners away. The room was empty.

16

The conversations with Father conducted on Maximum Security Row ended in silence, which, in Stefan W.'s opinion, was hiding stubborn, relentless disapproval. At first he felt bitter. Later he came to the conclusion that further argument was pointless. One cannot convince a man who lived through Dachau without resistance and later looked for justice in the prayer book *We Sing the Lord*. Therefore he turned to another person, to his father's mother. She was overworked and poor. She was being exploited by factory owners. She was the person Stefan W. and his friends wanted to defend from capitalist greed. She had to be an ally in his struggle. She had to understand him. He felt her compassion and addressed her with boundless trust. He longed for her. He did not know how old she was. He could not know that at her death she was younger than he, sitting on his bunk on Maximum Security Row. Had he known the story of Stanisław W.'s younger brother, about the attic room and the pan of burning spirit, he would probably picture her sitting in a chair. He would address a shivering woman wrapped in a blanket, with a blue flame at her feet like a sacrificial fire.

17

One day Stefan W. received a letter from an unknown woman. She wrote that she was twenty-three and fighting for women's rights. She was thinking of him and wanted to pay him a visit. He invited her over. She was tall, slender, and wore a black sweater and black leather trousers. They talked through the bulletproof glass about women's liberation, world imperialism, and love. From that time on she visited him each month, and several times a week she sent him letters and postcards. These letters had neither beginnings nor ends. She would start in the middle of a sentence, sometimes in the middle of a word, and break off in the same manner. They guessed each other's moods from their handwriting. They made an agreement never to pretend anything. When she was sad, she did not try to smile, and when she felt bad, she did not put on make-up. They worried that they thought each other better than they should, that they idealized and invented themselves. That was their constant worry and the constant subject of their conversations. 'Perhaps you think I am intelligent,' she shouted towards the glass. 'Please, don't think so. I am much more stupid than you would wish.' 'Perhaps you think I am good,' she shouted on another occasion.

For seven years they were unable to touch each other. They made love with their eyes through the bulletproof glass.

For three years they met in the visiting room under the prints of St Petersburg in winter.

One day she wrote that she was in love with someone else. Because they promised not to pretend, she wouldn't visit him or write to him any more.

She kept her promise.

He calculated that she had been coming to see him for ten years, so she must be thirty-three.

He never counted the letters and postcards she wrote to him during those five hundred weeks.

18

Daniel Cohn-Bendit, the student leader of 1968, has recently been nominated the Director of Intercultural Affairs in the office of the mayor of Frankfurt. He has a spacious room with a secretary who brings coffee and biscuits. He says that terrorism was the product of the fifties – the silence about the war. The young Germans wanted to know how it was, and their parents said: 'Why scratch old wounds?'

People started talking publicly about the crimes only after the trial of the Auschwitz henchmen held in Frankfurt in 1963. When the war in Vietnam started, Andreas Baader, Gudrun Ensslin and their friends said: 'We will not remain silent like our parents.' They started to kill. They thought they had the right to kill American soldiers in Germany in revenge for Vietnam, and German judges in revenge for their bourgeois justice. They believed they were on the side of right. If somebody is on the side of right, everything he does is right. Even murder becomes sacred. Andreas Baader summoned Cohn-Bendit, the hero of 1968, to common struggle. Cohn-Bendit refused. Andreas Baader called him a traitor. Cohn-Bendit told Andreas Baader and Gudrun Ensslin that using youths from reformatories in RAF activities was a crime. He condemned terrorism. First, he did not like killing. Second, he did not like Andreas Baader and had no intention of building a new, better world with him.

The government handled the terrorists ruthlessly. The Social Democrats assured the Germans that 1933 would never happen again.

The terrorists said: 'No one will ever accuse us of silence.'

The Social Democrats said: 'No one will ever accuse us of weakness.'

It was a psychodrama, says Cohn-Bendit. Both sides were trying to act out their post-Nazi complexes.

19

One of the postcards from the girl in the black sweater was a reproduction of a painting by a Mexican artist, Frida Kahlo. Stefan W. liked the picture and wrote to the publisher of the postcard. The publisher sent him more reproductions and a letter: 'You have a Polish name. Are you interested in Polish subjects?' The next package contained several German translations of Polish authors.

From that time Stefan W. started reading Polish books on the Second World War. He took special interest in the Warsaw ghetto. He discovered a similarity between the fate of Jews in the ghetto and that of prisoners in concentration camps. He read books by Bartoszewski, Moczarski and the poetry of Czesław Miłosz. Together with the girl he pondered the discrepancies in the accounts of Marek Edelman and General Stroop. Or the question of why Edelman did not like the communists, although the communists sent the first pistol to the ghetto – the one which was used against the commander of the police. He gave the books to the girl to read. She never returned some of them, perhaps out of absentmindedness, perhaps for some other reason. He was fascinated by Marek Edelman's statement about 'the human right to weakness'. For Stefan W., Edelman became the highest moral authority. He was said to have learned that Marek Edelman considered the terrorists' contempt for human life a post-mortem victory of the Nazis.

'It's a pity I didn't know it earlier,' he said.

20

Sunday is Gizela W.'s best day. She does not work, she does not help the old lady from the neighbourhood, and she does not meet the parents of the other prisoners from the RAF. (She does not like these meetings. Professors and doctors all, and she the sole working woman.)

First, she has her Sunday breakfast. Then she writes a letter. That her legs hurt a bit less. That she is still strong enough to help the old lady. That the chestnuts on the river bank are in bloom, and soon the Japanese cherry should blossom too. She seals the envelope and writes the address: Ossendorf Prison.

Then she starts to pray. She begins with thanks: for the coming of a new day, for legs not hurting, for the chestnuts . . . then she presents her request. Not to God. She would not dare to bother Him with her affairs. She turns to Stani, who suffered a lot, never complained, and each Sunday went to church. He must be in better relations with God than herself, and if only Stani asks Him, God would allow her to see the return of her son.

In just one issue does she turn directly to God, without involving Stani.

This is when she asks Him to forgive their son the most unforgivable sin.

Translated from the Polish by Jarosław Anders

Jerzy Pilch

The Register of Adulteresses

I was standing by a pay phone, I was leaning on it, cooling my burning forehead on its armoured case and frantically leafing through my appointment book. The gleaming eyes of a common drunk elated by his own immoderation followed the familiar string of letters and numbers, and I was becoming more and more convinced that the addresses and telephone numbers of my female colleagues from the Institute were in fact addresses and telephone numbers of biblical women of debauchery. The string of letters and numbers was familiar, even though I had no idea what some of those letters and numbers referred to. While writing them down my hand must have led an existence surprisingly separate from my own. I was not sure whether the treacherous date of 9 July and letters *cdefg* were the address of a young poet who bared the secrets of his beautiful soul to me during one long evening, the telephone number of a clochard – the Eternal Wanderer, with whom I shared a bottle of Hennessy on the lawn in front of the Lenin Industrial Complex – or coded co-ordinates of a charming bartender? I was looking through my appointment book wondering who, in the last resort, can be counted on, and recalling the great moments of my, Gustaw's, loneliness.

Whenever I was left alone, whenever the Good Lord bestowed upon me moments of great loneliness, whenever my wife Emilka departed for one of her training seminars or scholarly conferences, I would move a comfortable stool next to the linen chest, place my telephone on the chest, arrange an ashtray, matches, a brandy glass, a bottle of Albanian brandy and a huge cup of mint tea next to the telephone, and I would call, call everywhere. I would dial the numbers as in a trance, I would turn the dial as if I were dancing, I would desperately search my appointment book and call endlessly, I would hang up and call again, I would dial number after number at random, until, moments before falling asleep, I felt like the poet Broniewski, famous for his ceaseless, narcotic night calls.

I pressed the receiver to my ear and knew I was longing for those sporadic moments of great loneliness. Grass is always greener on the other side of the fence. I would be better off sitting next to the linen chest, kindling enormous inner conflagrations and extinguishing them with powerful gulps of brandy or mint tea. It would be nicer that way, although the present situation was not bereft of great promises and great literature either – doctoral students and young assistant professors appeared to me shrouded in the fog of suffocating ambiguity; the appointment book, published by the House of Books, was beginning to smell like accidental perfume, but first one had to decide beyond the shade of doubt, who, apart from Jola Łukasik, can be counted on, who should be called and invited.

I cursed the moment when my guest, a Swedish intellectual, started to yearn for feminine company, I cursed it even though his yearning might have been free of any unchaste intentions. As a writer says: 'Femininity, even without unchaste intentions, is always a damn good thing.' I cursed the moment, but after all no man is able to disentangle himself from all the encroaching contradictions of life. Therefore, just as I was cursing, I was humming to the receiver the first bars of the mad song of all procurers, I was humming and slowly composing a list of my female colleagues, I was writing an unattainable *Index adulterarum* – the register of adulteresses.

Who should we call, Gustaw? I asked myself in the plural because I was sinking into yet another narrative trance, this time in *Pluralis secundum*. Who else could we call? Let's bring some order into the chaos, Gustaw.

I had no complaints about that plural form – on the contrary. It was perhaps a bit uncomfortable, but still – the fulfilment of my dreams and incantations! So many times did I implore the material world: 'Speak!' So many times did I beseech my trousers, 'Speak', my shirt, my jacket, my shame, 'Speak my shame!' I adjured, I pleaded with everything at hand: 'Speak, speak, oh tea, lemon, ruled notebook, ink pot, watch, strand of hair torn from my own head, speak, talk to me!' and I implored so long that now I had the right to think: it was fulfilled, all my petitions were granted, it really happened, and everything that surrounded me, and everything that was in me, started to talk, and there was a great sound of trumpets and fanfares. We, Gustaw, were standing by the phone dialling number after number and trying to establish once and for all who can be counted on, apart from Jola Łukasik.

The Ugly Dark-Haired Darling! First of all we can count on the Ugly Dark-Haired Darling, who kept her vigil over the books in the Faculty Library in Jagiellonian University. Yes, the Ugly One was sure to fulfil our every whim, was sure to guess our each and every secret thought. Next, Doctor Agata Tlamsik. Then Iza Gęsiareczka – ah, Iza Gęsiareczka! – if only she could be found, if only she agreed to bring her swimming suit with the golden thread – the epiphanies of summer heat, down pillows, and foreign languages. Next, the red-haired receptionist from the 'Eagle' dormitory, why not, we can call her, next, Magdalena Maria Szkatuła. A simple yet intricate story, let's tell it immediately, perhaps it will sooth our shaken nerves.

Magdalena Maria Szkatuła always evoked our strongest desires. She was wearing dark, loose-fitting dresses, drapes and veils. This apparel enhanced the epic expressiveness of her body. It seemed enough to raise the seven veils, seven dresses, and she would spring from the nets of dark cottons and silks like a glowing, dazzling mermaid. Her body was shining through dresses, jackets and turtle necks. Everyone who felt her haughty stare had to bear immeasurable tortures. I, Gustaw, tried to defend myself by focusing on my higher aspirations; I chased away the physical man in me and summoned the spiritual one. But they locked immediately – the physical and the spiritual – in a deadly tug-of-war, and the physical always won in the first round, even, let's be honest, in the first minute of the first round, and having won so easily proceeded to torment me and force me to chase Magdalena Maria Szkatuła, that is, Doctor Szkatuła's wife. And chasing her was not an easy task! She was a mother of three and a woman of broad cultural interests. Chasing her consisted of waiting in front of schools, kindergartens, or the musical centre where her youngest child took lessons. It required attending shows, concerts, exhibitions, movie premières, and elegant receptions in old Krakowian apartments, which consumed a lot of time, raked my nerves and adversely affected my health. Besides, you must remember what kind of weather we had in Poland in the eighties: snow, rain, heat waves. Desperate and exhausted by the lack of results, or even perspectives, I finally resolved to try a time-honoured method and approach her, as one usually does a married woman, through her husband.

I, Gustaw, visited the office of Magdalena Maria Szkatuła's husband, Doctor Szkatuła, and in full awareness of being only a potential drunk, I presented myself as a mature and accomplished alcoholic. I do not remember if I had mentioned before that Magdalena Maria's husband, Doctor Szkatuła, was a psychiatrist. 'Please, sit down,' said Doctor Szkatuła, looking me in the eyes, and I felt that his blue, childish eyes burned right through me, exposing all my hidden intentions and designs, easily penetrating the most secret corners of my soul – a rented studio, a friend's apartment, a number in a secluded hotel – and that he recognized the fragrance of Magdalena Maria's perfume, and I curled up in anticipation of my demise at the hands of a jealous husband. But at this very moment, seconds before my death, Gustaw's most vile characteristics suddenly came to his rescue – fear, duplicity, hypocrisy, cowardice – all those dark muses sent their messengers of hope, and thick, cold sweat appeared on my forehead, my hands began to shake, my speech deteriorated into mumbling, and my whole body started to tremble as if possessed by an unspeakable wild beast, and Doctor Szkatuła immediately recognized the onset of *Delirium tremens*. With each consecutive visit I, Gustaw, did my best to make my wretched affliction even more plausible. I drank a sea of Albanian brandy and – but let's make the long story short because other candidates are waiting – while trying to come close to Magdalena Maria, I came close to her husband, I came close to him as a patient. I pretended to be a man ensnared by addiction, and I did it so convincingly that I became one! I did not come closer to Magdalena Maria Szkatuła, I moved away from her; I have built an insurmountable wall between us, although sometimes she was within the reach of at least some of my senses. Sometimes, behind the white door of Doctor Szkatuła's office, I heard the rustling of her dresses.

Let's call her, the voices tempted me, let's take the Swedish intellectual, call her, and pay her a visit. She will receive us, no doubt, in grand style – drinks, candles, fluent English – let's call her, Gustaw, and perhaps she will answer the call of the sinful Swede when he feels the burning glare of her body. Perhaps this obscure light will burn him to a handful of icy Scandinavian ash, so let's call her, Gustav.

All right, let's call her, but first of all let's see who we can count on besides Magdalena Maria Szkatuła; Jola Łukasik, Iza Gęsiareczka. Who else do we have in store? Let's figure out, for example, who hides behind the mysterious number 11–26–48? Perhaps some beautiful unknown met by pure chance? And Kubas? And Barteczko? Perhaps we should call them after twenty years? One of them had round breasts, the other the shape of pears. But which one had which? Or maybe Gustaw will simply call his wife, Emilka, and then he will not hum, he will not even sing. His throat will simply explode with the truly satanic air of a procurer.

Call your wife Emilka, Gustaw, the broken voices tempted me, call her, whatever happens then will only be the climax of your symmetrical marriage.

And the demon of vengeance? Perhaps we should combine the beautiful with the useful, and take the insatiable Swede to the wife of you-know-who, Gustaw? Perhaps we shall feed the hungry beast of revenge that has been sleeping inside us?

And perhaps . . . ? No this name shall never escape our lips. Gustaw's heart valiantly defends itself against the arrows approaching slowly in his direction, their heads dripping with cherry syrup. No, not her, never! Our emblem, our caress, our Ludwika. Spacious interiors, a thick, phantasmagoric garden behind the patio, her glance. Yes, one would not have to explain anything, mince words, suggest a fleeting intimacy with the Swedish intellectual, no, she would understand us immediately. Let's have a drink, then, in her celestial company, in her spacious apartment, let's have a drink heavy like lead and let's slowly turn ourselves, ourselves, into Swedish intellectuals.

Translated from the Polish by Jarosław Anders

Paweł Huelle

Mina

Mina had long since given the impression of an unbalanced person, but the sudden eruption of her illness and its violent progression took me completely by surprise.

She came by more and more often, and could talk without cease for two or three hours on end, chain-smoking the while. The themes of her monologues revolved around her childhood, seamlessly drifting into the realm of her religious life, finally, in an inevitable sequence, to wander the gloomy corridors of Eros.

Mina feared damnation. Her God, ever on the watch for every false step she made, every stumble and fall, was a cruel and vindictive God. He could punish, but He never forgave. He passed judgement, but He couldn't love. He was the Creator, but He prophesied death and destruction. Mina feared this God, and in her anxiety I recognized the terror of a five-year-old girl, awoken in the middle of the night to the sight of her father, drunkenly hurling oaths as he beat her mother with his fists.

I was never able to convince her or make anything clear to her. Her childhood, that far-off time, in which the monologue so often immersed itself, as if to draw breath from it, was a distant and unfamiliar land to me, though Mina was born and had spent the first twenty years of her life in the very same country as I. The small Silesian town, close to the German border, loomed out of her story like an exotic island. Here the men died young, regularly before the age of sixty; in the breaks between cooking and working on three shifts the women bore children, and the young men all left the place as soon as they got the chance; if no such opportunity came along, they drank vodka and went down the mines instead, for such was the pattern of life here.

Mina also used to talk about her father, who didn't love her,

65

her mother who died ten years ago and her brothers who had no interest in their sister's fate. She also talked about the Russians, a couple of thousand Soviet soldiers who were stationed in the town, and about the closed district where they lived with their families.

Mina was immured in a sensation of cold. She had felt it through her body from the very start, and it was a terrible ordeal.

'As if I were plunged in a well,' she'd try to explain, 'as if I were falling deeper and deeper down where the water's freezing, where there's not a breath of air.'

She had often spent whole months on end in this state, and even though leaves were budding outside her window, even if the warm rain of June was falling, Mina could feel her body being wrapped in a thicker and thicker shroud of snow, her hands turning into icicles, and a cold wind raging in her gut, her breast and womb.

'If only a ray of light would get through to me, if I were only to hear the word,' she'd explain, 'then I'd be saved.'

But HE WHOM SHE AWAITED didn't even want to look at her, he hadn't the least intention of imparting his word to her. At such times she gave herself casually to chance-encountered men, and the long-repressed flames of desire would erupt with volcanic force. Soon she became aware, however, that as her body reached the heights of pleasure, her soul would be filled with anguish and anxiety. To start with she couldn't explain this to herself, but in time this strange duality revealed its cause to her – every time she was yielding to the very same man. The Prince of Darkness did change his appearance – he might be dark and swarthy, a man she'd met in a hotel, or a blond from the commercial department – but at the moment of the most extreme elation she always recognized his features, where beauty and ugliness combined in a most astounding way. Then her shriek would pierce the air, she'd break glass if it fell to hand, or run on to the stairs to warn people. Then the cold stage would come on, and Mina would sink ever deeper into it, until the next time. HE WHOM SHE AWAITED never came, but the Prince of Darkness, his lust to some extent satisfied for the time being, was still on the look-out for the next ideal moment.

I sat and watched her tears. Mina was helpless, but my

helplessness to relieve her suffering seemed even greater. Should we talk about God, whom Mina feared so much and who in her mind was a replica of her father? She had run away from him, away from the town on the German border all the way up here, where she'd finished university, where crouched for hours on end over library shelves she earned a pittance for her keep, and where like an invisible force his gaze went on pursuing her.

All her schemes, all her magic tricks to elude his gaze, the embodiment of power and authority, were in vain. Mina had became convinced of this several months ago, when kneeling at the confessional grille she had done her best to explain the essence of her pain to the man in black cloth. She told him of the flame which burst forth unexpectedly from beneath her dome of ice and frost, she told him of the unquenchable fires of desire which inflamed her at those moments, and of the Prince of Darkness, to whom she must submit. The man in black cloth had dashed from the confessional and shouted words she couldn't understand, but it soon became clear to her – it was Him, vindictive, envious Jehovah in person! He ran chasing her right across the church, violently waving his arms, threatening her with damnation like her father. Mina had run off to the beach and lain on the dry sand till evening, listening to the wind blowing.

'But just one ray of light would have been enough, one single word,' she repeated, 'and I would have been saved!'

I made an attempt to say something. I told her that the ray or the voice she was waiting for might be very near by, just a moment away, so there was no need to despair. At that she would explode with rage. On Mount Armon, when two hundred angels had been inflamed with desire for the daughters of the Earth, the very glance of those unearthly beings had burned them up. Not one of them could withstand the heat, and that was the beginning of the end. Incorporeal angels, pure intelligences, joined with the dust of the Earth, for what is a woman's body, if not dust? So when the angels on Mount Armon joined with the dust of the Earth, that was the instigation of the Fall.

But Mina wasn't concerned with that sort of glance, not with the sort of light that burns up and destroys. Mina was waiting for a ray of light that would touch her body tenderly and permeate her soul; to strains of music – or maybe just to the sound of invisible breathing – it would make her blessed. HE WHOM SHE AWAITED had just this sort of glance. How could I fail to understand it? How could I possibly fail to see that such very different glances could exist?

I didn't know much more than that, however. The old mine shafts, the motionless wheels of inactive pumps or the Russian soldiers' quarters, whence the sound of gunfire or of a mouth organ and choral singing sometimes drifted, were just as far away from me as the story of Mount Armon and the fallen angels. Hovering in the midst of it all, as if Mount Armon were a slag-heap in Mina's little town, was the ghost of her father. This man with bushy eyebrows and hands the size of spades had hated Mina from the outset, from the very day she was born in their suburban house of bricks.

'I was meant to be called Helena,' she explained, 'but my father burst out laughing and shouted at my mother that you couldn't possibly give a name like that to such an ugly child. So he called me Mina.'

The man with bushy eyebrows and hands the size of spades had a craving for perfection. And just because the world, like Mina, their little town and thousands of other people, wasn't perfect, her father condemned it all, because wherever he looked all he could find was dusty, grimy, full of cracks, like the ones in the walls of their home before they moved to the new housing blocks. Mina could remember watching a bulldozer smash up the wall and red roof; she also remembered seeing a tree ripped up by its roots, gripped in the metal jaws and left swaying for ages after against a clear blue sky.

As if to spite her father, Mina grew up to be the prettiest girl in town. The men were bewitched by her breasts and her way of walking, and the Russian officers with golden epaulettes, emerging from their district now and then, soldiers smelling of eau de Cologne and polished boot leather, gazed after her with expressions full of despondency.

'The Prince of Darkness could be hiding in any one of them,' explained Mina, 'but I didn't know that yet. All I knew was that my father was just waiting for my fall.'

I looked at her tired face and her fingers, tarnished yellow by the cheapest cigarettes. She went on spinning out her story, leaping freely across the months and years, while her inner logic was like a labyrinth with a bricked-up exit. Mina was well aware of this, and maybe that was why a look of dread lay lurking in her eyes. She could sense madness enfolding her in its grip, and although she still had one foot on this side, where a lot of things could be explained without recourse to fallen angels, the other was already firmly planted over there, on the other side.

'It's like a vortex sucking me in,' she cried, without looking up at me. 'In a couple of days or so I'll latch on to the first decent guy, I'll grab him by the sleeve and say, "Why don't you give me one hell of a good shafting, what do you think?" Or I'll stand in the window, yes, I'll stand in the window and fling off my clothes until some guest appears who wants to remove them from me.'

She wept loudly, hiding her face in her hands. In fact our acquaintance was merely fleeting; occasionally she had handed me some books in the library, I'd seen her a few times in the long university corridors, and we'd swapped a couple of remarks on the weather or on the meals served in the canteen. I had come to know that she lived alone and probably had no one to talk to. No one ever wrote to her or came to tea in her empty little room. Finally, after several minutes' silence, she handed me a phone number on a scrap of paper.

'Call them,' she whispered. 'I can't do it myself. But mind you, tell them to keep their paws off – or I'll bite them like a wild bitch, get it? Just you tell them that!'

I realized that it wasn't the first time she had taken herself off to hospital.

When the men in little white coats appeared at the door, Mina calmly got up from her chair and went off to the car with them. Shortly after, one of them came back, wishing to find out some more about the patient. Had she had a seizure? Might the cause of her depression be conflicts with her family? Was this the first case in the family? I was reticent. When the car drove away from in front of the house I breathed a deep sigh, as if I'd been relieved of a massive burden.

Two days later she called me from the hospital. She encumbered me with a whole baggage of unsettled matters. I was to pay her rent, go and talk to the man who ran the library, fetch some books, her toothbrush, a towel and her slippers from her flat and take it all over to her. I wasted at least half a day getting it all done. So when on top of that she suggested I keep her key and water her plants for her, I refused adamantly. I did promise, however, that once a week I'd come and visit her; I told her that if she were suddenly to remember something, she should call me at once without waiting till Friday.

She looked sleepy, complaining of headaches and about the injections that the nurses kept stuffing into her. Her movements were slow and she couldn't bend her back or her neck all the way, because the medicine was making her muscles stiff. In the television room where we sat and chatted other figures were wandering about in their pyjamas. Though the expressions on their faces were transparent and absent, I found them highly disconcerting, because it seemed as if they were hovering around us, picking up what we were saying, as if we had something to hide. For the meantime I said nothing, while Mina, her gaze fixed on the window, went on and on about HIM WHOM SHE AWAITED. Why didn't he come? Was it because she, Mina, wasn't worthy of such a visit? Or was it because he was disgusted by her body? He must know that apart from her body she also had a soul, and what a soul she had! How strong she felt it was, that pure, immaculate soul – he could come into it, like entering a crystal vase. What if he found her here, in hospital, in the middle of all these beds and nurses' white tunics, amidst all this stench and turmoil? He'd fill her up, just like olive oil filling an empty jug. 'He, who can place his hand in a nest of serpents, who can open all doors and locks.'

A terrible shriek resounded from somewhere in the depths of the ward. I could hear shouts and comings and goings; approaching the window, Mina just went on whispering the words of her prayer, more and more quietly – she was completely absent, lost in concentration.

One of the patients; a dressing gown pulled on over his sweater, was raking a wide strip of ground by the wall. Mina appeared not to notice him at his labour. She went on talking to herself, while I observed his accurate movements, which from up here, at first-floor level, looked strangely solemn. Once in a while he broke off his work to inspect the fresh furrows in the earth he'd tilled. His eyes seemed to be looking for something, then he shook his head in a disbelieving way and set to work again. When the nurses came to lead Mina down the corridor, the man with the rake was standing motionless by the wall, staring up into the sky. Silvery clouds were gently drifting across the park, sunlight glinted idly in the leaves of the trees, and beyond the forest, in the direction of the airfield, a passenger plane went purring by.

A week later Mina's puffy face greeted me like the harbinger of bad news. She had dark rings around her eyes and a cut on her lip; her grimace made her look like a witch from a children's picture book.

The bag of greening apples fell to the floor. I started to pick them up, kneeling on the slippery linoleum. As if possessed by an evil spirit she began to curse me in a hoarse, low voice, hurling a stream of vulgar remarks. I was to blame for everything – all her rage came crashing down on top of me with savage fury. I was the one who followed her about the university corridors, it was I who made suggestive innuendoes as I returned the books I'd borrowed, I pursued her in the streets in the hope that eventually she'd give in to my impure desires, and just because she hadn't, I had packed her off to the hospital, where she was suffering all this torture, where they kept on giving her injections, electric shocks and 'all that shit that makes you feel ill'.

She wouldn't let me get a word in edgeways. Again she hurled the bag of apples to the floor. She waved her arms about like an automaton, making sexual metaphors. I was the Prince of Darkness, the leader of the lust-filled sons of God from Mount Armon, I was the Russian soldier who had raped her in the park just after dusk, as she was coming home from her first date; I was also the doctor who had performed her abortion; it was all because of me that her father had struck her across the face, called her a bitch and thrown her out.

I tried to get away, but Mina came after me, talking ever faster and tugging at my arm. Streaks of saliva spattered furiously in the corners of her mouth; I kept hoping the nurses would come running to put an end to this scene of my accusation.

And in fact that did soon happen, but with a strength which I never would have suspected she had in her, Mina battled with the three strongmen for a good long while.

'That's him! That's him!' she kept shouting to her tormentors and pointing at me. 'He screwed little Mina! Shut the doors! Don't let him escape! Where's his uniform? Where are his golden epaulettes?'

I cannot describe how I felt at that moment. The patients and their visiting relatives were casting furtive glances at me; though they were accustomed to such scenes, yet in the looks that clung to me I identified a latent question. The apples lay scattered on the floor, still as billiard balls. I didn't stop to pick them up, but soon after, as I was heading for the exit, I was held back by the doctor, Professor B., a notable figure among local psychiatrists who was also head of the clinic. He wanted to invite me into his office to question me about Mina, but I was already running down the stairs, as if I were one of the nurses or hospital attendants, without taking any notice of what he was saying. Yet he kept on coming after me, the hem of his white apron flapping in the wind, and our conversation was like an exchange of diplomatic notes, restrained and full of hidden information. Finally, when we stopped by a wall covered in wisteria, once I'd explained the true nature of my friendship with Mina to him, as he was telling me about the cycles of schizophrenia, its common symptoms and baffling exceptions, I suddenly noticed the man with the rake. He was looking at the violet flowers of the wisteria, or else at the freshly raked strip of ground that he was busy tidying, just as when I had watched him from the window.

'Such a state,' the professor continued, 'can last for a few months, then either the crisis passes, or it doesn't – sometimes it goes on for years' – he pointed to the man stooped over the plot of earth – 'as in that man's case. Do you realize how long he's been here? Over thirty years!'

I walked down the avenue of the old park, in between hospital outbuildings. Here and there the faces of patients were looking out from the barred-up windows. Only a few inmates, like the rake man, were walking about the garden at liberty in faded dressing gowns stamped with dark-red triangles.

At the open psychotherapy ward Professor B. stopped and offered me his hand.

'Young man,' he said, 'it's good of you . . . it's commendable that . . . especially since our patient doesn't seem to have anyone . . .'

When to finish with I gave him my name, he thought for a moment and remembered my father.

'We went sailing together on an old German hulk at the yacht club,' he said, smiling broadly. 'In 1946. Yes, indeed, do you know what Gdynia looked like in those days?' As he was walking away I heard him say that I should pay him a visit next time I came to see Mina. 'Don't worry,' he called after me, 'she should be calmer in future.'

For the next few days I tried not to think about Mina, her illness or the hospital.

But one night Mina came back to me in a dream. She was standing at the top of a tower made of bricks: all round it stretched a plain full of undulating grasses, and I was running towards her, through thistles and teasels. In her hand she held a flaming torch, and although it seemed to be daytime, my vision was blinded by its light.

'I am not Mina, I am Helena!' she shouted once I'd got there.

I awoke to find the sheets damp with sweat.

From then on the dream began recurring, and I could feel my own growing anxiety. I desired her body, but not the one I'd often seen in the library, or in the long university corridors, or the one I could imagine in the small town on the German border. I wanted her body as it was at the top of the tower of bricks – there it was beautiful, absolutely flawless.

Meanwhile alarming things were happening to Mina's real body. From week to week she was getting fatter and fatter; her puffy, bloated face reminded me of an image out of Bosch, and her total apathy and inertia further deepened the impression of remoteness, provoking me to feel a repugnance which in spite of my best will I couldn't altogether stifle.

Maybe she understood what I was saying to her, but she only

answered reluctantly, in fitful sentences. There were a lot of things I wanted to ask her about. What were her brothers doing? Was her father still alive? And what had it been like with the Russian soldier in her home town that time, as she was on her way back across the deserted park at dusk, walking on wings of joy from her date, when maybe she'd exchanged her first kisses with her schoolfriend from the year above?

But it was all to remain in the realm of hypothesis. There was a repelling force in Mina's gaze, and none of my questions was even so much as uttered.

I couldn't really explain why I still kept on going there. I had no obligations whatsoever towards Mina, and her condition, close to catatonia, was ever worsening, shutting out communication.

My visits became ever shorter; while there I avoided meeting Professor B., and it was only the rake man, whom I encountered every time in exactly the same spot by the wall, who held me more and more firmly intrigued. He was always raking the same strip of ground, then inspecting the tracks made by his tool. He was quite clearly seeking some sign in the narrow furrows, but he'd fail to find it and start raking again, stooping over his little plot. I watched his movements many times, stopping at the wall for minutes on end, but busy with his task, he never took any notice of me.

Towards the end of summer I recognized that Mina was no longer the real reason why I kept on going there, nor was it because of my dream about her – it was because of the man in the dressing gown stamped with the letter P in a triangle, the symbol of all hospitals for the mentally ill. His face expressed no emotion whatsoever. Never for a moment was it brightened by a smile, never was it crossed by a look of doubt, and only as he stood stooping over his patch of earth did I notice him frowning, probably in amazement that he couldn't find whatever it was he yearned to see there. Nor did he answer the timid questions I put to him once or twice: 'What are you looking for? Can I help you? Have you lost something valuable?' Sometimes, at the sound of my words, he turned round towards me, and I got a look at his eyes. They were the same blue as Mina's, but the look in them seemed to express a different kind of madness. Yes, his ascetic figure and Olympian calm presented a sort of challenge. The world I had come from on the other side of the wall all of a sudden seemed chaotic and random; in a constant state of change, in a non-stop stream of shapes and noises, it reminded me of a river, flowing God knows where. The rake man, meanwhile, was somehow not subject to this force as he continued to perform his ritual. His eternity, existing on a dozen or so metres of loosened soil, silent and inaccessible, lay elsewhere.

One day, maybe the last Friday in September, they stopped bringing Mina into the visitors' room. She sat in bed not moving, and when I looked at her face through the window of the isolation ward I realized that an invisible force, the same one no doubt as had persisted in torturing her for all this time, had cut the final thread that tied her to this world.

Right behind me I heard the professor's voice, talking of somatic and hormonal changes, of the tissues, chemistry and mysterious substances of the brain, the names of which I can't remember; he said that in a hundred, maybe two hundred years from now, when biochemistry has solved these mysteries, such illnesses will no longer be incurable.

I said nothing.

The professor's voice was calm and decisive, as if he were giving a lecture to a room full of people sharing his profession. On this side of the window the corridor resounded with 'the structure of protein', 'genetic mutations' and 'cerebral ganglia'; on the other side sat Mina, fat, ugly and slobbering, in a state of utter idiocy. She had to be fed, washed, dressed and undressed like a child; she had to be cleansed of her own excreta. To all this she submitted indifferently, putting up no resistance.

Hadn't HE WHOM SHE AWAITED come? Had the gods of darkness, led by the angel from Mount Armon, carried off her soul, stamping their sordid seal on her body?

Could there be any other answer? I was twenty-four years old and I'd never studied theology. My Catholic upbringing gave not the slightest advantage for considerations of this kind, and yet Mina was crying out for an answer. Especially over there, on the far side of the window, where she was utterly helpless and desolate.

Meanwhile the professor went on talking, and it was some time before I realized that he was telling me the story of the rake man. In the days when an ammunitions truck used to drive down the beach each evening the man had been a border guard. Every morning at daybreak he had patrolled his stretch of the route, and every morning, as he was later to claim during hours and hours of interrogation, he found the tracks of bare feet leading from the sand dunes to the sea. He didn't report it to his superiors – if the footsteps had led in the opposite direction, he might have assumed, in accordance with his orders, that a spy had emerged from a submarine. But why barefoot, and why in exactly the same place every day? He couldn't find answers to these questions, any more than he could explain why the footsteps always led to a point where the waves washed them away. So he spent night after night on watch, hoping for an explanation of this mystery. He never saw a soul, yet the footsteps were always there, as if someone were making fun of all the guards at once. These footsteps wouldn't let him rest; they became his obsession and his curse, and whatever he did besides his job he couldn't free himself of the thought that next morning, while marching along the wide strip of ploughed-up beach, with his gun slung over his shoulder, in just the same spot as usual, he was bound to find those imprints of bare feet. He followed them down to the sand dunes, but there the trail broke off, as if someone had materialized out of thin air with the sole purpose of crossing the sandy hill, cutting across the ploughed strip and then vanishing into the sea.

I wondered why the professor was telling me this story. Once I was sitting in his office, drinking tea from a china mug, it all became clear to me.

'Those footsteps,' he said, adjusting his horn-rimmed glasses, 'were never actually there. He must have already been suffering from certain disorders which, if discovered in time, might not have led to tragedy.'

It had happened in 1951, at daybreak, as mist was settling and the first rays of sunlight were shining on the sea. Lying in wait as he had done for many nights on end, the guard dozed off, and when he was suddenly awoken by the daylight, he felt his heart shudder. A figure was approaching from the direction of the sand dunes. It was moving lightly across the ploughed-up beach, barely touching the ground, and the guard, who couldn't tear his eyes away from it, afterwards claimed over and over again that two great wings were sprouting from its back. 'Stop or I'll fire!' he had shouted, but the figure – whether it was a man or a woman he couldn't see properly from this distance – took no notice of his shouts; it just kept on moving further from the shore. He squeezed the trigger once, twice, aiming slightly above the shoulder blades between the wings. When he ran up to the shore he found a young girl of about nineteen or twenty, lying motionless, gazing up into the sky. The waves were lapping at her bare feet, and dark stains of blood were rapidly soaking into the sand. She was dead, but he couldn't see the wings anywhere. That's just how they were found an hour later – she lying with her feet in the water, he kneeling beside her weeping, touching her cheeks and stroking her long hair.

'They never did manage to establish the girl's identity,' continued the professor, 'and to close the matter they recorded it as an attempted illegal border crossing. The guard was transferred to barracks so he wouldn't have to walk up and down the beach any more, but a couple of months later it came to light that he was quite simply a madman. "I killed an angel," he wrote in a succession of reports to his superiors, "and may God send punishment down on me and on this whole accursed country where such crimes are allowed to happen." That's when he was sent here,' said the professor, lighting a cigarette. 'In those days I was just an assistant and I was present at his examination. He couldn't explain why no one else had seen the footsteps on the sand, and as for the wings, he claimed they must have flown off to heaven on their own, because God would never have allowed them to fall into the hands of mortals.'

Soon after that he had asked for a rake and had started his daily ritual, tidying the same patch of earth by the wall.

'Thirty years,' said the professor, after a brief silence. 'Yes, that's exactly how much time has passed since he first asked for the rake. There was a journalist who was interested in his story,' he went on, 'you know the sort of thing ... digging about in the past, investigating that era. But he never managed to find the grave of the girl who was supposed to be an angel; he never even got hold of the records of the case. And as for him,' said the professor, pointing out of the window, 'he doesn't say a word. Ever since he began raking his plot by the wall he has ceased to talk entirely. There can't ever be any newspaper footage anyway, for who in their right mind would believe such a story?' The professor gave a short laugh, dry and ironical.

As we were walking down the park towards the hospital gates he told me that Mina might remain in a state of stupor for just as long as the rake man or even longer; as he was explaining what complex processes occur in the brain and throughout the nervous system, processes whose very essence we are unable to define, let alone control, I was thinking about the handle of the rake. It was smooth and shiny like the wood of church pews, handled in exactly the same place over and over again.

'Sometimes,' the professor ended his account, 'all it takes is a slight change in the chemical composition of the tissue or the fluid, and we start seeing angels and devils, we start hearing voices, and you never know how it'll end. Yes, indeed . . .' he said, 'please give me a ring some time, but there's really no reason to come here again for now.'

Indeed, there was no reason to come again. Mina was never getting any better. No miracle occurred to restore her health and her former appearance, nor has any biochemical substance been discovered that might cure her.

Eight years have now passed since then. I know that Mina, shut away in a special ward, has an attack of frenzy a couple of times a year, followed by a period of total apathy and passivity.

I often think of her, and every time I do, I recall my final visit to the hospital, which was the last time I ever saw her. Two months had gone by since my conversation with the professor. The trees in the park had lost their leaves by now, and at every step flimsily frozen puddles crunched beneath my feet. The nurse escorting Mina straightened her coat, thrown on over her dressing gown; Mina stopped and stood by the wall. Someone inside the building started calling to the nurse from a window; he hesitated for a moment, but seeing that I was standing close by, he left Mina on her own and ran inside. It was then that something most extraordinary happened: the rake man, wearing a woolly hat and a ragged old sheepskin coat, put down his tools and kneeled to the ground; folding his hands as if at worship he began whispering a prayer to Mina. There she stood on the freshly raked plot; the wind was blowing dry leaves off the wall and the first flakes of snow were swirling in the air, settling on her hair like a silvery net. They were gazing into each other's eyes, he praying to her, and she taking in his words in silence. When the nurse came up to take Mina by the arm and lead her back into the ward, it occurred to me that both of them had been waiting for this meeting by the wall for ages now, and both of them were very happy at that moment, if by happiness one understands a temporary relief from suffering, a moment when we can't feel piercing pain.

Translated from the Polish by Antonia Lloyd-Jones

Hungary

Péter Nádas

Vivisection

The model steps behind the screen. She steps out of her skirt, pulls her blouse up over her head, removes her brassière, pulls down her underpants. She emerges. She stands between the desk and the armchair.

On her feet are well-worn moccasins, and a cheap pendant hangs around her neck. The pose has not been decided upon yet; she is uncertain. The flat light provides no contrast; her body is exposed to view. The sun has delineated the white pattern of a two-piece bathing suit on her flesh. On her belly is an appendicitis scar. Her pubic hair is sparse. Her breasts stand up and apart from each other, limply, without passion. Her hands are red and swollen. Her buttocks shapeless. She is ashamed of her feet, but she must take off her shoes. She has fallen arches. Corns on her toes.

Beauty and ugliness mean nothing in this context. She is raw. Only the pendant between her breasts can be categorized, because it is an object. The body is defenceless and changeable. It exists.

But that bauble must be removed. Its existence is more pronounced than her own. It must be removed, so that she will be utterly naked.

My friend S. begins to move the model this way and that. He looks for the most unflattering pose. In the same way he could look for the most flattering.

But that by now is not the model's reality, or mine. This pose belongs to the painter, my friend.

These few minutes excite me: the no-man's-land between the clothed state and the naked pose, *that which is no more and that which is not yet, the in-between*. History suspended, vibrating. Only the few minutes without pose offer some certainty, amid universal uncertainty.

Maybe.

But now I speak for myself. From this sense of universal uncertainty a painful, all-pervasive distrust arises. Distrust of humans. And of objects. And even of phenomena. Groping to define them, I arrive at not one, but a series of logical and equally valid solutions. For what one solution could ever accommodate, what definition ever encompass, if not its own opposite, then at least the countless possible variations of that which it attempts to define?

If I approach my own thought processes with the necessary attention, and compare the rich open field of the mind with the necessarily narrowed approach of the written word, I stumble upon an arbitrary element of writing: *distortion*.

The model does not step behind the screen. In this studio *there is no screen*.

Her undressing? Certainly a nuanced series of characteristic movements, the momentary results of the blending of mind, body, and intention. I know nothing about it. Not the least distinguishing detail. Nor anything about the model. I only met her ten minutes ago. My description is no more than the dry rendering of the familiar process of undressing.

But even if I *did* know the model? At this point I can't raise her from her model's state – can't see her as other than a generality. And supposing I began by knowing her? If my knowledge of her were to overstep a certain border (and where exactly does that border lie?) she would cease to be a *model*. Then she too would have crossed a border, beyond which she could no longer be written about. At what point would my knowing her transform her from something into someone, into She Who Is?

And supposing I were to invent that which I do not know? But even invention becomes generalization.

This struggle is useless. In place of facts, I am left with formulae.

But the facts of distortion are also facts.

The model was not wearing a skirt and blouse, but a sleeveless summer dress. I changed that fact for a stylistic reason. I felt that *steps out*, *pulls up*, *removes*, *pulls down* lent a direction and a flow to the sentence. The point here was the rhythm of that second sentence, which seemed important to me.

And the naked model does not stand between the desk and the armchair. In the studio there is a desk, and also an armchair, but the armchair is not there at the moment. I arranged the picture thus after the fact. I thought that her body took on a reality, a palpability, between those two objects. For my original point (if I had one) in making my thought clear, would have been that the clash of the naked human body with the surrounding objects – in anthropocentric thinking – leads to a tragic realization: the object is always more stable, more durable than the living body. The object is inviolable, describable. This clash is diffused once the naked body is garbed with inanimate objects, and by virtue of its elastic continuity a pathway is opened between the two worlds, a sense of invulnerability awakened.

Bergson has written on this: 'It no longer occurs to us to contrast the vibrant flexibility of the living, uncovered body with the heavy inertia of its covering.'

The tragedy of the naked body, its vulnerability, would perhaps not be quite so apparent in natural surroundings. Only here is it so: between the desk and the armchair. I used the armchair only symbolically, by the way, casting it as the sturdy desk's wobbly companion.

I will start again. I will try to draw a clearer, more accurate picture.

'Shall I take my shoes off?' she asked. The silence, the lack of response, made it clear: they must be taken off. She blushed and kicked her shoes into the corner of the studio. Now only the pendant remained, foreign to her body. A few seconds hung in the air. Her blush faded and she stopped the awkward twisting of her toes. But she did not kick her shoes into the corner of the studio. I invented this action because I don't remember how she bent down, if she did bend down. So how could she remove her shoes? She simply stepped out of them. But then, how did they end up next to the stove? They did not end up next to the stove.

Yes. And neither did she stand in front of the desk, when she asked, 'Shall I take my shoes off?', but stood below a large sketch of a mural commissioned for the wall of a school. And she blushed. No one answered. She simply stepped out of her shoes. She twisted her toes together. 'I have blisters on my feet,' she said. My friend S., staring towards the corner, his eyes gathering, collecting, observing all the details, answered shortly: 'So do other people,' and gestured her over to the corner. The model obediently and hesitantly stopped in front of the desk.

I was waiting to see what would happen with the pendant. Her shoes stood neatly, side by side, under the large sketch. I'm not really sure about this . . . she pulled the pendant around so that it hung down her back, but she didn't remove it. In this way she finished her undressing, and if I remember correctly she quickly took the pose.

The whole thing came into my mind then, about the relationship of the object and the human body. Or maybe later.

Instead of the shoes, the desk. The armchair in place of the pendant. That is how I want to tell it now. But it's too beautiful and logical to be true.

She had no scar on her belly. I made it up, I must admit, because I thought it would be indelicate to write that I could see the marks left by her underwear on her waist. But I don't even know that I did see the marks. Underwear usually does leave marks. The appendicitis scar only served to emphasize her vulnerability, the rawness of the image. But even without the scar or the underwear marks the picture is raw enough. The corns on her toes were real. The fallen arches: I made that up. (She said she had blisters, but they were corns. Thinking back, I decided that she had said blisters because she thought it more refined to have blisters than to have corns.) I, on the other hand, used the image of fallen arches as a stylistic metaphor, to hint at the juxtaposition of object and body, to subtly introduce my theme. Thus, between her attempts at refinement and my attempts at style, the truth was left hanging. Or left out entirely.

I find it astonishing: the truth distorted for such trifling purposes. And so we proceed: the list grows. But as with truth, so we can hope only to approximate even the distortion of truth. And sardonic laughter echoes among the twisted ruins of all the facts bent in the service of some goal.

I wrote: her pubic hair is sparse. Now I must state: the model's pubic hair is not sparse.

When she emerged from behind the improvised screen – a stretched canvas propped up against one of the studio doors – when she emerged, the first thing I noticed was the unusual size of her mons veneris. In my description I didn't mention that. I couldn't decide if the model's mons veneris was significantly larger than average. As it seemed to be. But I'm not sure about this. That's why I covered my uncertainty with invented certainties. That her hands were red and swollen I don't really remember. Probably I don't really remember her hands.

I promise now to remember.

When she stepped into the studio and sat down a few feet away (approximately six and a half, but maybe more, maybe less) from me on the platform, I offered her a cigarette. And she? Did she take it? Light it? I don't remember. I'm sure that I didn't light it. If I had, then I would remember seeing her face close up. I stand up, I strike the match on the side of the box, I lean close with the flame. I did not stand, I did not strike the match on the side of the box, I did not lean towards her with the flame. I have absolutely no memory of her face close up. I did not light her cigarette. I remained seated, stiffly, on the platform, as if I too were posing. Although I did stand up once . . . a drawing pad fell from the easel of *the girl with the interesting face*. I picked it up. The drawing pad also knocked over the metal box in which she keeps her pencils, some charcoal. I think that she picked up the pad, and I picked up the box.

The next image is not accurate either, that of my friend S. preparing to paint. He had set up the pose for his students, two boys, and *the girl with the interesting face*.

I offered the model a cigarette. If I didn't light it, the model must have used her own lighter or her own matches. But I don't think she carried a bag. I'll have her make her entrance again, through the open door, against which S. later leaned the stretched canvas to serve as a screen. There she is, but I still can't decide whether she is carrying a purse, bag, or whatever it is women usually carry. Her shoulder, bared by the sleeveless cotton dress, I do remember: it was rounded. I don't remember her hands. We did not shake hands, not having been introduced.

I didn't light her cigarette. I can't visualize her manner of holding the cigarette. She probably doesn't smoke. She didn't even take the cigarette that I offered her.

One distinct gesture I do recall – the motion of her wrist as she threw her pendant over her shoulder. I had mentioned the action merely. It's a rash undertaking to venture an opinion on an unfamiliar hand. Although it's also possible that I was not mistaken; her hands probably are reddish and swollen. Her legs are. Thick-ankled, with strong ruddy skin. Pale thighs, sunburned arms, as if she always wears that faded, sleeveless cotton dress.

Another thing: there is no imprint of a bathing suit on her skin. In fact, the opposite: the sunlight has left only blurred, random marks on her body.

The sun has delineated the white pattern of a two-piece bathing suit on her flesh. This is no more than a well-turned phrase.

Finally: S. did not pose the model, she posed herself. 'Is this good?' 'Good . . . a bit more . . .' 'Like this?' 'Good.' The pose is neither flattering nor unflattering. It is simply a pose. She has to hold it for forty minutes at a stretch.

In the same way almost every moment described can be refuted. And even the refutation can be refuted.

In the attempt to do away with distortion, to clarify the relationship between the distorter and the distorted, it becomes impossible to avoid the multiple meanings of even the simplest fact. As preconceptions are torn down, the edifices of convention abandoned, we are left among facts, all elusive, fluid, resisting definition.

The model once again appears at the door. In her hand, on a key-ring, is a key.

Translated from the Hungarian by Judith Barnes Kerrigan

László Márton

The Sunken Apple Tree

One morning the apple tree in the garden sank. All I noticed was that the room was much brighter than usual. The light, which came from where the doctor's surgery is now, was no longer obscured. When I went out to the front of the house, I found that even the top branches of the tree had disappeared. The ground, having been loosened by the thaw, could no longer support the weight of the tree. The snowfall had been particularly heavy that winter; I can still remember how we trudged through it.

I even remember how the snow tasted, as the patrol was coming and we had to lie down in it. We were walking by the Church estates, which had been vineyards in those days. My little brother was sick with meningitis. The doctor had given him one pill – a dose of penicillin – and said that he would have to take at least another ten to survive. So we went into town. We knew a shortcut through the forest, which was safer than taking the main road because the soldiers didn't know it. But even when we got to town we found that there were no pills to be had and, sure enough, three days later my brother was dead.

And I can't stop thinking about how that huge old tree sank so miraculously into the ground. I have never seen apples to compare with the beautiful, streaked apples which grew on that tree. I was told not to go anywhere near it, in case the earth swallowed me up too. Mother tied a rope around my waist, and it was only when I got close to the place where the tree had sunk that I saw that the earth had caved in, leaving a large ditch. I didn't dare climb in, and neither did the men when they were eventually allowed home. Anyway, I had other problems, as it was then that I had to go for the doctor, and that wasn't easy in those days. It may sound silly, but Mother dressed me up as an old woman and dirtied my hands and face. The doctor roared with laughter when he realized that it was me. You see, once, when I was walking along the main road, I was stopped and told to go and peel potatoes. As it turned out, it wasn't to peel potatoes at all. All the officers were at the cinema and they made me watch the film with them. It was a very nasty film. How can I put it . . . ? It was amoral. Then one of the soldiers told me to go home, quickly. He was a nice man compared with the others.

A captain lived with us who loved to joke around. He was no more than a kid but, because they are moved up through the ranks so quickly, he was already a captain. The officers would sit in the room playing cards, and the captain's blond hair hung in his eyes and the lice hung in his blond hair. And he pointed at his hair and his lice and said he was Gitler. And they all laughed. They could really laugh at things like that. Then the captain died in a skirmish. Considering that those who came after him were of a kind I'd rather not talk about, we were sorry that our good captain had died.

He was one of the many who died in the German push to break through to the west. The town was surrounded, the Germans holed up in the forest, believing that from there the road to the west was still open. Or, rather, I really don't know what they believed, but they were all massacred. Not a single one escaped. They fell at the foot of Dog Hill, where later, when the first co-operative was formed, we were taken to plant saplings. We were terrified because as we dug we constantly hit bone. Sometimes the hair and remnants of clothing were still attached. Later they were all gathered up and buried in one place, but I couldn't tell you where. Since then, the neighbourhood has changed so much. There is nothing left to distinguish it. Even the trees we planted then have been dug up, without having had a chance to mature.

When the doctor visited and gave us that one penicillin, he looked at the ditch where the apple tree had been. He said that the ditch was part of an old cellar, and that all the cellars in the village connected. He was right. There is an entire labyrinth under the village; under the church, by the old school and in the courtyard where the Cistercians live. It may not have brick walls like the one at Eger, simply having been dug into the compressed ochre, but it's still quite a remarkable thing in such a ravaged village. When the children came to see it, we said: Look, the ground is eating apples!

I try to picture the people who dug this labyrinth. What use was it to them? Perhaps they used to hide in it. Who knows what momentous events may have caused them to shelter there. One day we too will be forgotten. New people will come who won't even know our names, let alone what made us happy or sad. Opposite the co-operative farm, near the spring, there is a cholera cemetery which we just call the Hajnár. We know they died in the epidemic because they were all buried there together.

But even that probably isn't interesting; there is little point in dwelling on the past, only on the present.

It was Sammy Bük from whom my little brother contracted the disease. We had no idea how dangerous a disease it was. He came over to our apartment when the building was hit. Uncle Johnny Bük had stormed out of the building after an argument with his wife just as the bomb was dropped. It took his head clean off.

There he writhed with no head. I can't begin to tell you what that was like. Sammy Bük is still with us. Sometimes strange shouts can be heard from the courtyard where he lives: hey-ho, hey-ho, hey-ho. It's Sammy Bük's voice. He's an old man now. They don't let him out into the street any more because if he sees building work going on or even bricks stacked up somewhere he goes straight over and starts saying hey-ho, hey-ho. Once he was almost run down by a truck. Well, that's what became of him. My little brother died because we couldn't get any medication . . . but maybe I've already mentioned that.

I forgot to say that after the cinema, when I had already taken shelter at my great-aunt's, they went looking for me and Mother was struck in the breast with a rifle-butt. She has been sickly ever since. And then, when I got married and we dug a new cellar, and Mother was so ill that nothing more could be done for her, in our despair we moved all the earth to the ditch and buried the apple tree.

Translated from the Hungarian by Barbara Egerváry

Péter Esterházy

Down the Danube

From time to time a vague smell of onions wafts into the compartment. I look outside: Szolnok.

People chattering. Making my silence somehow disturbing. Perhaps I should speak.

'You say, young man, that you're heading east? East and only east? But where do you end up if you keep on going? Well? Well? That's right, in the West! In the westernmost West. Remarkable, isn't it, that the world is round? Know what I mean? The hope. That there's no such thing as easternmost!'

A pig stands in a field, its head held high. A proud pig, look.

I'm trying to read. Jonathan Harper (Bram Stoker: *Selected Atrocities of Count Dracula*) confirms my suspicion we are now entering the East. I check the upper canines of my fellow-travellers. The male party of a married couple well-intentionedly suggests that I'd be better off addressing strangers in German rather than in Hungarian. 'Could be dicey.' But in Old-Romania, or in the region of the Danube Delta, I can, by all means, speak Hungarian. There it signifies nothing. Nothing. He wasn't trying to alarm me, only being helpful. 'Not a good idea.'

They tell me about their experiences in Budapest. The way they talk is the way we talked about Vienna in the seventies. The woman shakes her head; she can't understand how anyone could want more than Sunbeam, the department store, had to offer. 'To want more simply isn't normal.'

Later, they drop off to sleep. Presumably they all have the same dream, for their hands fall into their laps at the same moment.

*

At Biharpüspöki I step out into the corridor. The station building stands in almost complete darkness, illuminated by a single, pale yellow light, a mood-lamp from the saloon. I look down at the track where the light from our window falls. Rubbish, bottles, paper, a drying turd-sausage. And then, on a sleeper, two objects, two perfect, natural forms, like in a photograph for *Vogue*: an egg leaning against a small Chanel bottle (eau de toilette, Egoïste, for men). Bizarre still life. The nocturnal station of Kolozsvar (Cluj, Klausenburg) is crawling with people. It conflicts so strongly with my mental picture that it almost corresponds to it again. The same state of fright. As if in a time of war. Everything like the film *Brasil, Brasil* or the old, black-and-white Orwell *1984*. Behind the ruined façade a developed, hidden function. Developed, thus unknown. At first glance even the waiting-room seems immense, but shrinks the more I begin to find my way around.

All kinds of people. A man in an impeccable straw hat, as if straight from the beach. Thin as a reed, trembling from head to toe, reeking of sour alcohol. A girl in a mini-skirt. (Good.) A boy in the same. Pimps. A young girl, no more than a child, measures me with her eyes, and at once looks ten years older. (Or is she merely looking *back* at me?) Hawkers, lottery tickets, coffee, sandwiches. Wouldn't eat one if they paid me. Chatwin comes to my mind. Bruce Chatwin, who died from eating Chinese eggs. A great traveller. The vendors are ugly old she-devils; their lives have passed them by, they never sleep. It's two o'clock in the morning.

Bit by bit I find my way in the commotion: exit, information, WC. This way my fear diminishes. I'm like a finicky Westerner. I stop to ask myself: is there any other feeling inside me than *let's get the hell out of here*? No. Like Ulrich I'm not frightened, but everything is frightening here. Inspires fear.

From time to time the loudspeaker blares out. Then turmoil, people rushing in all directions. One corner empties, then fills again. Everything seems so fortuitous. Will I notice when the Kocsard train – my train – arrives?

There are gypsies, one blond, the classic 'eastern' type, in an inner-city denim suit. Counting money, changing money. In the embrasure of an alleyway, a couple. *Hard porn.* As the witchlike cleaning woman passes, she lunges at them with her broomstick. They step out in silence and readjust their clothes, skirt down, zip up. Then they stroll back. I look into their faces and see nothing.

Wandering on the platform I peer into another waiting-room. Bodies strewn over benches, fast asleep. Like the dead. Nothing moves. Pompeii. I watch them for some minutes. Nothing.

A black princess in a dark compartment. She's there whenever I open my eyes. Looking at me. Sometimes I dream the same. Night passes. As she gets off the train I can see them checking her papers in the distance. I can hear her laughing hoarsely. The policeman too.

I am in the home of Andris Tüskes's brother, György, on the bank of the Maros. A quiet, severe house at the end of the world – with a natural, self-evident claim to wholeness. I look at the Maros and pretend it's the Danube. Costs nothing. György tells me that the electricity supply was cut off in December. Which meant they were without water, too (electric pump). Even the nappies had to be washed in the Maros. 'The Maros devours its own banks.' They had to climb down a steep and shaky ladder. He shows me the spot. 'The river's changed beds. It used to lie over there.' The water is incredibly filthy. I dip my hand in. When I take it out again, I can see the water-mark. The river is heated by the nearby power station, pampering (spoiling!) the fish. 'Fisherman and hunter return empty-handed.'

Contours of a more severe view of life. Yesterday I, the eternal papist, sat through two Calvinist services. A bit much. Mother Mary, help me, I whispered to Andris as we entered the second church. Ecumenical snigger.

'I kept quiet,' says his grandmother the following morning. In the evenings they sing psalms together, the brothers and their wives, young women, young men. I share their silences. The thought I have now I have had for ages: how good to be able to sing, to really want to. A memory from my altar-boy days. To show willing, I sang a descant to the National Anthem. The priest thought I was simply out of tune. 'Superfluous, my child. We are plenty as it is.'

According to Grandmother, cholera spreads through the air. (Hence the proverb 'See a priest and die – he's probably just buried a choleric . . .') For this reason we don't set off for the Danube. To be precise, we both do and don't set off. Time means something different here. Perhaps that's why I accidentally stepped on my watch this morning, the springs crunching under my foot like a may-beetle. I sleep in the middle room. Now and then someone appears, as in an István Mandy novel, and makes a discreet gesture, nods, shuts his eyes, or sighs, then disappears again. Here all is quiet and delicate. Unlike the roughness of the grim and distant mountains, the roughness of the muddy courtyard, the river, the village, the dark, cold night. (Approaching from Kocsard Station: a car sliding through the lifeless darkness, manoeuvring between ditches and potholes, constantly braking as it winds its way past shabby houses and derelict factory walls.) As if nothing were alive here, nothing but us.

At the crack of dawn, the children (three and two) come and trample all over me. Still half asleep, they establish that I am some sort of fish defying closer identification, which they, in accordance with our common hopes, will fish out from the Maros. (Undine-beginnings.) Yesterday I heard one of them praying (a little tough-nut): 'Now, Lord, for the last time, *please make me good.*' The whole house is permeated by the presence of God – or, rather, by allusions to His presence, which is not the same thing. I find all this at once disarming and thoroughly exasperating.

I leaf through a book (a Bible commentary of some sort) and find a sentence by Oscar Wilde: 'I can resist anything but temptation.' Indeed, sir, indeed.

The flies crawl into my hair. As if they're building a nest.

Excursion to the Torda Gorge. Again the *exasperating* beauty of nature, mountain brook, sky-high rocks plus ancient Hungarian legend. ('We are now standing at the mouth of the gorge. Words are powerless to describe the scene. As if a storm had rolled a thousand Egyptian pyramids into one; as if a host of burnt-out towers and churches stood together before us; as if, under a narrow ribbon of sky, a mass of ruined temples and columns, burnt brown, red and white, towered up before our eyes. All is still. Only the gurgle of the brook disturbs the silence. The heart trembles at the sight of this almighty devastation.') I did, however, become familiar with the *mici*, the correct pronunciation of which is, I believe, 'mitch', but which I continue to pronounce 'mitzi' all the same – this is a region rich in *mici*, which are roasted far and wide, either on a grill or over an open fire, spicy minced meat, delicious. But no beer or wine. Only an improbably sticky, yellow soft drink, best described by the name 'horse-spittle'. A dead fly in the neck of the bottle over which the liquid unavoidably gurgles. The Danube at the Iron Gate? Not my exaggeration. Horse-spittle in Romanian is *suc*.

Scene: Fishermen on both sides of the Maros. Some have camped the night there in their tents. I fancy I can see their stubble. They call out to one another in Romanian. A kind of 'manly banter'. 'Wooden hands!' 'Whale hunter!' Then an argument begins. One gets undressed and prepares to swim over to the other side to demand satisfaction. By the time he reaches the other bank a young man has arrived, 'someone who commands respect'. As soon as the swimmer sees him, he backs down and, with excessive humility, begs forgiveness. 'I beg you. On my hands and knees I beg you to forgive me.' They throw stones at him as he withdraws. My hosts visibly enjoy my bafflement at this, for I simply can't understand how this passionate belligerence has turned so quickly into an equally passionate retreat. Hungarians, Romanians, the Maros.

Both Andris and György have offices, one facing the Samos, the other facing the Maros. I could already do with an office myself (together with a wallet, the title of doctor, a nurse and a secretary – especially the latter, who'd handle my correspondence, do the typing and some of the smaller journeys; she could hire horses, get hold of carbon paper, do the vacuuming, secure new contracts, translate, and ask for loans from the bank; she wouldn't want an affair with me, but would rest a cool palm on my tormented, burning brow; she'd smoke cigars and be only a little bit cleverer than me and, discreetly, without so much as saying a word, she'd finish my novels about the Danube). My office would face – what else? – the Danube: a virtual, imaginary, ideal K-und-K, Habsburg, Central European, East European, postmodern, realist, OK, if you insist, *narcissistic* office. In us the experience of three rivers meets.

Let's go, then. If there are too many problems, we can always turn back. I picture us cunningly avoiding quarantine. Gone without trace. We see someone in a wooden hut in a bare beech grove, like an incredibly boring (and undubbed) scene from a low-budget Russian movie. An old fisherman in the process of dying a torturous death suddenly springs up and rushes out of the hut, splashing through deep puddles screaming, slapping and chopping the water as he approaches . . . 'Listen, Andris, let's get out of here. I'll invent the Danube Delta for myself, just like I always do.'

In Vasarhely we run into their parents by chance. A small, bright thing, the mother. For a minute or two I can shamelessly indulge my mother-hunger. As if she notices this. Notices everything. Which is about as annoying as if she really were my mother. I introduce myself. She has heard my name, she says. A good name. But what about my heart? Is it good too? That's the question, I say with a cheerful grin. To this she replies, both teasingly and with severity: 'I don't like to meet people in the street. It's so much better at home, where I can take a good look at you and decide whether or not you need a good scolding.' 'I'm an eminently scoldable sort,' I reply proudly.

I had already heard much about their father. I listened with envy as they sang his praises. When he was released from prison, he'd spent all the money they'd saved over the years on a gramophone. Not on bread or milk, but on a gramophone. And he put on Mozart's G Minor Symphony. 'Mozart to give us love of life, and the G Minor so as not to spare us anything.' My own fatherhood comes to mind. I'll never put on records for my children, and they'll never tell such stories. Whenever I think of the Tüskes's father, I can't help feeling that my own paltriness is a great mistake. No, not a mistake, but something which will have 'dire' consequences. The name of this something is tragedy.

We tell them where we're headed. Then mention the business of the cholera. At this the father extends his hand: 'Good luck, my boys.' As if I too were one of his sons. 'May the best man win.' The mother embraces us. 'You're mad, the lot of you. There's no point. Go on, then. Go.'

The Child of State Socialism

The child of state socialism – which is what I am – took himself off one day to a neighbouring country, which shall for now remain unnamed. It was, at any rate, a country which had also just won its – so to speak – freedom. A country in which, to its eternal glory, the sun rises earlier than it does here.

Our man arrived in the tiniest of villages in the mountains, where he was met by two young men who would assist him in his travels. But it's not about them that I want to speak now, or about their quiet home at the end of the world, or about the energetic children who are left to play in the yard alone as there are no longer any other Hungarian (or Hungarian-speaking) children of their age in the village, or about the delicate womenfolk who float around the quiet house, or even about that unexpected wholeness (wholeness is always unexpected) which our man experienced there during his two-day stay, as he saw with pleasure – because he was allowed to see – how, even under conditions so very different from his own, one could none the less strive towards the same ends. It is about something much less worthy and much more modest, yet at the same time equally instructive, that I shall speak.

This child of state socialism thought a great deal about himself – or, rather, not so much a great deal, as many different things – but never in his dreams would he have imagined that he was a child of state socialism. Not that he thought himself free; he was far too cautious for that. But – we are bound finally to admit – he did think that he had not been corrupted by the system (the system which no longer exists). Everything had its price, and this he had duly paid. And that, he thought, was that. He was very pleased when the whole thing fell to pieces, seeing it as a kind of liberation. A liberation of energy, above all, for he no longer had to be perpetually on the alert. Or at least no more than was natural.

The first thing he noticed in the foreign country was the lack of beer. Then the lack of wine. Then the lack of mineral water. Which, after three days, was no laughing matter. Without anything to drink, we don't feel like eating. Our lips start sticking together, and so on.

After this, he suddenly noticed the poverty, which occurred to him rather like an afterthought. The wornness, the shabbiness, the dust, the horrific and manifestly superfluous monstrosities of factories, the destruction of nature, the barrages for which the valleys had to be specially made, the senseless canals to which the water had to be brought by the glass, and poverty, *bitter* poverty, the like of which he'd never seen at home.

This confirmed the traveller in his suspicion that the self-image of his own country, as one treated cruelly by fate, was utterly mistaken, false, and no more than a form of self-pity. Offendedness and lamentation as Hungarian national characteristics. The endless whining. The terrible Turks, the awful Austrians, the trickery of Trianon, the indifference of the English, and, to cap it all: the Russians. Oh, outrageous fortune. But wasn't this really just an average European destiny? Now and again countries disappeared from the map, were shunted around like furniture and sooner or later along came the Russians. We have no special cause to feel sorry for ourselves.

But let's finally get to the point. The three men arrived at a hotel one evening, looking for a room for the night. It was dark, they were tired, and the choice was limited. The child of state socialism had travelled relatively widely and, although hardly a man of the world, knew how to get by with the likes of porters and waiters. The hotel foyer was a cross between a Communist Party Headquarters and a railway station. Yet this did not in itself arouse our man's suspicion. But then the porter and the two young men entered into a series of peculiar negotiations. Whenever he interrupted with a question of his own, they gave him a dismissive wave of the hand, as if he were an interfering child. Suddenly fear began to well inside him. He could see that the porter was master here, master of time and space, and nothing could happen without his consent, unless some unfathomable intrigue were to bring change.

That was the first night. From then on he never gave the waiters orders, only requests. If they cheated him, he paid and said nothing. He was aware that he was in a strange land with strange laws, and was happy simply to be alive. Nothing dramatic happened, only that he began to speak more softly, grew more attentive, pricking up his ears, night and day, like an animal. And it was now that his defencelessness and subservience, his anxieties and inhibitions, really made themselves felt, as qualities which he, the child of state socialism, had inherited from the system after all.

Then he went back home again, where he lived happily ever after.

Translated from the Hungarian by Richard Aczel

Lajos Grendel

The Contents of Suitcases

For Jorge Luis Borges

No sooner had I set forth from home than I noticed I was being followed. I was somewhat surprised that I had found my way on to the list of 'observed persons', as these days I avoided publicity and lived only for my family and vocation. I hadn't moved in society for ages, or written articles for the papers. Even when from time to time a book of mine appeared, it hardly caused a stir. Rack my brains as I might, I simply couldn't remember a single incriminating act, or even the pettiest of offences that might have aroused the suspicion of the authorities. My past was absolutely spotless. I had never been one to contrive dark schemes to bring about the downfall of my greater or lesser superiors.

I was just going out to the shops. In the neighbourhood where I do my shopping, the houses are almost lost among the multitude of garden trees, hedgerows and bushes, and in the later hours of the afternoon there is hardly a pedestrian to be seen. Here, there are no resplendent supermarkets, and the area is nowhere near as elegant as the host of exotic plants, neatly pruned trees, and pretty gardens might lead the passing stranger to suppose. Coming out of the baker's, I made up my mind to confront my pursuer. He stood waiting at a respectful distance, his figure almost entirely engulfed by the twilight fog. But it was him all right; I could tell by his long winter coat and somewhat old-fashioned, broad-brimmed hat. Putting my best foot forward, I began to grow a little nervous as I contemplated what I should say to him. As soon as I drew near, he too picked up his heels and headed not towards me but in the opposite direction. I quickened, but he strode even faster, and the gap between us only widened. I broke into a run; so did he. I didn't know what to think. Up until then he had been chasing me; now I was chasing him. Two heavy carrier bags, each full to the brim, impeded my running, and although he was the older man, he managed to give me the slip, finally disappearing from view at a crossroads.

On arriving home, I immediately phoned my wife, who was spending the weekend at her sister's in Kassa. She had taken the children with her.

'Missing us already?' she asked, a little surprised.

I told her about the man who had been following me.

'You haven't been working on a new novella, have you?' she asked.

Thus it was she who, albeit unintentionally, gave me the idea of writing this present story, in which, I fear, it will soon become difficult to distinguish fact from fiction. No, I'll not talk nonsense. Of course I can separate the day's events from those appendages added on as afterthoughts. But even so, it is still far from certain that those events will be identical to the text that they become after writing. Well, of course they won't. Lies, when they are self-oblivious and to the point, can bring us closer to the truth than plain naturalism.

I had only just hammered the first letters on to the typewriter when all the familiar doubts and difficulties began to surface. As long as I stuck to the facts, everything seemed to go to plan. The only thing that troubled me was that the man could really have been anyone at all. And I had hardly even started. I turned off the radio so as to be surrounded by silence, like a trapeze artist before his perilous leap. I knew, of course, that it was all now up to him. Only he could come to my aid: the man who had first pursued, then fled from me.

A few minutes later the doorbell interrupted my thoughts. I poked my head out into the hall, and was not in the least surprised by what I saw. For there in the corridor stood my pursuer with a suitcase in his hand, as if he'd come in search of lodgings.

'I promise I won't keep you long,' he said, entering my room.

He did actually introduce himself first, but I couldn't catch his name. I only remember that it was some everyday name like Kovacs or Lovasz. He asked whether I worked for a publisher, and whether I'd written this or that short story.

'Yes,' I nodded. 'And you? What do you do?'

At first he gave a cautious reply:

'For a long time I worked on the railways,' he said.

'And now?'

'These days . . . how shall I put it . . . ? I've been pensioned off . . . Nowadays I deal with eternity.'

'Eternity?' I asked mistrustfully.

His face remained serious, then, after some thought, he replied: 'Oh, you don't have to take me absolutely literally.'

Thereafter our conversation was short and to the point. My visitor could tell that I wished to be rid of him as quickly as possible. He'd obviously had unpleasant experiences elsewhere, as he confessed that I was not the first person he had approached.

He wished, he explained, to speak to me both as a writer and as a publisher's reader. All he asked of me was that I read his manuscript and offer a few comments of my own. I knew his type only too well. A marauding horde of graphomaniacs would always take us by storm during publishers' 'open hours', and, if they had no success with their manuscripts in the office, they would invade one of our readers at his home. There were those who threatened us, or went crawling (not always without success) to higher quarters. And there were those who wept and whined and spoke of the poisoned cup that awaited them. Then there would be others who tried to exploit the vanity of our readers, or who always came equipped with 'a little token of appreciation'. My man tried neither flattery, nor bribery; neither threats, nor tears. His manuscript had already been to the publishers. The reader had offered no encouragement. Then my man had simply thought: 'No matter, there's plenty of time.' And if I were to kick him out without a hearing now, he'd bear me no grudge. He'd still simply think to himself: 'There's plenty of time.' So it was for me to decide, quite freely and without any pressure from him, whether or not I wished to take a look at his manuscript.

'All right, then,' I said. 'Where is this manuscript?'

We went back out into the hall, where he had left his suitcase.

'I do hope you won't think me too pushy,' he said in the same hollow and humourless voice. 'Actually I'm really a bit of a coward. As you saw this morning, when I turned and ran . . . Could you pick it up for me?' he said, pointing to the suitcase.

I feared the worst, and, a moment later, my fears proved not without foundation. My visitor snapped open the catch. The suitcase was packed full: not with articles of clothing, but with pages and pages of manuscript.

'Naturally I took a taxi from the hotel. I'm old and sick, and not as strong as I used to be.'

Noticing my expression of utter shock, a hesitant, if somewhat supercilious, smile appeared on his face for the first time. When he opened the suitcase a few pages of manuscript blew on to the hall carpet. I bent to pick them up and quite involuntarily read a couple of lines. It immediately struck me that the pages were unnumbered. When I put this to him, he answered with complete confidence:

'This manuscript has no need of numbers.'

'But which is the first page? Where does one begin?'

'Anywhere,' he said indifferently.

'So it's some kind of avant-garde text, is it?'

And then, for the first time that morning, he burst out laughing. 'If that's what the publishers like to call it, very well. The truth is that this is only one part of the whole work, so I haven't the faintest idea of which page I wrote first. It's quite likely that it isn't even here.'

'What?' I asked, in perfectly justified disbelief. 'You mean there's more?'

'Oh yes,' he replied, 'but as I'm sick and weak, I couldn't bring all the suitcases at once.'

'*All* the suitcases?' I asked, dumbfounded, beginning to feel quite faint. 'How many are there, then? A dozen?'

'Oh no, much more than that. More like twenty-five or thirty. Or maybe even fifty. I gave up counting years ago.'

When he finally left, I went over to the typewriter and read what I had written: he hadn't given me quite the help I had expected. I paused for a moment to weigh up the situation. It was then that I realized I had been the victim of a disastrous misunderstanding. My ambition as a writer had always been fuelled by the desire to get closer, through writing, both to reality and to myself. To understand the world more profoundly than others. For while most people only lived *in* the real world, I, in a sense, also lived above it. The events and experiences which hold my attention, and which are fixed by the keys of my typewriter, represent one possible – although not absolute – version of the way things are. Objects do not merely appear before me; I also have the power to transform them. Or, to put it more naïvely: there is a short and narrow path which leads directly from life to literature and from literature back to life. Now my confidence had been shattered at a stroke. To my astonishment, I realized that the only path from literature led full circle. What we see in the mirror is not life, but literature itself. If we smash the mirror to pieces, we discover there is nothing behind it. My man's manuscript began to fill me with curiosity.

I took a single page from the suitcase at random. And this is what I read: 'Each of the two boys had been called John, and the husband said that the last boy's name was to be John, too. Nameless chance-solitude, yes, that is what he saw before him, he who was preparing to plunge, but, at the same time, already stood plunging in the window. It filled me with a certain satisfaction to think that the fatty tissue of the woman's rear hemispheres was omnipresent throughout the inhabited globe, on each and every charted, or as yet uncharted, island (on the island of the midnight sun), the Happy Isles, the island world of Greece, the Promised Land, hemispheres which gave form to the eternal roundness of family life, exuding a gush of milk and honey blood, warm as the womb, while remaining entirely insensitive to the passions of passing moods and the debates of mortal minds, being, as they are, the silent, unchanging expressions of mature animality. On Sundays, beside the well in the municipal park, they would shake five small balls in a tin can, then roll them out on to a table; the balls represented five figures – a hunter, a stag, a girl reaping, a soldier, and a peasant – whose counterparts were sketched upon the board where bets were placed. The stakes are pretty high, the onlookers would jest, but the real advantage of the game was that the hunter never fired his gun, the soldier never got shot, the stag never dropped, and the peasant and the reaper never tired of their toil. When Count Leinsdorf ordered "parallel manoeuvres", the national minorities immediately sensed a secret pan-German offensive, and his lordship's insistence upon involving the law brought back vivid memories of the political police, allowing the inevitable conclusion to be drawn that the two "branches" actually stemmed from the same root.'

Any remaining doubts I might have had disappeared after reading that single page of manuscript. I had been the victim of an incredible delusion, and hadn't even the right to feel outraged. For even what I referred to as my vocation was itself no more than a form of self-deception. I liked to think of myself as reconstructing events which had either happened, or could have happened, in real life, when all I actually did was hammer out letters and words. What I saw before me was really no more than a sheet of coloured glass.

I lifted another handful of papers from the suitcase and threw myself wholeheartedly into reading them. I found myself in the middle of some totally unedited chaos. One description followed another for dozens of pages on end – descriptions beside which Michel Butor's *Saint Mark*, or the structural engineering and geometrical sobriety of Robbe-Grillet seemed no more than prepa-ratory sketches. As if on a river three times as wide as the Danube the pictures of a hundred different photographers, taken over a whole lifetime in every corner of the world, now billowed and surged for hours or even days on end. Images that would flash up for a single moment, then be drawn along with the current, never to be seen again. No two descriptions were ever repeated, and there were no two images that could be said to be connected in any way at all. Locations shifted without end: from Dresden, Prague, and Budapest to New York, Tokyo, and Cairo, from villages, farmsteads and thatched cottages in primeval forests to weir-keepers' lodges, train compartments and desert camps. This exuberant stream of dazzlingly inventive and graphic descriptions was so rich and detailed as to sustain the illusion that I had really been to the places described. I became acquainted with the pasts and presents of endless human settlements, meeting men and women who had lived a hundred or five hundred years ago, and whose bones had long been ground to nothing by the acidic soil. And then I saw my own contemporaries, from the humblest of guest-workers to the highest of statesmen. My visitor hadn't merely brought a handful of characters to life all over the world, but whole hordes of people and races. His characters would momentarily swim into view then disappear for ever, as if to illustrate that, from a certain absolute point of view, their lives lasted no longer than the flick of a switch. He condensed not only their destinies, but their whole lives, into a single sentence, leaving no sense of inconclusion when they vanished into thin air. I soon began to get the impression that the manuscript set out to portray every possible human destiny, and, in so doing, made one long procession of all the people who had ever lived. For no two living beings, nor any two human destinies, can ever be exactly the same. He never focused on the fate of one individual at the expense of another. Each destiny seemed equally light, or, if you prefer, equally burdensome. He left no destiny unfulfilled, as if wanting to show that all we think of as value, culture or civilization finally comes to nothing with the advent of death. That the worldly existence of the heroic priest who, defending his homeland, plunges with the Turk from the ramparts of the castle, like that of the cowardly informer, or that of Messalina, the nymphomaniac and common prostitute, and that of the gentle nun who, tending to lepers and victims of the plague, preserves her chastity to the very end, are all rendered equally meaningless by death. That our deeds have neither weight nor meaning beyond the brief span of our lives, and that all we have ever done will turn to nothing when our time is up. That outside of ourselves there are no principles, laws or regulations to guide us in the difficult moments of decision or even to question the wisdom of what we decide. In my man's manuscript events merged into one another, locations alternated from one sentence to the next, and, while he evoked an astounding variety of human emotions, ranging from happiness to the sense of mortality, from lovemaking to adolescent melancholy, he never for a moment sought to give the impression that he himself had ever reached the point towards which his hundreds and thousands of scattered stories all seemed to be perpetually striving. Only then did I fully understand why his text had no first page – just as it probably had no last page either – and why he hadn't thought it important to number the pages at all.

Believe it or not, I still hadn't even read a third of the contents of his suitcase. I looked up at the clock and was astonished to find that I had been reading for less than three hours. It had felt as though a whole day had gone by. I had supper, took a shower, but still feeling far from tired sat down at my desk, soon to find myself dipping once again into the chaotic manuscript of my morning visitor. I sat up all night reading, and only when my body began to feel as heavy as lead one minute and as light as a feather the next did I finally lie down and, as if I had received a blow on the head, slept until noon on Saturday. At best I had covered about a quarter of the text. But I'd already had about as much as I could take.

Waking up in a daze around noon, I pulled myself together and gulped down two cups of poisonously strong black coffee, one after the other. I was already completely convinced that my visitor's manuscript was an outrageous travesty of literature. And not only of literature. It was a flagrant insult to everything that sustained my faith in my own activity, and thus, in the last analysis, to everything that kept me alive. And yet – paradoxically – it was precisely this manuscript which served to restore my flagging faith. Even so, I couldn't entirely suppress the somewhat begrudging sense of wonder that I felt towards my visitor. I couldn't help feeling that he had done exactly what I was supposed to do – to venture freely and irresponsibly into the innermost realms of being. I knew that somewhere in his endless collection of suitcases the short story I completed that Saturday afternoon lay already written. And it was for this, more than anything else, that I could never forgive him. He had deprived me of the most vital of all illusions – the illusion of creation.

When he rang my doorbell at five in the afternoon I didn't ask him in, but simply took his suitcase out into the hall. By way of parting, I said: 'I don't feel qualified . . .'

I was left with a bitter but irrefutable sense of recognition. The short text, or, in literary jargon, the 'novella', that I had just completed, and that now lay before me on my writing desk, was, and could only ever be, the still paler reflection of a reflection of events. No paths or inroads connected it to anything whatsoever.

And if someone, somewhere, had made a note of my personal details, what in the world did I care?

Translated from the Hungarian by Richard Aczel

Czech Republic

Bohumil Hrabal

The Pink Scarf

Miss April,

A few days ago, on the 28th April, David Černý, student of
sculpture at the Prague School of Applied Arts, went over to
Smíchov, to the Square of the Soviet Tank-Corps, and painted its
green memorial tank a rosy pink. For, as he said to the journalists,
pink is the colour of an infant babe in arms, a symbol of innocence
. . . All day long onlookers flocked to see this unreal thing which
had actually come to pass . . . Cameramen rushed, while there was
yet time, to film this wondrous sight of Prague, which knocked
Allan Kaprow's one-time happenings into a cocked hat . . . And it
was some time before the army came to drape a green military
tarpaulin over the pink tank . . . Policemen went into the School of
Applied Arts, infringing sovereign academic soil, and all day long
they subjected a female student to forensic examination, all because
she wore pink boots . . . as Martin Šmíd reported in the
Metropolitan. Later on the soldiers painted the pink tank green
again. The things that go on here in Prague . . . I was only sorry
they demolished Stalin's monument all those years ago . . . Can you
imagine, Miss April, what a wondrous sight that would've been, if
David Černý had used his pink paint on Stalin as well? . . . In one
fell swoop this would've made Prague the world centre for pop-art;
a happening like this here in Prague would've set the crown on that
American school initiated all those years ago by Allan Kaprow,
Claes Oldenburg and the rest . . . not forgetting our own Milan
Knížák or Eugen Brikcius . . .

Miss April, on this last day of April Prague was on the march
again, just like in the November hurricane of '89. Hundreds of
thousands of people, young, old and lame, all rushing to feast the
Burning of the Witches, according to the ancient Slav custom,

inherited from the Celts, of celebrating the last day of April with drinking and orgies.

And I, in my 'girl's' pink scarf, struggled to the bank, to get me some Deutschmarks to purchase this video from Charlie, which features me as well as the rest of his wedding. I got hooked on the idea of having this video, because, says I, what if I were to die? What a splendid thing it would be to be seen going about at this wedding with a boa constrictor round my neck, adding to that myth of myself as a bit of a lad about town. You see, April, the wedding in question happened last year, I saw the video at the time, and I'd almost forgotten its existence, yet there I was in it, a treasure going to waste. What a wedding it was too! The bride was stunning in her wedding dress of Valenciennes lace, with a rose in her hair, the music was half-gypsy, the groom was in a DJ, smoking a cigar, with his hair in a parting, and the guests sat about drinking and eating, or wandered about from table to table, while I, Miss April, sat by the window, when all of a sudden something touched my ear . . . it did it again . . . And the guests opposite looked on with bulging eyes, staring at what I too soon found myself face to face with . . . I swung about, and there right opposite me was the head of a snake flicking its red tongue at my ear, over my shoulder and round my neck, and once more this beautiful great snake went and wound itself right around me, it was rosy pink and gold, gleaming like a head of corn on the cob . . . And it gazed lovingly into my eyes, so what could I do? It was my fate . . . my destiny . . . I stood up, and that snake was really heavy . . . A certain lady there, one of Charlie's guests, told me it was hers, that snake, it was a strangler, the last time it had strangled and eaten was only the day before yesterday, a boa constrictor it was, but she would keep a good eye on me, so that nothing would go wrong, the groom had refused to have it round his neck . . . So I walked about the place wearing this snake, and the wedding guests were scared, some were jealous, and at last I became what in fact I am, a bit of an old comedian, a bit of a ham, for, you see, art, Miss April, involves a certain amount of hamming it up, a certain amount of the old *Schmierenkomediantentum*, as Friedrich Nietzsche put it, writing on 'Why I write such beautiful books . . .'

Miss April, tell Dubenka I even took the snake over to the table beneath the Great Antlers where the bride was sitting, she'd just finished sharing a plate of dumpling soup with the groom . . . I sat myself down beside her, her dress of Valenciennes lace glistened like the skin of the pink boa constrictor, I sat beside the bride, who leaned her head over, and the snake's red tongue whispered words of love in her ear . . . The table was redolent with bunches of roses, and the snake clasped me so tight that I went slightly red, and just for a moment I had the distinct tactile sense that this boa was Dubenka, code for my attachment to her, a long arm extending all the way from San Francisco over to Prague . . . So I stood up again, and I walked through the festivities, the music moved along, now in front of me, now behind, bow-strings and gypsy eyes accompanied me, and I saw that nobody else would've dared to do what I did, for this snake was a strangler, it weighed six kilogrammes, it was cold, as though made of brass, it smelt just a little of musk and rosy perfume . . . And it would only have had to wind itself a little bit more round my neck and the coil would have strangled me . . . Moreover, I acquiesced in this, for I had the tactile sense that this snake was Dubenka, and I said – If I had to choose how to die . . . then this would be the right death, to be strangled by this boa constrictor . . . That's what I said, but its owner took fright, she said . . . 'If Sisa starts squeezing you any tighter than this, you've got to stick the fingers of both hands under its tightening grip, otherwise I'll have to run and get a knife from the kitchen . . . Look, I'm really geting a bit nervous about this,' she said . . . But I was just on top of the world, Miss April, I loved it, even though I could feel the boa gripping my neck and its little red tongue flickering ominously about . . . I saw its owner fling open the door to the kitchen – but then she went out the other door into the passage, with its steps leading up to the first floor where she was staying . . . I could see the illumined stairs rising, first of all her head appeared, then her ascending body, then her body disappeared, I only saw her knees and white stockings, till they vanished too, and only her shoes could be seen as she pattered up the stairs . . . Then she was totally gone, only her footsteps could be heard upstairs . . . Shortly after that she came back down,

leading by the hand a lovely little girl in a pink dress . . . She came
into the bar with this little girl, who was beautiful, just like Deanna
Durbin in the film *One Hundred Men and a Girl*. The little girl
bowed, bobbed a little curtsy, then she proffered her elbow, and
the boa constrictor slowly unwound itself from my neck, and
slowly it slid across my elbow on to the girl's shoulders . . . And
now the little lassie carried the snake through the bar, again my boa
constrictor was the centre of attention, while I turned pale, Sisa's
owner wiped the perspiration off me with a hankie, and I smiled. I
could only just manage to sit down beside the bride, I touched her
hip, my hand was shaking, and her dress of Valenciennes lace was
cold. Charlie came over with a glass of champagne, so we drank to
my having made myself an adornment of his feast . . .

Miss April, so now I've told you the story of what my friends
and I would see again on the video I've bought from Charlie, I'm
curious to see if I'll be as touched by it as I was six months ago at
Charlie's wedding, a thousand marks I shelled out for that
magnificent video, because I had this vision of me dying soon, and
the video would become the property of Prague Imagination, my
publishers . . . what a fine thing that'll be, when I die, and Prague
Imagination sell the video clips all over the world, earning money
for Mr Karafiát to print new writers' débuts in rosy pink jackets . . .
pink, like the 'girl's' scarf I bought in Strasbourg . . . My friend and
translator Sergio Corduas, whenever he came to Prague, always
without fail he wore a pink scarf . . . and just as they used to ask
him, so people in the Tiger ask me, why I wear this girl's scarf . . .

Miss April, then the day came for the screening of the video . . .
and it was defective, with a kind of snowflakes falling all the time
down the videotape, as if the Golden Tiger's ceiling had gone and
rain was showering down diagonally over the wedding . . . But the
main point of it was still there, what really mattered, it achieved
what I had in mind, a kind of death insurance, so that ultimately
these video clips of me, no more than ten minutes in all, could one
day be seen across all the screens of the world, making me number
one, for wearing this boa constrictor at the Golden Tiger . . . But
above all – since Prague is Golden Prague, where all kinds of weird

and wonderful things happen – it's so that Dubenka can be proud I'm not really such a wet rag as I like to make out in my letters . . .

Miss April, pass on the message to Dubenka that I'm starting to go soft in the head, tell her, when we showed this video of Charlie's wedding, I ended up agreeing with the words of Tomáš Mazal, that in view of what happened to that old girl of a tank, maybe the height of achievement would be just to wipe the video clean so that only the empty tape remained, with one great pink Nothingness on it, price a thousand marks . . . the Nothingness contemplated by Heidegger and the ancient Indian philosophers . . . Tell Dubenka also, that here in Prague we were captivated by that young German who, at the age of seventeen, on Soviet Air Force Day, crept in wolf-like with his aeroplane through guarded air-space all the way from Sweden to the Kremlin in Moscow, the traffic policemen even guided him in, to stop him hitting the overhead wires; he just glided over the bridge and straight into Red Square, bobbing up lightly against the Kremlin wall – and two women, carrying bunches of roses, going to pay homage to Lenin, gave their bouquets to the pilot instead . . . Just as, similarly, we were captivated these last few days by David Černý, who, using false papers, right before the eyes of the police, merrily painted the green Soviet tank pink . . . Miss April, tell Dubenka again that I, so often to be seen in my pink scarf, walked through Charlie's party at the Golden Tiger with a boa constrictor round my neck, charming all the wedding guests . . . Mind you! that boa constrictor wrapped around me like a pink scarf, that was nothing, but those two young men, one in Moscow, and now another in Prague, they have set the crown on our rosy velvet epoch, laid the foundation for a new era, in which they may reign over the world's future . . . Join the Society for the Restoration of the Pink Tank, as Martin Šmíd said in the *Metropolitan* . . .

P.S.
Miss April, it's the First of May, I'm out in Kersko, it's raining, the whole countryside around is permeated with the scent of blossoming trees and bird cherry, I walk up and down the white

fence, breathing in that scent, with my band of cats following after me, last of all comes quietly, timidly my old wet rag of a Cassius, a kind of little villein of his own emigration, he's always last, solitude has polished off the bravery and impudence I once loved in him so much . . . It's raining, it's getting dark, the countryside is quiet, dominated by dark green and blue, broken only by the white glow of my fence and garden gate . . . I'm standing by the fence, beside me rises a great bird cherry tree, its blossoms are white, the breeze ripples through the top of this tree, whose trunk stands there firmly like a great bride, that bird cherry tree shifts like a film projection screen, like a great curtain of Valenciennes lace . . . The band of cats sits round me in a half-circle, all absorbed in their own thing, what I'm doing now, all those girlish feline friends of mine do it, all my little children . . . they're gazing at the flowering bird cherry, sniffing that pungent scent . . . and there . . . last of all sits my Cassius, gazing at the same thing as me . . . all of us captives to Seryozha Yesenin, who also loved so much – to listen intently to the song of the bird cherry trees and the rain . . .

Miss April, I send, by the scent of all the bird cherry trees in the world . . . greetings to Dubenka.

Translated from the Czech by James Naughton

Eda Kriseová

The Unborn

*I see them enter the house, which is dark. He goes in first,
fumbling with upraised arms in the darkness, groping over the
walls and feeling for the light switch. When he finds it he turns
the switch, but the darkness remains. He has to find the fuse box
and the main fuse. This is his first task here, but by no means
his last.*

The plaster digs into his nails and he hisses, as if he'd hurt
himself.

'What happened?' asks Eva, who is standing on the threshold.
Eva is a name stretched on the cross, like Anna, Jana, or Hana. But
Eva is expecting something nice, because she hasn't yet given up her
girlish dreams. One of them is about a cosy cottage, where the fire
burns in the stove and she is there with her lover. Yellow light at a
distance gives the sense of a real destination, and they are inside.
You and me. Except that here it's cold and dark. It smells of mildew
and decayed rags, it stinks of rotting wood and something else too,
maybe dangerous. Martin has opened a door somewhere in the
darkness, and a draught of icy air now flaps against the drenched
trouser legs of the young woman, making the fabric cling to her
thighs and carrying away the smells. The woman is fair-haired, has
widely spaced eyes and prominent cheek bones, her figure is bony
too, with a broad pelvis, but inside she is shy as an antelope, fragile
as Chinese porcelain and querulous about life. Now she wants to
take hold of Martin, so she fumbles after him, but she reaches into a
cobweb and quivers with revulsion. She returns and slams the front
door shut.

I've got them trapped and I'll let them wander a while longer.

119

They put on the light and saw an L-shaped passage ending in that long porch which shelters such houses on high ground to the north. A bulb hung on a flex from the ceiling, and spiders scuttled off in all directions over the peeling walls. The house is dormant, everything is cold and torpid, like a reptile in winter, but storing up its poisons.

She saw her shadow poised in front of the door leading into the interior of the house and it seemed more substantial and courageous than herself. She gathered strength out of her dark recesses and opened the door. Beyond it was a whiff of mice, squashed hay and damp straw. And again that sharp, sweetish stench, whose quality she could not determine.

She felt for the light-switch casing. The room was square, constructed out of dark-painted beams with white infilling. The ceiling was black, timber, but almost invisible, because almost everywhere polythene canopies were hung, and each had a string from its lower end weighted down by a peg lying in a basin or a bucket. The light made a yellow circle in the middle of the room and there stood a billiard table, with three white balls and one red gleaming on the green baize surface.

She went up to the billiard table and took the red ball in her hand; it was cold, but at least it was reminiscent of blood. She squeezed the ball for a moment in her palm and then she threw it gently so as to hit the three ivory ones. After the impact they scattered, each bouncing off different cushions, but then they went back to each other, blood and bone. They collided in the middle and went motionless.

She opened another door and found herself face to face with a new unplastered wall. Stiff drips of mortar hung from the bricks, evidently the door led somewhere one wasn't supposed to go. She retreated back to the billiard table and leaned on it as something comprehensible. But she let go at once. Wasn't the billiard table in fact the oddest thing of all?

She went back into the passage. She heard a clatter, presumably from the woodshed, and chose not to go there. She opened the last door. The room behind it was full of empty tins, arranged according to size and kind, and some, at the end, still had their dirty torn labels. Beef in its own juices, frankfurters; the person who lived here evidently ate nothing but tins, but that was a long time ago. Here too the air was foul, perhaps because time had stood still. Perhaps time in a house stands still at that point when people leave it. Or does a house have its own time, which it lives, independent of people?

I watch her, and I like her even more than when she first stepped in. She is rounder and softer than I thought. She is scared and she is tender.

Martin came in with an armful of firewood. He knelt in front of the stove and pulled out the empty ash pan. Next to the stove there lay a pile of boots for use in the forest. On the coat-stand there hung various items of clothing for the same purpose. She took the boots and carried them a yard or so away to stop them from burning. Then she looked at Martin's back. It resembled a bird's wings with powerful attachments at the spine, with a hollow in the middle which looked like a river-bed, even underneath his sweater. The back was his nicest part. And then his legs, long and straight.

She went up to him, squatted down and stroked his back. After all: a cottage with yellow light, giving the sense of a real destination. And just the two of them, isn't that enough? Martin strikes a match and lights the kindling. At that instant thick blue, obviously poisonous smoke starts emanating from every cranny.

Eva retreats swiftly, opens the door into the passage, and a white figure comes inside. It wafts coldly past her, dampens her face like dew on a rose at dawn, and floats through the room, where Martin is driving out blue clouds of smoke with a towel. The thing goes after him and Eva is afraid for Martin. She is about to cry out 'Watch', when luckily the poisonous smoke surrounds the white figure on all sides. It overwhelms it, the white thing bedews the billiard balls on the green surface and then dissolves.

Martin is kneeling by the stove puffing at the fire.

'Did you always have central heating at home?

'Be quiet.'

'Have you tried all the levers?'

121

'Yes. And it was central heating at home.'

The stove exploded again and Martin jumped up, eyeing it like an enemy. Fat flies awoken from their winter sleep flew stupidly about in the smoke. War. Gas. She closed her mouth, ran back to the door without breathing and opened it. It was there on the other side. It floated in, leaning forward, its feet not touching the ground. Light-coloured, silent, dangerous. Eva slammed the door shut.

'What are you doing, for goodness' sake?'

'I'm scared, you see.'

'Scared of what?'

'Of this white figure.'

'What?'

'It comes in when I open the door. The first time you had it on your back.'

He opened the door and both of them looked in. Nothing lovely, or undeserved, was awaiting them, they could see that.

She hugged him round the neck from behind and pressed her chest to his back.

I see them both and I exult. Now he kisses her. And then he'll go on kissing, kissing, kissing her.

He shook her off.

Eva remembered her flimsy nightdress and started to laugh.

'Let me have a go at the stove!'

He didn't respond, but clenched his fists and went backwards towards the stove, as if it were a fortress he was determined to defend.

'We had central heating,' he said, 'and anyway I never really did anything much at home. Just sat about all the time and read.'

'Then let me have a go,' she asked. 'When I was little . . .'

'Even then you knew how to do everything?'

'Give over.'

Eva is hurt, and I, hidden behind a beam, suffer. What if they quarrel and break up? What if they quit the place in a furious temper?

122

But the woman hauls a feather quilt out of a painted chest, carrying it over to the bed in the corner; the quilt feels chilly against her hands, but she still takes off her wet jacket and shoes. She slips under the quilt, but finds that the feathers are bunched up into a cold lump inside the cover. She tosses the feathers from corner to corner, then catches it and shifts it on to her tummy, but it's still chilly there, so she puts it on her chest, which seems to emit greater warmth. Martin has gone out somewhere, while the stove is gently reeking like a stick of Christmas incense.

I inhale the smoke and it drugs me. If only I weren't so powerless, if only I weren't condemned to wait. My arms are drooping, actually no arms and no breath.

Eva lies in bed and listens to accelerated time ticking away in the nibbling of woodworm. They are eating away at the house and won't stop until they have eaten it up. But, before that happens, something has to be settled, Eva can feel that. She senses the tension and thinks: Someone is waiting for something. Someone is longing for something so much that his longing is making my body tremble.

Eva turns to the wall and stares at the plaster. She wants something white and empty to face her eyes, but the wall is stamped with the paw of some animal, which possibly walks about on the walls and the ceiling.

The stove, into which Martin has meanwhile poured paraffin, is burning fiendishly, now radiating even warmth. Martin dances a little dance of thanksgiving around it.

'Come to me,' Eva's voice invites.

He'd have picked up the billiard cue now, if she hadn't called him. He stands for a moment, rocking on his feet. He looks at Eva, who sits up in her corner and watches him, like her prey. Even the woodworm have stopped nibbling, they await the snap of the trap. Or evasion.

Eva is the trap, and Martin knows it. She wants to be with him all the time, she weeps when he leaves her. Martin doesn't see why women can't get involved in any work enough to forget about everything. They keep waiting for something beautiful which cannot not come, they want it to be complete and final. Me and you, you and me. In a little cottage. Eva still believes that the whole tree is in the leaf, all mankind in a beloved being. She doesn't want to relinquish the idea, she resists when Martin talks about things becoming humdrum. For a long time she's wanted to have a child, and he doesn't want to give her one.

Now he's standing by the billiard table, where he's in the middle of a game. He's always in the middle of some game, Eva thinks bitterly. And I have nothing. Nothing but him.

The light shines down on his head from above, he'd look like a saint, if it weren't for his wary instead of humble expression. Why is he always so afraid?

'Come to me,' Eva requests, knowing that once in her embrace Martin will start to laugh, say loads of stupid things, be innocent and uncrippled again. Be happy.

'Come to me,' Eva repeats, wanting to expel her own fear, every disagreement and apprehension.

I'm trembling all over with anticipation. I need flesh and bones, in order to live. I watch with eyes which I am yet to acquire. She's been making towards childbed for years, but he always resists. The flesh is willing, but the brain is on guard and always intervenes in time. It never falters, its will is iron. But I'm the one in charge here. I am the longing of life for itself, and thus I shall win. I shall wear them down by persuasion, or creep by stealth into the womb and nestle there.

Martin sits down on the bed beside Eva and takes her head in his hands.

'Dear head,' he says, 'forgive me.'

'What for?'

'For bringing you to this dump.'

'I'm happy with you wherever.'

'Sweetheart,' says Martin in the deep voice her father used to employ. 'Are you afraid of ghosts?'

'I'm afraid of death. Maybe that's why I want a child, in order to forget about that.'

'You've got your work.'

'I wanted to tell you ages ago.'

'Tell me what?'

'About the child.'

She felt Martin's back stiffen in her arms. The computer in his head is doubtless now active, selecting and sorting out the best answer. At that moment Eva hears a tapping sound. She pushes Martin aside and props herself up on her elbows, listening.

'What is it?'

'Someone's knocking.'

'Whoever would that be, round here?'

Eva admits she might have been imagining it. She's always hearing things. The house is full of life, of which one knows nothing. As if there was another time here, or it was counted differently. Sometimes she gets the notion that maybe people from ancient Babylon and Egypt are living simultaneously with us in another time. That we could be born into any millennium or century out of the millions of years lived by this planet. It goes forwards and backwards, because everything that was, is, and shall be, must be encapsulated in a single instant.

The tapping came again. This time Martin heard it as well.

He jumps up from the bed, grabbing the axe by the stove in his right hand. His shadow breaks twice between the floor and the wall, and the wall and the ceiling, and is enlarged against the polythene bags, which rock and swell in the warmth.

The door opens slightly and an old fellow sticks his head into the crack. His face is narrow, pointed above and below, his skull bald as a monk, cheeks red and nose beaked. He stares for some time without saying a word. He looks like a marten inspecting the inside of a chicken run and choosing a big fat hen.

'Hello,' he greeted them shyly, without coming in. 'I was just passing, wondered who it was.'

'Come on in,' Martin invited.

The old chap slid his body cautiously through the crack in the door. His raincoat dripped on the floor. The ceiling also let the rain in at this point, and water began trickling noiselessly down the strings into the prepared containers. You could tell by the gleam of the strings.

'I'm the neighbour,' the old fellow said. 'Růžička's the name.

He explained how he came over to lend Mr Hošek a hand from time to time. His wife had died five years ago last spring, he was all alone and lonely. This evening for instance. He'd peeped out the window and seen a light across the valley. He'd said to himself he'd go and have a look at how they were getting on, in case they needed something. If they were okay.

He choked. Either this speech was too long for him, or else there was still smoke in the room. Martin laid aside the axe and said, 'Sit yourself down.'

Eva watches to see if the chair-leg will sink into the floor like it did to her before. But the old fellow sits down slowly and ceremoniously and settles himself. He looks up at the ceiling, inspects the quiet simple operation of the arrangement. Meanwhile Martin tells him he's a friend of Mr Hošek and introduces himself. The man evidently isn't interested. His face has twisted into a grimace, he's evidently cottoned on to the feeble makeshift nature of the system.

'He should've left it to fall down,' he said. 'I told him, but he wouldn't pay any notice, and now he's got this albatross round his neck. Pospíšil, who lived here before Hošek, was on his own too. This is his cottage, inherited from his parents. We were left on our own, both of us, after the time his wife died. We got our water from the same spring in the little valley, but he never used to go at the same time as me. He was grumpy, and odd.'

Martin sat down on a chair, and its leg subsided. The old fellow gave a brief sharp chuckle.

'It's rotten,' he exclaimed. 'All of it's rotten, through and through. I told him, only he wouldn't take no notice.'

Martin pulled the chair out of the floor, with a guilty expression on his face, as if it was his fault. He's always so careful, Eva thinks to herself, he likes to work out anything that happens well in advance.

'Pospíšil never talked to anyone either,' the old chap continued.

'His dad and mum were just the same. They only lived for themselves. We Pospíšils don't need help from anybody, that was their motto, till it drove them round the bend.'

He lapsed into silence and gazed about the room, his glance falling on something invisible. Perhaps he was seeing the dead. She wished for him not to summon them, for maybe it was him they were waiting for.

I, the being behind the beam, am trembling with anticipation. How long are they going to spend telling these old stories? Time flies, the room is sweltering with heat. I'm all bedewed, glistening cold and lifeless as a pearl. I'm practically alive, I only have to slide into the kindly fertile darkness, where I can grow and ripen.

'He lay here dead for quite some time.'

'What happened to him?'

'Who knows how I'll end up myself' – the old fellow waved his hand – 'but Pospíšil was so decomposed they had to take the carpet with him. He never let anyone into the house, you see, it was the postman told the police he hadn't been seen. His parents never let anyone in either, they never sent the children to school, and when the parents died, no one went to their burial. Pospíšil took them up to the churchyard himself on a wheelbarrow, wrapped them in a white bedsheet, didn't even get them a coffin. He dug them a grave himself and buried them without a priest or a sexton. They're lying by the wall like dead dogs, there's not even an inscription saying who they are.'

The old chap lapsed into silence again. It occurred to her he was deliberately stringing out his tale, to make the most of it. He didn't want to be left alone, and he'd long ago forgotten how a man and a woman like to be left alone.

Martin urged him to go on. He liked listening to stories about the good things and bad things that happened to people.

'So then the brother was left living here with the sister. They worked in the field, took the barrow to the woods to fetch firewood, otherwise they were never to be seen. The sister maybe even baked bread at home, because they never went to the local shop. That day it was raining just like today, I was already in bed, ready to sleep, and all of a sudden I hear someone banging on the door and calling out: "Václav!"

'I didn't know who it could be. Nobody ever came to visit and even less in such weather. I lit the light, opened the door and saw Pospíšil standing there, wild and unshaven, eyes crazy as the forester's Baruška passing in the straitjacket on her way to the asylum. Pospíšil was all covered in mud, from falling over. It's heavy clay round here, and when it rains it turns to sludge.

'"Come quick," he shouted. I asked him what had happened, but he didn't want to say anything, he just kept urging me to hurry. He drove me along in front of him, both of us falling, and him spluttering behind me like one being strangled. He was crying and muttering with it all the time, "Quickly, quickly."

'The bed was there,' said the old chap, pointing at the corner where Eva was lying. 'And Mařena was lying on it. The bed was soaked and blood was running into the middle of the living-room. Pospíšil pushed me forward to the bed, uttering something, and I saw blood everywhere. Her belly was laid bare and her legs apart. The moment I'd come in, she'd lifted a hand and tried to cover something bloody between her legs. From close up I saw it was a baby, it was wriggling on the cord, but it was quiet. It looked like a skinned rabbit, and Pospíšil stuck a kitchen knife in my hand, for me to cut the cord.'

In the living-room there was an age-old silence, in which something was waiting.

A bloody knee?

Eva remembered how she used to hold hands with the other children when she was small, playing that game, they walked round and round wickedly calling out: 'One o'clock sounded and still the lamp shone . . .' and it didn't go out till midnight, when the bloody knee was supposed to come. She was afraid at that time even to think of someone's death, in case the someone might die. Every evening she used to pray, maybe for hours, that everyone she loved might stay alive. She tried to ward off night and everything that closed in on all sides after the lights went out, which maybe one day prayer would fail to avert. Infinitely cold space spread out on all sides. She was not yet aware that space lessens and constricts with age, you hold it with your elbows and it ends in smallness.

Eternity merged at that time with life, because there was plenty of it before her, and little behind her, the day was long, and night too long to be slept through.

The old fellow said he'd run that day down the muddy track to the village, thinking he'd seen the worst, but that was still to come. When he came with the doctor, Mařena's body was still covered with blood but her face was wiped, as if someone with a rag had wiped the pain from her face and the colour from her eyes, till they were white. She was gazing vacantly into space; perhaps her eyes reflected the white vacuum she had seen, and that glowed so strongly that it bleached even her hair which only an hour ago had been brown.

The baby lay between her legs and was dead. They took her off to the hospital, the infant boy with them. She'd probably strangled it. She came back, but soulless now, if soul is what causes us to laugh, to work, to love and to hate.

He would see her walking about the cottage, formerly she used to work all the time, now she went from tree to tree, stroking the bark, embracing the trunk and going on empty-handed to the barn and from the barn to the woodshed. Once he'd met her at the spring, but without a jug. She was like a skeleton cased in dry skin; she looked at him, but her glance was blurred, or misted over. Who knows what she saw in the mist of her existence. She got thinner, sickened, then stopped coming out of the house, till one day he saw her, wrapped in a bedsheet, on the wheelbarrow. She was so light that he was practically running uphill with her. Perhaps he wanted to rid himself of her quick with this wild rush to the cemetery, wished to have her swiftly buried.

It was said that he never slept from that day on. Thus was he punished for living like man and wife with his sister.

Finishing his story, the old fellow sank his hands into his lap and drooped his head forward.

'Time I went,' he said.

'Stay for a bit,' said Martin. 'We'll make you some tea.'

The old chap stood up, stamped and his foot did not subside. He took his raincoat from the hook, fastened it up to the neck and put on his beret with the turned-up edge. He leaves the same way he arrived. Once he's made his mind up, he can't be induced either to leave or to stay.

Martin locked the front door and stoked up the stove. The wind was splashing rain against the windows on the west, the water rose in the containers. The wall, towards which Eva turned, smelt of winter, fungus and damp, and now it also emitted a curse. Perhaps they'd never get out of here. The tracks would get wet and they wouldn't have anything to eat.

Martin poked at the billiard balls, they collided and sometimes one fell with a hollow impact and a bounce into a corner hole and rolled with a dark thunder down the inside of the table.

'Want to have a game?' he asked, his voice coming from far off.

'I'd like to get out of here.'

'Now, just when it's warmed up nicely?'

'But I'm afraid.'

'Afraid of what, I ask you.'

'Afraid of that murdered born child.'

'Don't be a baby.'

He put the cue down on the edge of the billiard table, came over and slipped his hands under the lump of quilt. By now the old fellow was slithering off through the night to his cottage.

'Why did you bring me here?' whispered Eva.

'I liked the place. I was here once before, we played billiards and drank grog all night.'

'Didn't Hošek say anything?'

'Maybe he doesn't know.'

'He does.'

'How do you know he does? Maybe it's not so important for him. You're the one with second-sight.'

'Come to me.'

As he undressed, he watched her as she also undressed. She never had to tell him twice. Martin knows of nothing better in this world, after all. He also used to say he was united to her with all the cells in his body, because it came from nature, from God. He thanked God for her, God in whom he cautiously believed and did not believe.

'Give me a baby,' she begged him, hearing the voice of the being that had chosen her from amongst all others. It was something stronger than either she or Martin, it wasn't important who the two of them were, because they were only the instruments of some higher will, whose voice she heard and wanted to obey.

Thy will be done, she replied to someone, she didn't know whom, nor did that matter.

Everything was making ready within her, mounting and culminating to a high peak, whose dizzy slopes she conquered with all her might, and there at the summit in the cloudless blue she would take a child from that man from whom she would have taken death, not to mention life.

'Give me it,' she begged him, trying to restrain him in her arms, but his resistance was too much. She let him go, and he finished into her flat belly, which had been ready to swell.

Somewhere near the ceiling she heard a cry resembling that screech of a dumb rabbit smashed with a log behind the ears, eye turned bloodshot. The body twitches for a while, the eye glazes over ruby-red.

She burst into tears, warm tears, while the body turned cold and solitary. She folded petal after petal and eased them back into the bud, like a flowering autumn rose does, feeling the onset of frost.

Petal adhered to petal, and hardened into something durable with a firm core in the middle, harbouring the last hope of survival, living to fight another day.

'What's wrong with you?' he asked, stroking and kissing her. He hadn't heard that thing, and if he did, he left it in its state of non-being. It will take years, for another man and woman to come. What if they don't hear? What if they never come at all?

'Why didn't you do it?'

'Because I don't want to. You can't want me to do something I don't feel.'

She said nothing and heard the silence. No one was expecting anything now, no one was impatient. It was all over, she realized with a silent pain in her brain. She lifted a hand and looked at it.

'You're shivering?'

'We shouldn't have come here.'

'I didn't know you were afraid of the dead.'

'Something was lying in wait from the very beginning. Then that old man. We ought to have lifted the spell. Not left it in the house, when it's gone wrong once already.'

'Don't be frightened,' he said. 'I'm here with you.'

Should she tell him, or leave him his hope? How painful to condemn someone we love, how impossible to tell the truth. She rocked him in her arms like a mother. We hide death from a child also, don't we, so as not to horrify it. And why tell him I'm afraid of the death in you? Why me?

'You're my dearest. You're my nearest,' he replied, as if in his sleep, and fell asleep.

It was warm in the living-room and the rain had stopped outside. The woodworm had stopped nibbling, and the impatience of frozen time had evaporated. No one was expecting anything, death ruled, only the stove door gleamed. A fiery frame, behind which flamed the purgatory fire, which one day would burn up everything anyway.

He slept on her shoulder, his forehead and temples damp with sweat. She warmed him with her own heat and suddenly there was so much that she couldn't stay lying there. She lifted the man's heavy head from her shoulder and laid it carefully on the pillow. She got up, dressed, and started walking about the room. Six metres from the bed to the door and six back, she stepped lightly so as not to sink into the floor. Every time it was fifteen steps there and back, always past the billiard table, where the four balls lay still on the green baize, just as it was in the beginning. By morning the metres were kilometres, taking her further away from this man who would never draw level with her ever again, even as a headless knight, a rider on a horse whose hooves re-echoed in her empty body like a fine trot and a gallop, but over and done with.

Eternity did not interest her, she was no longer afraid of death or of solitude. Her mind was intent on free hands, and free, still swift-moving legs. She waited for dawn to come, because she couldn't yet see in the dark, and after rain all the tracks in the hills are heavy with clay.

Translated from the Czech by James Naughton

Alexandra Berková

He Wakes Up

He wakes up on his hard bed without a pillow; lying on his back with his hands by his sides he'll look at the white ceiling, at the fly by the lamp, at the shallow plasterwork, or just look; he'll be awake without moving. If he was twelve, he'd find his hands sweaty under the blanket, but he'll be more than four times twelve this time now when he opens his eyes,

his wife rolls over to the other side, sighs and gives a snore and turns,

he gets up and picks up a little speck from the floor, placing it in a box with a capital S. Then he'll stand by the window: spread his arms and breathe in the air of the grey or white or blue day,

his wife pulls the quilt over her head, she'll try to hold back her vanishing dream, or just yawn, click her tongue, stretch herself,

then he straightens a book or a pen, something not lying along the edge of the table, maybe only now he picks up that little speck, and goes out of the room. He passes the door of his wife's bedroom, or stops, taking a look: through the half-open door perhaps he sees over to the hump of quilt and the night shirt and old jumper which his wife sleeps in,

his wife squirms and sighs into the pillow,

he will stand and look: but quite possibly pass by the door, it may be shut this morning.

In the bathroom mirror he bares his gums at his more-than-four-times-twelve-year-old face, leaning close over to the glass he makes two sucking movements: spits out blood. Then with the small round mirror he looks at the light-coloured circle on the top of his head, today again it's a little bit bigger, he will be examining it attentively when his wife comes in.

In her old jumper and night shirt: she yawns, without covering

134

her mouth. Are you up? she says, or, what time is it actually? or, I'm absolutely whacked. He answers something and goes into the kitchen, his wife comes in after him: I'd like some too, she says. He takes the kettle, which he'd put on the ring, adds more water and puts it back. He'll watch his wife's little eyes blinking as she says, another day, or, I'm knackered; as she wrinkles her face at the light of the white or grey or blue day, yawns and scratches herself on the back. And the water will be boiling: he pours it into cups with blue butterflies, *Nicht Ende, Verwandlung nur*, it says beneath; he sits down opposite his wife, hunched in her old jumper and yellow shirt with white polka dots.

He feels that look: maybe he slumps deeper into the chair, maybe he straightens up, bends his head: Dita's going to be twenty now, she says, or, are those teeth of yours any better? or, ask today at the travel agent's. He answers something, finishes drinking, stands up, rinses out his cup and goes to the door: take your scarf, she says and goes after him. He answers something and then goes off.

She stays there, behind that door, she'll stand there and look through the white glass at the slender figure, as it walks solemnly and slowly, she'll look with sleepy eyes.

He steps straight-backed into the calm street, the air will be sharp and the trees bare, the white thread of a low sun pricks at his eyes; he breathes in and slows down.

His wife then pulls up the blind: get up, it's nearly seven, she says and the daughter with a pillow in her embrace and a blanket between her thighs whimpers, what is it? oh coming, and yawns at the wall.

He'll stand with his legs apart; with his arms behind his back and his head up he'll half close his eyes and think of his list of activities for today, similar to the list for tomorrow, similar to yesterday's: this list is on a slip of paper in his breast pocket; he thinks of it and excludes the first thing, for which there won't be time; perhaps it's the dentist or the travel agent or visiting a friend who's getting divorced, or is ill – this thing will be transferred to tomorrow's list, as soon as he gets home.

The wife in her flannelly night shirt goes to wash: she'll feel chilly, have some grog and lie down again.

He goes into his office: your table is over there now, says the girl, or, the new man's going to Finland now, or just taking a look in, she calls out, good morning, he's here! and the new man comes in.

And the wife will read a story about love: he loves a younger woman and she knows it, understands him, leaves, he dies in a car accident; I ought to try to write really, says the wife and falls asleep blearily, she'll have a strange dream: her husband kills her father, they go somewhere by train, there's some kind of meaning to this, that scene by the water, she says half awake, I mustn't forget.

We're a bit over what's-it round here, the new man says, taking him by the elbow, what was I – ah, yes: I'll take over that introduction in one oh six, if you've no objection. But of course, he says, just what I was thinking. The new man goes from the window to the door, runs his finger over the corner of his mouth; it doesn't really amount to any change, he says, spreading his arms, it'll be, so to say, a pure formality, he claps his hands and goes back to the window; of course, certainly, says the other, nodding his head gently; in any case, one has to make a start somewhere.

The wife wakes up with a headache; perspiring, she goes to the kitchen: don't wait for dinner, it'll say on the slip of paper, or, tell K. to come tomorrow, thanks, D. And the wife rubs her eyes, takes some Aspro: forgets that dream. He'll go to the dentist's or out, maybe he'll visit a friend: glad to see you again, you faithless old fellow, says his friend, well come on in, come on in right away, don't take your shoes off.

And the wife will walk with full bags: buy some food and a tie or socks for her husband, lipstick for herself: I think this one would just suit you, says the young salesgirl, twists out the little red stick from the white holder, makes a line with it on the back of her hand, and she nods: a tee-shirt for her daughter: that's like something for a child, says her daughter, then takes the lipstick, and the tee-shirt stays in the cupboard till the wife starts wearing it.

I've got it all written down, the friend calls from the next room, here it is, he says, bringing the file with a heap of papers, look here, do you see? And he will listen to what was wrong with the first diagnosis, see the grey knitted waistcoat and the collar of the grey shirt and the yellow face with wrinkles round the mouth, and it's useless, says the mouth, would you believe it? totally, it says, and it smiles. Look, here and here, the mottled hands roll up the trouser-leg, here, right? And it's getting bigger all the time. Not quickly, mind, and he shrugs his shoulders, raises his eyebrows, nods his head, nothing, he says, absolutely nothing has any effect, and he closes the file; maybe a bit later, he says, maybe the effects will begin to show later, he says, and that will be the sentence he prepared beforehand. Rubbish! exclaims his friend in a high voice, it's the other way round! it should've worked right away! he laughs softly, they're helpless, completely, do you understand?

His wife under the dryer fills in the questionnaire: you have a well-balanced marriage, it'll say, you might perhaps achieve better harmony by – she finishes reading and closes the magazine. My husband's away on business, in Bogotá, says the woman on the right.

So I play, says his friend then, slowly covering the big table, where there was a landscape with woods and fields and a railway station, houses and chalets, a big tunnel and a little country pub with a red roof, tiny white chairs and tables outside, a red parasol over each and a teeny green railing round about; it cost a fortune, he says, carefully smoothing the rubber cloth, but it does give me a lot of pleasure, would you believe? it really does, he says, smiling a little, it takes all sorts, he says, tapping his forehead, and since I'm a sick 'un, he waves a hand: anyway, it doesn't matter, he whispers, just be glad you're still healthy, a person doesn't know what he's got. He nods his head and says it solemnly again.

My husband's meant to be going on business to Finland in a month's time, she says to the woman on the right, I'd go with him, if it wasn't for the child, you know what I mean. The one on the right sighs, oh, absolutely, a woman I know: she lowers her voice.

Maybe he makes an excuse to his friend, maybe he went to the park: excuse me, says a pensioner with a dog, if you wouldn't mind, just for a moment, I'd like to, ach, and he sits down next to him. Children come along the path, tripping each other up and shouting: ouch, miss, Urban bashed me! and two boys maybe whisper together: you've got curlers! and you've got a bun! and you've got a bonnet, a nylon one! and they'll laugh falteringly and shudder allergically. The dog will sit and look solemnly in front of itself: watch out children! don't tease the dog! says the young teacher, that's right, let's go nicely round him. Urban, what did I say? And with her back to the bench and the man and the pensioner and the dog, arms outspread, she chivvies along the wavy double file and the children will call out: hello, doggie-woggie! goodnight, mister doggie-woggie! *guten Appetit*, mister doggie-woggie! and laugh and cackle away. Small fry, maybe the pensioner says; he will say nothing and look at the trees, Urban! calls the high voice, Urban, what did I tell you? somebody repeat to Urban what I just said! The pensioner strikes a match and turns to him; thank you, I don't smoke, says the husband and he will chew his unlit cigarette.

You have a nice quality of hair, says the young slip of a hairdresser, it would suit you better like this, she says, sweeping some hair forward over her forehead with one hand and taking a hairpin out of her mouth with the other, she bends over her: it'll be better like this, won't it? she says, and the wife in the mirror sees the brightly hued face of the young slip of a hairdresser, her own red forehead, wrapped in a hairnet, with a grey sweep of hair deep over her eyes. I ought to lose weight, she says to herself for the hundredth time; I'll leave it up to you, she says then aloud.

She gets up and it'll be two o'clock. Maybe there was a meeting, or he went to the park, or to see his friend; maybe he went to the dentist and he said: it's the gums, it's all got to come out, come back when there's more time; he gets up and goes to see her.

She comes to open the door, small and pale; hello, she says and blushes, or doesn't say anything, maybe she whispers, come in quick, we've only got an hour.

It really is better like this, she says, dropping a coin into the large pocket of the white coat, and she goes out. She stands for a bit in front of a plate-glass shop window and lightly pats her new hairdo: it springs back under her fingers.

He will lie there tired and smoking and listening to things he doesn't want to hear, does Jindra know? she says to him suddenly and he nods silently. She looks at him, then says, you're joking! and she laughs quickly, bending her head, and she'll laugh, laugh so much that the tears'll start flowing and she'll weep. He'd like to go, but he has to comfort her and say various words, he'll caress her and talk, a lot, quickly and in a whisper, so as to stop the choking sobs.

She returns. Makes some coffee, dials a number, sits down, says, well hi there Danny, how are you? or: I was just coming back from town and I saw it on the way, terribly nice and really quite cheap, so I thought I'd tell you now.

He goes down the corridor; dark and long, with girls in short coats, one turns to look at him, he walks quickly with his head down, in the doorway he answers the greeting of the woman who lives with her, it will be a loud greeting, he answers with a nod and hurriedly leaves.

Well and what did you say? she moves the receiver to the other hand, you had to say something to him about that!

He'll take the tram. He still had a lecture, or he was at his table in the office and a student came, I'd like to do my diploma with you, she said, but I still don't know, so I'm coming to ask, she said and smiled; he'll take the tram. He'll stand there straight-backed and tired, he'd like to have a bath, he'll stand there looking at the grey nape and brown wrinkly hand next to his own, and suddenly someone shoves him from behind into the lap of a sitting girl: she looks up with a grin, please, she says, have a seat!

He returns home. He empties his pockets and takes out his list and the scrap of paper from his wife, where it will say *'Čedok!'* or 'Plumber!', screws it up, chucks it away, opens the door, and a sharp stench of paint wafts over to him. Over by the window his wife will be standing in her tracksuit with a transparent headscarf over her crisp hairdo, which makes her look older. Look, she says, pointing at the chairs, the table and the dresser, carelessly painted white, look, she says, nicer isn't it?

And he will stand amongst the furniture, on which the paint is tearfully drying. It needed it badly, would you like some coffee? says the wife. And he says: where's Dita? or: I fancy a bite to eat, or: it really is nicer, that was a good idea. And he sits down slowly to the two little cups with the blue butterflies, *Nicht Ende, Verwandlung nur*, it will say beneath.

Translated from the Czech by James Naughton

Ondřej Neff

Brownian Motion

The library entrusted to the care of Jan Kaufman occupies four large halls in the spacious Žerotín castle of B., decorated with ceiling frescoes by the Italian mannerist painter Nicollo Sacchini, renowned for his attempts, tireless as they were unsuccessful, to emulate the voracious imagination of the great Arcimboldo, and who even here, in B., failed to emancipate himself from the classical strictures, so that this work, though high up on the ceiling, hardly lifts the spirit at all, and today if it has a certain value, this is alas merely because it is so old, and even this doubtful value is still further set in doubt, for Sacchini's work is damaged by damp, mould and the hapless efforts of men of diverse trades, especially bricklayers, electricians and plumbers, so that, for example, Juno's swelling breast is pierced by a sewage pipe; and maybe that is the reason the goddess gazes down with such melancholy, at the four ample canvases of Peter Brandl, which depict life in the castle kitchen, stable and servants' quarters, almost totally obscure compositions, which Brandl painted clearly just for his own amusement, casually, as it were, in the intervals between work on the altar painting for the adjacent chapel of St John the Baptist.

Jan Kaufman, a most erudite man, is custodian of all these volumes brought to the castle of B. from six other castles and aristocratic summer seats over a wide radius, shifted here thanks to the fortunate, in those days even rather risky decision of a responsible official, who for some reason took pity on these books, earlier destined for transport to the paper works in Štětí.

Twenty-two years ago a catalogue was produced of this library, but there is no record of its subsequent fate, so that it may be assumed this catalogue has been lost. However, Jan Kaufman retains several filing cabinets of correspondence conducted with various specialist institutes in the capital, which – as it emerges from the correspondence – propose to embark on a thorough re-cataloguing project, based on extensive research aimed at making these literary treasures properly acccessible, taking advantage of the most up-to-date methods, such as computer technology employing bubble memory, so that one day it will be possible – metaphorically speaking – by simply pressing a button to convey electronically to some scholar's table, situated in Prešov, say, a xerox copy of any page of any book, without obliging the said scholar to travel laboriously all the way to B. and consult at length with Jan Kaufman, a librarian of the old school, whose qualifications are – regrettably – inadequate, and not up to the demands of the modern era. As yet, however, these numerous institutes based in the capital have failed to decide which of them should take on this responsible task, and under what conditions, so the library is still being looked after by Jan Kaufman, who airs the place in summer and heats it in winter, lays mousetraps from time to time, and occasionally embarks on a struggle with the airborne armies of moths, parasitic upon the spines of books.

Most of his time Jan Kaufman spends sitting on a chair with a carved back which is extremely uncomfortable, so that it can only be tolerated for any length of time by someone whose spine has become insensitive through long practice.

Jan Kaufman sits and gazes at the particles of dust which dance in a broad strip of light falling into the largest hall through a half-closed shutter. The particles are innumerable, certainly hundreds of thousands, maybe millions. Some of them rise, others fall, but mostly they just hover inertly in space, supported by molecules of oxygen, nitrogen, carbon dioxide, water and rare gases, in wintertime also carbon monoxide, for the stove is not exactly in the best of repair. The librarian stares at them fixedly, with great interest, motionless, for hours on end.

Everybody in the whole of B. regards Jan Kaufman as a nutcase. The librarian knows this, but he doesn't mind. True, years back, when he began his observations, he tried to explain the aim of his behaviour to his fellow citizens, and he gave improvised lectures on the subject in the local Jednota hostelry, mostly greeted with derision, sometimes pitying indulgence, but never sympathy and understanding.

'Alongside the infinitely great and the infinitely small there is also the infinitely complex, and though it may seem paradoxical, this third infinity is greater than the other two,' Jan Kaufman explained to the local tractor drivers and tenders of calves. 'Of course from the physical and philosophical point of view the number of particles of dust in the strip of light observed by me is not infinite, however, their mutual relationships vary over time as a consequence of the molecular motion of the gas particles in air, so-called Brownian motion, named after Robert Brown, called the prince of botanists, who achieved fame when in 1827 he observed the motion of microscopic particles in liquids and correctly associated this with the movement of molecules. Dust appears to the human eye as an uninterrupted grey surface in the strip of light penetrating the crack between the shutters, and there is a reason for this – the particles are more or less evenly distributed in the air. But the motion of molecules is constant and infinitely complex, and equally infinitely complex are the interactions between the particles. In the course of time it may – indeed must – happen that some of them will approach each other and others move apart, so that in their totality they will form an image.'

At the thought of this, Jan Kaufman went pink in the cheeks and raised his voice, likewise in order to make himself heard over the snide comments which people were starting to make.

'Observe any picture in the newspaper. It is likewise composed of dots! At some point the moment will come, maybe fleetingly short, when the particles of dust will group themselves into an image composed of dots. It may be an image of some trivial scene, but in view of the infinity of possibilities it may just as probably be an image of some mystery from the past, present, yes, even the future. I may see an image of my birth or the burning down of this inn, the murder of Julius Caesar, Libussa prophesying Prague's future glory, or the face of the inhabitant of another distant world. It may be the image of a scene which is real or unreal, so that one might imagine that you, Mr Znamenáček, will appear to me in the shape of a woman, a beast or a tree. I may see the image of the death of the universe, I may . . .'

The rest of this account, by which on several occasions Jan

Kaufman attempted to explain the sense of his ideas to his fellow citizens, sank in a clamour of voices, as the fellow citizens began to vie with one another in their suggestions of all the things that might appear before the eyes of the castle librarian, and insofar as any children were present, come with a jug to fetch beer for their dads, they pricked up their ears, for many of these suggestions were spicy, and humorously coloured.

In time Jan Kaufman realized that he would never overcome the barrier of incomprehension, and when anyone asked him, 'Well now, Mr Kaufman, how's infinity doing, seen anything yet?' he would smile shyly, shrug his shoulders, and reply that he'd seen nothing yet, but that since the probability of success heightens with the passing of time, his hopes were growing, rather than being undermined by his lack of success so far. He would only leave the castle on dull and rainy days, haunted by the thought that the dust, invisible in the prevailing light conditions, might group itself into the desired configuration right at this very moment, and it might be necessary to wait a long time, a very long time, for the next occasion. But as he was basically an optimistic person, he managed to dispel his gloomy feelings, and buttressed his optimism with a further rational consideration: the dust was in a more active state of motion in sunny weather, because the sun's energy causes the molecules of air to move more quickly, whereas in cloudy conditions the molecules are somehow lazier and sleepier.

On sunny days, however, Jan Kaufman was never to be seen on the village green or in the neglected castle garden. To find him, one would have had to creep softly into his dominions, peeping over his shoulder, carefully, so that no one would spot us, not even he, since we are not equipped with the proper letter-headed document permitting access, for – it goes without saying – the only matter upon which all those highly important institutes charged with the fate of this treasure-house of books could agree, was the strict prohibition of access to all individuals, authorized or unauthorized, quite without exception, subject to applications for exemption.

Let us call on Jan Kaufman today, perhaps, when the sun is shining beautifully, as in any case is the usual habit in this blessed wine-growing district.

The librarian sits there stiffly, his hands folded in his lap. We hardly dare to breathe and we proceed in a shuffle, our feet equipped with the usual felt over-slippers. We are so close that Jan Kaufman is bound to hear us, but he gives no indication that he is aware of our presence.

Now we notice a peculiar slanting of the librarian's head.

Cautiously we walk round him and look into his face.

Jan Kaufman is staring in front of him, blissfully smiling, but his gaze is fixed on nothing, for – as we have just realized – his mind is extinguished, life has departed.

We rush off hastily to fetch help, but in vain, for Jan Kaufman is truly dead, and only living water could return him to life.

'He looked odd,' those who saw him in that posture of death say to the others in the Jednota pub.

'As if he could see something?'

'As if he could see something.'

'What could he have seen, the dead don't see anything!'

'He might have seen something just before he popped it.'

A year or two later on sunny days B. seems deserted. When we look in at the window of one of the cottages, or sneak into a stable or granary, here and there we find a figure sitting motionless, his eyes staring straight ahead.

Local farm output is allegedly suffering as a consequence, to the annoyance of many bodies, especially the District Agricultural Administration, who in their letters to the regional authority complain about the presence of the library in the castle of B., and attempt to draw a causal link between it and the farms' lamentable economic performance. Officials at meetings call down fire and pestilence on the 'inkhorns who caused all this'.

But sometimes, when they are alone at home or in the office, and rays of sunlight penetrate the room in a wide strip, illuminating quivering particles of dust, they start meditating and a question flashes through their mind:

Why was old Kaufman smiling so blissfully?

Translated from the Czech by James Naughton

Slovakia

Pavel Vilikovský

Escalation of Feeling

A young girl – that is to say, at that loveliest female age, when her female charms have just fully developed – a young woman like that sat at a lime-wood table.

The little nurse who fetched her at eight was called Elenka, like herself; she wasn't scared of her. She brought the wheelchair up in the lift, tapped her on the shoulder. So, how did we sleep last night? A more awkward moment came when two hefty nurses lifted her up at the baths. Every time her body . . . I'll get undressed by myself. The body all of a sudden . . . Yet all the women were naked. It wasn't the fact of being naked, it was the helplessness of it, that the body at that precise moment couldn't express itself . . .

It was all inexorable, there could be no negotiation. The wheelchair at the door, the bathing book. The two hefty nurses appearing at the end of the corridor. They smiled at you from close up. Actually not always.

But these are just moments. Everyone dreams of being able to fly, and on waking up is not therefore unhappy. Again, it was the little nurse who carries her into the showers. But it's all just a moment. A sick moment.

Dear diary, she thought. By half past nine she was in the yard of the institute. The wind blew. The sound of the leaves rustling about her head pleased her. There was something about it, something . . . in that movement from one leaf to another, like passing on something fragile, there was something . . . Dear diary, she thought. Excuse me, said a grey-haired lady in a white hat (she was holding it on with a false, outdated charm), I wanted to ask you this yesterday, don't take it as an impertinence, I have a woman friend who . . . just like you . . . that wheelchair, it's not from round here, is it? I thought as much, chrome, you know. And excuse my asking,

147

is this leather? Well, doesn't matter. Twelve thousand Austrian schillings? Dear diary, thought Elenka. She'll be wanting to have a ride next. She watched her go: one hand holding the hat down, the other the skirt. Really blowing now; lovely, as if the day was suddenly a bit larger.

Dear diary, she thought at last, you are the only one to whom I can confide all my griefs and joys. I got this checked blanket here from Mum. Not that it was cold or that, but she didn't like it when they looked at my legs.

Vlado said to her: Legs aren't ⁄ . . aren't vital. But that's a lot of talk. Vlado won the school long-jump competition. Legs aren't vital! Sweet boy, Vlado. She smiled, somehow much older. Today, in the age of cars and aeroplanes, legs aren't at all vital. Sure, sure, if you close your eyes to it . . . A tree grows on the spot. She opened her eyes and looked: true enough. She laughed. Silly girl, stupid!

The Váh flowed peacefully along between two ranges of hills, stretching away down to southern parts. Look at this countryside any time, it must enter and move you; look at it when the sun sets, and the soul is drenched in waves of desire and the heart melts into ecstasy and blissful peace.

Dear diary! Legs aren't so vital. What's vital is, that on a bright September morning . . . She opened her eyes and convinced herself with a single glance. On a bright September morning, on the threshold of life . . . She laughed, somehow much older than her years. Legs aren't vital. Vlado, sweet boy, is not vital. What's vital is, that a certain sixteen-year-old girl, on the threshold of life, a silly girl, on a bright September morning, on the threshold of a huge day, meditates about her legs. That you talk, a sixteen-year-old girl on a bright September morning, about a chrome invalid wheelchair. Twelve thousand Austrian schillings! Who said so? What for? On the threshold of life!

Dear diary, she began carefully, for she knew it would be a difficult sentence, and at the same time, with lowered eyelids, she rose from her wheelchair and began walking over the grass, dear diary, after a series of emotional shocks . . . Yes, she was pleased by this, that's what's vital! After a series of emotional shocks . . . Somehow older than her years, she laughed at this boastful little girl.

'A sleeping princess,' said a man's voice somewhere very close by. She contemplated that voice for a moment with closed eyes. It was a mature voice, sort of . . . weary. It was addressed, evidently, towards the invalid wheelchair. She did not respond.

'I know you're not asleep, girl,' the voice said again.

The sixteen-year-old girl took fright, squeezed her eyes even tighter shut, and she, hidden inside her, thought: Oh-ho-ho! Since when have we been friends?

She felt a slight jolt to the wheelchair, shifting it forwards a little. She caught the arm with her hand.

'The sun's been shining right in your eyes. What are you reading?'

Oh-ho-ho, she thought. She opened one eye and saw, right over her head, a branch with a few leaves. 'A book' she said.

'I can see that,' the voice said without anger. She opened the other eye as well and looked round. He was standing next to the wheelchair holding a book in his hands. It was a sort of handy-sized book. It was . . . but that really doesn't matter. She hadn't even noticed him take it. Hadn't felt. She'd had it lying on her knee just before.

'Good?' he asked her. He was a lot older than her, he might have been about . . . twenty-five maybe? Maybe even thirty. Long fair hair. When he leaned over the book it fell over his brow.

'And though they saw one another but rarely, yet the flame grew so in their breasts, that all at once it flared up and their mutual plighting of love that same evening joined the souls of both for ever and eternity,' he read aloud; it surprised her how fluently. He shook his head. He turned a few pages at random. 'Love is powerful, wise and prudent, when the enemy lies in wait for it.' He uttered a kind of sound, she couldn't find a word for it on the spot. 'T-gh,' let's say. 'Love.' He closed the book and put it back on her knees. 'Yesterday you were reading the same one.'

Dear diary, she thought. I have a relationship. We took a walk beside the river, he clasped me by the hand . . . She laughed, the tears welled up in her eyes. In those eyes that look in the other direction.

'You could get through a thin book like that in a day. If it was interesting. Don't you feel a bit hot under that blanket?'

Quickly he caught her by the hand. Only after that, reassured, did she shake her head. 'This isn't a very interesting conversation,' she said in a half-stifled voice.

'It'll do,' he said without anger. 'For a start.' He eyed her directly. He went on looking at her for a moment. Defencelessly, she thought, feeling somehow much older, and averted her eyes. Amongst the trees the rear wall of the Napoleonic Baths gleamed white.

'I saw you here yesterday, girl. Do you always go to the same place?'

'It's nice here,' she said, as if it mattered, as if she understood. 'I don't remember us agreeing to be friends,' she added peaceably.

'I saw you here yesterday.' He was still eyeing her. 'I liked you the minute I saw you.' He flicked his head. 'It's mostly older patients that come here.'

Dear diary! she thought. Today he declared his love for me. I shall never forget this day. A black bird hopped over the grass. A thrush? With a yellow beak? A step further, over another strip of grass, the wind gently passed. Without a backward glance.

'Agreeing to be friends?' the man asked suddenly, as if only now remembering. 'You what? Come again? Anyway, what's the point of that? What's your name?'

I must write to Alena about this, she thought. For a split second it seemed to her that it was the loveliest thing about the whole situation: she could write about this to Alena. 'Denise,' she said, for she could see her sentence in the letter already: *Just imagine, I told him my name was Denise!*

'Denise? Really?' He looked at her. 'Denise,' he repeated slowly. 'Is it out of a book? You've got a lovely straight nose, Denise.' All of a sudden he ran his finger down it. Down the ridge. She flinched her head. Although the finger ended up hanging in the air, for a moment she could still feel it warm on the end of her nose. As if a big goose-pimple had just sprung up. Maybe that too.

'What are you, a male nurse?' she said quickly. She grasped the

150

book in her hand and mentally crossed her legs. That helped. One bright September day, she thought. That also helped a little.

'What? A male nurse?' He looked at his hand, left hanging in the air, looked at it absentmindedly, preoccupied with something else, and laid it on her bare neck. 'Yes,' he said abruptly. 'Good.' He gave a laugh. 'You've got a nice face here from the side, have I told you that already? Yesterday the minute . . .' he gave a wave of his hand, but the other, not the one on her neck. 'How do you like Piešťany?'

'I can't walk,' she said. 'I'm here for treatment.'

'I can see that. What happened to you? Polio?' Questions, right enough, but only questions.

'Put that hand away,' she said to him. Somewhere in the distance, in front of the Thermal Baths perhaps, a car engine roared. In Piešťany, she thought. An ordinary normal September day. Clear.

'But why?' the young man asked and shifted the hand up through her hair. 'Is it unpleasant for you? Really, is it unpleasant for you?'

'Yes,' she said, 'yes, and . . .'

For a split second she stopped. She knew what she ought, what she wanted to say back, but for a split second she stopped, as if she wanted to be genuine, to convince herself again . . . What was this? Such a stupid thing! Was he really asking? Seriously? Did he really think, just like this, as simply as this . . . with a movement, the laying on of a hand . . . ? Leaning forward like this she could see in the distance in front of the spa post office two young men with a large parcel. Young men? Maybe only because they were slim. She stared at them fixedly. They too? Is that how it is? Is that how men actually ask? Pleasant! Yes, when all's said . . . That is the word! Pleasant. Unpleasant. Is this supposed to be for real?

The man waited for a bit, but it was as if he too had forgotten the question; he lifted his hand off her neck and put it on the handle of the wheelchair at the back. Then the other. He laughed.

'No, and no,' he said. He began to push the wheelchair, slowly, even tenderly almost. 'No, and no.' Again he laughed, and she observed in surprise, with a kind of hyper-real precision, how the wheel parted the blades of grass, the taller ones, and simply squashed the shorter ones. It didn't seem rough or cruel, that motion; it was almost as if the wheel were handling every blade specially. It was the right-hand wheel, the one she was looking at.

'If only you women,' she heard behind her back the voice, hoarse and somehow deeper, as if he had been talking for a long time, 'if only you could ever be honest with yourselves, honestly admit it . . . No, and no. But you're all alike. No. Good lord,' he exclaimed, suddenly louder and yet seemingly from a great distance, until she couldn't help turning her head round, 'it's simple as ABC! What is all this, come on tell me, all this round here, this green stuff, well what is it?' All of a sudden he bent down beside the wheelchair and started plucking whole clumps, two or three of them he left lying on the ground, then the fourth, as if he liked that one, as if he was satisfied with it, he lifted up in his fist and brandished before her eyes. She noticed that his nails had picked up a bit of earth.

'Don't do that,' she said. 'Where are you taking me?'

'Well what is this, this stuff I've got in my hand?'

'Grass,' she said. 'Take me back. The nurse'll be coming to get me any minute.'

He nodded, but maybe not to her. 'And this, what I'm standing on now?' He stamped his foot, and then once more. He laughed involuntarily. He reminded her of some animal, she couldn't right-away say what, all in a huff . . .

'Earth,' she said. 'Soil.' She tried to turn the wheelchair round, but she was holding the book in her other hand.

'And that there, that's a tree. Don't you believe me?' He strained against the wheelchair, the wheel moved again, faster and faster . . . 'Simple as ABC. Don't you believe me? If I take this chair and push it, if I start running like this, what does it do then?'

She put the book in her lap and caught hold of the arms with both hands. 'It bounces up and down,' she said. 'That hurts.'

'It bounces up and down.' He was panting audibly, but he didn't slow down. Not right away. 'It buckets along.' Suddenly, just when she was about to cry out, he stopped several inches away from a tree. The wheelchair gave another bounce, as if willing to carry on by itself.

'A tree,' he said gaspingly. He touched the bark with his hand. She heard a special crinkling noise, as if the trunk were made of paper. 'This is a tree. And that down there,' he stamped, 'is earth. Grass. Is that clear? Let's get it agreed once and for all. A tree. Don't you believe me? Go on, get a feel of it,' and she scarcely had time to utter a quiet little astonished 'no', before he was holding her in his arms, all at once she was light herself, incredibly, and when, automatically, as a reflex, she put her arms round his neck, she felt him slippery with sweat. 'Don't be afraid, eh? A tree. And this here, everywhere, there,' he pointed around him, finally the hand stopped with his finger indicating the other bank of the Váh, and above the tree-tops she saw with abrupt, even painful inward perception the roof of the Hotel Slovan . . . that's where Mum took her, once every Sunday, when she came to visit, 'that's Piešťany. Easy as ABC. And this here, this is love.' She didn't understand him right away, she didn't know what he was talking about, she was just thinking of something else, some words her mother always told her; she tried to remember, in the park in the middle of the flowers there was a statue of lovers, two rather angular bodies, leaning away from each other, she had just thought to herself, why lovers?; she was thinking of something else, and the movement wasn't even abrupt, there was nothing alarming about it, the body was preparing itself to sit down in the wheelchair. 'This is love.' The words didn't scare her, but suddenly it seemed to her she felt cool air, a breeze on her knees, and she realized . . . but that's the sentence, and she felt like when, in the dark, a bat flits past, close above your head: The blanket! Where's the blanket?! 'It's love, and all that various stuff that's talked about, described, in that book of yours as well . . . is this.' With sudden panic she tried to resist, but that only meant that her arms, holding him about the neck, clasped him even tighter, and on her cheek, very vaguely, she felt something warm. 'Don't be afraid.' The body sank, tenderly and softly, suddenly it leaned; at once she let go, fumbled with her hand . . . 'Don't be afraid. That's grass. Don't you remember? We agreed about that. You said it yourself. And this now, when I touch you, like this, this is love.'

She shifted herself a little with her elbows, felt them dig into the ground, a blade of grass passed thin and sharp like a knife across her skin. Earth, she thought. But what's it supposed to be, all of this? Nurse Elenka had taken her to the park . . . 'I'm going to shout.'

'Yes.' Suddenly, as if with some silent mechanism, a face descended over her. With surprise, for it was her first sight of it close up, her first real sight, presently and with surprise she realized that it radiated something . . . He's nice-looking, she thought . . . not in terms of his nose or mouth . . . nor his eyes, the eyes! what is it, how do you tell, nice-looking eyes! . . . she couldn't think of it any other way, only with this particular word: nice-looking. 'I'm going to shout.'

'Yes,' he said, his lips seemed to enlarge, swell, had trouble in parting. When they did, a black strip remained on each. 'What? Fine. Shout. This is love. Go on and shout. You imagine, I don't know what . . . everybody imagines, but in the end . . . always, but always, don't you believe me . . . ? it's like this.' He pressed up suddenly with his lips, with the black strips, but at the last moment she turned her head, they touched her ear; it was such a precise touch, such a . . . touch, genuine, that she thought: maybe he meant it? And knows? Suddenly she felt tiny hairs on her neck, as if they had sprouted just this moment, they quivered all damp still in the warm breath. Is there such a place? On her, about which she didn't know before? At least, not like this? The sculptor was called, he had some sort of funny name . . . there was a name plate, she sent Mum to have a look . . . Mum muttered, they stick things like that, lovers, out in the park . . . and there you sit, getting wheeled about, she said, and you never even think of my sore legs . . . they weren't really even bodies, just sort of . . . imitations, like when a child crudely draws an apple . . . not when it draws on its own, its own apple, but when it draws one lying on a table, teacher's table, on her raised desk . . .

She was startled by a hotness, it was his lips, hot, she licked herself: really. But what is this? she thought. She felt him slide his hand under her sweater, a movement like . . . it didn't even scare her much, not that, she just couldn't comprehend it: right here? in

Piešťany? in the park? on the grass? What is this? What does he want? What does he mean? Like when at some party one of the guests pulls out a pack of cards and asks you to pick one. The selfsame question: Why? What's this about? And he keeps on insisting: Just pick a card. Don't be afraid. You'll see. Pick a card and . . . Hard to refuse, silly in fact. Really, what is there to it, picking a card? But then you ask yourself: Is it some kind of a trick? What's going to come of it? Will they laugh at me?

He can't mean it seriously! Okay, we know, we've all heard what it's about, but what's he bringing this up for now? He's said his little piece, and now . . . Lovers! It struck her that the sculptor's name was Bártfay. But that didn't matter. Bodies . . . but not real ones, only square blocks, symbolic like . . . they were far apart too, even leaning right away from each other, each the opposite direction. They only touched in the middle. 'Help!' she shouted quietly. Not for real, she only wanted to try it out. She didn't like it. She wouldn't be able to shout that out loud. She'd be ashamed. 'You can't,' she said. 'You can't, not like this.' The man lifted his head, but his arms stayed where they were: one with its elbow leaning on the grass, the other under her sweater.

'But it's always,' he said, a little surprised, as if cross about having to repeat it so many times, as if he had thought she was more understanding, 'always like this. It's the same, on the grass, in bed . . . even then it's all the same in the end, love is, like this. You get various situations, the positions differ . . . but the thing itself, it, it's always . . . Try closing your eyes. Some do that. Don't be afraid, I won't hurt you, don't you believe me? I . . . It's no problem, getting hold of a bed here, if I thought, if that made any difference . . .' 'That hand,' she said; that hand under the sweater was confusing her, misleading her. It was so precise, so insistent, always at the same spot. 'But that's what it's about, that hand, see . . . Doesn't it feel good? Like this? Honestly: doesn't it feel good? I can tell it does. Eh?'

'It does,' she said crossly, 'but what is this? What are you saying? Take me back. The nurse'll be looking for me, and when she sees you here . . . Where's my blanket gone?' She lost her patience. Such jokes! 'And my book's fallen down somewhere.' A year ago, before

155

the accident, she would simply have stood up and left. She tried it: mentally she stood up. It worked. She still knew how. She felt the muscles tighten on her back. But why am I so much older? she thought. And this one here, this man, how old can he be? twenty-five; how come I'm older all the time?

'There's no point,' again it was that hoarse-sounding voice, she lifted her gaze and looked at him, 'in all that talk, women just don't admit it to themselves, they don't have the honesty to say it . . . not to me, that doesn't matter, but to themselves,' she was still looking at him and she saw him give a smile; nice-looking! she thought, as if watching from a safe distance, there's no other word for it, nice-looking! and she couldn't have described, she wouldn't have been able to define any feature in him. 'They don't admit it, that's excluded, but how they like it! Those sighs! And shouts! Don't you believe me?'

Why can't we just have some silence at last, she thought, a lot older, afraid, or what? She wanted to remember . . . not that she was paying attention to what he was saying, but all the same those words, that voice . . . there was something about that occasion, she wanted to remember, for instance the way Mum slewed the wheel-chair round, masking it from the side, that was why she spotted the statue in the first place: Lovers! What's this? she thought at the time in that little park, what is she up to? Are we even going to start hiding statues from us now? So as not to upset me? That was why she sent Mum over right away, asking her: 'What is that statue over there? Who's it by? Please go and look.' Mum muttered, 'Go and look, I ask you, your legs hurt, fit to drop, and there she sits in her wheelchair, and she tells you to go and look . . .' She detected it now, this manoeuvre, when Mum suddenly turned at an angle, bent down over her, quickly began talking about something, like she did when a disabled person went by on crutches, and every time she thought: But why? So as I don't envy him? There were lots of them in Piešťany like that, with crutches.

'Again?' she said to him. 'That's enough! And you can pick me up now as well!' She noticed that her skirt was tucked up, a very long way; she wasn't scared, not of him, but the legs . . . those legs, objects, just legs there on the grass, lumpy knees in the middle . . .

'Aren't you ashamed of yourself? A cripple? That people might see you? You've no . . .' But the heavy body bore down on her, at first seeming only to have one dimension, weight; she began to stifle, turned her head in order to free her nose: 'Help!' cried the sixteen-year-old. Across one blade of grass (she saw it close to) a ladybird crawled. It went slowly, uncomplainingly, patiently. Don't expect miracles, her mother had said at the time, as if it had something to do with the statue (lovers!), all of a sudden: Don't expect miracles, the most important thing for now is patience, just be patient, and gradually . . . She thought, when the ladybird had clambered right the way to the top, it would open its wings and fly away; as they say. Be patient! that's the most important thing! They said on the threshold of life. To a sixteen-year-old girl. But what do they mean, and how? 'Help!' The shout seemed to her a bit off. It was all sort of undignified: those white legs, the man panting, the grass, the earth, the tree . . . and now this shout. Legs aren't vital. Said Vlado. The ladybird didn't fly away. It simply fell off the blade of grass. For a moment you couldn't see it, then it appeared at the foot of the same blade of grass, crawling so slowly, so systematically, it seemed to be counting stairs. Where there were none. 'Shout. Do you feel like it? Shout away.' His lips were pressed to her neck, she felt her heart suddenly throb in an artery under their weight, it eased again. Don't expect miracles! Who do they take her for? Even this one keeps going on about this is how it is, it's nothing else but this, nothing more . . . don't expect anything better, no miracles . . . What's going on? she thought. I mean I reckon it's up to me, only me, it depends on me, I'm the one that decides. How can he? Don't expect miracles! I'll expect whatever I like, everything, she thought, just as it is, as it usually is, as it comes, everything, everything . . .

Then he began to tremble. First of all she heard his loud breath in her ear, she heard it for a while, loud, louder and louder! Oogh, oogh. But she was just thinking of something. Suddenly he began to tremble. Involuntarily she put an arm on his shoulder, he was trembling all over, violently, disharmoniously, as if separately with every muscle. What is this? she thought. What's happened to him? She caught him with both arms, squeezed his shoulders: let them stop shaking, let them stop . . . He's not going to end up lying here, is he? What is it doing to him? I mean he can't . . . Why's he sighing like that?

'That's enough,' she said, but he didn't hear, 'enough! Just stop it right now!' With surprise she was aware of a sob, his? her own? and another, others, thick as raindrops. That's all I needed, she thought, to start blubbering like a kid, and she burst into much louder weeping. She averted her head, covered her cheek with her elbow.

'Don't cry,' the hoarse-sounding voice said again. 'There's no point. It's always like this. You think, if it was with someone else, with some other boy, some other place . . . Did it hurt? Sometimes the first time it does . . . That's nothing. It soon goes away. I know it does. Stop crying. It'll always be like this, you'll see.' She felt him lift her, so light again. 'Wait, I have to adjust you. Don't squirm, or you'll fall out. Denise. Tell me then, Denise, did it hurt? Tell me then.'

He spoke from somewhere below, and when she opened her eyes, she saw he was lifting the blanket from the grass. He caught one corner, then another, shook it out vigorously. The blanket flapped like a whip, with a deep bass. 'Get everything in order,' he said cheerfully. 'So, tell me: sincerely: did it hurt? Not very much, right?'

'It didn't,' she said. 'I didn't feel anything.'

'Well, there you are. What did I tell you?'

He bent over her and covered her up; it surprised her how considerately. He folded the blanket in half, tucked the end behind her back. Then he wrapped it round her feet. 'You've got nice legs, pity to hide them.' What does he mean by that? Is that all it takes? A single remark? And if she shook her head, he'd probably only ask her: Why? Don't you like what I said?

'Well, there you are,' he said, down there again. He was squatting in the grass, she could only see his back. His shirt hung back from his shoulder blades. When he stood up, he had her book in his hands. 'It's always like that. No, no, they say, and in the end they like it. That's love for you. Take your book. If I thought it was something bad, something that would harm you, I would never . . .'

'That's not it,' and with one sob she seemed to split her anger in two: anger at herself, for her stupid tears, and anger at him, for his stupid talk. How come? she thought. Is it possible? Only a moment ago he was shaking away so . . . hatefully? Despairingly? As if about to die? Where does he suddenly get this cheerfulness? Because it was love, is that it? Is that why he's feeling so good? Why doesn't she? Right opposite the wheelchair there was a tree. Perhaps it was the same one. Evidently. When he touched the bark, it crinkled. Dear diary, she thought, you are the only one to whom I can confide this experience of mine. 'That's not it, not at all. Far from it. What do you know?'

'Because of this,' he said and pointed his finger; 'because of these legs? This polio of yours? But don't cry for that, I mean, that's . . .' he patted her cheerfully on the shoulder, 'well, what is it, just this once, that one moment . . .'

'It's not polio,' she wailed between her sobs, as if she was sorry just for that; equally, at the same time, she hated herself for those words. She'd start telling him all about it next, complaining, that's all she needs . . . She heard him behind her back, the river Váh was now on their right-hand side. She didn't hear the Váh, she was only aware of it. Mum had taken her along the embankment once, then no one did. True, you could see the Váh from the Colonnade Bridge. What's so special about the Váh, she thought, just because I'm stuck in a wheelchair surely I'm not going to bother my head about the Váh. Anyway the Danube's much bigger.

'One day I'll die,' she heard him behind her back, 'and so will you. Both of us will die. Everyone. And till we do, just for that while, we'll last out somehow. Even on one leg. Just this once. Don't be afraid, it won't happen again. Don't you believe me?' He laughed at that himself. 'I like you, Denise, really I do. Here's a hankie for you, wipe your tears. There's no point. People will stare at you unnecessarily.'

'I'm not Denise.'

'No, of course not,' he said cheerfully, 'you're not Denise, and this isn't the river Váh, and,' she heard, with the wheelchair moving along so quietly, it sounded as if he had stumbled; she heard him kick the ground, 'this isn't gravel, and what we made, wasn't love.'

They turned the corner to the Institute. He began to whistle quietly, almost inaudibly. The Váh, is it? she thought to herself. But why? She looked back over her shoulder at the water; she couldn't see that far. Why the Váh? Because we agreed on that?

He placed her in the shade. 'Tomorrow I'll come here again. If it rains . . . Never mind. It won't rain. Tell the nurse to take you to the same spot.'

He raised a hand, five fingers, presumably that was meant for goodbye, since he said nothing else. Dear diary! she thought. He can't live without me. She watched after him, he was younger from the back. If he had looked round, maybe . . . she didn't know what. Maybe it would have been more bearable. He bent down, picked something up from the path, a stone probably, and threw it into the water. From the distance like this, it was like a silent film. She didn't even hear the splash.

She watched after him, and from the distance like this it's almost . . . Lovers, she thought. I suppose that's why those statues lean apart, if they were close together they couldn't . . . such a love just wouldn't even be possible. I suppose they have to be estranged from each other first.

If . . . if it was only that moment of shaking, that helplessness, she'd still manage to believe. She'd still find herself able to like it. Said the dumb man to the deaf . . . But the way he goes now! The way he walks along, on his healthy legs! He comes up to this love of his, has it, and goes . . . No, legs aren't vital. But the way he says: It won't rain! And the worst is, what if he's right?

'So there you are!' She heard the sister behind her back. 'This won't do, you know, Elenka. I've been looking for you. Next time you want to go off somewhere . . .'

She wasn't angry really. She caught the wheelchair by the handles and turned it round. 'It's rice pudding for dessert. We must hurry. Where have you been all this time?'

'I was . . .' she said, considering. With one hand she caught her book to stop it falling. Then she raised her head and looked over her shoulder into the nurse's face. 'I was raped. I didn't feel a thing.'

'Sorry?' the nurse asked, uncomprehending.

'I didn't feel a thing,' she repeated with amazement. 'Nurse, I didn't feel anything.'

ASSAULT ON PATIENT

Last Saturday at Piešt'any Medical Institute one Jozef P. (age 27) accosted a female patient (age 16), who is immobile and confined to a special wheelchair. From the Institute he took her to a nearby park, removed her from the chair and raped her. Later he put her back in the chair and returned her to the Institute. On leaving he said he would fetch her again the following day. But instead of the girl, he was confronted by police officers, who took him into custody. He explained his actions by saying he liked her . . .

(Smena, 5 Sept 1973)

Translated from the Slovak by James Naughton

Ján Johanides

Memorial to Don Giovanni

One day — just when I was starting out as a young singer in a second-rate opera house — fate accosted me. It posed a question, to which I have so far failed to find an answer. Fate has surprised one since time immemorial: it always has an ample store of coincidence ready to hand, ever freshly attired and newly disguised. It has always adopted the habit of being the unexpected guest. But at the same time it always strikes a common note in all its mouths: the tone of the Pied Piper from the age-old notorious town of Hamelin. Fate accosts you with primordial words, analogous to the action of a dream. It confronts you in a foreign tongue, one you have never studied: it interrogates you in a language which has another grammar, sentence structure, different nouns, verbs, conjunctions and attributes from your trusted mother tongue, yet it insists that you grasp its questions, urges you to respond with your own actions. To reply with deeds, for it speaks to you through events.

A colleague of mine — the prima donna at the opera — invited me to her birthday party, which was attended not only by all our group, and the actors from the drama section, but also by retinues of unknowns, notables, and enthusiastic well-wishers. During all this celebratory, laughter-filled, frivolous time amidst the fragrance of abundant flowers, I behaved practically like Cinderella: now and then I cautiously swallowed a bite-sized canapé, sipped wine in tiny little gulps, and helped to multiply the giggles. I can't remember when my stomach started aching a little, but after a good half-hour the pain was unbearable and I felt an overwhelming sense that any moment I might just faint on the spot. I apologized stammeringly to my hosts, kissed hands, and staggered off to the hospital, where at first I got absolutely nowhere. The doctor on duty claimed I was just drunk, and waving my arms about aggressively, whereas I was only trying to persuade him I'd probably got meat-poisoning. He became more and more irritated, threatened to call the police, and when I realized he'd decided to get rid of me at any price, I clutched at my last straw of hope: I finally demanded with angry emphasis that he summon Mr H., the head consultant, on my own responsibility, since I knew him personally. I'd met the head consultant for the first time after the première of *Don Giovanni*. He'd offered me his congratulations and invited me later for a Cognac. 'Your performance of Giovanni was quite remarkable.' I always remembered these words. From that time on we met now and then at chess.

At first the doctor was reluctant, though by now I'd introduced myself, but eventually he agreed and telephoned the consultant at home. Only then did he take my blood sample and send it to the laboratory. The spasms continued unabated and I contemplated death for the first time.

The consultant, who had 'rushed over in the car straight out of bed', as he expressed it, kept on wanting to know exactly which people from our 'pocket atlas of the *grand monde*' (who knows why he insisted on calling them that?) had been present at Alexandra's party, and he did not omit to tell me that he too had sent a telegram and a bouquet. The birthday guests, half of them at least, were his friends and acquaintances. As an outstanding physician – and specialist in gall bladders, pancreases and livers – he was well received amongst the people of the theatre, and he knew not only the actors, but also many of the local district politicians and members of the Regional Communist Party Committee personally. Along with all this he also asked me (for about the tenth time) if I hadn't perhaps eaten something else I'd forgotten about, a fixed smile playing over his lips.

'Do me a favour: admit that after dubious sausage, slices of veal Marengo, say, and wine, you nibbled a little soupçon of something else: at least half a savoury stick.' He laughed. 'Let's work it out together: how about the hostess's pickled mushrooms maybe? You know what human memory is.' So spoke the consultant, examining the laboratory result, as it was handed to him by the nurse. 'No Cognac? Alexandra's watching her purse-strings. Your guardian angel's definitely due for a big bonus. You're still pale as a rusk, but it'll pass, all in good time. Don't worry!' Then he added, rather too loudly: 'Were there plenty of tables? Or only the big round one? Did you sit – sort of in a circle? Were the guests in a circle? You know – like a garland or a wreath?' His kindly, but always mischievous laughter, suddenly resounding, seemed to me ever so much sadder than his voice.

'Tenor! Baritone! Bass! Mezzo-soprano! Alto! A good pathologist is what I need! Not a diviner of entrails – we've more than enough of them already! Why are you a singer anyway? At least tell me a good joke, now I've been dragged out of bed specially for you! Look: Alexandra wanted to poison her rival, female or male, and she mixed up the sausages. How come this particular poisoned singer's got no sense of humour? We'll get down to business in a moment. As a great man once said: hurry slowly.'

The first time I was introduced to him, I noticed the way he was able to control his facial expression, but now he carried on, quite relaxed, with the same vociferous joviality which I least expected at that grey hour shortly before dawn, for the pains were still very much with me, though I also had the feeling that the consultant was mocking his own mistrust, which nevertheless he couldn't afford to exist without.

'Try to put up with it a bit! You used to sing in the Army Ensemble, remember! Stomach-pump – yes, but it'll wait three minutes. I'm telling you this on my own responsibility. The lab result's rather curious by the way.' He spoke with a strange half-smile on his face, which annoyed me exceedingly, for it felt rather like scorn.

'Rather curious? What do you mean by that, consultant? – Like *Alice in Wonderland*?'

'Food-poisoning, meat-poisoning. Meat. Botulism.' The consultant bit his lip. 'Meat, old chap. *Atropa belladonna* – deadly nightshade – that'd be more theatrical – I know. "The murderer whets now his thirsty blade, craving ravenously innocent blood"? – as the poet says. Nurse, make me a deadly strong coffee, please!' (She was just watering the dried-up, mud-grey soil in the flower pot, and I would have sworn her action had another motive.) '"With ever higher honours the toady longs to edge his showy garment's hem"?'

He clasped his head in his palms and gazed ahead. 'I always had a good memory for poems. I was taught literature by one Alexander Jezevec.'

'Aren't you trifling a little – with my life – consultant?' I asked him with suppressed hatred.

'Not at all!' he said, and I couldn't restrain my laughter in spite of the pain when, in a singing voice, but especially with gestures, he imitated me in the role of Giovanni, continuing: 'You definitely must have wanted to destroy someone! You swore revenge upon him! And now you've been poisoned for it! Creeping up the sweet laps of wives! You must've struck below the belt . . . and how! You must have been seducing the soubrette, state property of the Regional Committee! The cock bade farewell to the hen – but watch! the final line ends with chicken paprika! – a sad loss for the pathologist. A win for you. Toxicology today is as broad as an emancipated heart.'

At that point I saw he was about to start another theatrical performance and I had a good mind to stand up and take him by the throat, but this time the consultant didn't laugh, he continued in a much gentler voice:

'Anything true often looks like a bad joke. Did you know, for example, that a stingy man can suffer impotency? I mean it, seriously. A psychiatrist colleague just came back yesterday from an international congress – he told me. You don't believe me, Don Giovanni? You'll have to grin and bear it a little while longer. Terrible, the things I say, eh? Don't make anything of it: the unbelievable is really quite normal.' He looked at the laboratory result again. 'You don't believe me? Then I'll prove it to you – even the unbelievable is normal.'

I felt as if I were going to faint again, but I clenched my teeth, leaned the back of my neck against the curved upholstery, and the consultant fixed a reassuring glance. After the nurse had gone, he lit a cigarette and his voice became more subdued:

'You'll just have to grin and bear it for a bit. Let me tell you the following story: during the War we had air-raid alarms. And various Civil Defence exercises. Just like now. I was a student. First-year medic. On vacation. I was roped in by the powers that be: you're going to be a doctor, you have to set an example to your native town, and so on. In short, I didn't want my father to suffer any unnecessary unpleasantness, so I went on this exercise. Moreover: I wasn't in Hlinka's Academic Guard. I didn't stay in the Svoradov hostels.

'During this exercise I received orders to stand at a certain place and wait for a green signal from a torch. So there I was, stuck. It was in front of a synagogue. In the evening, I stood there contemplating my own things. All of a sudden – I don't know how – a storm sprang up. It began raining furiously. Absolutely pelting down. Naturally I didn't want to get soaked, so I retreated towards the door of this synagogue. Beneath the arched doorway. Don't worry about your botulism, all in good time. I remember precisely, as if it were today, how there, on the door of the synagogue, there hung a lock. A hasp and a padlock. A padlock – for the two halves of the door. I leaned against the door – and it immediately gave way. The lock was hanging in the sense of: I'm hanging here, but just for appearance sake. And terrible rain. So I went in, into this synagogue. The alarm was over, I knew that, but I couldn't go home yet. I switched on my torch: in the middle of the synagogue there was a pile of sacks of cement. Maybe a hundred. Or more. Aha, that's the point of the lock, I thought. Broken windows everywhere, everything upside down. A mess. It was the first time I'd been in a synagogue. Close by the door I spotted a discarded armchair. Something like that. I ran the light of the torch once more round the synagogue. Totally wrecked. I sat down in the armchair by the doors – which I'd left open – I put out the torch and gazed at the rain. Into that rain. I sat and meditated about everything. I don't know how it happened – but I just dropped off to sleep in the rain. Not feeling any better yet? I was tired, I suppose, that's why I fell asleep so easily. Suddenly I woke up, as if I was choking. Kind of coughing. I was choking. Choking dreadfully. I'd got this fit of coughing, such as I'd never had before, nor after. You know when you feel as if you're drowning – don't you? Surely you can imagine.

I clapped both hands over my ears – I remember it precisely, as though it were today – and I dashed out into the rain. I breathed in: ordinary air everywhere, but continued coughing. I couldn't explain it to myself, not even a week, or a month later. Even after the war. This exercise was in '42: there was no word of any gas chambers going round here at the time, or anywhere else, I suppose – nobody yet knew. So why was I choking in there like that? At the time I had . . . I had the feeling in there that it was my last moment on earth. I don't know what I dreamed about. But I went on coughing even afterwards. I ripped off my Civil Defence band, stuck it in my pocket and hurried off home in the rain. In the rain, coughing. Even at home I was still coughing, right till I fell asleep. – Unbelievable? – Definitely not. Interesting? – Certainly. I didn't catch a nasty cold or anything. Tell me, why did I start choking in this synagogue, when the door was wide open in front of my very nose? Feeling any better yet?'

His eyes went visibly sad and immediately took on an expression of astonishment. Who knows how I got the feeling that was how he stared at everything when he was quite alone and no one was watching. But my pain was as bad as ever. I no longer even felt angry with him; gradually I was overcome by surprise, like the time I saw my friend's open fracture and my breath quickened.

Then the consultant opened a cabinet door, he took out a half-full bottle of Martell and two glasses, and he continued:

'Always – in medicine as well as in life – when I encounter something that can't be rationally explained, I remember that synagogue. That choking feeling. The gas chambers. Don't imagine only rationality helps me to live. How good that we can now share a glass of brandy together.' He smiled gently, gave me a fatherly glance, then very slowly he said: 'You haven't been poisoned by anything. Aha! Here's the piece of paper! And it speaks clear enough!' He picked up the laboratory result and waved it in the air. 'Do you see? You're fit as a fiddle!' Again he smiled gently and continued: 'Now if you can explain my coughing – I'll give you a detailed explanation – ' here he giggled ' – of your own so-called poisoning! All your symptoms of botulism! Can you do it?' Then his glance suddenly went solemn, he grabbed the bottle of Cognac, poured us a large glass, and went on in his matter-of-fact tone of voice: 'Go home, strip off everything you have on, down to your dirty underwear, and then – please take a shower, for at least a whole hour! The pain will go. You don't even need half a painkiller!' And after a moment's silence he whispered: 'And never – do you understand, never again sing Don Giovanni – or any other role in this opera.' Then he added, out loud: 'But, first of all – let's drink this bottle of Cognac together.'

Translated from the Slovak by James Naughton

Dušan Mitana

On the Threshold

MYSTERIOUS DISAPPEARANCE

Bratislava (date) – Chalet owners in Koliba have been disturbed by a strange event. A father and daughter vanished without trace on the night of Friday to Saturday. According to witnesses from the neighbourhood who spoke with them as recently as late Friday evening, there was no indication that they planned to go anywhere. They were quite relaxed and there seemed to be no conflict between them. Fears of both neighbours and the former wife and mother of the missing persons are heightened by the fact that the man was once under psychiatric care. He became 'famous' to the public a few years ago after publishing certain very eccentric 'theories'. A search is on for the missing pair. The man's name is Vít Nehoda, he is medium height, with short chestnut hair, brown eyes, symmetrical features. No particular distinguishing marks. The girl is four years old, her name is Dana. A letter was found in the empty chalet, evidently from the missing man. We publish here the full text of this letter, entitled 'Report of a Superfluous Person'.

I was told I had to revise my theory of light's dampening effect on sound. I have convinced myself that for most people night means silence, as if light were louder than darkness. I am surprised most of all that people for whom I have great respect are also affected by this illusion.

When I issued my proposal for research on the interior of air, they prescribed treatment. I proposed that this research should be conducted by leading world philosophers, painters, musicians, poets, and myself. Patronage over the entire project should be adopted by the UN or UNESCO. My inspiration for this proposal was the word 'inscape'. Everyone claimed that this was a useless piece of stupidity, because science has allegedly identified all the various components of air. I discovered that my proposal was not properly understood, and considered it useless to try to convince anyone of its value, especially in view of the fact that I had proposed the whole project precisely due to its apparent pointlessness.

Naturally I was not insane, but I was happy to enter the mental hospital: I had always longed for such an experience. Once I tired of the constant electric-shock therapy, I renounced all my theories, although I was convinced of their accuracy. In any case I realized it was futile to try to force people to believe in the truth of my theories; they had to work it out for themselves.

In the mental hospital I learned many things from my new friends and I knew I would miss them very much. For this reason alone I proposed a mass break-out, but they explained how this would be an irreparable error, for after a time they would be bound to catch us, and the work they had already done would be reduced to nothing. They regarded the hospital as an ideal environment where, in peace and absence of fear, they could bring influence to bear upon the doctors and nursing attendants. I can confirm that this method was even starting to show the first modest results. It is an effective method, though its success will take many generations. My friends are convinced, however, that a few people in every generation will be found to pick up the baton.

After discharge from the mental hospital, I spent some time in the circle of my family, but my attempt at co-habitation was not successful. It suited neither my family nor myself. Most of all, people were worried about the effect on my three-year-old daughter. Gradually I gained her unbounded affection, which was evidently love. I have never been obstreperous, and so the solution proposed by my relatives sounded ideal: they bought me a timber chalet with a plot of garden above the town, in what is termed the summer district. As soon as I arrived at the chalet, I realized it was what I had always longed for. I am surrounded by many similar chalets (some are even solid-walled) and by similar or larger gardens. But I am the only person who lives here permanently. The owners of the other chalets visit only on Saturdays and Sundays from the onset of spring. On the coming of autumn they usually make their last visit. Some of the dedicated fruit-growers come out even later, but during the winter I am generally alone.

At first I had a neighbour who lived here permanently like me. He was very old, but I never found out his real age. In fact, I never actually asked. He always kept himself to himself, but for some reason he took a liking to me. Initially I thought it was from a sense of fellow feeling, because it soon turned out that he too had thought about the interior of air. He was much further on than I was, but he never shared his insights; clearly he sensed I was unable to rid myself of doubts about the point of such thinking. Thus he did not consider me a proper devotee, perhaps he even thought I was just trying to curry favour. I know now that we were brought together by my daughter, who continues to visit me to this day. The old man left us, however, without even saying goodbye. He kept various livestock, poultry and domestic animals. Apart from that he had the wreck of an old bus in his garden, which he claimed was a space ship. From time to time he used to bring all sorts of old metal parts which he found on rubbish dumps or bought from scrapyards. Using some designs quite incomprehensible to me, he was working on the inner mechanism of the bus. He never let me inside, but my daughter had free access. When I asked her what she saw there, she only said how lovely it was. One morning, when she came to see me as usual and we wanted to visit the old man, the chalet was empty, the chicken runs, cages and sties were empty too. I wasn't terribly surprised, because I'd always reckoned on the possibility that one day he too would be taken away to the mental hospital. At that moment, however, my daughter pointed to where the wreck had stood. The bus was no longer there; there was only a rectangle of yellowed grass distinguished from the surrounding green. 'He's flown,' said my daughter, shading her eyes with her hand and gazing at the sun. Involuntarily I too looked up: the sky was clear, and blue, though some dark, heavy clouds were beginning to scud along on the far horizon. It didn't look like an ordinary brief thunderstorm, it looked like prolonged rain. After that indeed it rained for two days on end, but no flood came. With relief I realized the old man was no Noah.

Since then I've had no permanent neighbour. My wife has divorced me. That is understandable. But she doesn't stop my daughter from coming to visit. Now that I'm not living with my wife any more I like her much better than before. She got on my nerves for a while, though, and once when she tried to please me by praising my nice white teeth, I seized the pliers in a fit of rage and pulled out a tooth on the spot. I'm still sorry about doing that to this day. Initially I was afraid she would set my daughter against me, and raise her in hatred and scorn. Luckily I was wrong.

Apart from my daughter I am also visited by a thirty-year-old woman and every Monday we make love together. It's natural and that's how we both see it. Probably she has a number of other lovers, but that doesn't bother me and I'm not jealous at all.

So as not to be a financial burden to my relatives, I started keeping hens, some hares and two pigs. Apart from that I have three hives of bees. It doesn't cost a lot of money, the hens find plenty of worms and other nourishment in the garden, and the hares graze freely on the grass, which I've sown with clover seed for variety. I fetch slops for the pigs from the nearby pub, which I get for nothing, because the woman I sleep with on Mondays is the manageress. I needn't mention the bees. They fly from flower to flower, flower to flower, flower to . . . I've forgotten how I meant to end this sentence. It happens now and then; the memory of the electric-shock treatment. But I believe even someone who's been under treatment has a chance of recovery. I obtain some indispensable extra cash by card-playing.

Thanks to numerous tricks I learned in the mental hospital I regularly win smallish sums.

I remember that as a child I was appalled by the killing of hens and hares. Now I chop off their heads and wring their necks as if I'd done nothing else all my life. I'm quite convinced they're not angry with me, for like me they know it's only natural and I help them fulfil their mission. Every winter I slaughter two fattened pigs, make yards of sausages, bacon and ham, which I smoke, or I preserve the meat and it lasts me till the next winter.

At first I thought a lot about death and sometimes it seemed as if life had come up to me and said: 'Nehoda Vít – you're in the shit.' One morning, when it rained and it looked as if it wouldn't stop all day, I decided to commit suicide. It seemed a bit impalatable though on an empty stomach, so I got out of bed. I spotted an egg. And I actually drank it. Raw. Meanwhile, however, it stopped raining, so I gave up the notion of suicide. I have thought a lot about this experience. If the rain hadn't stopped, I'd be dead by now. An ordinary raw egg saved my life.

Ever since then I've been convinced the world is not chaos; on the contrary, it has fixed laws. Yes, these laws exist, it's just that we don't know them all, and there lies hope. I have realized life is dangerous and inscrutable, but at the same time there's no use in being afraid of it. And so the thought of death, I hope, has left me for ever. It was then I understood Spinoza's saying, which had previously caused me so many sleepless nights: 'A free man thinks of nothing less than of death, and his wisdom is not in reflecting on death, but on life.'

And so I sit out on a summer afternoon on the threshold of my chalet in the sunny silence and I contemplate my theories. The hens and hares wander about the garden, the pigs wallow next to the sty, the bees fly about with their quiet soothing buzz. The chalet has two rooms and a kitchen. My daughter's room has a settee and a chair in it. My room is empty. I sleep on the floor in a sleeping bag. I'm afraid that one day I'll give in, buy furniture, fill the empty space with it and thus deprive myself of all possibilities. This is probably my most natural desire.

I have convinced myself that my old theory about light's dampening effect on sound was correct. Previously I reached this conclusion more or less by a process of speculation, but now I am able to prove it by experience. The day is quiet, but the night is full of unbearable noise. The rustle of trees and grass, snuffling of a hedgehog, chatter of crickets, creaking of timber in the chalet walls, barking of dogs, whistling of locomotives, tremor of rails, the swish of falling stars. Yes, darkness is a sound amplifier.

Now I am thinking about the interior of air and I regret very much that I was unable to gain the trust of the old man who solved this. What a lot of time I would have saved! At the time, however, I doubted the point of such thinking, so I don't blame the old man at all for his distrust. Today I believe it does all have a point, and I know that even the old man would deem me worthy of his trust. However, the solution is lost with him, and I am left with no other course but to work it out for myself. It is very important that I solve this, because with great difficulty I have finally obtained the wreck of an old bus. I only succeeded in getting hold of it thanks to my daughter, who is my great support . . .

Translated from the Slovak by James Naughton

Rudolf Sloboda

The White Dog

Now that I'm someone, I'm writing my autobiography. I became someone by my own efforts, through work – but thirty years ago who would have said these efforts would one day bear fruit? Who? During those thirty years of work many of my enemies came over to my side, so that now when I remind them sometimes how sceptical they were, they laugh heartily and consider these remarks a sign of my willingness to speak about them. I am a man who sleeps well. I am guarded by my white dog, that idiot, who alone thinks that life is without end. His animal limitations prevent him from getting depressed, like a lot of people do, even if they are idiots. This ugly white dog is my servant, he is the offspring of a disobedient bitch, later killed by my enemies. When I first appeared with this white dog on the street, everyone expected me to shout at him when the white dog jumped into some flowerbed, these cheerful graves which everyone has created in various ways, but all basically the same, in front of their houses, following the recommendation of the members of the local council. I thought I hated these people. But ever since I've known how low a man can sink, I've viewed them as saints. They behave well. Each has a hobby, works like a donkey, and then sits down sweating on his bed wondering if he can't avoid the duty of washing his feet. It's unbelievable how much I resemble these people, how I am one of them and how at the same time they can regard me as one of their masters.

Their daughters adore me, but mind you, not one of them is afraid of me. These people have a high opinion of me and consider sex something I have only under strictly legal conditions, so they don't even bother to distrust their daughters when they sit with me for two or three hours. And it doesn't occur to them that, although I've never so far caught a single one of them in a tight, inexorable grip, from which there is no escape, I really haven't; nevertheless, though I haven't done it, I easily could, quite out of the blue. On the first occasion I suppose they'd take it as a joke maybe or some kind of misunderstanding, which could even have been caused by the white dog, that monster I don't even want to name.

This autobiography of a man who became a master by his own efforts may one day become an item of great curiosity for the historians. Unfortunately, I still can't get it moving properly, I'm still stuck in my childhood. And I can't remember properly many details which would create a continuous picture of childhood. It shrinks to just a few episodes and someone might think, on reading my biography, that I had no childhood. I must devote more space to descriptions of the countryside. It was a bit different from what it is today, but I don't even remember about that properly. I don't know which houses have been knocked down. I ought to know how each house got built – but at the time I didn't pay attention to such things.

I know that even back then we had a white dog. Someone might think it was a pointer. My uncle, when he came to visit, used to say, 'It makes me sad to see that animal. And that name: Duntcho! You must be nuts! A white dog ought to be called Harry.'

He was an idiot. He used to blow smoke in the dog's eyes. I would be glad if I could remember some continuous episode about Uncle. It's difficult for someone to make out from the reaction I mentioned to the dog's name that Uncle was an idiot. How come I am so certain? Something must have preceded this conviction of mine. There must have been far more of these incidents.

It might seem to some that the fact I'm about to mention ought, in the proper hierarchy of values, to have come right at the beginning of this paper. However, I wanted to give everyone a surprise. I ought indeed to have begun with the fact that recently I got married. This did not disturb my life of a master very much, or my work. My wife introduced a few changes, for example we started drinking coffee and eating cakes. It was pleasant (and still is) to have for breakfast something we didn't have before we were married. After this, however, I've usually had to go and have something else to eat. My wife is glad I'm fat. She can't hold me on her knees.

When I sit down, I can see how happy my wife is; like when we're afraid a huge plane isn't going to land. (By the way, sometimes a man secretly longs for some aircraft to land right in his garden.)

We don't talk much about food in our new household. All the latest research can only prolong a person's life by a few uncertain years, during which, indeed, this old person has to watch his special diet to an absurd degree. It's true that a man can't do just what he likes – but in the end, why not just rely on the most reliable regulator: income. Income enables you to eat bread and soup, cook vegetables from the garden, enables you to appreciate the kohlrabi you buy for a modest sum from a smallholder. From off-cuts you can fry half a kilo of fat and warm crackling, which the white dog will eat, even if it is slightly burned. But that doesn't happen. We put some bits of crackling in his rice, one piece on top, so he knows, and his food takes on an air of luxury. It's true, of course, that in many countries people are starving, but even there dogs have to be fed somehow. And why should a dog, a creature who was in the world before man, why should he suffer for the fact that people take the food out of each other's mouths, that they beggar each other. My white dog eats fairly little. Just like you have to feed horses, to make them pull, so you have to feed the guardian of your yard and your surroundings. Sometimes the kind of people who criticize dogs don't even realize they are actually worse than dogs. If people like that weren't around, maybe there wouldn't be any hunger in this world. The kind of person who criticizes a dog for liking meat calmly goes, for example, to the theatre or the cinema or the seaside, and it doesn't even occur to him to send the money (if he knew the address) to some poor person, some place where people are starving.

So the fact that I and my wife have a dog is a certain sort of culture; it's maybe not even such a luxury as someone going to the hot baths. We can manage without that as well. If the people who serve the visitors in hot baths worked in the fields, we could increase production. They could go down the mines as well . . . But what's the point trying to show it's absurd for us to consider a dog a luxury?

I couldn't bear for no one to be in the yard at night. I'd rather put up with three dogs there than none. When the old bitch was still alive, the one from Hungary with a name like a Hungarian river – Tarna – a problem arose sometimes with the larger puppies. The mother would drive them out of the kennel and they had to sleep by the door. There they lay down in a heap, and the one in the middle, covered with live fur coats, soft as velvet, had the best of it. At that time the black dog Uro was still alive too, and he always lay down beside the heap. But he never stayed there long, for the heap was constantly quivering, and an old dog can't stand that in his sleep. He had his own kennel under the window where we used to watch television in the evening. He knew it wasn't us talking (me and my wife), but in a certain way he felt the presence of human communication. Tarna again knew when we would go out into the yard, so she guarded the house at the other end.

Uro got killed; he disappeared. Tarna too, about a year later. I gave the puppies away and suddenly only the white dog was left me. He still didn't have a name. I wanted to give him to somebody, so I didn't give him one. (Otherwise, without meaning to anticipate, he does have a name: Iris. But everyone thinks it's derived from Irena, so I'm considering whether I oughtn't to change his name to Uro. Names can sometimes be the same for both sexes, you see.)

In the morning, especially in summer, when I lift the blind, I see the white dog standing by the fence staring into the distance.

Everything is peaceful. On such a fresh summer morning the clouds, which are always different but can always bring back some day from our childhood, if similar, are a promise, a hope, that the day, even if it is unbearably hot, will be freshened up now and again by a little cloud. It is well arranged, would it might last like that for ever. My wife opens her eyes a bit, it's uncertain whether she will feel like telling me her dream. I don't like conversations with women. Even in books. I have always talked the same way to women as I do to men. It was dreadful to hear one day one of my teachers talking very sweetly to a female colleague in the staff-room. Particularly awful was the fact that when the teacher saw me in the door, he jumped up and said sternly, 'Did you knock? Go and knock on the door properly.'

I was shaking all over with disgust. He looked at me, a little schoolboy – (ah, God, was I ever a little schoolboy?!) – as if he was looking at a dog. I don't read novels, they show all sorts of funny behaviour. A man always has to flirt with a woman, he always has to try and win her, in small steps, with a smile . . . (He said, smiling.) The women mostly resist the men's attacks ingeniously and one party goes after the other. However, when they get to the bit about reaching the real love, the sex, they mostly say how next day they met again at the same place as before. And we've no idea what gestures they made when they said goodbye. That's why I haven't read many books, because they are stuffed with lies. I mean, what else but lies is all that talk?

So that's why I'm glad when my wife keeps quiet and at the same time does a bit of useful work. In the morning she eats her breakfast silently and goes to work. It takes her a long time. Even when it's been quiet for ten minutes after she's gone, I'm still not sure whether she's really gone, whether she hasn't forgotten something. That's why I help her get to work in the morning; I hold her watch for her, for when she winds it up, she mostly forgets it. Fortunately she only notices once she's at work, and they don't let her out again. So when I've made sure she's not coming back, I tidy things up and go to the pub. There I have some goulash, drink some beer and smoke two or three cigarettes. About nine o'clock I enter my supervisor's kiosk, check the telephone, and start working. It's a master's work. All day I don't have to talk to practically anyone. The drivers nod at me and say hello. They know I see them and won't answer.

Now that I sit all day behind glass in my master's role, watching the hubbub of traffic at the crossroads, I see that those thirty years of being an honest man were not wasted. I was honest before, too, but that was when I was still at school. Now I see all the things in the world that could be changed. I see that here at the crossroads you get a kind of extract of life, something we don't see so easily elsewhere. And as long as we don't see it, it doesn't even occur to us to think about it.

Sometimes I see a neighbour or somebody else I know in a packed tram. Sometimes our eyes meet, but the neighbour isn't sure it's me, for I wear an uniform cap. That evening in the pub, when I drink some more beer and smoke, my neighbour tells me how he saw me in the kiosk at the crossroads, was it really me? I have to laugh. Who else could it have been? I don't know, ever since I've been doing this work, people have been more inquisitive somehow. Everyone can't be a supervisor, though; somebody has to do the actual work. It's the same as if a hundred people came to a building site and all wanted to do the same job on the same spot. Somebody has to give the orders, and so he doesn't have time for the actual work, because he's overseeing it. First you have to make plans. That can't be done by simple-minded folks, for what if others came along and wanted to start work according to this simple-minded plan, they'd find out they'd been duped by this idiot who wanted them to build something that wasn't properly thought out.

It's just the same with transport. There too you have to have organization. Organization means some people work, driving passengers, while other people organize the transport. It's the only way. My wife thinks people like me are superfluous. But just let her try telling that to her manageress. If I wasn't a traffic supervisor, somebody else would have to sit there. But me and my wife don't quarrel about such things. The dog doesn't like it either, when people quarrel around him. It's like a thunderstorm to his ears. (A dog has fifty times better hearing than a man. It's pointless for us to shout at him.)

When I tell my wife she can go and take my job then, she shuts up at once. Not everyone has what it takes, the nerves. It turns out sometimes a good driver can't be a supervisor. The psychologists have their own special terms for this, but I know all about it anyway. I can't put my foot on the accelerator. I have to wait for someone else to do it for me, and at the same time I have more worry about a vehicle getting damaged than the driver does himself.

So I have to write this autobiography of mine, in case one day anyone was to think I didn't realize the place I occupied. I have insight into these things!

What I'd prefer to do is skip my childhood and go straight on to the bit about how for a long time my present wife didn't want to marry me. We've known each other by sight for a good ten years. When I was still a driver, and it happened that she saw me working, more than once I found the time to say to her a couple of words.

Mostly about the weather. Then, when I found out that she'd seen my dog and liked him, I asked her why she didn't get married. She said it was because nobody wanted her. (Actually she was just leading me on, for now we're married she says her boss wanted her, some foreman or other, but he had too many bad points. Who knows what these bad points were . . . ?) I kept this to myself and watched to see if I ever saw her with somebody, with any man. After a few months I knew she was totally on her own, I said to myself a piece of stuff like that would suit me just fine, I wouldn't have to feel ashamed of her at all. It happened subsequently I was taking their firm on a trip to a harvest festival in Nitra. She was still free. She was sitting right behind me, she could see me driving. I made up my mind: I was damned well going to find out today whether she was willing to consider marrying me. After locking the vehicle, I went off to the harvest festival and found her after a while. There some man turned up who was drunk already and he started chatting her up. I couldn't get rid of him, for she didn't show him the slightest disinclination. She giggled and simply pushed his hands off her. During the official entertainment he tried getting his arm round her waist. I followed them for about an hour and then I went off somewhere else. I played cards with my colleagues. Then I walked over to the castle, and dozed off under a tree. I was supposed to go off with the second load at about half past three, so when I woke up and it was only half past one, I was fed up, because I didn't know what to do. I went back over to the platform, and the chap was no longer there beside my wife. I behaved as if on duty – I had to hang about somewhere – so I sat down next to her and watched the endless entertainment.

Fortunately Pal'o Bek was there – that joker with six kids, these days he drives a 101 – and he was making snide remarks about the programme, so a little group of us got together. He was there along with his wife, who ignored him totally, except once or twice when she drank from his lemonade. Pal'o said how the programme wasn't up to much and he was amazed people bothered to come at all. At that point my wife suddenly bent over to me and said, 'I couldn't stand living with him.' I felt a bit taken aback, because I get on well with Pal'o, but on the other hand I felt it was a good start. I said I was sure she must have quite different views on men from other women. She didn't know how to reply to that. Then I went straight on to say I was more the silent type. She said she didn't know about me, but she knew about drivers, they were very wild to women, especially strangers, and she wouldn't want to marry one. (She didn't know one day I'd be a supervisor and she'd envy me.) I didn't go on with the conversation, for I began to fear she might be stupid.

But when we set off home from Nitra, I saw her pushing her way forward on to the bus, just so as to be able to sit behind me like before. I didn't say anything.

About a month later I went round to their place to see if she was at home. She wasn't, I was glad, and they told her I'd come. She asked me, when we bumped into each other again, what I'd come for. I said I was still a bachelor and I might want to get married. To her, what's more, if she wanted. She said it wasn't so easy and why did I want to get married to her anyway. I said because she was pretty, that is to say, I liked her, and would she think it over.

But instead of agreeing to meet, I waited again for a number of weeks, until we bumped into each other again, and I told her that maybe now she'd had time to think. Few will believe it but she went on another two years still thinking about it; in fact I'd forgotten her, because while I was away on manoeuvres a certain widow came into my life. But she didn't want to get married, because she'd have lost her widow's pension. As soon as the manoeuvres were ended and I was on the train back, I cast her out of my mind.

I bought myself a dictionary of foreign terms. It contains a huge number of these fancy words. I know some of them, I've heard them on the radio or on television, but there are lots of others I don't see the reason for.

Of course I know words like tragical, apologetic, conceivably, and so on, which people use all the time on the buses. Especially when some educated lot on their way back from a night out or a get-together finish off the discussion they were having on the street, which probably started in a wine bar or café. They shout at one another noisily; the rest of the sober passengers all frown; the driver keeps silent, but when they get off, he starts cursing them. If anyone disagrees over something, he gets what's coming to him. I don't study these foreign words just in order to be able to record in my memoirs all the conversations I've heard in the bus. Every word a person learns, or even just finds out about, awakens in him a whole series of thoughts. This is because every word is a sort of an idea, a sort of fact. And though it seems as if words lie next to each other in the head, like stones on the beach for example – when we start dealing with words more closely, we find they are like a bird's plumage. To stop the water running off the wrong way the plumage has a particular slant to it, and each feather helps to remove a drop. That was just for example. Words are also arranged in other ways, however. They are like stitches on a jumper. That means, the more words we learn, the stronger the jumper is. Every foreign word is like a double thread, so the stitch is harder to unravel. You can't write your autobiography without words. Nowadays I know, for example, that my aunt was bigoted. But if I didn't know this word, I wouldn't know what was so odd about that aunt of mine. Because I didn't find the other women who went to church so unpleasant. But she was bigoted – and everybody who knows that word, knows right away what kind of person she was.

Nobody knows I'm writing my autobiography. My wife thinks I'm doing some sort of accounts, something supervisors have to do after their shift.

If anyone happened to ask me why I'm writing my own autobiography, I'd tell him I do it for fun. But there is a deeper reason. For example, this week I washed the dishes twice, and my wife only once. Who is going to remember this, if it's not written down? Years later people will be able to find out what I was like, and if I become a criminal it could serve the lawyer as evidence of my path to crime. On the other hand, if, for example, I am wrongly accused, the court could find out by comparison with my autobiography that I am innocent. It's terrible how people just don't realize the value of having their own autobiography. You don't have to quarrel with anyone, the truth is there, everything is noted down, recorded, and this is the only way the truth can emerge, like oil to the surface of water. How else can we take the saying 'Truth will out', if not as meaning how one day all the documents will be compared and lots of people will grasp where the truth lies? For absolute truth cannot be in the present. Every fact may look like a lie, but years later it becomes a truth. That's why it's necessary to write a lot and unceasingly.

It's quite possible, of course, that everyone who isn't illiterate, and has a bit of time to spare each day, is writing his own autobiography. They don't talk about it to other people, though, and gradually, as they don't have anywhere to store the paper, they burn their own writings. But a month or so later, when they are convinced this was a mistake, they start writing again. Meanwhile they get hold of some hiding place to put their writings, and when they see that nobody is interfering with the stuff they go on with it till the day they die.

You need to know, however, that some people who find this stuff after the writer is dead destroy it, for they find things against them in it. Or they chuck it out with the rubbish and keep only that part of it which seems harmless. It's logical to suppose that when some inheritor like that has been writing his own memoirs, he attaches the stolen part, from the dead person, to his own writings, later copies it out in his own handwriting, and gets the feeling of having gained someone else's life. Unfortunately, human memory is weak, and conscience bad. Soon this person starts believing that it all happened to him.

True, it's not clear how many people write their own autobiographies. When you go to visit someone, you mustn't conclude from the fact that the person has a pen in his hand, and paper on the table, that he is writing his memoirs. He may be writing an application. After all, you can't go round every day checking up to find out he's been writing this 'application' all year long. People can't discuss the subject of their memoirs in the pub. That way memoirs would get stolen, and someone could get his hands on a grand set of memoirs without doing any work, without writing a thing, just sticking his name on somebody else's stuff. Of course someone like that works on his own autobiography for one reason only, which I've started to look at – but it's not fundamental! – that is to say, in order to show himself in a good light for the future. Everyone does all his deeds for the future. I mean, nobody's going to bother his head for the past. Nor for the present either, I mean, the present doesn't even exist, it's only a second out of our lives. For the next second, however, in other words for the future, we are willing to do more. Even when we're cooking the dinner, we do it for eating in the future. Not to mention keeping supplies. But we make supplies for the future, so as to live longer, and we want to live longer, so as to be able to correct or improve more and more of our actions. For if we were perfect, we wouldn't think about the future. I repeat, however, if someone is capable of falsifying his own autobiography, that's not a happy person. Deceit is another matter. We deceive in a given situation. Not realizing that we could tell the truth. Or we deceive for a joke. But why should we deceive for the future? Who are we trying to deceive? By doing this we are deceiving ourselves.

A person like that, who falsifies his own autobiography, is a criminal. Nobody can convict him, for he hides his writings, but he's a criminal all the same, and it's clear, even if he gets off scot-free for the rest of his life, his falsified autobiography is a crime, one way or another.

Obviously there are going to be lots of people who copy their autobiography from the writings of others. Not that they praise them. Their manuscripts are full of anger and abuse, every day they note down all the bad things they saw, how other people insulted them, and they plot how to insult others, and kill them.

In all this, it is true, there is one thing constant. A person's own autobiography is a matter of enormous importance for him.

If my wife happens to find out I'm writing about myself, I've thought up a very neat little trick. I'm writing this autobiography of mine as if I were describing the life of the white dog. The pages where I wasn't yet writing like that, I've cut out. My own autobiography is thus formally speaking the life of a dog. It won't even occur to my wife, when she finds a mention of our white dog, our (second) Uro, being in the pub and listening to the bells striking midday, that it was actually me. True, I mustn't ever write that the white dog spoke to anyone. Or that he laughed. I did read one story in the newspaper where some author wrote about dogs talking, but my wife hasn't read this story, and she'd find it suspicious right away that the dog was talking. She'd start digging further and discover I was writing about myself.

How simple it is to describe what I am doing. After all, the white dog sees me when I wash the dishes. Nobody can prove the dog doesn't see it. And he also sees when my wife washes him. And when he starts thinking, that's just the white dog again, and my wife won't guess these are really my own opinions. Similarly, I don't write what I saw from the kiosk at the crossroads. I write that I was sitting in the kennel ('The white dog watched intently from the kennel') and everything I see in the yard, that's really the crossroads. People are sparrows. Each resembles some animal. In this way my wife won't realize, if she happens to read my memoirs, I'm writing them about myself and about her. But the proper reader in the future will find the key to my own autobiography. He'll find everything there.

Then I have another trick. If I want it to be convincing that the white dog heard us quarrel – I always call him in and make him listen to us. Sometimes I also tell him, 'Uro, did you hear? Did you hear what she was saying?' That's when we quarrel, but that's only seldom.

That's why I often tell him whole sections from my childhood, so that my wife, if she found my papers after my death, would know where the dog got it from. He, of course, knows nothing, but my wife will tell herself, 'That husband of mine was crazy. First he tells it to the dog, then he writes about it as if the dog had understood him.' In this way the whole of the memoirs hang together, it has its own logic, and no one can blame me for making a dog think. After all, for the future reader it's not important whether I thought this, or the dog. It's important for the future reader to know how this could have been seen in our own time. And this way I don't even have to worry about someone who can't understand any of my memoirs calling me an idiot; he'll simply blame it all on the white dog.

Translated from the Slovak by James Naughton

Bulgaria

Ivailo Dichev

Desires: The Erotica of Communism

And that which we can today predict as the forms of sexual relations after the forthcoming removal of capitalistic production is primarily of negative character and is mainly defined by that which will fall away.

FRIEDRICH ENGELS

What Zheni experienced when she caught him for the first time with the maid in the closet had nothing in common with bourgeois possessive feelings. No, her astonishment had more of a theoretical nature. Of course, the philosopher is, as Fonerberg said, only a man among men, and yet . . . That passion, that distorted, blazing, terrible face. Why had he never experienced with her, his comrade, this state in which she saw him now with a simple servant who spends her days on all fours washing tiles? There was something there she did not understand.

'Tell me, Fred.' She ran that very day to his best friend for advice. 'When there's no more exploitation and women are completely equal to men, won't sexual attraction die off like the State and everything else?' 'No, my dear, it's primal,' said Fred, looking at her suddenly, with an odd expression on his face. He kissed the tops of her fingers, then her wrist, then his lips climbed up to her marmoreal shoulder. 'How could you?' she whispered, overwhelmed. 'That's base . . . If Karl finds out . . . So this is how it is.' That was her last thought before her consciousness was overcome by the hot, pulsating lie of existence.

*

189

It was not just a few delegates but the common people themselves who passed through the doors of the Winter Palace in order to decide its future. Common in the most literal sense of the word (and precisely in this lay Ilich's genial contribution: in that unprecedented qualitative leap through the abyss between signifier and signified, and in the leading out on to the historical stage of the thing itself instead of its forms, representations, signs, symbols, etc.).

'Just look at this riff-raff,' exclaimed the cook who first ventured to turn away from the procession of framed portraits along crystal corridors and crack open a door at random. At first all the gleaming faïence and the mystical echo made her think that she had come upon a church. Then something, perhaps the drip percolating from the gold pipe before her, led her to think that it was a royal bathroom. But why did they have a vase in the bathroom, she murmured, running her fingers over the pale emerald-encrusted alabaster. 'We'll fix this,' said a smiling peasant from the guard, waving his rifle.

'Wait, comrade,' the cook stopped him, 'this is a work of art.' Then, as she winked at him devilishly, she threw her skirt over the alabaster vase and sat on top of it. Several seconds passed before the peasant's red face broke out in comprehension. Then he winked at her too, undid the belt of his coarse trousers, stuck his lips forward as if to whistle and let out a powerful stream, forward and up – on to the golden faucets, the balms, the gargling glasses, the perfume atomizers, the steps of the bathtub which were decorated with Byzantine mosaics, on his own face and on the crystal mirror.

Years later, the historians would reconstruct those revolutionary times. In the Winter Palace there remained no empty fruit platter, drawer, soup tureen or powder case. The needs of the people, both small and large, were not spared: grand pianos and cellos, royal teapots, potted palms and cacti, baldachins covered with bearskins, the niches for statues and fountains, latches, chandeliers, livery aprons. Royalty had been defeated decades in advance.

The illegal love of the illegals. They are proud, handsome, and clean. Sometimes during the act, a lock of her hair touches a lock of his and she blushes, he blushes, and the two of them squeeze their thighs together even tighter beneath their student tunics. But for the real poet, their love does not remain hidden. This impatience in the accomplishment of errands, this effort to scratch, hurt, wound and cause pain with a heated face. This need to display one's body to hostile bullets, yes, comrades, to hold their breath. That reckless breaking of hoops, concealing of deviation. The eating of sheets of paper marked with passwords. While the line of policemen rapes her in the basement of the station, and while in another basement they pull out his fingernails and send electrical shocks through his sexual organs, the two think of each other.

Who knows better than Comrade Lenin that love always involves three!

At night, when a male comrade and female comrade are lying somewhere in the boundless Soviet land in order to fulfil their responsibility to Biological Materialism, he is with them. Because at every moment, at every caress, asleep or awake, they are waiting. Things must be left to chance: in a threesome there is no more erotic third party than fate. Suddenly, out of nowhere, the patrols pull up in their vehicle and the male comrade is dragged out in his underwear and carried off to some unknown place. And the female comrade begins to write letters to Comrade Stalin to explain how much she loves him. The Party and life, or vice versa, win over the female comrade and the next day the male comrade, the old Bolshevik, goes to work pale, trembling and castrated. Stalin sucks in his gut and waits: Will he ask? Will he dare to ask? Will the traitorous feeling pulsate on his face? Will love and hate mix in a self-destructive explosion? And so days, months, years fly towards the future and the Bolsheviks, carried away in their thoroughly erotic game, remain eternally young. (If one day God is filled with lust for the world, communism will win in an instant.)

In 1968 we hid our long hair behind our ears and seduced girls with blues from the *White Album*. In August, our plane landed at Prague airport and from inside, instead of electric carts, came soldiers who occupied the area in order to prepare for the landing of the Warsaw Pact operation code-named 'Zhivkov'. As a sign of protest, we organized mass gatherings all over the country where we participated in promiscuous sexual acts. The Czech men and women stood together in chains against the lines of approaching, brotherly tanks. We moved on to intercourse in the open – in parks, entryways and public toilets. Among the forms of our taking the law into our own hands were the most amazing objects: belts, whips, desecration of holy sites, and, of course, orgasms. Orgasms everywhere.

And in spite of everything, one fine day they broadcast the news that the Czech student Jan Palah had doused himself with petrol and burned like a torch in the centre of the city. Then, filled with furious powerlessness, I set off towards Party Headquarters in order to masturbate so that the splashes would reach the star on top and everything would collapse and end. Today I still wander around the centre of town with my hand busy deep in my pocket, caught in a mismatched battle with weakening resolve.

Secret thoughts of a secret agent: the task is to sleep with her in the light, because the film is *Orwo**, which is to say, garbage. The camera is mounted on the lampshade to catch her in a classic pose with her face clearly visible. But there has to be some dirt, because the classics don't impress anyone any more. Yet I must not forget that Comrade will also look at the film and he gets angry at perversions; after all, he is a man of the people. If I give the impression that I'm enjoying it, he might begin to suspect me of some more peculiar relations with the embassy. And, besides, Elena will see the film and if my performance really pleases her that will be the end of me (how many boys from counter-intelligence have suffered!). So, that means that I must at the same time both please the ambassador's wife and not please Elena. On the other hand, maybe the ambassador is playing both sides, just waiting for an excuse to divorce her, which I will give him. Or perhaps he knows about the camera and is waiting

---

* A film manufactured in East Germany during the communist era. This was the most commonly available film in all of Eastern Europe at the time, and was of generally poor quality.

to use it as a pretext for a big diplomatic scandal. And it's possible that the Russians are involved: the ambassador's wife isn't just a wife, but their secret agent whose mission is to give herself to the first courter-provocateur (that is, me), in order to cause a crisis in American–Romanian relations. Yes, but maybe the ambassador has understood their game and has recruited his wife, charging her none the less to allow herself to be seduced so that Comrade and Elena will think they've got him in their hands and will show their cards. By the way, why does it seem to me that something about this woman's face is reminiscent of Yasser Arafat?

The Semiotics of Jealousy

Here is the edifying story of our friend Mechev. Mechev had impetuous desires, but unfortunately – no intuition. Some women would incessantly greet him with indignant slaps in the face, while others blushed every time they saw him coming near. Mechev lay panting and sweating beneath the summer sheets, touching his enormous body unhappily.

Only a single advantage had been awarded Mechev by fate, and that was the incredible jealousy of his wife. What kind of advantage is that, you'll ask? An enormous one. Just remember that even the sun is defined by the shade.

The woman had an impassable black forelock beneath which her angry eyes blazed when she got excited. In rare moments of benevolence she would let out a stream of air up past her nose and the forelock would wiggle almost playfully while she closed her eyes against the light. This is what Mechev discovered: in her jealousy, his wife could faultlessly sniff out those young women who showed a tendency to like him. In practice, that meant the end of the systematic approach: sweating in dancehalls and planned drunkenness. It was enough for him to watch his wife. When she began to notice runs in a woman's hose, sweat spots under her arms or pores on her nose. If she began to make malicious remarks about saggy breasts, jiggling flesh, protruding ribs or uncombed hair, Mechev knew that the woman liked him in some way. How stupid on his part to argue in those cases, to assure her that she wasn't being objective! That just increased her suspicions. He had only to agree and follow her emotional involvement to plan his own strategy. When his wife reached the level of metaphors ('As if they were keeping her in a box!'), his chances were nearing 100 per cent but he still had to start with an invitation to a restaurant or something similar.

When she began to make diagnoses ('Mechik, she's suffering from seborrhoea. She scratched herself three times while we were talking'), he knew that without any preparation he could lead the common acquaintance to their first secret sofa and squeak the springs of desire. Her selection was perfect, if we exclude a case of identical names. Mechev was absolutely irresistible.

After a while his wife began to beat a retreat. The tones grew softer, the common acquaintance was shown understanding. Most unexpectedly she did a small service, showed up with a really nice piece of clothing, or was just caught in the moment, standing and staring sadly through the rainy window. Such occurrences were a sign to Mechev that he should begin preparing manfully for the separation. Then one day, while bringing in the potatoes, his wife blew on her forelock and said: 'Oh, what fine skin she has!' and Mechev knew that the affair was over. He filled their wine glasses and clinked the crystal rims together in a secret farewell ceremony. Then he asked, 'Don't you think that Z. is plain?' 'You're being unfair,' his wife said, surprised. 'The girl has a lot of problems with her mother.' And she entered into the difficult situation of the acquaintance. That's clear enough, thought Mechev. It would be like hammering on stone. He waited a few tactical minutes and tried again: 'And that F., isn't she ashamed to go bra-less? She's no spring chicken.' 'That slut,' jumped his wife with her eyes glowing behind the agitated forelock. 'She's ready to jump on the first gypsy that asks her. You know, she's been treated for gonorrhea three times.' A diagnosis! Mechev thought to himself happily as out loud he said, 'What filth!' And again he discreetly clinked two glasses together, in an effort to control his smile.

*

Communism reduced the known dissident Mr N. to a constant state of agitation. You could see him in the coffee-houses, dishevelled and angry, circulating his petitions, which threw the philistines into heavy torment. They fidgeted in their seats and went to the lavatory for no reason. 'Sign that you demand they arrest me,' he fired at a line of acquaintances. 'Let them dare. Let there be a scandal.' Then a satanic grin would appear on his face and he would move the ashtray in order to say to the table (where the supposed microphone would lie): I won't leave you without work, you bastards. Then he'd rush off to other cafés, in order to confuse those following him.

And it was the same at home. When he passed the telephone in a good mood, he never failed to lift the receiver and whisper: 'Comrade mayor, shall I whisper in your ear?' or he would take off his trousers in order to display his hairy arse to the plaster ceiling. And if he brought a woman home, he would perform such acrobatics that even the Kamasutra would be jealous ('Let them go crazy, let them come in their green drawers!' he'd whisper, panting, into the ear of his astounded partner). He was happy, and his happiness was his battle. How grey his life is now that communism is gone. He paces alone through his haggard home, passing the dead telephone, uninterested in the objects which are now just plain objects: he has no desire for anything.

A Story of Desire

Everything has the right to occur at least once, without destroying natural law. That's why, when at the moment of our first meeting I was seized by the uncontrollable desire to show her my penis, I said to myself OK, maybe those are the real relations between people.

You know well what madness love is: but imagine the double madness of lust, about which no poetry, operas or tracts are written and about which it is practically forbidden to speak – lust in which I was completely alone. I functioned like an automaton. I kissed hands, ordered Campari, expressed a neoconservative position, but my thoughts feverishly sought a way out. To remove my trousers in a public place would mean getting arrested ... If I lured her somewhere alone, I would risk getting a vase broken over my head ... Perhaps I should turn the conversation somehow to a theoretical plane so that showing it would just be a demonstration? My God, I had no ulterior motives and I didn't want to seduce my new acquaintance who was, by the way, slightly cross-eyed. My desire was completely platonic. That is to say, afterwards we would continue to use formal language with one another.

And so day after day was filled with calculations, torments and hopes, until the most unexpected event took me to an international semiotics conference on the sea coast and I used all my talent to arrange paid trips for us both. I went straight from the plane to the beach saying, 'No semiotics until I see the sea!' The beating of my heart resonated through my entire body.

Of course you can already guess that everything was pre-planned and sketched out. No matter how many times the taxi stopped so that we could choose the best spot, we didn't get out until we were at the nudist beach, and by the time we realized where we were, we had already let the taxi go and had to act like modern people. Thus, while I was still expounding my thesis on the utopian character of pure denotation, my fingers shaking from the excitement, I took off my tie and jacket, and hung my trousers on the bushes ... and finally the damned organ jerked towards her in its natural state, filling me simultaneously with shame and pride. (I couldn't tell whether she was staring at what I had in mind the whole time, or whether she never even glanced at it, focused on her thesis about the psychological character of pure connotation. The ambiguity of her differently aimed eyes exasperated me, disheartened me, titillated me, and depressed me.)

Whether it was because of the intense pressure or because of the sun's rays and the sea breeze, all of a sudden I felt that my penis was beginning to grow, and no conscious effort would stop it. The only option left which could save my dignity in that absurd situation was to fall at the last moment and glue my belly to the hot sand. 'Wouldn't you prefer to lie on my sheet?' she asked. I mumbled something about being thirsty for real things and waited for my organ, buried in the hot sand, to fall voluntarily and the scandal to pass.

But there was no sign of that happening. Had she suspected something? In her decision to undress in turn was there not a hint of preparation? Her breasts were as uneven as her eyes. One was soft, spread out and shapely, the other sharp and purposeful. (Picasso, I thought, in my efforts to distract myself.) Her undressing had a strange effect: it increased my secret, underground erection due not to any attraction to the sight of her naked body, towards which I felt nothing more than curiosity, but the discomfort which arose from the growing ambiguity of the situation. Who would believe now that my erection was not due to her disrobing, to her asymmetrical breasts and all the rest? (How uncivilized, an erection on the nudist beach!)

And I still didn't know if she didn't know, if she was pretending not to know (or was pretending not to know that I knew she knew). I just could not judge the strategic reason for her decision to enter the water. In any case, lit up with deep-felt hope, I began to drag myself imperceptibly towards my clothes, ploughing through the sand and carefully following the reactions of the other naked people.

Disastrously, just at that moment a swarthy compatriot dressed in drill work clothes set off towards the beach on the scree which passed directly between me and the bushes where my suit was hanging. When he saw the smiling flesh rising up from the sands, he took off his clothes, winked at me for who knows what reason and, to my great disgust, lay down next to me on his belly, matching my position.

This development put me in an even more difficult position, in which my erection was a painful element. 'This is absurd,' I repeated to myself. 'Let's be sensible. My condition has no reason, no referent. The referent is at least a hundred yards away in the water. She may have already drowned. Yes, she's drowned and the awful, unmotivated, painful hardness continues! There is nothing more dangerous than unmotivated things: they can attach themselves to any motive. What will this grinning cretin think if I am uncovered? What will the people around us think he thought? How will I convince them that there was a woman here, but actually she is not the reason, just a desire to be seen with her help.'

Then the worst occurred. Two militiamen appeared on the strip of beach in full combat uniform. The naked people pulled on bras and underpants, fled, or sank down to their necks in the water. And as the two continued steadfastly forward, I lay pinned down with my organ in the sand. They were going to tear me out and force me up, and everything was going to be exposed. They were going to demand that I cease the outrage but, of course, I would be unable and they would lead me forward across the beach and through the town with the painfully throbbing evidence, to display me in some cage, and only God knows what else.

The area around me had cleared. Only the militiamen remained, approaching silently. They stepped on unfinished games of solitaire, sandcastles and half-eaten salads, because they had already fixed their eyes on me. I pressed with ever-more energy into the ground, praying that somehow the problem would pass. I pressed, their figures grew larger and I grew smaller until – what a miracle – 'Give me your passport!' they commanded, and just at that instant, by some absurd joke of physiology, a delightful shiver ran through me and everything ended. I sighed, relieved, and to the surprise of the authorities, I was almost grateful as I rose to pay my 20 leva fine.

When my new acquaintance left the sea, she found me happy and alone, lying on my back with my hands and feet pointing in the four cardinal directions, having forgotten completely about my penis in its sandy shell. Her wet, uneven breasts were at a loss.

Afterwards

The guillotine: the machine which makes people equal. The mythical brigand Prokrust, who put people on his couch, cut off the legs of the tallest and stretched the shortest, is an allegory, created by the imagination to scare and educate. The machine of equality created by the genius of Dr Guillotine is completely passionless. It does not express anything. It does not symbolize anything. It simply reduces equality to an action, removing those heads that tower above others in a maximally human fashion. Literally.

N. Fyodorov, a Russian dreamer at the end of the last century, taught his concept of the universal resurrection of the dead. In fact, resurrection is promised by the holy scriptures, but the modernizing Russian soul could not stand with crossed arms waiting for the Day of Judgement: it thought up an integral system for the regulation of nature. With the cosmologizing of the sciences, which is to say their unification under astronomy, every molecule of nature had to become the object of conscious management and thus, in final account, to fulfil the supreme duty of the sons: resurrection of the fathers, the guilt for whose deaths weighs on their shoulders. Whole generations will carry out these daring dreams.

But before all the molecules were regulated, the father of the Soviet state died. From all over the country, letters flooded in from the afflicted workers: Don't give the body of our beloved Ilich to the ground. Leave it in the central museum for the next generation. Science was mobilized: biochemistry, restoration, parasitology, refrigeration, upholstery, etc. (for the grandiose achievement, Lenin's chief embalmer was given the Order of Lenin). Ilich's brain was preserved separately in alcohol in a glass container which they placed in the newly created Lenin Museum. Now, the workers reasoned science was still powerless to resolve the secrets of such a brain, so it had to be well preserved so that future generations could study it and return Ilich to flesh and blood. That possibility weighs on the world up to our day. (By the way, years later, many American millionaires, including Walt Disney, pay dearly to have themselves frozen with liquid nitrogen in the hope that in time science will make their resurrection possible. In the refrigerated cases, they are also awaiting the Last Judgement of the universal regulation of all molecules of which Fyodorov dreamed.)

Literalisms

Asian literalism: blast furnaces in all educational institutions. Every citizen kills one sparrow, one fly, one earthworm. The Party employees measure the economic effect. The throwing of parties in the streets, the killing of everyone who wears glasses, the return of all people to agricultural work (because labour is an action done with the hands, and necessarily connected to sweat, corns and other appearances). The leader is the author of all the films in the country. The bench where he sat to rest is preserved under a glass cover.

The literalism of the sixties: the cosmonauts realized the cherished metaphors of humanity. Flight, conquering new worlds, looking for brothers in reason, the contemplation of the Earth from above. And together with that came competition in metaphor: who first, who most, who the longest. In a variant which is less expensive for the taxpayers, the same emotion was caused by Guinness's book (that bible of literalism). Victory, the interesting, the important, the exciting is carefully measured and recorded. The best is faultlessly defined. The rest can only make themselves more.

On the other hand, there is the sexual revolution which literally realized the Christian call to love one's neighbour: in practice they just decided to fuck and leave it at that. Similarly, the narcotics boom: how can we explain it except as a direct, literal realization of the basic principal of European civilization, the right to happiness? Better, stronger, less toxic chemicals equals more happiness for the individual. The breaking of guitars on stage is the literalization of ecstasy. Torn jeans is the opposition to culture. Remember Khrushchev's corn, a literalizing resolution of agrarian problems. The freeing of the insane by the Kennedy administration under the influence of a sort of anti-psychiatry in support of the freedom of the individual. The students in West Berlin who surrounded the radio tower because they wanted time on the air to tell the whole truth. (They were given time, but I don't remember exactly what they said.)

If communism was a literalization of metaphors (that the cook must lead the country, that the people will be brothers when everything is taken from them . . .), its fall was naturally no less literal. The Berlin Wall fell. Anyone can buy a piece as a souvenir. The masses invaded Romanian television. We saw them cluster there needlessly before the screen, as if they wanted to participate directly, physically in history. Words were assaulted, articles of the constitution were besieged. The five-pointed star, mummies and statues were attacked. Literalism has been defeated. Literally.

Translated from the Bulgarian by Robert Sturm

Victor Paskov

Big Business

... When the millionaire Koleff called, I was in a depression. My novel about Germany was dragging along like a worm. It was not going well – that's for sure. Not that this came as a surprise to me; questions of its immortality were not torturing me, but still . . .

Marie, pregnant to her ears, looked at me with understanding eyes and every morning put a bottle of beer on my desk. It didn't help. I was pulling out my hair, crumpling up sheets of paper, showering an atmosphere of genius – but nothing could fool Marie. She is well aware of the mystical Slavic soul. She is a doctor of all things Slavic. She has read Dostoevsky, goddamn it.

In response to my depression, Marie sat down at her computer and, after a bit, from her corner, came tsk-tsk-tsk-tsk . . . tsk-tsk-tsk-tsk . . . six hours, seven hours! It was maddening! – and then suddenly the millionaire Koleff calls.

When at one end of the line sits one for whom things are not going well and at the other the type who's worth a hundred million – who knows how much a millionaire can put away? – the conversation is not equal. 'Of course,' I said. 'Yes, yes!' and, 'I am flattered, sir!' and thus I take the Métro from Boissy to Les Invalides, shaking with claustrophobia. What the hell does Koleff need with me?

Marie wrote the station stops down on a scrap of paper, how to get off the damned Métro, how to take the stairs to the right, heading for a street I don't know, how, afterwards, to cross Alexander Bridge, and when I see the golden cupola of Les Invalides, to think of Napoleon; again to the right, and there is the street where Koleff maintains his establishment.

In the moment when I stopped before the pink building, a sunbeam pierced a bit of cloud, spread over Les Invalides and lightly

202

fell upon the complicated system of bells, another kind of computer; I stood there, staring foolishly, I, who cannot even change a fuse.

I threw away Marie's directions and took out Koleff's. 'Push number three, then X,' I had written. 'After that, enter code 249. Wait for a while, and say your name to the apparatus. Articulate clearly. The door will open. The porter is Spanish. Give your documents to her. She dials the code and opens the inner door. Enter to the left, and there is my elevator. You dial code so-and-so. You enter the elevator and lightly touch the button. Don't push hard: it's photo-activated. The fifth floor. It's as simple as that.'

In a glass booth, with a glass face, the pathetic Spanish attendant was sitting. *Buenas dias, señora*, I said. She looked at me crookedly. She pushed something. A small metal plate was thrust towards me. On to this I dropped my card from the Writer's Union. There, inscribed in English, it says that I am a member. She was turning over my card, looking at the photograph, her look sliding over my jeans and jacket, as she lifted her moustached upper lip.

After performing all these Spanish manoeuvres she dialled the code. I went in. I swung to the left. I saw his elevator and dialled the code. So far so good.

Here I am in front of Koleff's apartment.

I pushed a button. An explosion of music. Someone had programmed the bell to play the Fifth. After fate had pounded a full five minutes on Koleff's door, it opened.

Koleff was about seventy years old. One of those vital seventy-year-olds, who, as if born seventy years old, travel all their lives back to their forties. On his nose were balanced blue eye-glasses of the latest half-lens style. Without adjustment. His wide, flowing shirt fell in elegant folds upon his beige trousers. *'Appelle-moi!'* was written on the shirt pocket. Hand-embroidered. On his feet were sneakers worth about five hundred francs. A thin moustache was twirled upon his bluish upper lip. A wrinkled, powerful neck, the colour of roof tiles. He was short, but gave the impression that he was tall. I don't know how.

'Hi, Mr Paskov!' he said. His voice – hoarse yet glottal, as if he were gargling with thumbtacks. 'Happy to see you. Do you speak English?'

I mumbled that I too was happy, but that I speak German better and, of course, Bulgarian as well.

'Good,' he said. 'Fine. *Ich habe in Deutschland studiert.*'

The intercom buzzed. He picked up the receiver. The porter, with her Spanish obsessions.

Koleff gave me a sign to follow him. We started down a wide corridor. I gazed at the marble statues and also at the tapestries on the walls. Motifs from ancient Greek mythology.

'My den is a little messy, Mr Paskov,' he whispered. 'In Paris I am a bachelor. In Paris every man must be a bachelor. In Madrid, of course, no. Because of the religion. Are you religious? I have an apartment in Madrid, in which . . . however, in Hawaii, my little girlfriend sits in my hacienda there and keeps it cosy. In New York my home is a haunt of hooligans. I left my son there last year, who – you know – hashish, women, scandal . . . youth!'

After some wandering we reached the living room. The Boston Philharmonic could give a concert in it. Magnificent acoustics. Slowly we crossed it. Our feet sank into the carpet, thick enough to slow our movement. We went out on to the balcony.

'Look, Paskov . . . is this not an obscenely beautiful view?'

Obscenely beautiful it was.

From the spacious balcony a manicured park could be seen below. Across from us – the golden cupola of Les Invalides, behind – Le Grand Palais, Petit Palais, the bridge, the Seine, cars and people scurrying along the wide boulevard, and above us the blue sky. A view worth millions.

We sighed. We went back into the living room. And we looked into each other's eyes. I lowered my sight. He went to the bookshelves, took down a thick volume and gave it to me. Rabelais. Leather and gold. A rare antique. Koleff took out book after book, rubbed the covers, held them to his cheek and quietly growled. Ronsard, Corneille, Voltaire . . . all first editions.

'Let us sit, Paskov!'

I sat down on something soft. My legs flew up. An obscene sprawl. I apologized. On the walls paintings. Painting after painting. I recognized Vasarelli, Picasso, a small Paschen, not that I under-stand so much, but I recognized a large Gross! – by its collage and academic style and, most of all, because with this same Reiner Gross I got drunk in Berlin, in Kreuzberg, and his wife was going to publish my book in New York, she was going to publish everything I had written. But she did not. Be that as it may, I was very pleased with Gross.

Upon the elegant coffee table, with baroque legs, was a row of bottles. Whisky, vermouth, gin, pastis, grappa, Pernod, vodka, tequila, white rum, red rum, Armagnac, even Bulgarian grape brandy. They were shining softly. A sorrowful constellation.

'Do you drink tea, sir?' he asked. 'I can offer you Spanish tea, from strawberry leaves.'

I wouldn't have minded a whisky, after all the stress, but I said, 'Yes, I love tea. And most of all – herbal tea.'

We went into the kitchen. A space station. We sat down on tall stools. Some computer made us tea.

'I could offer you some sugar, Mr Paskov, but it is bad for you. Salt as well. Do you read the natural science magazines? No? It's a pity. Take this . . .' He dropped a miniature sweetener into my cup. Ssssssst . . . it hissed and dissolved in the tea.

'Sir!' he said briskly, as we went back into the living room. 'You are a talented young man. I have some information. I was told about your book. Congratulations.'

Quickly I pulled out the book – in Bulgarian and French, with an inscription in both languages, respectively, and handed it to him. He took it and placed it on the coffee table with the liquor. Not that I expected him to put it next to Rabelais, but all the same . . .

'Not long ago, I financed a book, Paskov. *Moments from Bulgarian History*. You have heard of this? Fine. It was written by an acquaintance of mine, a journalist, also a Bulgarian, hmmm, now a Frenchman. Have you also become French? Not yet? Become one, Paskov, become one. I am an American but I feel that I am a Spaniard . . . yes. All those travels, Berlin, Rio, hotels and nego-tiations, not to mention the profits – do you understand? – big business, Paskov. For it, not for me. A man must not forget that he is Bulgarian – unless he is Chinese, ha ha.'

'Ha ha . . .'

'The time has come for this book to belong to the Bulgarian

people. They don't know history, Paskov. The communists falsified it and the people grew dumb as donkeys. You are *not* a communist?'

'A monarchist . . .'

'Oh . . . how does your Frenchwoman see this? As a matter of fact I don't care about that. And neither should you. Communists, royalists, leftists and rightists, high and low – all are trash.'

'*I* don't care!' I lied.

'And so: a publishing house . . .' – he mentioned the name of a great Sofia publishing house – 'made contact with me. They want to publish my book. I am to retain all the rights. How much do you think they could pay? Tell me the truth, sir.'

This same publisher had paid me three thousand leva for my book. One year ago. On this money I lived for a month or two. And damned well. But I am I and this, here, is Koleff.

'How many copies?'

'Two hundred thousand.'

'Mine was twenty thousand. That means a bestseller.'

I had heard that during the sweet years of totalitarianism some writers had received a hundred thousand each, a huge amount of money for our trade.

'Look . . .' I said. 'Maybe two to three hundred thousand?'

Koleff leaned back and laughed quietly.

'Paskov, what are you saying? Two hundred thousand? Three hundred thousand? One million, Paskov! A million!'

The hell with him. The year was 1990. The country was writhing in an economic crisis, like an epileptic. Various world organizations were promoting humanitarian aid and this guy wants a million.

'It seems to me,' I replied, very carefully, 'that this is beyond the resources of Bulgarian publishers.'

'They will find the means, Paskov, they will find it. Let them borrow the money from their grandmothers.'

'But what will you do with this million?' I burst out. 'These are leva – not francs!'

He removed his blue glasses. He scratched his cheek with them.

'I'll tell you, Paskov. Even though it is not your business. I will buy an apartment on a street in central Sofia. I will furnish it.

Appliances, computers. I will establish a firm. Business will flow. Big business! I will establish a foundation as well. Named for me. Capable young Bulgarians will study agronomy at my foundation. They will cultivate our abused Bulgarian soil, which the communists have ruined. I am a patriot, Paskov! I will tear this million out of the paws of the communists!'

I wouldn't mind if Koleff tore a million out of the paws of the communists, except that the communists had previously stolen the million from a torn packet of that donkey, the people. And already deposited it in a Swiss bank. Communists are also in big business! It's a vicious circle.

'What, do you think, the people have need of now?'

'Of cash,' I answered without thinking.

'Cash, cash!' He was angry. 'So you're like all the rest! You're all dreaming of cash! And do you ask yourself how it's made, this cash? You don't! The people, Paskov, have the greatest need for a moral example. These people are desperate. They need models.'

Les Invalides was bathed in blue. Upon the walls played mysterious shadows. The hues of the paintings were everywhere, refracting, as in a fish-bowl. His voice was gurgling.

'At one time, sir, forty-five years ago, before you were born, I began from nothing . . .' this model whispered in the half-light. 'I wandered from country to country – what do you think, Paskov? At last, I fell upon America. Have you been to America?'

No, I haven't been to America! I have lived twelve years in the German Democratic Republic – what do *you* know, Koleff? – as far from America as cow's teats from the milky way. I knew what was coming next. I was prepared to listen to this enterprising young Bulgarian being praised, who had overcome everything to grow taller than the Empire State Building. I know how the millionaire is made, Koleff! Give me the shorter version!

He couldn't give the shorter version. *He* didn't want the shorter version. His thoughts bouncing from politics to construction (Koleff had been a contractor), to the King, from the King to Hamburg and the whores of Hamburg, from the whores of Hamburg to the whores of St Denis, then back to the communists, a short visit to Bulgaria thirty years ago, the memorial service of his father, and then – *boom!* – the Canary Islands! New York! Senators, presidents! A German wife, whom he had made a lady, but this dirty bitch had left him (be careful of women, Paskov!), dark lawsuits against mighty governments for a pile of millions . . . God! – it made me dizzy.

'Mah life, Paskov,' he concluded. 'That is mah life. An edifying example to an aimless people. Tell me, as a literary man, what's selling best now?'

'Crime. Stephen King. Thrillers, the erotic so-so, maybe dissident literature from the East? – but soon there will be inflation.' I was boiling, I swam in my waters. 'Beckett is expensive, but they don't read him, the Americans spew out loads, but they repeat themselves.'

'Wait a minute, wait.' He was getting bored. He was tapping his fingers on the coffee table, yawning. 'Nonsense, nonsense . . . melodrama, dissidents, Stephen King. *Biographies*, Paskov! They read biography. Do you know that?'

I knew that.

'It's interesting to me – what do you remember of all the things I've just told you.'

'The memorial service.'

'The memorial service. OK. Why don't you jot down a few pages. But you haven't taken any notes, Paskov! Don't you know shorthand? What? But you have total recall? We'll see, we'll see. We will talk again. Business, Paskov. *Big business!*'

From the Métro at the Grand Palais I called Marie. In a tone defying objection I told her to go at once to the Arabs and to buy a bottle – she knows what to buy, yes, and peanuts, of course! Who drinks whisky without peanuts? – no, I'm not crazy. They don't let crazy people do business! As I was travelling to Boissy, I finished the memorial service.

'*Big business!*' I told a startled Marie. I took the bottle and the peanuts and locked myself in my room.

By three a.m. I had finished eight pages of breezy dialogue à la Raymond Chandler, a little Proustian sorrow, a little dirt in the style of Bukowski, patriotic outbursts I took from Hugo, and poked into the mouth of Koleff – a pageant. Of my depression – nothing remained. 'Rio!' reverberated in my hollow head. 'Hawaii! A million! Hey, Paskov! Do you know how to write biography or not!'

Koleff called at ten the next morning.

'Do you know, Paskov? – tonight I will have guests. Some Bulgarian MPs from the anti-communist opposition visiting here. Yes, you know them. And they know you. I invited them for dinner. I need some advice. Ask your French wife what's to be done. I'm a bachelor.'

'Why not take them to a restaurant?'

'*Merde!* Do you have any idea what one dinner costs in a Parisian restaurant?'

Merde – I had! From time to time Marie and I had lived the good life; afterwards I had heartburn. Not from the food, but from the prices. Well, damn it! I am better known as a gourmet chef than as a writer, and we agreed that I would go to his place and fix dinner myself. Before that I would go to the supermarket and buy groceries, in order to save time. The millionaire Koleff insisted on beans. After all the steaks, salmon, caviar, baked sausages, between New York and the North Pole, now he's longing for beans, like those his mother had fixed for him.

'And the memorial? Are you thinking about the memorial, Paskov?'

'It's finished,' I came back, in the vigorous tones of a youthful American.

'Wow! You don't fool around! I'm impatient to see it,' said Koleff, 'very impatient.'

I went to the supermarket. I bought beans, onions, carrots, tomatoes and a green pepper. From the Chinese I picked up sage and dill, chilli peppers – everything needed for bean soup, which would be like Mama's.

Koleff hovered in the kitchen quite helplessly. He didn't know anything about it, its how, what or where. A long time passed as he tried to solve the riddle of the kitchen, its machines and technicalities, but no kitchen in the world could give *me* such difficulty.

He was reading the memorial service and sipping strawberry tea, his blue eye-glasses perched on his forehead. I was chopping onions, carrots and a green pepper into tiny pieces. He was excited, as if he really had lived out my brazen fantasies. And I too was excited. Literature is literature, but making bean soup is not easy either. Especially if one wishes to make it like Mama's.

'Good, Paskov! *Sehr gut*,' said the millionaire, raising his eyes. 'I like it, especially at this moment, as the sparrows peck wheat from the grave and carry it in their beaks to the sky. Only – father died in 'sixty-five not in 'fifty-eight, and the German woman was named Klara, not Gretchen.'

I took a pen and made the corrections. When the beans began to boil, I grabbed the pot and poured the water off into the sink.

'What are you doing?' He was agitated.

I explained to him that the first water from the beans is thrown away, because it makes you fart. And therefore they call it the 'farting water'. It causes gas.

'OK, Paskov, OK!' He was looking at me with astonishment. 'How do you know this?' The millionaire was getting in my way in the kitchen, humming, droning, flattering me, whistling through his teeth, and slowing my work. I hate anybody who gets in my way when I'm cooking. So it was good that the phone began to ring. They were calling him from Frisco. Later from New York, from Sofia, and from I don't know where; and, later, he called his little girlfriend at the hacienda in Hawaii, then returned and began again to read the memorial. He kept asking me when the beans would be ready. He was extremely hungry. And I wanted a beer. In his refrigerator I had seen a Tuborg, but how should I say to him that I needed a drink? – since the liver turns beer into sugar and sugar is bad for you. And when I recalled the Spanish tea, I decided to go downstairs to the bistro and have a secret beer. I was getting angry. 'The hell with him!' I will tell him I'm going out to drink a beer.

'Fine, Paskov!' Koleff said agreeably. 'While you're gone, I will slice up the pickles.'

'What pickles?'

'Pickles. For the soup.'

'Koleff!' I was outraged. 'What do you mean – pickles? Downstairs they sell fresh onions, radishes, green lettuce! Wasn't everything to be like Mama's?'

'Paskov, you're like all Bulgarians!' he said sternly. 'Let's say that we go to buy lettuce, radishes and onions. But we will also see oranges, melons, kiwi. Let's take some of them too. And why not sit down, after our great shopping, to have a beer in the bistro as well? All this time the pickles have been rattling around in the refrigerator waiting for someone to eat them. Business doesn't get done this way, Paskov – forget that beer.'

'Is that so?' I asked, needling him. 'But pickles go with apéritifs.'

'What apéritifs?'

'Pastis. Maybe Pernod. You put a Spanish olive into each glass and pour a French apéritif over it. On to the pickles you dice Chinese dill, but before that you pour over it some Greek olive oil.'

'Nonsense! I have Bulgarian grape brandy.'

'Sir – you are giving a reception! The opposition has been chewing on beans and pickles for forty-five years! It needs a moral example – come, sir, let's go and get some lettuce, OK?'

'Apropos of moral examples' – he was slurping beans from the pot, growling approvingly – 'wonderful beans, Paskov, beautiful . . . like your little memorial of me . . . yeah! Leave the moral example to me. I am full of moral examples. Don't think about the opposition. It doesn't even deserve these beans. Think about our book!'

'What book?'

'The book about my life. A bestseller. Look, Paskov . . .' The millionaire Koleff settled himself comfortably upon a high stool and looked down on me. 'You will come here every day and cook. And while you cook I will tell you stories. Afterwards you will go home and sit before your typewriter. You have convinced me, Paskov. With your technical skills and my experience . . . there will be no problems with the publishers. You may have problems with the ideas. Ideas, Paskov, are expensive. You may use my ideas' – he spread his arms expansively – 'create a bestseller. We'll sell it to this publisher of yours for a million dollars and not a cent less. This is big business! The book will be called *Thunder in the Rocky Mountains*.'

'Why *Thunder in the Rocky Mountains?*' I asked him, completely nonplussed.

'Why not? Do you want to make a contract? Now?'

I flung myself downstairs faster than the elevator. I forgot that the door was computerized. I began tugging like a peasant at the doorknob. The Spanish porter was gloating behind my back. I turned to her and put my hands on the glass booth. 'Open!'

'One moment! You are Mr . . . Mr Paskov?'

'No!' I shouted. 'How did you get such an idea? I am Don Miguel de Cervantes, José Ortega-y-Gasset, Miguel de Unamuno! Open!'

. . . I was hanging around on Alexander Bridge, spitting into the Seine, watching how the winged and golden horses were dashing, in communist style, towards a glowing future. Below, small boats passed, bathed in coloured light and filled with carefree tourists. Splendid. Searchlights were scoring the sky . . . music, laughter, noise, men, women . . . Parisians acting like butterflies. I resolved to name my future son Alexander, after the bridge.

I wished him to be as cheerful as this bridge, and not a gull like his father. When he grows up I will tell him how I was fixing beans for a millionaire. A moral example. No, I was not cut out for big business. I was not, and I was not! I started slowly across the bridge, and passed Le Grand Palais, Petit Palais, which had a Picasso exhibition and a huge American crowd, with all their . . . ah, how annoyed I was with all Americans.

I wish that Koleff's history were a plot for at least a short story, but it was not. A heap of writers have described these Koleffs, from the Renaissance even until now, this very evening – why should I take a place in such a crowd?

'Ah, Rio,' I thought bitterly in the Métro for Boissy. 'Hawaii? Haciendas?'

Everything was to be blamed on my writer's block, in combination with this idiotic million, which in turn combined with my life of the free-lance artist in Paris, which in turn combined with my writer's block, oh, stop it!

It was not crowded. I tried to doze off, but how could anyone doze with such rage in his stomach. A line from Eliot about the Métro passed through my head – how everything sinks into the dark – Eliot was right.

And this, Paskov, Paskov! I grew angry. Couldn't he turn his tongue around enough to pronounce Pas*kov*, properly? Why hadn't I told him that? Because I lack character. Art requires strong personality, character, sacrifice.

. . . 'A victim of Ceauşescu! A victim of Ceauşescu! Ladies and gentleman, have mercy on a victim of Ceauşescu!'

I was outraged!

Think what you will, I hate the Métro. Only those who enter it to earn their bread with dignity, reciting poems, singing, with and without guitars, doing magic tricks – only these make it bearable.

With the collapse of communism, the Métro filled with the victims of Ceauşescu. The victims of Ceauşescu could neither sing nor recite poems nor pull pigeons from their sleeves. They disguised themselves as movie Draculas, wearing tatters, and painting bags under their eyes. Under their arms they carried apathetic and anaemic children, who squealed from time to time, because the victims of Ceauşescu were secretly pinching them, those virtuosos of indigence, those laureates of despair.

They were sobbing with a fanatic professionalism, these victims of Ceauşescu.

Killers of style, marauders of tradition, disrupting my reverie.

They chased from the Métro the fiddlers who played Brahms. They drove out the old men with music boxes. They displaced the bums with green moustaches. They pushed outside the meek Indian yogi, the black Bantu, who had never whimpered so, the zombies, acrobats, jugglers, fire-eaters. They rushed into the Métro with the flame-throwers of their revolutionary incompetence, creating an atmosphere of horror, nervous tics, teeth-gnashing, apocalypses – hell!

Oh, you, victims of Ceauşescu!

This one was my age. About forty. Hunched over, dressed in a sack. Under the sack, pyjamas, the legs torn off. Sticking through the openings were thin hairy legs covered all over with ketchup. No doubt Ceauşescu had cut him with a saw.

But I worked in German opera for thirteen years and in Bulgarian cinematography for three years. So I know what ketchup is all about.

'A victim of Ceauşescu, sir!' He thrust his dirty palm under my nose.

I stood up.

I gave him a murderous look, from head to toe (the way I should have looked at Koleff). I smiled cruelly, derisively (the way I should have smiled at Koleff), and I said, emphatically:

'A victim of Todor Zhivkov!'

Silence.

People were looking at us. We were swaying towards each other, without touching. The Métro was tilting, now in this tunnel, now in another.

His face was stunned with surprise. It became wooden. Then it stretched, somehow, and stuck forward. He stared at me. His look grew opaque as if he were viewing a rare Chinese vase, or a magnolia, I don't know what. In the corner of his eye a tear formed. It swelled, grew larger, and then it broke, sliding down his cheek, making a furrow through his victim's make-up and lipstick. He was breathing heavily.

'Brother,' said the victim in pure Bulgarian. 'Brother!' He opened his arms, grabbed me, and began to kiss me, as if I really were his brother. Love radiated from him, of a kind no one has ever shown me before . . . generally speaking, I am not so lovable. But this one here . . . I let him squeeze me. So great was my surprise . . .

The train stopped. He began dragging me by my sleeve. I followed him. My will was paralysed.

'How do you know Bulgarian – aren't you Romanian?'

'I am a Bulgarian,' he said. The yellow light was playing over the mixed paints of his face. Absolutely grotesque, and, at the same time, as in a fairy tale by Charles Perot. 'I am Bulgarian, see!' He shook his fist after the departing train. 'How long have you been here?' the victim asked.

'For two weeks,' I lied. I don't know why.

'A novice . . . you shouldn't be wearing those clothes. Don't you have better clothes to wear?' He began to look at me like the Spanish porter.

'What's wrong with my clothes?'

'They shine with newness. You won't earn a torn franc. Why don't you tear them a little, wrinkle them, put some dirt on them, get a more human look. You are green, still green.' And he dragged me towards a bar.

'My soul is full! A victim of Todor Zhivkov – did you hear that?' he shouted at those hurrying to the Métro, pointing to me with pride. They walked even faster.

The first two beers we downed non-stop. He treated. He'd had a big day: 100 francs.

'Here in the Métro there are about ten of us Bulgarians,' he bubbled. 'Kircho, Vancho Kyorata, Grafcheto, all from Ceauşescu's team. Give me a cigarette. Do you see? You reveal yourself again by showing Marlboros. You have to take out Gitanes, without filters. If you smoke Marlboros it means that you have bucks. You won't get even a franc. *Do* you have bucks?'

'I don't.' I lied for the second time. I don't know why. Probably 100 francs were burning my pocket.

'How could you have, since you are smoking Marlboros?' he concluded logically. 'Where do you sleep?'

I lied for the third time. I don't know why. I told him a story – am I not one who can tell a story? – according to which I slept in the basement of an acquaintance, a cousin of my brother-in-law, a writer. He is married to a Frenchwoman, a doctor of . . . well, a doctor – you understand? And this acquaintance of mine, the writer, has established a big business: he was writing the biography of some millionaire and the millionaire would take him along to Hawaii,

Rio, New York, in order to convey more accurately the atmosphere of his life. He stuffs him with bucks. And I sleep in his basement – where there are rats.

'And you call that business?' said Mircho, pursing his lips (Mircho was his name). 'You are so stupid. This millonaire – if he is a true millionaire – he could buy an American writer, a French writer, an English writer. This is the first time I ever heard of anyone buying a Bulgarian writer. He will look at him for a while, listen to him for a while, and then he will kick his arse so hard that your writer will land in front of the National Assembly in Sofia. What do you know about writers?'

'Nothing,' I confessed. 'This writer is the only one I know. I am a singer. I have sung in the opera. (A half-lie – I have sung in some operas, but not in the Opera, in Sofia, which is bad luck for *it*.)

'I'll tell you what. You're a nice guy. You are a patriot. This is the first time I've seen such a patriot, a victim of Todor Zhivkov. But you are a fool. That's why I'm buying the drinks. I, my little brother, I know the Bulgarian writer. I am a taxi-cab driver in Sofia. Many Bulgarian writers have puked in my cab. The Bulgarian writer has needed only something to gobble, something to slurp, and the chance to say how sweet communism is. Now, however, it is no longer sweet – it is shitty. That is their business. And your friend is a pederast. What's his name?'

'Victor Paskov,' I replied timidly. I'd grown sick of lying.

'Who? That one?' Mircho was angry. 'Do you know how many times I have given him a ride from the Writers' Club to the home of Todor Zhivkov?'

I was speechless. 'Who – me?!'

'Look, look. So he married a Frenchwoman? Surely she is an ugly bitch.'

'No – she's not . . .'

'She is ugly, she is ugly, ugly.' He was certain. 'Listen, trust me. He was the left nut of Todor Zhivkov. He's been paid big bucks to write *his* biography. And you call him a writer? Fat, bald and wall-eyed? . . . a pigmy, talentless, a boil! . . . a hireling, a cop, a whore! . . . a lunatic, a syphillitic, a kleptomaniac!'

For some time we cursed Victor Paskov, and we grew more and

more friendly while doing so. We drank lots of beers. I told him that this one, my writer, may be a terrible shit, but he is a great chef. They are all great chefs, he said, I know them. And oh my, what apartments, what women, what parties – so it is with them, the writers. Garlands, confetti, whores, caviar, whisky! – and my little gypsies meanwhile are eating bread made from cow-feed. That's why their dad is here. Mircho sniffed. 'You had better leave your writer and go. We will find you a big cardboard box, and you will sleep, with us in the Métro. You are a proud bum. What did you say? – *A victim of Todor Zhivkov!* – I kiss your hand.'

'Why are you crying that you are a victim of Ceauşescu?'

'Because Todor Zhivkov doesn't sell well. You are the only patriot here. Ceauşescu is business. He took out a handful of wrinkled banknotes and pushed them under my nose. 'Smell! See how nice Ceauşescu smells. This is a dictator, and, sorry, ours is only a crotch-louse. You may wander in the Métro for a year, shouting that you are Todor Zhivkov's victim, and no one will look at you. You will starve to death. Ceauşescu – peace to his dust – may his memory live for ever – God forgive him – he will feed you. Everyone knows this.'

He poured several drops of his beer on to the floor and said, entirely mellowed: may the earth rest lightly upon you, Ceauşescu – and may the filthiest devil fuck your mother.

Oh, Todor Zhivkov, Todor Zhivkov, Todor Zhivkov, you awful shit! What would have happened had you offered me such big business as this two or three years ago – like the millionaire Koleff? Would you have sent me on a writer's retreat to Capri (where Maxim Gorky was sent) to describe your struggle? Great numbers of nutless literati were spinning around you (isn't it true that you like litera-ture?), you went hunting with writers (isn't it so that you were hunters?), they were baying, flushing game out for you like dogs (isn't it so that they were dogs?), they sang folk-songs for you (didn't they emerge from the people?) – isn't it true that in the final accounting you would have opened your great mouth and swallowed up my little writer's head the way the python swallows the bunny?

In Bulgaria they were readying a trial for him. Who could possibly serve justice on Todor Zhivkov? His millions were in safer places than Koleff's millions. His grandchildren and the grand-children of their grandchildren were secure unto the second coming.

BUT

Do you hear the judgement of the Paris Métro? – you are not selling, my man! Nobody knows you here. You are not worth a torn franc. Ceauşescu is a hit, but you are – what did Mircho say? – yes, you are exactly that. The only thing you are able to provoke is this absurd war between comradely Bulgarian and Romanian citizens in the Métro.

The real victims of Ceauşescu have occupied Nation, Châtelet, Montparnasse, St Lazar, Les Halles – all major central stations, where business is booming.

The Bulgarians are pushed into the suburbs, but Arabs live there, Indians, Greeks, none of whom give a damn – not about Ceauşescu, nor Buddha, nor Homer, not to mention Todor Zhivkov.

The Bulgarian, in response, smuggles himself into Romanian territory and steals away their Ceauşescu. And the Romanian, a great patriot, beats up the Bulgarian and does not yield up his tyrant. Look at Mircho, beaten three times by the chauvinists, but he continues to risk his life for Ceauşescu, who feeds his children, doesn't he? After three months, he will go back to Bulgaria with big bucks. Who cares if at the border he will be fined for over-staying his visa? The Frenchman is reasonable, unlike the Romanian. He won't steal the bread of the little gypsies.

'This is business,' he concluded. 'Severe, merciless, hard. The rest is a lie. Are you hungry?'

I was hungry. I had cooked beans for a millionaire. I was starving to death. Mircho bought me a fish sandwich. He was so generous, so good to me. He was ready to help me, even to give me his soul. He has never before seen such a proud bastard. Nor such a fool. We, the singers, are not like the writers. Mircho knows the singers.

Honest!

Independent!

They sing!

I told Mircho how Chaliapin bowed neither to the Russian czar nor to Lenin nor to Stalin and was buried here in Père Lachaise.

'In Père Lachaise – of course,' he said. He wouldn't let them put him in some mausoleum, like a fool. We drank two beers to Chaliapin. And do you know what we will do, from tomorrow on?

Big business!

We go into the Métro straight down the Champs-Elysées, where the real millionaires are – Mircho knows them – and we will sing.

Like Chaliapin!

We won't pretend to be Romanians any longer. Ceauşescu may go to hell. We will put an end to this shame.

From early morning we will sit down in the warm corridors of the Métro, as in a concert hall. And I will begin to sing ballads (am I not a singer of ballads?), with my bass-baritone, and a good thing I have my bass-baritone. Mircho will wander about and he will cry, *a victim of Todor Zhivkov, a victim of Todor Zhivkov, ladies and gentlemen come closer, closer!* And he will gather our clients. Honestly. Professionally.

And, as you know, the Frenchman is curious and will stop to see: who is this who sings so sadly and so well? Then we will tell him swinish things about Mircho and his little gypsies, about me, about Todor Zhivkov – the Frenchman will be excited, the francs will pour forth. The Frenchman's little dog will also be moved. And if the government of Mitterrand passes by, it too will be excited. Wow! they will say, these people have suffered a lot. And they will give a part of the cake to this poor donkey, the Bulgarian people. Wasn't it their queen who said if there is no bread let them eat cake? Isn't it for this we live in the final accounting, you fool, to know who we are, where we come from and where we are going?

We have also given something to the world!

The truth, the whole truth, and nothing but the truth!

Ah – this is business.

The rest is illusion.

Translated from the Bulgarian by Lyubomir Nikolov and Roland Flint

Ivan Kulekov

My Past, My Future

Once upon a time there was a fabulously beautiful bird. She lived in the dreams of artists, poets and hunters. The artists tried their whole lives to draw her, but never succeeded in capturing her image. And the people said to them:

— If you can't draw her, it means there is no such bird.

The poets tried their whole lives to describe her, but did not succeed.

And the people said to them:

— If you cannot describe her to us, it means there is no such bird.

— What do you mean she doesn't exist? — cried the hunters.

They grabbed their rifles, fired in their dreams and killed the bird.

Then they stuffed her.

And the people said nothing.

*   *   *

A man had a cow.

She gave him milk.

The cow died.

The man built her a monument

and continued to milk her.

*   *   *

A homeless person from Varna was sleeping on the main street in a cardboard box from a 'Sofia' television, dreaming of the West.

Activists from the Nationalist Party moved through the street and smashed his ugly face, but, to the joy of the homeless man, members of the European Party also passed by and gave him a cardboard box from a Phillips refrigerator.

*　　　*　　　*

The sixth-most-important man in Bulgaria went on an excursion to New York. It was noon when he set off wide-eyed down Wall Street, turned right on Broadway, had his picture taken in front of the world-famous financial centre and then continued along Broadway until he reached Canal Street. There he found a place where you can eat for just 99 cents and there for the first time in America he felt he was among equals.

*　　　*　　　*

The people of Bulgaria ate and drank with their overseers three times a day. Then one day the overseers didn't come to dinner and the people were afraid. They were so stunned with fear that they couldn't eat a crumb or drink a drop. The people of the world heard that the people of Bulgaria weren't eating or drinking and began to send them all kinds of foods, juices and money. But the news from Bulgaria on CNN and in *Le Monde* remained the same. Then the people of the world came in person to Bulgaria and found that in Bulgaria there is food, drink and money, but no people.

*　　　*　　　*

A lonely ruler had a nation and ruled over it from morning to night. He spoke to it, he sang to it, he fed it, he moulded it, he spread it out person by person to see what each was made of, then he gathered it together again on a table, shoved it first into the refrigerator, then into the oven, took it out into the street, played war with it, made it cry or laugh, say 'mama', get drunk, groan or do something until the batteries were completely exhausted. Even at night, the lonely ruler did not leave his nation, but lay down to sleep with it.

　　And when all of this tired the lonely ruler, and he threw his nation somewhere and forgot it, the nation did not feel free, but alone.

*   *   *

When the lonely ruler was walking in the park, threading fallen leaves on his cane, he noticed that among the fallen leaves he had begun to pick up fallen people. 'What a problem,' the lonely leader said to himself. 'What shall I make with the fallen leaves?'

He knew what to make with the fallen people – a party!

*   *   *

Millions whiled away their time in servitude.
Hundreds perished for their freedom.
The heirs – are proud.
They know their history.

*   *   *

We have land.
We have water.
And we make mud.

Translated from the Bulgarian by Robert Sturm

Stanislav Stratiev

A Bulgarian Tourist Chats to an English Pigeon in Trafalgar Square

You've got it wrong, my English pigeon! . . . Not only am I not
going to give you any crumbs, but you are also in danger of coming
to a sticky end yourself . . . Inherently hungry as I am and having
been regularly underfed in Bulgaria, I am just about ready for the
ultimate pigeon pie, back at the hotel . . . Hard to believe, isn't
it? . . . Well, just come a step or two closer and we'll see . . . No, we
Bulgarians are not that desperate as yet but the way things are going
we soon might be . . . This sandwich I'm eating now is my breakfast,
lunch and dinner . . . if only these Japanese with their cameras
weren't around . . . Oh, yes, we Bulgarians are real Europeans and,
yes, we are part of Europe . . . Look at the map if you don't believe
me . . . I couldn't even begin to explain it all to you, you wouldn't
understand, it's too complicated . . . It's all that post-totalitarianism
. . . It's the historical conformity of Bulgarian social behaviour . . .
Don't you dare eye my sandwich . . . The specific social psychology,
formed by the living conditions at the Balkan crossroads . . . This
perpetual state of fear that made survival the main historical value,
is in our blood . . . Wait a moment, you can see I've got my mouth
full . . . How can you help but find this fascinating? . . . Wish you
could stay in Bulgaria for just a while; you'd find out for yourself
how very fascinating it all is, you would curl up and die before the
end of the second week . . . Now to continue . . . It's all due to the
immature social awareness of the Balkan people, the lack of a
Hungarian Uprising, a Prague Spring or a Lech Wałęsa . . . The
combination of historic and ad hoc influences . . . the social muddle

... why don't you come a bit closer? ... based on hunger and desperation while lacking an historical perspective ... here, park yourself on this nice bit of stone ... the moral degradation ... the wanton plunder ... the endless lawbreaking ... Will these Japanese tourists never go away! ... The political speculation with national problems has been reduced to a level of absurdity ... the aggravation of Balkan contradictions ... I wonder if I could fit you in this carrier bag ... The ever throbbing Balkan nationalism raises its soiled banners again ... At last, those tourists have finally gone ... Quiet, now, quiet, don't flutter about or you'll scratch my hands ... keep still or I'll wring your neck ... I'm definitely going to eat you; did you think that we'd continue our highbrow discussion until lunchtime? ... I don't care, I honestly warned you at the start ... Come, get into this bag and don't waste any more time ... So ... Where were we? ... Democracy, yes ... the magical word that you find on the lips of diehard Stalinists and extreme liberals alike ... Old and young both swear by the word democracy ... However, at the moment in Bulgaria this is a word devoid of meaning ... Sorry, my dear pigeon, I should have said this at first but then you'd have run away ... Keep quiet, keep quiet, now I'll tell you about the mysterious Slavonic soul ... and as you wish ... also about the Bulgarian Enigma ...

Such a being as a Bulgarian should not exist according to the Laws of Nature and Physics.

However it's not the way it turned out.

There we were, clutching our horses' tails, we arrived safely.

Being outnumbered seven to one by the Slavs we not only assimilated them but proceeded to give them our name.

To top it all we also called 'Bulgarian' a language which retains only eight Bulgarian words.

However, the first of them is *toyaga* – the stick.

Even today it remains for many of us the basic word in the vocabulary.

The habit of naming and renaming became an established Bulgarian custom later on.

And usually the process began by using the first of the Bulgarian words.

There is nothing more powerful in nature than the instinct for self-preservation.

So amongst Bulgarian sayings you will find this one, which sums up our philosophy of life:

'If I can't get what I want, I'll learn to want what I can get.'

Dear pigeon, one can understand the enigmatic Slav soul only after it has been wrenched out.

It is not able to know itself, so what hope do you have of knowing it.

Even as a reader of *The Times*, you still wouldn't understand it. Very well, by way of explanation I shall use the Bulgarian Experience.

If we have given anything to this world – it must be the Bulgarian Experience.

It is – as Cheops's pyramid or the Tower of Babel – our contribution to the treasury of mankind.

Defining it at a higher level – this is a specific state of mind. A certain way of thinking. A kind of spiritual make-up. Defining it at a simpler level – the Bulgarian Experience is the opposite of everything.

Columbus set out for India, but discovered America.

We set off for America and we reach India.

In every corner of the world the king in Andersen's tale is found to be naked.

With us at home, it was just the opposite – the King was dressed while the subjects were naked. And hungry. And jobless.

Throughout the world the insane are accepted as ill but decent people.

At home decent people are regarded as insane.

All over the world you'll find cheeses with holes.

At home holes are a feature of the establishment.

Around the world people are having a grand time.

At home we have a Grand National Assembly.

Everywhere there is only one step from the sublime to the ridiculous.

At home there is no difference.

Over there the people are liberated, at home – the prices are.

This is the Bulgarian Experience.

The Bulgarian Experience is worse than the Bermuda Triangle.

In the Bermuda Triangle things simply disappear.

And one knows they are no more.

Within the Bulgarian Experience things still are, but they are not what they seem.

And no one has a clue.

A place calls itself a petrol station, but it supplies neither petrol, nor oil, nor do they check the tyres, nor do they wash the windscreen.

All you know is that we stand for the best and most of everything in the Balkans.

The Bulgarian dwarf is the shortest and the Bulgarian man the most macho in the world.

One could also have detected the long hand of the Bulgarian Experience when Charlie Chaplin's buried body was stolen for a ransom.

Following the Bulgarian Experience the peasants come to town to buy milk while the townsfolk go to the country to harvest the crops.

A symbol of the Bulgarian Experience could be a retrievable coin tied onto the end of a string to be reused in a lift or a telephone box.

The Bulgarian Experience is indestructible.

It will only be finished off when all of us have emigrated to Canada.

But then Canada itself would be finished.

However, for all these misfortunes we have the Occupation to blame.*

We had no luck with our occupiers.

Norway was under foreign rule too, for nearly as long as we were. Only now their unemployed get 1500 dollars a month. But let's face it – the occupiers were Denmark and Sweden.

Wouldn't you be glad to groan under such a yoke?

---

* The Ottoman Turks occupied Bulgaria for nearly five hundred years, between the fourteenth and the nineteenth centuries.

All around the world, when a people emerged from foreign domination, it came out speaking English, having acquired a civilized way of life and being left with an underground railway by its occupiers.

Now our occupiers happened to be even worse than we were.

Otherwise how could they have ruled us for five whole centuries? Any sensible occupier would have run away from such a people by the tenth year.

So, we have the Occupation to blame for still not having an underground railway.

And also for not having learned English.

Not only have the common people not mastered the English language but the People's Representatives have not mastered the Bulgarian language.

That's the kind of Occupation we've suffered.

We did not have much luck with the Liberator either.*

To think about it, we could have waited three or four more centuries for a better one to come along.

We couldn't have been worse off.

We did not have much luck with the country's geographical position either.

Would any sensible people settle in the Balkans?

The old adage goes that one should not even attempt to pee at a crossroad, but – lo and behold! – there we were attempting to set up a state.

We were not successful in finding suitable neighbours either.

Not a single Scandinavian country next door.

Nor even a Switzerland.

No – all of them just Balkan states.

Under the circumstances what could we attempt except to organize some Balkan Games?

Or alternatively – a Balkan Summit Meeting.

We did not have much luck with our industrial upper classes either.

They didn't leave much behind.

* Bulgaria was liberated from Ottoman rule by Russia in 1878.

Just a few cotton mills and saw mills.

And one safety-match factory.

Had we at least been left with industries comparable to Siemens or Krupp or Sony our place in the world would have been quite different.

Not to mention how things would have turned out had we been left with colonies, protectorates or overseas territories.

Let's not even speak about supplies of black pepper and guest workers.

So now we ourselves have to wash our own dishes.

And also the dishes of North America.

We weren't lucky with our working classes either.

Nor were we blessed with intellectuals.

Nor with immigrants.

Nor with dissidents, nor the necessary ores and minerals, nor with the level of the Danube's water, nor the fauna, the flora, nor the subterranean water level.

Whatever we attempt to do in this situation the same result is inevitable: a banana republic with no bananas, an emirate without oil, a sultanate without diamond deposits.

And there is absolutely nothing we could do. The Occupation is to be blamed for everything.

Until very recently, when the word 'free' was mentioned we used to make the following associations:

Free range.

Free verse.

Free fall.

Free-for-all.

Free and easy.

Free Europe.

Free Agent.

Freelance.

Free association.

Freebie.

Nelson Mandela.

And yet, strangely, it never dawned on anyone that they could think of themselves as free.

We had come to the stage of accepting the famous revolutionary slogan 'Freedom or death', embroidered on the green flags of our Haiduks*, as almost as trivial as the 'Good morning' welcome on bath towels.

Following some tacit agreement we never spoke of freedom. It was not so much the result of fear, as of shame.

For us freedom was a chimera.

I write 'chimera' but the word means one of several things: a beautiful and ineffectual dream; a desire impossible to fulfil; and a mythical monster with three fire-belching heads. Whoever approaches is doomed to die.

I still cannot understand which of the chimera images represented our freedom.

The dream or the monster.

Things seem to be changing now.

We are being told we are free.

Aye, there's the rub . . . What are we to do with this damned freedom? Because, as a Serbian satirist puts it: 'A free man thinks what he wants to but eats only what is at hand.'

And we have always wanted it to be the other way round.

To eat whatever we want and to think whatever is at hand.

I find it so unfair that we were never consulted. Someone comes to liberate you and that's that.

Were we to strike an average, we would be the most frequently liberated people in the world.

And all our genetic mutations spring from this.

Every now and again, there comes a new liberator.

And then we are obliged to erect a new monument.

Or, someone devises an alphabet for us.

At that time, we are told, Emperor Charles the Great dared to speak German only to his horses, but someone took it upon himself to create an alphabet for us.

---

* A name given to rebels and guerrilla fighters against Ottoman rule.

Well, whatever possessed them – would we have been worse off if Charles the Great had spoken to us in German too?

Now that we speak Bulgarian, so what? Even our horses cannot understand us.

Or, someone took it upon himself to write our History. The Slav-Bulgarian one.

So what is the use of this History?

What is the practical use of our Revival?

Had we not been so deeply into the Revival Experience we could have been a Baden-Württemberg province.

And as a consequence being paid 8000 DM per month.

Instead of just being free.

What did you say, dear pigeon? . . . You still cannot make head or tail of us Bulgarians? . . .

Wait, here is another clue for you.

The Bulgarian is a very sensitive person.

Let's take Stoyan, for example.

He's into selling empty bottles.

He's worked at the bottle bank for two years.

He's earned enough to buy himself a house, a car and a place in the country.

Fortune has smiled on Stoyan.

He sings while collecting the bottles.

He sings as he arranges them in the crates.

Stoyan is also acclaimed as a singer.

During his third year of arranging the empty bottles, he finds a letter in one of them.

Stoyan opens the letter.

It contains a cry for help.

This goes over Stoyan's head.

Neither an address, nor a name is included.

Stoyan shakes his head and throws the bottle into the crate.

Within three days a second letter arrives.

And in a similar bottle.

Another cry for help.

Stoyan is having a hard time deducing something from the label.

Nothing. It's just another grape brandy bottle.

Something begins to stir in Stoyan's soul.

Three days later a new letter comes in a bottle.

Someone is desperate for help. They are perishing.

At this point Stoyan breaks down. He tries to find moral support in a full bottle.

Next week they are calling out for help again.

Stoyan's mind is in turmoil.

If someone out there is perishing, he cannot possibly live a contented life.

At the bottle bank the number of full bottles equals the number of empties.

So Stoyan proceeds to lose his singing voice.

And after that – everything else.

He now drinks heavily day and night, having had to sell the house, then the car, then the summer house.

And still, the letters crying for help continue to arrive.

Stoyan continues to drink.

Stoyan is surrounded by mountains of emptied bottles.

All the white mice descend on Stoyan.

Delirium tremens sets in for Stoyan.

Stoyan is perishing.

In one of his rare lucid moments he writes a letter asking for help. He seals it in an empty bottle and sends it to the bottle bank . . .

Translated from the Bulgarian by Galina Holman

Romania

Mircea Cărtărescu

The Dream

You get up from beside me and switch on the light. A wriggling, sharp pain shoots through my pupils and, as I peer from underneath the sheets, I see you as in a sea of flames that seems to be devouring the whole chamber. Suddenly, everything strikes me as hallucinatingly real. Another world. The shelves crammed with books, our clothes strewn all over the place, the basket on the coffee table with only two apples left in it, the ashtray in which three apple cores are slowly turning brown, the coffee-mill, yourself searching for something under the armchair in which the portable TV set is reclining, your naked body, yellow-pale-pink-golden in colour, erect and making me wonder at the width of women's hips when seen from behind, everything expresses and suppresses its facets in the light. Facets in the light, I say to myself, dazed, this is our world. Your cropped hair is ruffled. Your face is old, your skin as soft as buff and all wrinkled. I'm filled with nausea at the sight of you, yet I give you a mechanical smile and you smile back with very little hope. An old woman. Your breasts are still shapely, but what's the use of it all? I am devoid of love and your story is draining my strength. Day is beginning to break. Come on, Nana, break through. You return to bed with something like a shoe box. You open it and from beneath a layer of cotton wool you take out an egg the size of an ostrich egg, with a rough, yellowing shell. The lightbulb casts a bluish shadow upon it. The egg has a red fading smear on one side. Probably the place marked with the star. I cup my palms around it and carefully weigh it. It is heavy and bulky and its shell is lukewarm as if someone were sleeping inside. You place it upon the table and leave it there, on the striped tea-towel, where breadcrumbs can be seen, each of them casting a tiny coloured shadow. You switch off the light. Through the window, the sky no longer looks pitch black. All things in the room have become dark bluish and the walls are beginning to show in the gloom. My ears are ringing with your voice, which I'm no longer perceiving as sound but as a pure succession of images. I am exhausted after this sleepless night, I feel as if my entrails were a mixture of acid and rubber. The moment you resume spinning, the yarn of your story passes unnoticed. Your narrative has the same temperature as my body, I succumb to it and suppress all my senses, I succumb to illusion, I make for the entrance to the cave on the emerald island. The narrow opening is overgrown with bone-like brambles, as tough as barbed wire, with hidden purple flowers scintillating from beyond the thorns. I enter the rock corridor leading into its depth. Translucent larvae are scurrying across the walls. The low ceiling is staring at me from myriad ocelli. The stream is the abode of the eyeless Proteus with the tiny arms of a man. And deep in there, at the very centre, cocooned in your night like a silk worm, you, as nobody knows you, you with your jaws bristling with crooked, curved fangs, you with your flaring nostrils, breathing out plumes of pure fire, you with your devouring jade scales, with dragon wings and anaconda tail. You, cocooned in your sulphur stench, you amongst bones and skulls . . . You, in your woman's silence, in your lack of communication, in your violence and fear.

In the evening, I took Marcelino up by the hand as usual, and, pleased as could be, made for the watch tower. Only a day had gone by since we had last dropped in, yet I felt guilty as if I had wasted one day of my life, nay, not one day, more like a whole year, I felt like I hadn't been there for ages. I was missing Egor and even his mother. When we entered the house, we could hardly believe our own eyes: the place was packed full of flowers. All the bottles, glasses, jugs, not to mention the vases – from cut glass or china ones to worthless replicas – had been taken out of the cupboards and stuffed with flowers. The sideboards, coffee tables, mantelpieces, the tops of the oak newel posts, the stools and the floor itself were decked with rows of flower-filled vases. Upstairs, in Egor's room, one could hardly breathe: there were white and red lilies, their petals unfurled to the limit, overspilling with stamens, heavy with pollen, there were yellow roses, there were whole sheaves of snapdragon, clusters of elderflowers, camomile flowers on tangled stems, cornflowers. There were also blossoming cacti and some contorted blue and red flowers with sticky tongues, orchids, of course, whose names I didn't know at the time and which I had never seen before.

In a pot of muddy soil, a plant called 'heaven's dew' was wallowing, its beauty not of this world: its corolla consisted of very fine pricks, each ending with a bead of transparent liquid, gleaming in the penumbra of the room. 'This is a carnivorous plant,' we were informed by the elongated man, who had taken his favourite seat. With a finger almost as long as my forearm, he touched the centre button surrounded by pricks: as if obeying an order, the pricks all rose at once, and then, one after the other, they curved inwards towards the finger, clinging to Egor's finger with their sticky beads. 'If I left my finger here, they would soon mangle it to the bone.' That was a spider plant, and a delightful spider at that. I recounted to him my dream about the river, and the one about the goblet and Egor gently nodded his approval, no longer enthusing as in the beginning. Now he knew. I was, without a doubt, the chosen one, I was fated to enter the REM. 'Here, all these flowers are for you. People from all over the place have come here to bring them to you and wish you luck through me. They have been waiting for you for a long time, they would come here every year, they take my mother and myself for some sort of priests of the REM. But they know neither of us could ever enter it. Because the REM, the only one in our world, is made for the dreamer of dreams alone, that is, for yourself.' Egor went on to tell me the existence of the Exit, as he would call the REM, was known to people from all over the world, connected to one another through the revelation of the mystery and through the oath not to reveal it to anyone else. 'The REM is, in a way, like this heaven's dew plant, a kind of snare that reaches everywhere and has infinite patience, a passage waiting for years to be discovered and then for more years to be reached by the one and only being who can enter it. There are secret books on the REM, written by hand, there are a number of competing sects recognizing the REM, but interpreting its meaning in a host of ways. Some claim the REM is an infinite apparatus, a colossal brain regulating and co-ordinating, according to a definite plan and for a definite purpose, the dreams of all beings, from the inconceivable dreams of the amoeba and the crocus, to the dreams of humans. According to them, dreams are the true reality in which the will of the divinity hidden in the REM is revealed. Others see the REM as a sort of kaleidoscope in which you can read the whole of the universe at once, with every detail of each moment, as it evolves from Genesis to the Apocalypse. I have recently read a story in Spanish where the REM seen in such a way is called El Aleph. Some people strongly believe there is only one REM, others think there is one for each man and woman and they have gone to far as to invent a curious writing consisting of a sequence of signs through which everyone would be able to come to his or her REM, provided they know how to interpret these signs. But what the truth is, whether the REM is Salvation or Damnation, you alone shall know.'

Egor was speaking to me in a voice fainter than usual, his ugly acromegalic's face resembled an emaciated mask. 'I am terribly tired. I didn't sleep a wink last night and today I've been writing far too much. I had no choice, though, I'd lagged behind more than I could afford to.' I asked him what he was writing and his answer came naturally, accompanied by a nauseating mien: 'Literature. I am a writer, curse my fate.' I told him I found it a rewarding profession, and in order to show him I was not alien to the subject I went on to ask him, echoing words which I seemed to have heard somewhere before: did he want to become a great writer? I expected him to smile, the way grown-ups do when a child meddles in serious matters, but Egor, paler than usual, his nose cartilages translucently glaucous, his eyes lacklustre, answered me immediately, as if he had asked the question himself. Anyway, he was talking both literally and figuratively, way above a twelve-year-old girl's level of under-standing. 'A great writer is nothing other than a writer. There is a difference in nuance, rather than a radical one. All high-jumpers, say, jump two metres high. One of them jumps two metres and one centimetre and becomes a great sportsman. No, it is not worth the trouble to bother about becoming a mere great writer, a pathetic author of genius. Take the best books ever written. They are hardly a fraction above second-rate books. Basically, they are still books, nothing else. You might derive enhanced aesthetic pleasure from reading them. Like from a cup of coffee which is slightly sweeter.

You'll still put them down, thirty pages later, to make a sandwich or go to the bathroom. You'll read them in parallel with some detective novel. In a few thousand years, they, too, will turn to dust. Under the circumstances, to aim at becoming a genius, you, a man, a being granted the staggering chance of existing and reflecting upon this world, is humiliating, it is insignificant. It is like turning your back on everything and retracing your steps into the forest again. In each of us there is a potential against which the ambition of being the world's greatest writer is downright dishonourable, through its very facility. For is there a miracle greater than the miracle of existing and knowing you exist? From this point to being the wealthiest, most powerful, most talented in the whole world is like going from one billion to one billion and one, even less, much less than that. No, I don't want to be a great writer, I want to become Everything. I dream incessantly of a Creator who, through his act, will truly come to influence the life of mankind, of the whole of mankind, and then the life of the entire universe, to the most distant stars, to the end of space and of time. And then he will come to replace the universe, to become himself the World. It is the only way in which I think a man, an artist, could fulfil his destiny. The rest is literature, a collection of tricks, mastered to a greater or to a lesser degree, pieces of paper scribbled with tar nobody cares for, no matter how brilliant the rows of graphic signs, which soon enough will no longer make sense, anyway.' He had uttered these words passionately, with bitterness in his face. Then he was silent for a long time, in the golden night . . . 'But most people, or rather most writers, will not become everything. They will not even become genii. They will become nothing. I . . . I am the first among them. But at least I know it, and through my writing I am trying to express my inability. I know nothing can be said, nobody expects you to say anything, but I also know you do have to say it. I know you have to resist somehow the injustice of being human and thus unable to be Everything. I am doing this with all my might. Look.' He stood up from the yellow veneer chair and opened wide the two exquisitely inlaid doors of the stately escritoire. It was vaster than I had imagined. A red, fragrant wood coated its depth. The whole inside was taken up by several thick piles of writing paper, thousands of pages stacked high. When, thrusting his fingers in them and toppling them on to the carpet, Egor spread the pages all over the floor, I was able to see they were covered in an even writing, strangely characterless. But it was only when I attempted reading a few lines from the work of the elongated man that I understood the immense horror it contained: over thousands and thousands of pages, with an ant's patience and persistence, Egor had written just one word, repeated constantly, tens of times on each page, in a sequence without beginning or end. It was the word 'no'. 'I've been writing since I was sixteen and I've hardly completed over fifteen hundred pages. Sometimes I write for eight hours a day, but at times I can't write a single line. You might think it's funny, but on occasion I dry up, and though you might find it easy to write such things, I've undergone crises which almost made me give up writing. I'm also terrified by writer's block and by the inability to keep up with myself. Because I am not writing mechanically. I want each, and I mean each, of these "noes" to be pondered upon and felt to its very marrow. To be experienced with all of my flesh, with all of my nerves. And don't imagine it's easy. There are times when I ponder for a whole week before adding one more word, for I want my work to be perfect, to reflect me entirely.' I didn't understand a thing. I was shifting my eyes from Egor to the sheets of paper which the dusk coloured a pink shade of mother of pearl. I attempted to pick up the sheets from the floor, but the elongated man, taller than ever (he had risen to his feet and was looking out of the window), would not let me. I went downstairs, paid my respects to Mrs Bach, who, in her lurid négligé, besieged by flowers, was listening to a ridiculous romance, sung with a marked nasal twang, on the radio: 'What shall I write to you, now that we're parting?' and we found ourselves once again on the path across the field, leaving Egor's smoky silhouette behind. As I was walking unhurriedly, hand in hand with my cousin, I was suddenly overcome by a new surge of sadness.

That night I dreamed of a key which someone had left in the forest. I had just descended a gentle slope into a dell where the beeches had grown sparse and slender, and the black soil between their trunks was dappled with bright white and yellow patterns of light. The sun shone dazingly through the branches swaying in a green breeze. The trees' bark was peeling off and it gave forth a bitter tannic fragrance. A mist, caused not by vapour but by ennui and nostalgia, was coolly spilling into the eternal morning. I had spotted the glimmering key from afar, and I had taken a short detour to reach it. I kneeled and picked it up. The wine I had sipped in my previous dream, mixed with the spider venom, had inebriated me, had instilled in me a state of exaltation which I could hardly control. I picked up the key. It was a gold key, twice as big as my palm. In the contour it had left on the ground, an earthworm gave a fleshy, lazy wriggle, then it was slurped into the ground with a set of contractions. I wiped the key clean with the seam of my dress. Its head was club-shaped, over-ornate with gold twisting stems. The rod of the key, thick and sparkling, reflected my face and the surrounding trees in a distorted way. At the lower end it had a plate with three equal teeth, which I dreamily caressed with my fingers. I kissed the key and put it into my pocket with joy. I broke into a run down the path, which led deeper and deeper towards the bottom of the dell, where the air grew cooler and cooler. I could hardly wait to use the key. I did not care whether behind the door Pleasure or Terror would be waiting for me.

Translated from the Romanian by Florin Bican

Ana Blandiana

The Open Window

Back in those days, whenever artists were arrested, they were allowed to take their paints and brushes with them into the jail. Thus, on entering the dark cell at the top of the tower, the first thought that struck the hero of this story was to have a window painted on one of the walls. He got down to work and painted an open window through which a dazzling blue sky could be seen. Thus his cell became much brighter.

The following morning, entering with bread and water, the jailer had to shut his eyes against the blinding light pouring in through the painted window.

'What's going on in here?' he yelled and rushed to shut the window, only to knock himself against the wall.

'I have opened a window,' the artist answered, undisturbed. 'It was too dark in here.'

'Heh, heh, heh,' the jailer laughed, feeling humiliated because he had allowed himself to be hoodwinked. Then he started mocking the artist spitefully: 'You have opened a window ... You have painted a window, you fool! This is not a real window, it is only yourself imagining it is a window.'

The artist went on, undisturbed: 'I wanted to make light in this cell and I did so. Through my window the sky can be seen; you yourself, coming in, had to close your eyes because of the light.'

This time, the jailer was really furious: 'Are you trying to bamboozle me or what? This tower has no windows whatsoever. Whoever enters here will never live to see the light of day again!'

'And yet, daylight is pouring into my cell through the open window,' the artist said.

'Oh, yes?' the jailer mocked him. 'Then why don't you escape? That way, you could persuade me your window's for real.'

The artist studied him for a while, then took a few steps to the wall and jumped out of the window.

'Stop!' The jailer rushed after him, frantically trying to check him, but again all he did was bang his head against the wall. 'Alert! He's escaped!' he started to yell, as the artist's body could be heard hurtling down through the air, smashing itself against the slates at the foot of the tower.

Translated from the Romanian by Florin Bican

George Cuşnarencu

The War

Some five years ago, where the blocks of flats are now standing all
in a row like trams in a terminal, there were lush apple tree and pear
tree orchards, giving shade to tiny white houses in which two to
twenty souls were living together. The turmoil of Bucharest stopped
short of the ring road, as soon as you climbed the Cotroceni Hill.
Here, drama would flare from a match, and was quenched with
plum brandy. In the evenings, old people would gather outside their
houses and tell stories sitting on benches. Children would play with
rubber balls, and sometimes, out of carelessness, car accidents
occurred, which nobody wanted. Some would die, some would
survive, as is known to have happened in the case of Matei Vladescu,
today a student at the Polytechnic. About two streets further, there
used to live Marioara Petre, who one night eloped in a lorry with
her future husband, all because of old man Petre, who wouldn't hear
of weddings in his family, at least not in his lifetime. And he was a
strapping sort of man. It also happened at night that Teoharie Nucu
flipped his lid. He had returned from the bar in the evening, rather
tipsy. Whenever he returned in this state, he would go straight to
bed, without saying a word, and his parents expected no trouble, at
least from this direction. Nobody could explain what had come over
Teoharie that evening: he talked and talked. He recounted everything they had said at the bar, even some spicy stories from his
school days. Teoharie Nucu's folks split their sides with laughter
over his stories. After three hours of mirth, they all went to bed.
Teoharie slept in the kitchen, in an iron bed, next to a pile of
firewood. About seven o'clock in the morning, Teoharie suddenly
sprang out of bed, upset the stove, and stormed into the courtyard,
bleating like a wounded beast. His father and mother, who were
working in the garden, rushed to see what sort of creature had

invaded their courtyard. They found Teoharie rolling in the dust, with a piece of iron in one hand and a stone in the other, trying to knock in his teeth. With the help of their neighbours, they succeeded in fastening Teoharie's hands with the clothesline. Then the ambulance arrived. Teoharie spent three weeks in hospital, and three times a week the Nucus would visit the hospital, questioning the doctors about their son's chances of recovery. When they were allowed to take him home, they weren't any the wiser as to the nature of their son's affliction; but they remembered that the doctor had told them repeatedly the boy was all right but they would have to remove from the house any sharp object: tools of all descriptions, nails, wire, the whole lot. They had brought Teoharie home from the hospital, and all the way, the boy's behaviour had been perfectly normal. Nevertheless, an expert would have construed the meaning of Teoharie's staring eyes. He was taking in the rails of the tramway. Things were going all right, but a few weeks later Teoharie was found in the backyard, his mouth bleeding profusely, as he was trying to pull out his teeth with a pair of forks. From that moment on, they understood that the illness would eat into their son's soul like a drill. Overnight their house turned into a place where paper was substituted for whatever hard materials there were around. In the house of the Nucus, the windows were paper, the cutlery cardboard, there weren't any knives, axes or padlocks. Door handles, hammers and cupboards all had to go. So had the chairs, poker and piping. Everything was either paper or cardboard. Their hopes included. Yet the dramatic part of all this turmoil with no future was the merry-go-round of their daily routine which, to the eyes of their neighbours, had to appear unaffected by troubles and unchanged from the days before Teoharie Nucu became ill. Teoharie would still go to the bar, the old folks would still gather in front of their gates every evening, children would still play with a rubber ball in the street, and sometimes accidents would occur.

Somehow, perhaps due to living in a paper and cardboard world, which was exactly what the Nucus' house had become, Teoharie recovered, so that, ten years after his first bout of illness, everything returned to normal. Teoharie found employment on a construction site, as a welder. In the meantime, where the orchards had once stood, a whole new quarter was erected. Teoharie Nucu got married, and he was living in a two-room flat, less than five hundred metres away from his folks' house, still white, only slightly leaning to one side. The previous winter, its chimney had toppled. And it was the previous year, too, just before Christmas, that they had slaughtered the pig. The pig weighed nearly 150 kilogrammes and had to be slaughtered by a professional, who was simply not allowed to make a mistake. They had called upon Mircea Constantin, said Flocea, to do the job; by trade he was a car mechanic and the only expert on pig slaughtering in the quarter. There were others who could manage it, but they were known to have failed on frequent occasions, and people had tacitly dispensed with their services. Mircea Constantin entered the Nucus' courtyard about lunchtime. 'How is Teoharie, Uncle Titi?' he asked old man Nucu. 'He's in good health, my son, so keep him God,' Dumitru Nucu replied bashfully. 'How come you have a pig this year?' Mircea Constantin asked next. 'Well,' Uncle Titi replied, 'now that Teoharie's out of trouble, we've started to have everything in the house again. You don't remember, because you were a mere chit of a child way back when we kept two cows and around five pigs. They would graze at the back of the garden, see, where that block of flats stands, or thereabouts. And now, well, times are harder, leaner, sort of . . . More and more people are asking for food, that's why.' 'True,' Flocea said, 'quite true. As for that meadow, that plot of land behind the house, I can remember it all right, what the hell, because we used to play all together there, Teoharie, Rodica, Vlad and myself. All day long we would chase each other, all over the place, and get all muddy. Now my little ones give chase on asphalt, and come home all bleeding, their knees and elbows grazed raw. So it goes, Uncle Titi, we're living in a block while you still slouch in front of your house dreaming of all the things you once had. Want to know something? Fifteen years ago, I'd leave one bird's bed only to hop into another's. That's life, Uncle Titi. Where's that pig?'

The pig was rooting about in the dirt mixed with piss and excrement in its sty, as it had been doing for over ten months. 'I say, Uncle Titi, go and get that plum brandy to drink to the pig's health, or else the crackling will be no good.' Dumitru Nucu fetched the demijohn out into the yard, together with a wooden stool. Out of superstition, he still kept no knives in the house. Carefully, Mircea Constantin opened the pig-slaughtering kit. Carefully, he laid out his implements on the stool, then lifted the demijohn to his mouth and took a long swig. 'Aw, c'mon, Uncle Titi, do get us some plum brandy, not water, or the pig will start squealing worse than a fire engine.' Uncle Titi shrugged his shoulders in defeat. 'That's how we drink the plum brandy, Flocea, weak, for we are not so young as we used to be,' said old man Nucu. 'Never mind, this one will do,' Flocea said, fastening the demijohn of plum brandy to his lips. Two people from the neighbourhood were hovering around the pigsty, wishing to give a hand, which wouldn't have gone unrewarded, of course. 'Hey, you, blockheads. Haven't you got a house of your own? Go and get me some straw, someone, and spread it down here,' Mircea Constantin said, pointing at his feet with the knife blade. 'Well, Mircea, we thought you might want us to help you get that pig down, hold it fast till you stick it, but if you don't want us to, then peace be upon you.' The two withdrew, muttering, keeping close to the fence all the same, so as to see what was going on, and (so they thought) finally be asked to lend a hand. All along the street, their heads peeping from behind gate posts, other neighbours were carefully watching the pig slaughtering. Although an hour and a half had gone by, Flocea had done nothing to prepare the pig for slaughter, thus kindling with the passage of time the excitement of the crowd gathered round Nucu's yard. Mircea Constantin had drained the three litres of plum brandy and was now sitting on the stool in the middle of the yard, only ten metres away from the pigsty, his eyes riveted on the knives. His eyes were bloodshot. He was drunk. A quarter of an hour later – all the time he seemed to have sized up the tools for the slaughter, going through every stage of the impending action – Mircea Constantin stood up and stretched his left arm in front of his eyes. He could see there was no hint of a tremor. Next, he took out of the kit beside the leg of the stool a thin-bladed knife, tested its tip for sharpness, and thrust it under the belt of his trousers. He grabbed a five-kilo hammer in his left hand. He straightened his back, and before making for the pig he admonished the lot beyond the fence: 'What are you staring at, you nitwits, as if you haven't seen such things before.' He was fifteen steps away from the pigsty.

He set out with his knife in his belt and the hammer in his hand. The onlookers strung along the fence swayed with the thrill like sea waves stirred by the breeze. A woman covered her mouth with her hand. Halfway to the pigsty, Mircea Constantin changed his mind. He staggered back to the stool in the middle of the yard. He took a deep draught and chose another knife. The folks beyond the fence were watching his every move. Some of them started at the sound of Mircea Constantin's voice. 'C'mon, look, look on, because it's yourself you're looking at, and you're going to look death in the eyes, brrrhp!' He belched. Then he made a second start for the pig. He entered the pigsty, and his feet sank in the muck. The pig had retreated to the far end, giving weak squeals. In order to get into the pigsty, Mircea Constantin had to bend down and advance, stooping precariously, towards the far end where the pig had flattened itself against the wall. He dismissed this hazardous approach, especially since in those cramped quarters the pig had greater freedom of movement than he. The forces in that confrontation were unevenly matched, and neither side could afford to forfeit whatever advantage it had, not even for a second. Mircea Constantin climbed on top of the pigsty, whose flat rooftop stood one metre above the ground. Thus started a long wait. Mircea Constantin was squatting on the roof and grinned at the people he saw from up there. Every now and then, he would produce a flask from the pocket of his body-warmer and swig some plum brandy. 'C'mon, boy, out you go, boy!' he mumbled under his breath. It seems improbable, yet none of the loiterers watching the show would relinquish their position, not even for a hot meal. The sun was ready to set. Dusk was slowly taking over and long shadows were replacing sunshine. An acrid mist had descended over the yard of old man Nucu, a sort of haze thickened by the smoke from the straw pyre built at the far end of the garden for singeing the pig. Old man Nucu had expected the job to be over much sooner, so he had to keep the fire going. During the wait, silence reigned over both camps, no one uttered a sound.

Against this background of weird silence, Teoharie Nucu came through the gate, in good spirits, sucking on a tooth pick which he kept moving from one corner of his mouth to the other. 'What's going on here, Father, huh? Is this a travelling circus, has a comet dropped in your backyard or what?' he called to his father, cheered up by the sight. 'No circus, Teoharie, we're only slaughtering a pig, lad,' his father answered from the far end of the garden. Mircea Constantin was still squatting on the roof, biding his time. Inside, the pig was also biding its time. Teoharie made for the pigsty himself. On the way, he passed the stool in the middle of the yard, and, in spite of himself, his eyes suddenly fell on Mircea Constantin's kit, where a few knives were gleaming. For a moment, Teoharie stopped and sat on the stool, covering the knives with the sole of his boot, in order to obstruct the gleam of their blades. His illness had given him a nudge, and he had to acknowledge it or not. He was sitting on the stool and looking at the world around him with a hint of panic. His cheerfulness had vanished. He removed his foot, and the sharp-pointed blades of the knives became visible again. With robot-like movements, Teoharie Nucu bent over the slaughtering kit. He spit the tooth pick out of his mouth. He selected a knife. Ran the tip of his thumb over its point. His mouth widened in a leer, revealing his brownish teeth, decayed and crumbled to mere shards. He got to his feet and made for the house, walking unsteadily. At the very moment he was about to enter the summer kitchen, still furnished with the iron bed he used to sleep in as a boy, old man Nucu's voice broke the silence: 'Te-o-ha-ri-e, bring that gas cylinder over, my lad.' Teoharie Nucu looked first to one side, then to the other, spotted the gas cylinder by the stove, hoisted it on to his back, and made for his father. He had vaguely heard his father asking him to bring the gas cylinder. On his way, he passed Mircea Constantin, who was still waiting, perched on the rooftop. 'Here, have this one too, it might come in handy.' Teoharie said, lobbing the knife on to his lap. Mircea Constantin muttered something, and threw the knife towards the kit by the stool. 'That's it, lad, stick around, we have work to do,' old man Nucu said to Teoharie. It was getting dark; the shapes behind the fence were hardly discernible in the evening air. Everybody's nerves were on edge. They could feel, actually they strongly desired it, that the pig would eventually give up, that it would finally leave its cramped and dark nook and come into the open.

Mircea Constantin had emptied his flask of plum brandy and cast it over the fence. A hen scraping in the dung pile was startled by it, and fluttered away cackling. Then it stalked the bottle with hesitant steps and took a few pecks at it. All it could hear was a dull unknown sound. Everyone heard the sound, but no one cared about it. And then, when quite a few had come to believe that the show would drag on into the break of the following day (not that they seemed to mind the prospect in the least), everyone could distinctly hear the pig grunting under the open sky. It went round the enclosure a few times, sniffing at the pales. Mircea Constantin straightened his back and focused his clouded eyes on the back of the pig. He stood motionless like a rock, his muscles strained, his regular breath making not a sound. He waited for five minutes, during which the pig was supposed to make sure it was safe, free, and under no threat. It had five more minutes to live. At that moment, Teoharie Nucu appeared by the pigsty enclosure, on his way from the garden. He threw a chunk of stale bread to the pig, in the mud mixed with straw and urine. The pig took the bread in its jaws, and started munching on it. For an instant, Mircea Constantin thought that Teoharie Nucu would spoil everything, all the toil he was going to be paid for. Just to be on the safe side, he tumbled on top of the pig, grabbed its ear in his right hand, and, quick as lightning, he dealt the beast a heavy blow between the eyes with the hammer in his left hand. The pig crumpled into the mud. Mircea Constantin removed his knife from his belt and cut its throat. In the mud running red with blood there were two beings: Mircea Constantin, who was watching the pig's final spasms, and the slaughtered animal, whose eyes had come to rest on Teoharie Nucu's bland face. Teoharie turned his back on the scene and started to retch. Although nothing much could be seen any longer, people were still clinging to the fence. Mircea Constantin dismounted the pig and left the enclosure. He walked to the stool, dragging his feet. After a while, he stumbled against a rock and fell flat. He struggled to his feet, then collapsed again. He asked for something to drink, but nobody heard him. He crawled to the stool and gathered his tools. A knife was missing, but he was too drunk to care. 'Now it is yours, take it and do what you will with it,' Mircea Constantin shouted to the audience, then crawled out of Dumitru Nucu's yard on all fours. When the Nucus started singeing the pig, the audience started scattering to their respective pursuits. Each of them had children, a house, family. No matter what events occurred, they had to go on being decent folks, with duties and responsibilities to attend to.

That night, the Nucus saw to the pig; they cut it up into equal parts for each member of the family. They were finished by daybreak, and Teoharie Nucu made his way home with two bagfuls of pork. His wife and child had good grounds for rejoicing. On entering the flat, Teoharie Nucu warned his wife: 'I've brought you some meat from the old man, but I don't know what's wrong with it, because it tastes rather funny. I think it's got something to do with that drunkard, Mircea, I don't know what the hell he's been doing to it.' And his wife replied: 'It tastes all right as long as we have it, Teoharie, let us give thanks to the Lord.' She was a pious woman.

Translated from the Romanian by Florin Bican

Ştefan Agopian

The Art of War

Day was dawning sluggishly that Saturday and strove impotently to scrape the dark off our bodies like a blade, a blunt one at that. The bells tolled half-heartedly and a thin film of light spread over the city. Whatever zombies were around had one last dance, sniffed at the milky light as if in doubt and took to the road. An angel unseen by the eyes of this world quickly brought them together, herding them off towards another night and there they hastened, without a care.

Zadic the Armenian and Ioan the Geographer were left alone on the brink of the morning that had dawned upon the world. A few rats laboured playfully at their feet, a rather dim-witted one, attempting to climb up the Armenian's leg. The latter gave it a rather bored clout over the muzzle, thus chasing it away. The rat moved over to Ioan and was grabbed by its tail and lifted to the window. The beast wriggled its pink paws to its greatest advantage, squeaking for mercy.

'Let it go!' the Armenian said. 'For it saddens my soul.'

But Ioan did not let it go. He placed it on the windowsill instead and watched it for a while, as it froze, rigid with fear.

'How about eating it?' the Armenian asked in a starved voice. He produced a bulb of garlic from his pantaloons pocket and showed it to Ioan. 'We'll have it stewed.'

Ioan pondered for a spell, then nodded his agreement. The idea slightly cheered them up and, fired by it, they caught three more rats and wrung their necks. They eyed their carcases with glee and the Armenian started to recite some doggerel . . . Ioan managed to stop him in time, for a large ear had opened into the wall, inquisitively. They urinated into the cup of the ear, then spat into it and the ear changed back into a mildewed, wet wall.

'I was a cook in Anatolia for three years,' Zadic said and sat down on the floor with his legs beneath him.

Ioan aligned the four carcasses before him in an orderly fashion, and stared at them.

The Armenian picked up the first rat and, pumping up his lungs, blew into its bottom until it became twice as big, bunged up its hole with his finger and heaved a sigh of relief. He suddenly took out his finger and the animal's body was expelled from its skin with a cannon-like boom which startled Ioan.

'Heh, heh, heh!' laughed Zadic the Armenian, repeating the same routine three more times. He ripped the rats' bellies open with a fingernail which he had whetted at length against the wall and cut out their bowels.

'They're not all that plump,' Ioan said, just for the sake of conversation, although he was no longer in the mood for anything at all.

The Armenian stood up, retrieved a tin pan from a dusty corner and placed three chunks of meat into it. Ioan had already started peeling the garlic, and soon an enticing fragrance reached their nostrils, thus dispersing whatever gloomy thoughts they might have had. They had to stop for a while at the arrival of four thugs, dim-eyed with lack of sleep, who started beating them up till they got bored, then left them senseless in a corner and went away.

Ioan was the first to come round. He couldn't for the life of him remember where he was, so he had to ask the Armenian. Ioan's voice persuaded the Armenian to open the huge eye he had right in the middle of his forehead, Cyclops-like.

He blinked that one eye in confusion and said: 'I don't know.'

He tried sorting out his eye for a while, but in vain. Ioan said, from one side: 'Those afflicted with a disease in keeping with their constitution, humour and age, and with the season as well, are under a lesser threat,' but this did not put the Armenian's mind at ease in the least. He looked upon the world in confusion with the one eye in his forehead and the vile world was thrust into it, startling him.

Seeping in through the wall masonry, a big bird billowed into the room, under their very eyes.

'Who's this here bird?' the Armenian asked as an afterthought.

The bird sat down before them, crossed his legs, and watched them with compassion.

'I am Ulysses-the-Bird!' he said after a while, and folded his wings, voyage-wise.

Translated from the Romanian by Florin Bican

Albania

Ismail Kadare

The Concert

Mao had a file, perhaps the one he cherished most, labelled 'Letters from the Rice-fields'. In the last few years he'd received letters of every kind from all sorts of people: from prisoners on the eve of execution, from widows, from fallen ministers begging him for clemency, from unemployed embalmers, and so on. But those from the rice-fields were the only ones he enjoyed looking through again from time to time. They were from writers deported for a period of re-education in the provinces or in out-of-the-way villages. 'Thousands of us here in the water and the mud thank you, O God, for delivering us from the demon of writing . . .'

Mao liked to get out the file and compare recent letters with earlier ones. He noticed that they grew more and more scrappy, their sentences thinner and thinner, akin to the dullness of the earth. Lord, he thought one day, soon they'll only be sending me senseless ramblings like the blatherings of someone with apoplexy. And after that I shouldn't be surprised if one of them just dispatches a piece of paper smeared with mud, a few scattered characters like grains of rice miraculously left behind after a flood.

He smiled at the thought of it. Then he *could* be said to have got the better of the writers! He'd always felt a deep aversion for them, but after he married Jiang Qing, and especially after she began to get old, his dislike had become almost unbearable. He knew, as the foreign press had recently reminded him, that she was influenced by her past as a third-rate film actress, and the jealousies, failures and permanent humiliations she'd undergone, though she probably hadn't told even him about the worst of them. He knew or could imagine the real reasons why this belated settling of old scores had become an obsession with her, but as it chimed with his own ideas he didn't disagree with it. One day he went so far as to tell her so.

'You're an out and out egoist, and it's a personal matter with you. I'm a poet myself, but I don't hate other poets out of jealousy or spite. It's because they do harm that I can't stand them, not out of any personal animosity. And when I've got rid of them all I'll even feel a certain regret, as one might after having to pull up a beautiful but noxious weed. You, on the other hand . . . But you're a woman, so I suppose one mustn't be too hard on you . . .'

He well recalled that unforgettable July night in Shaoshan when they'd sat up till dawn talking about the future of the world.

It was an oppressive, damp night, stifling the end of every sentence into groans. They'd both been excited at the thought of the world of the future, purified of art and literature. 'How marvellous it will be to purge the world of such delusions and unhealthy emotions!' she had cried, though she cracked her knuckles with a certain amount of apprehension. She knew it was a difficult task, and kept asking him, as if for reassurance, about the chances of success. He duly reassured her, and she replied, almost as if she were actually drunk: 'And music too – on another night such as this we'll rid the world of that too, so that the whole planet is as deaf as a post!' The theatre, the novel, poetry – they were all to be dealt with in the same fashion. The only subject left for the imagination to work on – she didn't say this explicitly, but he could guess what she meant – would be their own two lives. Or rather hers. And was it such a wild idea, after all? What other woman since Creation had had the leader of a billion men for a husband?

All these things could be brought about somehow or other. Autos-da-fé had been common throughout the history of mankind, and it was quite feasible to close theatres, smash pianos, drag thousands of writers through the mud, and even return the human brain to a less complex state and make the imagination wither away. These things were all interconnected: the elimination of one brought about the destruction of another, just as the fall of one beam can lead to the collapse of a whole roof. But there was still one thing more difficult to dispose of than all the rest. Twice, almost trembling, she had asked him: 'What about life itself? What are we going to do about what people call the good life, with its after-dinner conversations, and love . . . ?' More out of fear than anything else she'd had to make two attempts at explaining what she meant by love. After much beating about the bush she'd finally brought it out: she was talking about love in the usual sense of the word – the relationship between men and women. Mao had listened to her in silence, then, with the same deliberation as before, he explained that all the aspects of life she had referred to, not excepting love itself, would eventually fade away. After-dinner conversations would disappear, if they hadn't died out already, for the simple reason that there wouldn't be any more dinners (you couldn't describe a mere bowl of rice as a dinner!). As for love, that was only a question of time . . .

Except that his ideas were untinged by any personal ambition, their views had recently tended to grow more and more alike. True, Mao had been very much in love with his first wife: when he dedicated one of his most moving poems to her, Jiang Qing had responded with hysterical tears. But in the course of the last few years his opinions about love, as about a number of other things, had changed.

Jiang Qing, glad to see love relegated at last to a place among the other undesirables, began to talk more passionately, more fanatically even, than before, for hours and hours during a night which he would always remember as *hers*. She whispered in his ear that love was their personal enemy (she no longer bothered to call it the enemy of China or of the Revolution), as ruthless as the rest and in many ways more unrelenting than they because more insatiable. She maintained that this wretched relationship between the sexes used up a large part of the world's total resources of love, thus depriving him and her of their own due share: it hijacked the love that should rightly come to *them*, she went on tearfully. Again he interrupted her calmly. 'Don't worry, Jiang Qing,' he said, 'love will be abolished too.' And he explained that love wasn't as powerful as it might seem: it hadn't even existed until comparatively recently. In the ages of barbarism it took the form of mere sexuality, and even in classical times its affective content was limited. It was the European Renaissance that had fostered the disease and turned into the most widespread epidemic in the world. But the winged monster would eventually die as rapidly as it had been born, after having already said goodbye to the things that had nurtured it – the arts, literature and all the other nonsense. He described the various stages of the war to be waged against it: the first thing to do was reduce love to what it had been before the Renaissance. The second phase would deliver it a fatal blow by reducing it to sexual relations pure and simple. Thus the danger would be, to all intents and purposes, eliminated. 'But how long will it take, for God's sake? How long will it take to finish it off?' she asked impatiently, almost in anguish. He had given her some sort of limit, he couldn't recall exactly what, but he did remember her sighing because she didn't think they'd live to see it. Soon afterwards, when he first heard of lovers in Cambodia being summarily executed after being found talking about love instead of politics, he'd reminded her of her sceptical sigh that hot damp night . . .

They'd talked till dawn, that strange summer night, discussing subjects that had probably never been debated since the world began. 'Anything that might encourage love must be abolished,' she murmured. 'Women's shoes, jewellery, dresses, hair-dressing . . .' 'But we've done that already, practically!' he answered. 'Such extravagances haven't existed in China for a long time.' 'Not in China, perhaps,' she complained, 'but we must look much further – the rest of the world is full of them!'

Then she suddenly stood up and went into another room. After a while she came back wearing a uniform that was half military and half more like that of a prison warder. For a moment he had to shut his eyes: he couldn't stand the sight of her got up like that, with that wretched cap covering her sparse hair, those trousers clinging to her body – it was horrible, as if there were nothing left of her, not even bones. He was well aware why she adopted his ideas on the reform of mankind so eagerly, but seeing her like this he realized she would go on trying to translate that dream into reality until she died. 'From now on,' she whispered, 'I shall dress like this not only when I'm with you, nor even just at meetings of the Politburo, but everywhere – in public, at the big parades in Tiananmen Square, and even at official receptions, under the very noses of the foreigners.' Her words convinced him that if her sacrifice was going to be complete, the reward she expected would be no less so. I must be careful, he thought: this woman is consumed with ambition. But she shall have her reward! He couldn't remember very clearly now what he'd actually said at the time, nor even what he'd thought. No doubt he'd made a few half-joking, half-serious remarks: 'As you faded, so beauty too faded from the world'; 'The world must mourn for your lost youth'; 'It's not you, but the world, that has grown old' – that sort of thing. And: 'I once heard of a book about a young man whose face remained unchanged, while the effects of time could be seen only in his portrait . . . Someone must pay for the passing of your youth, Jiang Qing. All the women in China aren't enough for you? I knew you'd say that! Very well, let all the women in the world pay, then!'

He reminded her that some women in Europe thought as she did.

She listened eagerly, feverishly. 'Some women,' he said, 'have lost no time in adopting my ideas, even in the heart of Europe, in Paris – people call them Maoists. Don't you think that's wonderful?'

'Of course,' she answered, 'but there aren't very many of them – just a drop in the ocean. What a task it will be to change all the others! Perhaps it would be a good idea to start with the women in Albania? The alliance between our two countries would make things easier.'

'Yes, you're right,' he answered. 'That's what we'll do. The Albanian women will be the first ones in Europe to be de-feminized. I'm told they managed to throw off the veil after being forced by Islam to wear it for five hundred years. But we are much stronger than Islam!'

Translated from the French version of the Albanian by Barbara Bray

Mimoza Ahmeti

The Secret of my Youth

She had a rather curious name. They called her Eyes. I don't know whether she was given the name at birth, the time at which our parents give us names without taking our wishes into consideration, or whether she acquired it as a result of her big eyes. Whatever the case may be, it is true that those eyes of hers had a sense of perception much keener than normal people could possibly imagine.

I had avoided those eyes for a long time. I could not help feeling a shudder down my spine when I heard someone whisper that her eyes sometimes underwent a perilous disfigurement. Quite normal people, for instance, had complained that they had seen themselves reflected in her eyes as a drop of water. Other people, serious, respectable and admired individuals, had found themselves not reflected, but grotesquely mutilated in her eyes.

No, I certainly did not want to see myself transformed into a monster in the eyes of a girl.

I had taken a decision. Whatever should happen, I was resolved not to let myself be captured by her eyes. But . . . I had taken this decision before ever being seen by them. And, indeed, I was seen by them. Every time I try to avoid something, it homes in on me. Now there is nothing I desire more than to be captured by those two eyes, and this time totally.

I am presently convinced that everything beautiful on earth is an exception, an 'anomaly' of sorts, towards which everything normal or average is attracted, in contradiction to its nature. Yes, and those all-possessing eyes could do nothing other in the essence of their activity than to constitute an 'anomaly'. They offered a precise reflection. Yes, I realize there is an element of illusion in most human reflections. It is perhaps for this reason that knowledge as a process is so long and infinite whereas human existence is so short and ephemeral. Because the reflection in her eyes was so precise, many people were confused by them.

They were the most marvellous eyes I have ever seen in my whole life, the meeting of physical beauty and functional perfection. When I praised her eyes, that is, when I told her I loved her, she replied simply, 'My eyes were not always like that. Experience has made them the way they are.' She had never spoken to me of the particular quality of her glance. Perhaps she regarded it as a matter of course. And for her, it was one. But not for me.

I did not understand that when she observed something, a city, a flower or a face, for example, a certain space in her eyes remained empty. The objects she observed did not always fill her eyes. It could very well happen that any object, however big it might seem, would leave a void in her eyes. This unoccupied space in her eyes she often filled with blue sky or with dreams of the future. Such was her life.

I did not realize either that I was one of the rare human beings (though I doubt very much that I was alone in this capacity) to fill almost all the space in her eyes with my reflection. Almost. But almost is not the same as completely. There was a bit of space left over, a little bit of space, indeed so little that, had she wanted to, she could have filled that little corner with the reflection of a tree or a bird in the spring. But, then, total bliss would have been beyond reach. It was only when her eyes were filled with the person reflected in them, only when no space was left over in them, that bliss could be attained. It was a strange game played between her eyes and her brain. Only now am I beginning to understand why she gazed so long at the sky. It filled her eyes. She loved it.

I allowed my happiness to be jeopardized, the happiness of the two of us. I was incomplete. There was something missing in me, something that created a void, a tiny unfilled hole in the corner of her eye, but it was room enough for a reflection, and by no means the most unusual of reflections: the boon of happiness.

I could not understand, and I thought a lot about it later, why a girl with big, bright eyes should have made such a sacrifice. Perhaps it came about since, though I was incomplete, I was the most complete of all the incomplete persons she had known up to then. I was almost 'the one' destined for her eyes. I was not completely 'the one', but almost. Do you understand now? Is it not terrible? It was simply a question of a little tiny something missing, but something which jeopardized everything.

And so she sacrificed herself. I did not realize that she was constantly reducing the size of her eyes solely to rid herself of that little hole which was always left over beside my reflection. If only she had told me, if only she had mentioned the problem, I would have done battle with myself and, why not, done battle with the others to grow in her eyes, or at least to become sufficient. What a shame! I was insufficient, and I did not even know it!

I did not realize that she was reducing the size of her eyes for my sake. I noticed nothing to begin with. Perhaps she had not started reducing their size at the start, since she was waiting for me to grow, to become 'big'. It was later, when she had given up all hope of my growing, that I spotted the wrinkle in the corner of her eye, a fold in the muscle under the skin which disturbed me somehow.

The days passed. Her eyes became more and more disturbing for me, not in their beauty, but in the way she used them. They had withered, had decreased in size. And all the time, my love had withered and decreased in size. They were not the same two eyes I had caught a glimpse of at the start, eyes which people, both young and old, would gossip about at length. For me they had fallen into a morass of normality. Even worse. They had become devoid of all beauty. Deceptive eyes. That is the impression they made on me.

Anger began to take form within my breast. It looked as if she were making fun of me. And anyway, what significance could my love possibly have without her eyes? My words of reproach turned into insult. I could not understand why she put up with me. Her patience made me believe that I was right. I did not realize, as I now do, how rare, how extremely rare people were who could fill her eyes. I had attributed this rarity to my virtue. How ridiculous! She seemed to realize this and therefore put up with me. I was not 'the one', but I was 'almost the one' . . . So she put up with me.

The more I reproached her, the more patience she showed, and the more her eyes withered and wrinkled, the more their glance grew faint. Finally one evening I seized her by the shoulders and shook her in rage: 'You're lying, you're lying,' I cried out. 'You have ugly eyes, the ugliest eyes I have ever seen. Leave me alone! I've had enough!'

She was stupefied. As I shouted, her eyes slowly opened. To my surprise, they grew big and bright, penetrating and pure, just as they had been when I saw them for the first time, when . . . they were still free of me. I don't know why, but I was now speechless, something stuck in my throat like a bone.

She gave no reply. She departed with eyes revived as I stood there benumbed by what I had done. No, not by what I had done. In reality, I was overwhelmed by the metamorphosis in her eyes. For one moment, a flash of lightning had illuminated the dark clouds of my doubts, a flash which proved lethal to my hardly profound conviction that I had been the cause of the withering and shrinking of her eyes, the most beautiful eyes on earth.

I called her name several times over. You will never believe how hard it was for me to call her by her name: 'Hey, Eyes. Come back, Eyes!'

But it was in vain. She did not return. Having turned her eyes away from me, I regained the place that I deserved in them. Soon thereafter my happiness dissipated. I had been almost complete, but not complete. I was insufficient. The game played between her eyes and her brain was now interrupted.

She had no intention of returning. There was to be no more bliss. Perhaps there never had been. She had created it with hard work by wearing out, indeed by damaging, her eyes. Bliss is the only thing that we have still not learned to appreciate when it is bestowed upon us. A weakness? Perhaps. But because of it, I still feel human in my suffering. I suffer to become sufficient, to become perhaps something more.

Some people say that bliss is impossible, unreal. But I got very close and I know what it is, even though I did not succeed in mastering it. I believe that I can do it, though. I want to take possession of bliss! Let them laugh at me all they want (laughing at someone else is often nothing more than a painful reflection of our own impotence). I want to attain the impossible. I want to be complete. I want to fill those eyes to the full. To attain total bliss.

This is the secret of my youth. One more reason for living.

Translated from the Albanian by Robert Elsie

Teodor Laço

The Pain of a Distant Winter

Each autumn, as soon as the days began to shorten and the forests were covered with a blanket of golden leaves, the man began the long journey to his native village. It was a tiring journey at his age and in his precarious state of health. Neither his wife nor his daughters could understand what attracted, indeed compelled him to undertake the trip. He had begun making these visits at a time when, though still full of strength and vitality, he looked back with pain and regret at the long-gone days of his youth. Eleven years had passed since that day in March. It had been a muddy spring, the time of year before the leaves begin to bud under a clear sky, though one not without a hint of grey from the cold weather which still held sway. He had sold his mother's house for a ridiculous sum of money. It was an old cottage, so dilapidated that had it been left unoccupied for a year it would have collapsed. Up to that day, the spirit of his mother had kept it standing.

He left part of the money from the sale of the house with close relatives to pay for the upkeep of the grave and placed the rest in a savings account. When he married, he used it to buy some bedroom furniture and a refrigerator.

The sale had been a perfectly normal transaction, the kind made by dozens of people, so there was no reason for him to feel guilty. And yet, the muddy spring and spending the money had cast a shadow of culpability upon his soul. This feeling seemed to him to be due less to the sale of the house than to the death of his mother in his absence, for he had been unable to persuade the old woman to leave her village. He was still a bachelor at the time, living in cramped rented quarters he shared with another man, and thus was unable to invite his mother to live with him. But he could have organized his life differently. He could have married earlier, as his mother had wished, found an apartment and invited the old woman to come and stay. Although she was strongly attached to her village, she was even more attached to the prospect of grandchildren. But no one can change the past, and so he had no choice but to come to terms with reality, which he did, though not without a certain regret for that which might have been. He imagined the long lonely nights his mother must have spent in her room all alone, the unbroken silence that must have weighed more heavily upon her than the layer of snow on the rooftops. The day he received the money – proof that the old house no longer belonged to his mother – he was filled with a sense of shame . . . Over and over again he had plunged into a whirlpool of memories and endeavoured to recall the events that first caused him such anguish. Strangely enough, though, his memory had never taken him back to that incident in his childhood of which he had only become aware during his trip the previous autumn.

It had been a long autumn with an ever so gradual transformation from green to gold. There were still warm days like those at the beginning of summer. Indeed the illusion of summer was perturbed only by the autumnal colours and by the rarity of birds. He persuaded himself that, with such weather, it would be a sin to go by vehicle and decided to set out on foot. He had been walking for two hours and still felt full of energy. Like a child he delighted in taking short-cuts down untrodden paths through the long grass and bushes, not knowing if they would lead him back to the road. Resting on one of these paths in the shade of a lonesome fir tree which had not grown quite as high as the others, his childhood seemed to surface out of the past and sit down beside him. There it squatted, insolent and stubborn, and began telling him a story, like a long-forgotten folktale . . .

Once upon a time there was a little boy who was so in love with books that he quite forgot his childhood friends and their games. At night, when the light from his petroleum lamp began to waver and shadows appeared in the dark recesses of the room; as the fire in the hearth, singing an interminable song, crackled and hissed, characters would arise from the yellowing pages of his book and climb into his bed as if to warm themselves under the woollen covers. There was room for everyone under the covers and he could make them do whatever he wished. Robinson Crusoe could climb into a boat with Long John Silver and play hide-and-seek and other games. Slowly his eyelids would close and he would tremble, in anticipation of the dreams that would make everything easy and possible. At dawn, he would abandon his night of wonder with a sigh of relief that he was now awake, and at the same time with a sigh of regret at the knowledge that daytime would be so much more mundane than the adventures of the night.

Gradually, the boy began to read hunched over his books as if to devour every one of the letters that opened to him that wide world full of mystery. His mother scolded him, though only half-heartedly, for her son was at the top of his class in school and no good student could do without books. To please his mother, the boy would raise his head and hold the book at arm's length, but then the letters would begin to move like a trail of sluggish ants, causing the magic to vanish. He was ashamed that he was unable to keep his promise to his mother and, in order not to appear disobedient, he stopped reading while lying on his stomach. His mother would perhaps notice that he no longer drew his eyes to the book but the book to his eyes.

The mother mentioned the problem to his teacher who told her that he thought the boy was a little short-sighted. This disability could be remedied with a pair of glasses, but to get them she would have to take him into town to see a doctor. She had decided to wait until the snow melted, but by the middle of February the boy had begun to suffer from severe headaches. She became frightened. It was clear to her that she could no longer wait until winter was over. She had made the trip from the village into town several times since becoming a widow and was not at all bothered by the cold weather or the solitude of the journey. The only obstacle was the snow, for every afternoon from sunset until late at night there would be a heavy snowfall that covered all traces of the paths. Every morning she rose early and heard herself say, 'More snow again.' She waited a whole week for the snow to stop until she heard from other travellers that the road was clear.

The boy felt a chill run down his spine the moment the path led them into the semi-darkness of the grove of fir trees. He shuddered and felt a knot in his stomach. The forest was large and little light penetrated this far. They were surrounded by silence, like that which reigned in the middle of the night when he waited for his dreams. But the silence was full of sounds, the incomprehensible language of nature which not even the snow could muffle. It startled him, like a covey of partridges beating their wings in preparation for flight. He gasped for air, realizing that the panting that followed him like that of an invisible dog was his own. He glanced at his mother. Her cheeks were red with cold but her face showed no trace of anxiety. He thought to himself that she probably could not hear the noises in the forest. Perhaps there weren't any, after all. But perhaps she was growing deaf in her old age or perhaps the sounds were muffled by the black shawl that covered her ears.

Suddenly, he held his breath and bent forward. He thought he could hear a voice, different from the noises he had been hearing, a voice that sounded like a long howl of anxiety, a lament and a threat at the same time. The savage howl resounded down the bare face of the mountain but the raging storm prevented him from determining quite what it was. Did she hear it or not? he wondered. His mother had stopped a bit farther on and had her back turned to him. He was not sure whether she was waiting or listening. He trudged on through the snow to reach her.

'Did you hear that?' he asked in a strangled voice. His mother took off her woollen gloves and stroked his hair, which was covered in melting ice.

'It was nothing,' she replied.

'Take off your shawl and listen,' he stammered.

The snow, melting under the warmth of her hand, trickled down his forehead.

'Perhaps it was a dog,' she said.

'Or a wolf!' replied the boy.

'Wolves are afraid of people.'

'But not in the winter. They are hungry now, roam in packs, and . . .'

He was about to add that in February the pack follows the she-wolf and that he had heard that a pack of wolves had once torn a hunter to pieces somewhere, but he thought better of it and bit his tongue. His mother must know as well as he that a pack of wolves might be coming their way. She seemed about to say or do something unpredictable. But she said nothing and did not move from the spot. Her face grew pale. There was not a shadow of doubt in his mind that the danger he had conjured up was now a reality and that the evil was approaching with awesome rapidity. Tales about wolves flashed through his mind and, horror-struck, he rushed towards a fir tree standing alone in the middle of a clearing. Its trunk was thick and the first, half-withered branches were high up, but in his desperation he managed to heave himself up on to a solid branch. From here he could see his tracks in the snow below, like those of some slithering reptile. His mother followed him, taking short steps. She leaned against the trunk of the fir tree, resting just long enough to get a grip of herself. He climbed up on to a higher branch, shaking snow down upon her. She brushed the snow from her shoulders without looking up. He felt she was unwilling to look at him. He climbed still higher. From here, he could see the wintry white expanses of the bare forest with a few dark spots here and there. He could not make out whether they were moving or not. If they were not moving, they were probably juniper bushes which had managed to shake off their covering of snow. Otherwise . . .

He listened again, and again heard the muffled howl borne by the wind through the dense fir trees. His mother heard nothing and remained silent. She looked so small and defenceless below him. He was ashamed of himself for having gone so far up and climbed back down to the withered branches below.

'Can you hear anything?' he asked again.

His mother gave no reply. She seemed to shrug.

'Come up here into the tree. It's safe here,' he said.

'No, I can't,' she replied.

The boy could hear the howling again, this time closer than ever. It was not echoing off the face of the mountain but coming straight out of the dark forest towards him.

'Try anyway,' he insisted. 'Here, can you reach my hand?'

'No, I'll never make it,' said his mother. 'Don't come down any farther. Stay where you are, son.'

On hearing this, the boy realized that his mother had no intention of moving from the tree trunk she was leaning against. Even if one of those miracles from fairy tales occurred and the cottage of a woodcutter with a solid door appeared before them, she would not budge from the tree. His hands and then his whole body began to freeze. His lips grew numb and his teeth started to chatter.

'Mother, my hands are freezing. Where are my gloves?' he asked.

'You dropped them when you ran off,' she replied.

She rolled her gloves into a ball and threw them up to him. For a moment, neither of them spoke a word. Absolute silence reigned in the forest. The boy looked up and spotted a squirrel on a branch. It sat there proudly like a host receiving guests. It stretched and shook its bushy tail, sending a shower of snow down on to the boy's face. He wiped it off. The squirrel scurried farther up the tree and a whole branchful of snow tumbled down on to his face. The little animal scurried about, quite at home, with little concern for the huge uninvited guest freezing in the cold down below who could not punish the animal for the chilly dusting of snow on his hair and shoulders.

The wind came up again and he had the impression that it had taken the eerie howling off with it in the direction of the stream. The squirrel launched a pine cone it had been holding in its front paws. He climbed down slowly, his cheeks aflame as if they had been slapped, and the tips of his fingers freezing and aching terribly. The stiffness of his limbs caused him such pain that tears welled up in his eyes. He could feel them turn to ice on his cheeks. He wanted to say something but was incapable of uttering a word. His mother took his hands and rubbed them in the snow until he could feel them again. Neither of them spoke a word.

They continued on towards town.

The boy never did learn whether they had been in great danger that day. He remained quieter than ever for long afterwards, roaming about the house as if searching for something he had lost, but his mother never brought the matter up again.

Many years passed before the anguish of the incident surfaced from the recesses of his mind where it had slumbered so long to burgeon forth into conscious pain.

Every autumn when the leaves began to turn, he visited the grave of his mother in a distant village.

Translated from the Albanian by Robert Elsie

Lithuania

Jurga Ivanauskaitė

Two Stories about Suicides

1
Pranas N. (1958–87)

Pranas N. slunk along the edge of the sleepy river. The thick sooty August twilight soaked through his eyes, nose and mouth. Elastic riverside plants broke under Pranas N.'s soles, crackling strangely, unpleasantly. Suddenly, as if frozen in mid-air, he stopped in front of a blindingly yellow Black-eyed Susan bush. It appeared to him as though illuminated by some faraway, unattainable star. He lit a cigarette. Pranas N. still had the entire night before him. Tomorrow morning, or maybe in a few days or weeks, they'll find him in the river's murky marshes – in the kingdom of vague hope and tolling despair. Pranas N. will have taken on the grotesque pose of a giant fish staring at the heavens with glass eyes (ah, the clouds are so close suddenly!). His blue fists will clutch bloody tufts of grass; dark holes covered with flies (that doesn't occur to him yet) will gape in his wrists. Meadow larks will circle around him screeching hysterically that he has overturned their nests. People will bow their heads, will gaze through their tears at the river's murky marshes, the kingdom of vague hope and tolling longing, at the bloody tufts of grass covered with droning flies in his spasmodically clenched fists. A suicide! Let's bow our heads before Pranas N., who dared to open the azure EMERGENCY EXIT door in the grey wall of our existence! Let's not hide it! Every one of us dreams about it, thirsts for it, desires it! At night, with quivering nostrils, we catch the bitter smell of non-being – with our mouths gaping open, our eyes shut, our ears tensed, we try to catch the silent chirping of emptiness! And always we stop, bathed in cold sweat, our eyes bulging, our palms bloody and painfully cut from digging our nails into our skin, having felt that *we are standing on the edge*! So let's bow our heads, brothers and sisters, before Pranas N., our prophet; the embodiment of our hungry and thirsty longing!

Pranas N. took a deep breath. Casting one last glance at the river's dark waters, he headed through the dew-covered fields towards the cemetery. (Dear Readers, why are some of you smiling? Do you find this ironic?)

Ancient trees creaked and snorted on the hill. Pranas N. breathed in the cool night air. He glanced up at the sky, moon, clouds – they spread like sour milk spilled on a black table top. He felt a blessed weakness – nature never let him down.

Pranas N. pulled open the green-painted gates. They whined softly, sadly. He carefully tiptoed down the footpath, coloured white with sand taken from the river bank. All around him crosses swayed and rustled like tropical plants.

Night covered the angels in their pale blue garments, drooping under the weight of their bright white wings; the Mother of God's blood-coloured painted robes, partly peeled off like the feathers of a moulting bird; the pale wooden faces of saints traced with trails of carpenter ants; proud black, red, and blue marble monuments in the same deep grey. Pranas N. liked the night. It levelled everything, made it equal. Even sparkling nasturtiums in bright orange clusters and sadly mottled pansies were covered with a matt grey pellicle at night. White ceramic plates containing photographs of the dead, fixed on to the tombstones according to the river people's custom, glowed faintly in the grey.

Pranas N. struck a match and gazed at one of the photographs: dark eyes full of longing, set in a perfect oval face; a sad, slightly opened mouth; a heavy braid, a wreath of flowers poised on a proud forehead – oh, what serene peace, how sublime, what beautiful wings, poised in anticipation of that black ascent into the night! When the match went out Pranas N. shuddered unpleasantly and crept into the darkness. Coughing, he approached another grave: a close-shaven head; sarcastic half-closed eyes; an aristocratic nose with gentle nostrils; an ironic smile on narrow lips – oh, what serene peace, how sublime, what beautiful wings, poised in anticipation of that black ascent into the night! The match went out again; Pranas N. was overwhelmed by a feverish anxiety. His hands trembling, he lit match after match and walked, led by the gazes of dead eyes, the subdued smiles of dead mouths, intoxicated, horrified by the bitter beating of wings. Oh, kingdom of vague hope and tolling despair! How beautifully we beat our wings leaving you behind! How beautifully we beat our wings leaving you behind!

Pranas N. lit his last match, then started. There were dozens of graves in front of him – more fog-covered stares, more sombre whispers, more breathtaking, fluttering wings!

Pranas N. froze for a moment and bit his lips thoughtfully. Suddenly he pulled out a pack of cigarettes and set the pack on fire. Running with this strange torch, he rushed from one tombstone to the next, from one face to the next, from one gush of wind caused by the beating of wings to the next. Finally his 'torch' started to sputter and singe his fingers. Pranas N., screaming hoarsely, tossed it to the ground and dived into the pulsating darkness. He was extremely depressed and worried. A tremendous uneasiness took hold of his heart! Those people! The beating of their wings . . . Understand? Of course you're shrugging your shoulders, how could you understand?!

Pranas N. cowered, feeling a bitter wave of horror pour over him. What an irreparable mistake he would have made! Seeing his pale, apprehensive face with its faded features, meaningless eyes, unfeeling lips under a sparse moustache on the tombstone photograph, people would turn away angry and disappointed. A suicide? Ha, a suicide! How can one step through the EMERGENCY EXIT door without leaving behind one's proud, sorrowful image to beat its wings and take one's breath away? Why didn't he think of that before? Now I suppose you understand?

Pranas N. rushed out of the cemetery. But no! Maybe it was just the night?! Maybe in the daylight those maddeningly perfect faces will lose their allure?

Pranas N. turned back. He seated himself on the cold polychrome stone fence and waited for dawn. He leaned back against a damp tree trunk and wrapped his hands around his knees. With his head hanging, he fell asleep and from afar looked like a big, ugly, tailless bird.

The intense sunlight and cawing of crows woke him the following morning. Pranas N. crept out of his pitiful shelter covered with dew-drops, dried leaves, tiny worms and dead ants. Again he slunk along the graves, brushing his chewed fingers across his dew-filled eyes. The smiles and hair on the ceramic plates dissipated into the cool mass of eternity.

He coughed. Jumping up, he ran towards the gates, wildly waving his long arms. White petticoats shone from underneath several elderly women bent over prayerfully before the burning nasturtiums and the quiet God of loss. Murmuring, they escorted him out of the cemetery with their angry glares.

Pranas N. ran down the river-village's main street barely able to catch his breath, choked with tears of joyous revelation. Oh, what a terrible mistake! What a terrible mistake he would have made! You are rejoicing with him, aren't you?! Rushing into his house, he grabbed his wallet, a fresh pack of cigarettes and an apple. He yelled something hoarsely to his elderly mother and ran out. He made off towards the highway. Like a madman he jumped into the middle of the road, waving his arms wildly, bellowing with rage at any car that dared whistle past him.

Eventually a small, sputtering, sickly car picked him up.

'To Vilnius! To the capital!' Pranas N. forced out, choking on his words. After a few indescribably long hours, he arrived in the capital.

He ran down the street pushing the calm, orderly citizens out of his way. In three bites he finished the river-village apple, redolent of his elderly mother. Finally! A foolishly smiling beauty stared at him from a huge shop window. Finally he had reached that magical place which preserves our faces for all eternity! *The photography studio!*

He crept inside shyly. He submissively suffered the photographer to twist his head, tousle his hair, pluck at his moustache, stretch his mouth, lift his eyelids, fold his hands, twist the upper part of his body into impossible angles.

When this photographer was finished with him Pranas N.

headed towards another, then towards another and yet another. Everywhere he went, smiling blondes, healthy, frowning infants, charmingly sarcastic men, newlyweds, idyllic couples, inseparable friends, wonderfully harmonious elderly couples, having made it to their golden anniversaries, greeted him from the shop windows. Pranas N. was seated in worn plush recliners, on red painted boxes, torn motley coloured carpets or coffin-like boxes covered with black velvet. They were either hostile towards him, or sweet, or indifferent, or apprehensive. 'Look this way, don't move, don't blink, soon the birdy will pop out, thank you, you may go.' In this manner evening fell on Pranas N. In the morning he began the entire procedure all over again. Eventually it became his daily routine. At night he would dream the same phrase: 'Look this way, don't move, don't blink, soon the birdy will pop out, thank you, you may go.' He would dream of sitting under the same hot, sweat-inducing lamp.

Soon his room began to fill up with annoying rectangular pictures. They convened under the glass top of his desk, filled his drawers, forced their way between the books on his shelves, lay all over the windowsills, occupied his wardrobe. Neat piles tied together with pale blue or pink ribbons arranged themselves along his walls. Sometimes, when Pranas N. was overcome with sadness, their mean, formless shreds would fly through the window and perch themselves on pedestrians' heads, hats, umbrellas or on the worn cobblestone streets of the ancient city.

In this manner the year flew by. Pranas N. forgot about the respectable, horror-inducing image – the body taking on the grotesque pose of a giant fish, staring at the heavens with glass eyes.

All the city's photographers knew him. From behind their black curtains they'd stick out their heads: 'Look this way, don't move, don't blink, soon the birdy will pop out, thank you, you may go.' It became as routine as a daily cup of coffee.

Soon Pranas N. could no longer sleep at night, sorting through, examining, gazing at the depths of his graceless image, either with Persian ornaments in the background, or a fake forest, or a dingy sky. Yet, for shame, where was that breathtaking, heartrending beating of wings?

'How embarrassing, how embarrassing,' Pranas N. thought. 'How will they, how will you, look at my unfortunate suicide's image on the white ceramic plate? How they will, how you will hide your smiles in your fists, pretending you are just coughing. That poor, poor, suicide.'

Then one day it occurred to Pranas N.! The thought came upon him with such force that the suicide even knocked over his cup of boiling hot tea! That's it! He'll punish them! He'll punish *you*! You use the azure EMERGENCY EXIT doors in the grey walls of our existence! You become the centre of attention and admiration! And he will live without feeling the rustle of wings on his back! So there! You may giggle, shrug your shoulders, wrinkle your noses, but let someone else take on the grotesque pose of a giant fish floating in the river's marshes, staring at the heavens with glass eyes – in the kingdom of vague hope and tolling longing! Let someone else clutch bloody tufts of grass, let someone else's wrists gape with dark holes covered in flies (think about it!), let the hysterically screeching meadow larks circle around you!

Pranas N. feverishly tore his images from the walls; pulled the bundles tied with pale blue and pink ribbons out from under his bed, out of old wooden suitcases, out of dusty cardboard shoe and sweet boxes. He dragged all the gloomy reflections of his loneliness into the bathtub. Piling up a huge sacrificial altar, he set it on fire! Perched on the edge of the tub, he listened and watched the captured fragments of his life drone disturbingly, curl-up and disappear. Then suddenly! Suddenly he saw IT! Something moved, creating a gust of wind which caused the fire to burn even more greedily. Something in the fire was beating its wings! Pranas N. extended his hands towards the fluttering. Oh, where did IT come from? Why hadn't he noticed it before while examining his images during those endless, eternal nights? And where is that scalding, maddening pain in his arms coming from? Pranas N. grabbed his burning left arm with his right, then lost his balance and fell forward into the droning flames.

What maddening pain! How deliriously beautifully I am beating my wings, burning in this singing altar of desperation! Pranas N. opened his eyes for the last time. An infinite number of Pranas N.s

engulfed in flames and eternal greatness beat their burning wings, creating a strong intoxicating wind, causing the fire to expand
　　and expand
　　　　and expand
　　　　　　and expand

2

Danguole L. (1960–87)

All week long that feeling had tormented her. It would pour over her in a sudden gush as she walked down the street, or rode the trolleybus, or sat at work, or stood in line at the store. It would envelop her in the middle of a conversation, while reading, while sleeping, or the moment she awoke. It even infiltrated her dreams. That feeling floated up to her outside the context of time or space. It tore Danguole out of *here*, only to thrust her cruelly back again, leaving her to sort out painfully what had just happened to her. (Danguole, our heroine's name, means 'of the heavens', but that has no bearing on the events described here. It doesn't say anything about the woman. It is simply customary to call people by names and I don't intend to deviate from this tradition.)

At first it seemed to Danguole that she had remembered something extremely important. She'd feel obliged to tear that something out of herself, give it a precise description, find a concept for it, give it a framework, close it up in a box, classify it and stick it next to all her other experiences – real or imagined. Only later did she realize she was trying to remember something that hadn't yet happened but inevitably would. Finally, with unspeakable relief, Danguole understood and described it as *Waiting*.

She'd run to her postbox several dozen times a day expecting a letter (from whom, unfortunately, I couldn't tell you, because she herself did not know). She'd jump as if she'd been scalded with boiling water every time the phone rang. She'd answer with a sonorous yet high-pitched voice. Not attempting to hide her disappointment, she'd speak to her friends apprehensively; those who said something tactless would be hit by a litany of anger, which continued whether the party on the other end was still listening or the phone buzzed off the hook. (After all, she had great expectations. Danguole's heart would flutter if she thought she heard an unfamiliar voice over the receiver. How could one expect her not to be upset, not having anticipated a miracle?) The same thing happened when the doorbell rang. Danguole would lunge to open it; the more sensitive guests (you must agree, not everyone is in tune with the vibrations of another's soul) would be overwhelmed by her relentless sorrow and desperation.

That evening Danguole felt absolutely calm. The painful sensation of waiting for a miracle had subsided. She was certain that if something was going to happen it would happen tonight. And if not, that strange feeling would slowly, slowly, subside, until it disappeared altogether, leaving behind only the sediments of hopelessness and bitterness. Then finally everything would remain as it was. (That is probably how you feel on the first days of the New Year when once again you have to admit that nothing has changed and everything will flow along in the same manner.)

That evening it grew dark quickly. Danguole stood smoking by the open window. She watched as the city drowned in moonlight. It sank like a huge ship burning with a thousand lights and it seemed endlessly strange to her that all the people hid in their cabins (excuse me, apartments) or calmly wandered around the deck, not even trying to save themselves, unconscious of their own tragedy. The moment the last lamp blinked from the city's highest mast, bobbed under and drowned in the moonlight, causing a beehive of tiny air bubbles to rise towards the sky and waves of water to flow outwards in small ringlets, the doorbell rang.

Danguole started. Throwing her unfinished cigarette out into the moonlight, she slammed the window shut and walked into the hallway. Without even checking the peep-hole, she opened the door and let her visitor in. She wanted to turn on the light so she could examine her guest's face, but he said to her in a voice unknown yet somehow familiar: 'Don't turn on the lights. The moonlight is so perfect tonight.'

Danguole nodded her head obediently. The visitor took off his jacket. They both went into the living room. He walked over and stood next to the window, again positioning himself in such a way as if purposely not to let her see his face.

'If you want, go ahead and smoke,' she said. 'I'll bring some coffee.'

Danguole addressed the stranger in the familiar form, even though she was seeing him (more likely, not seeing him, if seeing depends on seeing the face) for the first time.

Her calmness surprised even her. Her heart was not pounding, her hands were not shaking, her voice was not cracking, her legs did not tremble; rather, her movements were light and graceful. The objects in the room took on a weightlessness in the moonlight. It seemed you could rearrange them with your thoughts, gaze, desires.

The visitor was still standing beside the window smoking when Danguole carried in the coffee. Only his silhouette was visible. The moon, now directly over his head, looked like a halo behind him. (This last detail seemed a little funny to Danguole.)

Moonlight trickled through the half-closed window like water through a sunken ship's port hole, only moving somewhat more slowly, babbling quietly. Danguole felt the moonlight rinsing the soles of her feet, reaching almost to her ankles, as she walked towards the coffee table.

Silently she filled two coffee cups, poured wine for herself and the visitor, tore open a new pack of cigarettes and lit one. (Tell me, which one of you would behave this way with a complete stranger, whose face you can't even see, at midnight, when everything is sunken in moonlight?)

Although the silence was not oppressive, the guest broke it: 'How are you doing?'

'As always,' she answered.

Danguole strained to see the visitor's features, then suddenly realized he did not have any! She wasn't frightened or shocked, didn't gasp or jump, more likely she felt relieved. This unfamiliar face (if it's somehow possible to call something that doesn't have any features a face) was completely familiar to Danguole. The face gave off a strange sense of satisfaction, like a clean sheet of white paper on which you could write whatever you thought, or a newly stretched, freshly gessoed canvas, waiting for the first touch of your paintbrush, or an infinite expanse of sky in which you could read your lover's letters whenever you wished. Yet, you could almost see something in that face – faint shadows, which looked like the face some people, especially children, might see on the moon.

While we were examining this face (if it seems unpleasant to you, don't call it a face), the moonlight kept on pouring into the room, reaching the seated Danguole's knees.

'Do you recognize me?' the visitor asked.

She took a sip of coffee before answering.

'I know that you didn't come here to hurt me, rape me, rob or murder me.' As she uttered these last few words Danguole realized that she was not being fair to him, or to herself.

Shrugging her shoulders she turned towards the mirror and gazed at her graceful reflection in the moonlight. She noticed the visitor cast no reflection, but even that didn't scare her.

'You probably enjoy my company?' the guest uttered sarcastically, swallowing some wine. 'You like the irony in my tone of voice, my features, which do not exist, my reflection, which does not appear in your mirror, my shadow, which does not fall on your floor.'

'You're not the devil after all!' Danguole stated firmly (although this statement probably should have been more of a question).

The stranger nodded his head, yet it was entirely unclear what his nod confirmed.

Danguole pulled a chrysanthemum out of a black lacquered vase, broke off the stem, placed it on the table, squeezed the white head tightly in her fist and scattered the tiny white petals over the place where his shadow did not fall. (But then again, all the other shadows of objects in the room looked more like reflections rolling gently in the water. I can even firmly state that the objects in the room did not throw shadows, but rather reflected them in the floating moonlight. Indeed, the objects took on a sort of tangible unreality, a pale luminosity, which normally we are incapable of noticing.)

As Danguole stared at her reflection in the lulling moonlight, she suddenly recognized the stranger. He was her Sorrow.

'This is the first and last time I will come to you in this form,' he said. 'You were waiting for a miracle, and it has happened.'

Danguole shrugged her shoulders and broke the head off another chrysanthemum.

'I wasn't waiting for you,' she said, squeezing the petals in her fist, 'not that kind of a miracle. You are with me always. I was waiting for something else . . .' Her voice trailed off as she strewed the petals downward. They floated off in the moonlight, never reaching the floor.

'No. Indeed, it was me you were waiting for. I know how you search for my features in the face of every person you meet. You search but never find them. You know you will never find anyone who could replace me.' Sorrow leaned back as Danguole flung a handful of petals in his face. Still he continued: 'No one is capable of pushing me out of your life, of taking over your thoughts, emotions, soul, as I. If someone else had come here tonight, someone you thought you were waiting for, the two of you would have talked, maybe even made love, but the next morning, day, week, or perhaps a month later, he would have been chased out of your life. And again, you would run, falling on your knees, back to me, convinced of how weak they all are.'

Her eyes filled with tears. Danguole lowered her head, not wanting her Sorrow to see them; yet the gleaming droplets fell on to her open palm which lay resting on her knee, unnaturally white in the moonlight. Sorrow smiled. (You're right, there are no lips on his face, still, I repeat, Sorrow smiled.)

'You love me after all and are afraid of losing your one true emotion. You believe in your love for me and I believe! What more do we need? I fill that emptiness in you, that looming, screaming abyss which is called loneliness. You never feel lonely when you are with me, but if you leave me for just a few days, spend some time with someone else, the loneliness becomes unbearable. Again you run to me, falling on your knees, convinced of how weak they all are.'

'You're repeating yourself and that phrase sounds absurd on your lips.' She realized how fiercely absurd her own statement sounded, threw back her head and started to laugh loudly.

She finished her glass of wine in one gulp, still laughing, and started to cough.

'You're twenty-seven years old already. You've died of love twice; both times I resurrected you. There's no point in your trying to run away from me. The third time never lies. You won't rise again!'

'I won't run any more,' she answered calmly, clutching several chrysanthemum heads at once.

Sorrow poured himself some more wine, clinked his glass against her empty one, and continued: 'After all, you read somewhere and copied into your diary: love of an idea is stronger than love for another person. Admit it, you didn't really love the other two, even though you died of love when they left you. You didn't love them, but me: my features, which you thought you could see in their faces, my intonations, which you thought you heard in their voices, my thoughts, which you believed were in their heads. They left you because they understood that you were not meant for them, but for me. Now everything is the other way round. You leave and others die of love.'

'Nobody dies of love any more,' she answered, again turning and crushing a chrysanthemum head, the petals sticking to her teary palms.

'Maybe they don't die any more. So be it. But this phrase none the less produces strong currents in your soul. When you heard me say you'd died of love twice already, you felt sorry for yourself and grew even closer to me. Isn't that so?' he asked very, very gently, leaning towards her.

Danguole bit her lip, not knowing whether she should laugh or cry. Her hand reached for the chrysanthemums, but the vase containing the sharp, pointy stems bounced back from her touch and floated across the room. The moonlight already reached to her chest and Danguole stood up. (You must agree, it would no longer be pleasant to sit.) Moonlight flooded over the coffee table and rose to Danguole's waist. The chair in which she had just been sitting bobbed up and started to float away. The porcelain cups decorated with greenery, and their saucers, painted with grey flowers, silver spoons, cut-glass wine goblets, the coffee pot, all floated head over heels deep into the room, where the other things were already suspended in the moonlight.

Sorrow opened the window and more moonlight flooded the room.

Danguole approached Sorrow, gripping the windowsill so that the steady waterfall of moonlight would not pull her under.

'Kiss me,' she whispered.

Sorrow bent down and Danguole saw that his face was not just a pale flat void. His face was made up of a thousand faces: faces she had seen every day in passing, faces she had never seen and would never meet, faces that lived in other people's paintings, music, dreams, imagination, day dreams, which will never appear *here*, faces she loved, said she had loved, faces she had died for or could have loved, faces she had had her doubts about, didn't notice, didn't like, hated.

Danguole felt the cool light touch of her Sorrow. She felt herself dissolving between his fingers as if she herself had been turned into tears, water or moonlight; she felt his reflection in her rippling depths. She saw how she was rising and flowing together with Sorrow out through the open window; she saw how the moon reflected, shone, blinked, rippled in him and in the thousands of open and frozen dams, lakes, rivers, seas, oceans, streams, swimming pools, wells, puddles, dew-drops, eyes and hearts on this earth.

The room was left empty.

By no means do I want to prove to you that Danguole melted in her Sorrow, flowed into him, drowned in the moonlight, flew out (or jumped out) of the window.

But if you're curious to find out how this story ended, try this: some time, in the moonlight, while the cuckoo birds are singing, when the apple blossoms are falling together with the first hail, while burning candles on an unvisited grave on a windy All Souls' night, while wandering over broken-up ice floes on the edge of a river, gently take your own Sorrow by the hand and gaze into his face. Remember, *in the moonlight*! Perhaps it will help you escape, from *here*.

Translated from the Lithuanian by Laima Sruoginis

Valdas Papievis

I'm Going Out, to Buy a Lightbulb

I'm sick of this city! If I cared to look out of the window I'd see how the wind is herding clouds of dust, cigarette butts and shreds of this morning's newspapers through the streets; how people are shoving one another at the trolleybus stop and how once inside the trolleybus they sway down the street, splashing the lower half of the kiosk despite the sleeping newspaper-woman inside it. Slowly it will become evening and it's an awful mess in here. Well, of course, what more can you expect of her – she's lying on that dilapidated couch pulled out of the landlord's woodshed, because we don't own anything ourselves, and is lazily rocking herself back and forth, one leg thrown over the other. A half-empty tube of toothpaste, cap missing, a pile of baby nappies, yesterday's paper and a torn sock lie scattered about the room. Unfortunately, we communicate with one another just about as successfully as these objects do.

'He's crying again, well, what is he crying about this time, he cries and cries all day long and all night, I'm completely exhausted, I'm afraid to look in the mirror, what do you want my little darling, my little sweet pea?'

He looked out of the window and this time actually saw how the wind was herding clouds of dust, cigarette butts and shreds of this morning's newspaper through the streets; how people were shoving one another at the trolleybus stop, how . . . air! Suddenly it was so stuffy in the room. *I need air, you could suffocate in here!* He didn't even realize that he stretched out his arm, that he unhooked the latch, that he pushed gently at the window, and that a blast of wind, along with the stench of petrol and the screaming noise of the city, burst into the room.

'Now you're going to get it! What are you doing?! Are you out of your mind? Do you want to finish the baby off?!' She jumped up and slammed the window shut: 'Psycho!' She bent over the crib: 'Now, don't cry, don't cry.' Picking the baby up, she pressed him to her breasts. 'Your father's a psychopath, your father doesn't know what he wants, what's worse, no one knows what they want, the least he could do is screw in the lightbulb.'

Slowly it became evening. He pulled a plywood box out from under the couch: a torn nappy, a rattle, a bent aluminium spoon or dreams. *Crash – and the lightbulb burns out – and there's nothing left. Crash – and it's dark, and your father doesn't know what he wants, and everything gets mixed up like the objects in this box of useless things: the torn nappy and eternal love, the aluminium spoon and the university. Well now, where the hell is that lightbulb?* He finally found it. Elated to be doing something, he pulled over a table with loose wires hanging out from under it, climbed on top of it and lifted the lightbulb over his head. All he had to do now was twist it into place.

But the glass is so thin and slippery and the thread-like wire inside is so fragile. Crash – two worlds, two opportunities – stay or leave? He unclenched his fingers and watched how, slowly across his palm, touching his wrist – crash! It fell. It broke.

'You did that on purpose! On purpose! Anything to get out of here, just so you can get out, just so you don't have to be here. Why should I have to grunt around in the dark with this child, you'll see, one of these days I'll just leave, I'll run away, all of you should keep that in mind! My little darling, my little sweet pea, I'm exhausted, I can't take it any more!'

He got back down on the ground and pulled the table back into its place. She pretended that she was crying, she'd already learned how to fake it. *But you can't change anything; out of two opportunities you may choose only one, because, after all, you can't be in two places at once, crash! and reality itself solves the problem and that's how it is now, that way and no other way, nobody is to blame – you see, I have to go out.* He put on his shoes, his overcoat and at this moment she looked just like a neglected rag doll.

'I'm going out, to buy a lightbulb.'

It was miserable and empty in the street. Dampness rose from the water. A biting wind smacked him right across the face. It would be an understatement to say it was cold. He walked along the embankment. It was the third day in a row that had been overcast and windy. The city was even greyer than usual and had sunk even deeper into a tedious boredom. He crammed his frozen hands into his overcoat pockets and slowly walked, kicking pebbles, unable to believe any more that anything could be any different: just a pile of nappies in the corner, a shattered lightbulb, a grey day. He kicked an empty bottle and it clattered down the pavement until it plopped into the water and floated off with the current.

That bitch at the juice counter gave me such a dirty look when she opened up the bottle, as if I had asked for a handout! The burning pavement – summer, did it really happen? The trees fainting from the heat, their conquered branches reaching almost to the ground, the green of her dress, just at that moment – green with little white polka dots. 'No, I can't, not tomorrow either, or the day after tomorrow, I've got exams, I've got to study, at the State Library, no, really, I can't, my name is Irena, Irena, well, maybe on Sunday, but then I don't know either, Sunday.' The romantic love story of a provincial boy – Gediminas Castle and the valley of Sventragis, the old city, the hill of three crosses. We'd wander all over the place. In the evenings, when it cooled down, it was so nice just to be on the shores of the Neris – did that summer really exist? Did those evenings really exist? Was that nervousness I felt before our every meeting real? And those long minutes of anticipation, the quickened pace?

He leaned against the guardrail of the cement bridge and stared out at the flowing water. He was always overcome with a strange kind of mourning here, probably for the mysterious short breath of a time that had already passed, which he felt every time he looked at a stream of water sinking in the mist.

I don't know why, but at those times you really feel the need to have a drink – to toss down a shot, let's say for the summer that is past, along with its evenings, for our faded love – just as romantic as this toast for the days that have long since passed, when coming back from my wanderings around town I wouldn't find you sitting by the window, your eyes red from crying – try and understand, I can't be with you all the time, I need to be alone sometimes, everyone needs to be alone sometimes. Your wounded ego, all sorts of accusations, strange innuendoes, and then tons of reproaches: 'What kind of a life is this? This place is a fire trap, it's too horrible to tell anyone about, just look what's become of me, you good-for-nothing daydreamer!' We are what we are and when I lie down I could stare for hours at that sickly lightbulb right above the couch. Love is probably not a pile of nappies after all, not a plywood box full of useless objects, not this dilapidated couch, love is more likely the bottom of the river, and all that is just water which flows above it plunging through those nappies, past those half-empty tubes of toothpaste, past those burnt-out lightbulbs and torn socks, past all that junk, confusion, chaos, in which you drown every day, towards the bottom, towards peace, towards understanding, towards a bittersweet stability, and if not . . . if not . . . You won't find anyone to blame for it, because the reason – the result – is just a burst soap bubble in your grandmother's dowry chest. Often, let's say you're shocked when you realize that you've done something completely reckless unintentionally, completely against your own will, you feel as if you are possessed by some uncontrollable force from the other side and it's completely hopeless to try and figure out why, for example, you broke the last lightbulb, or why, having climbed up the stairs from under the bridge, you turned, as if on purpose, towards the cafés in the old city.

Shoving his hands into his pockets he moved on. Everything was running according to its usual schedule: people were going home from work, it was rush hour.

'A light? sure, no problem.' *The cathedral and the bell tower clock, it's getting even darker. Isn't it silly to believe, every evening, as if it was likely, that you'll meet the Messiah in one of these narrow streets – a prophet who'll help you to find all the answers to the questions troubling you?*

He scraped three kopeks out of the seam of his coat pocket and bought the evening paper: 'Franco's Family Affairs', 'Who is Agitating the Extremists', 'The Moral Position of Man'. A gust of wind jumped up and almost snatched the paper out of his hands. Folding it in half he rolled it up into a tube and stuck it under his arm. Suddenly something occurred to him, started to burn at his memory and then he could no longer run away from that strange mood, from the contours of that pale face, from those long graceful fingers with painted nails – like blossoms glued to her fingertips. All that appeared in front of his eyes in the evening's twilight, thrust through his thoughts like disjointed days or events. It was all so close – right here! He stopped for a moment, opened the newspaper again: 'Who is Agitating the Extremists', 'The Moral Position of Man' – and suddenly an arrow of light pierced his consciousness – *I write on moral issues, I am a journalist, Monika, it's true, I'm still a future journalist, but I've only got two years left, it's nothing, it'll speed right by, it'll fly by, you won't even realize how quickly, you just put one foot in front of the other.' For some reason her gaze had been fixed the entire time on her foot, which she didn't stop swinging for one moment: back and forth, back and forth like a pendulum and again she'd take a deep drag on her cigarette and again in a tragic voice, woven together from a beehive of the most pretentious phrases, back and forth, back and forth: 'It was nice meeting you, here's my telephone number, in case you ever need it some time, some time . . .'*

A telephone booth – clink went a two-kopek coin dropping through the metal slit: 'We definitely should meet, yes, now, right now, in the same café.'

He left the phone booth in a cold sweat – long graceful fingers, a pale face and a sweet surprised voice. *What good will it do – revenge, or maybe a necessary defence against loneliness, anyway, you can't say it won't be pleasant to sit in a cosy café and listen to some old worn-out record; they always play the same ones there; her face, although not entirely new, is at least not the one you see constantly in front of you in the grey of everyday existence.* Then he grew excited in spite of himself at the thought of a new encounter. Without even realizing it, his footsteps picked up speed. *Castle Cross Street. DADA is written in large letters on the wall with a red blotch next to it. You never know where the current of the secret rivers of the subconscious will take you. Inner life can be marked with the symbols of chaos and disjunction, disjunction and chaos – that is freedom, and freedom is disjunction and chaos, of course. Irena would never agree with that, of course, tears, hysterics, a line which divides us, which neither of us will ever be able to cross again.* He kicked a pebble and walked onwards. *Stereotypical thinking, prearranged formulae for life: every self-respecting young man or woman, having dragged themselves through five years of the University (Technical Institute) system finally receives a diploma, a warm spot, the staircase to a career, a nicely furnished little apartment and a cosy family life. Heaven forbid something should go amiss – an artist or a psychopath – 'Your father is a psychopath, your father doesn't know what he wants.' At first it was wonderful, at first it was pleasantly surprising, that you could do it that way – what a mysterious room, what a strange sofa, romantic love had wandered in from the summer's adventures. 'It smells of the past here, the room is redolent of faded postcards, we'll be happy here,' but really even then the writing was on the wall, eventually, in due course . . . Because you need a strong hand that would be strong enough to stop the chaos from spinning in front of your eyes at a dizzying speed and then paint everything in black-and-white stripes and label it: this is good, this is bad; because you need a lightbulb that will never burn out, because you need a roof over your head and your own things – your own; it's a joke, you just take a look at those tired people running out of breath, people trying with the last of their strength to curb the world. It's nonsense, of course, it's not even worth thinking about, in those moments you want to tap some solid elderly citizen over the head or, whistling loudly, walk on your hands down Castle Cross Street.*

Finally he reached the appointed café. Getting up on tiptoe he gazed through the small square window cut into the wooden door. Overcome with a strange feeling, almost as if he had just escaped into freedom, he walked inside.

'A hundred grams of vodka, Russian vodka, and coffee.' The bartender glanced around the corners of the room with his pale eyes, then opened a bottle and poured exactly the amount required, not a drop more. Boredom, twilight and boredom, rose together with the steam from those half-finished cups of coffee, from the empty glasses of dry wine, from the talking in subdued voices. Once he had tossed the meticulously measured one hundred grams down his throat, he took the cup of coffee, found an available seat, which was also out of the way, and pulled a cigarette out of his pocket. *Good thing they let you smoke in here.* An amber light shone from the yellow, almost like turn-of-the-century victims of tuberculosis, faces of the girls seated next to him. They wore tragically worn-out faces, which were tragically fading, and tragically put on an act – tragically tragic in its own tragic demonstration of the display of tragedy. *Monika is somehow similar to them – her long face and fish eyes. 'I write on moral issues,' one leg on top of the other, back and forth and back and forth. Splashes of light, the play of the shadows on the wall, quiet laughter, you can't say, no matter with how much irony you looked at everything that was happening around you, that you don't still feel some kind of a faraway spiritual connection with those yellowed faces, those protruding cheekbones, those tired eyes. Underneath, the mask of sham reality breaks through: the romantic dream which is crushed under the burden of everyday life, that quiet longing.*

He lit his cigarette and took a deep drag, feeling how a faint lightness slowly overcame him. *The devil take it, you talk to yourself as if you were talking with someone completely foreign, as if you had split in half, doubled, one half here, the other there – somewhere on the other side, in the fog, in the mist, in the haze, far away and unreachable, hiding in the rivers of the subconscious, everything goes just about this way: a carefully put-together mosaic, crash – and thousands of pieces of glass break on the cobblestones, a pile of nappies, a torn sock, unfortunately, a plywood box full of useless objects. Of course, it's best not to think about it, forget it, is it important? – Monika should be here soon. 'I am a journalist,' eyes the colour of ash and long eyelashes; 'we definitely must get together,' well, and what can you say to her, a fireworks display of a beehive of the most pretentious of statements and one leg thrown over the other, back and forth, back and forth – like a pendulum.* Suddenly he shuddered; a chill ran down his spine. *What is Irena doing here? Irena, bending over the crib, stretching out her arms towards the baby, cuddling him to her breast, she was prettier before she got pregnant: 'my little darling, my little sweet pea,' up and down, go to sleep, fall asleep, child – she swings him back and forth, up and down.* The coffee cup came crashing down and he pushed his chair back noisily. Surprised yellowed faces; in the doorway.

'Where are you . . . ? You called me, after all!'

'I'm sorry, I really . . .'

He found himself sitting in a neglected park. The bench was wet – it was drizzling. *Idiot, idiot, idiot.* Only old people and bums came here – across from him sat an old woman chewing her cud and pulling scraps of bread out of a dirty cloth bag. A flock of pigeons milled around her feet shod in old, untied men's shoes. *Idiot. Back and forth, up and down. It smells like urine and unwashed socks. I've got to go. I need to find a lightbulb. Just try and find one now, when it's already dark, when it's drizzling, when all the stores have closed long ago and the city is so empty. Unless you climbed up a pole and unscrewed one, unless . . .* He stopped and threw his head back: a halo of bluish light pulled large drops out of the evening sky, they fell slowly on to the ground. *It couldn't be raining. It's a joke, of course, the lightbulb, ruined hope.* He pulled his collar up, shoved his hands deep into his pockets and walked on, trying not to think about anything; trying to make the place where his thoughts came from turn into a puddle and be empty.

He walked through the empty city and at a distance looked so shrunken and lonely. Every once in a while he kicked some small pebble; every once in a while he stopped and gazed through the window of some souvenir shop – it seemed cosy and warm inside. Throwing back his head, he saw the silhouette of the Cathedral of St John's loom up into the darkness; beside it stood the bell tower, the great courtyard. *I studied there once: lectures, seminars, professors, everything is in a fog now, the road through the back and out and Irena stumbles in crying – who else but Irena – 'I told you, I told you it would turn out this way: skipping classes, you lazy bum, you good for nothing, you spend all your days on the sofa!' Just don't try and dramatize everything, everything is really a lot simpler, an aluminium spoon and the university. A fly was crawling around the windowsill and unexpectedly got it right there, crash, there, it's been squashed, and nothing more, just squashed, let's think globally. Let's think globally – aspirin, that you drink down with water, immunity towards all sorts of tablets, unfortunately, though, no immunity towards contradicting reality. What happened in the café, that was idiotic. One leg thrown over the other, go to sleep, fall asleep, child, after all you just pretend to be faithful, jumping rope in the unkempt square in the Old City. Who is stopping you from crossing the line, who is stopping you from whistling loudly and walking on your hands down the main street of the Old City and why not, after all, one day tell her and yourself that everything was over long ago, that it blew up, broke, spilled out, floated away, glided past with the wind and the garbage through the streets. The baby was our last hope, both of us are crazy, for the time being the only thing holding us together – which later will fly apart into a thousand threads – woven together, knotted together, one with the other, an unrepeatable tapestry, the wonderful harmony of two souls, a joke, childish dreams, a red lump screaming on a pillow, sleepless nights, Irena's world begins and ends with him. It's like a play: you stand over there and I stand here and between us is this infant – a part of you and a part of me, and beyond that everything is very funny: you stretch your hand out to me; I stretch mine out to you, but they never touch, you want to tell me something, I want to tell you something, but we never talk sincerely with one another, you want everything to be all right and I want everything to be all right, but everything always turns out bad, you could just sit and cry over it or sit and laugh, there it is – a black comedy.*

He ended up in a dark, completely unlit part of the city. The houses leaned together, almost touching, along both sides of the street, leaving only a very narrow passageway between. It began to rain even harder. Long trails of rain looked like live spider webs on the walls – they moved, pulsating, flowing together only to separate, then expanding again, until finally they turned into one long stream of rain pouring down from the top to the bottom. It was raining.

Therefore – a black comedy. He unbuttoned his overcoat, turned his face towards the rain and walked on. Not a soul was out; he threw his soaking wet cigarettes into the gutter. *What can you do, sit and cry over it, sit and laugh. The lightbulb – light.* Fiat lux! *As if on purpose – it's dark, you could poke someone's eye out.* Then he suddenly came to a halt, leaned against a telephone pole, ran his hand through his wet hair, over his face; looked ahead of him again and started to giggle. He hugged the pole with both arms, threw his head back; streams of rain fell painfully on to his face, then flowed over his forehead, through his hair, down his neck and he just kept on giggling like a madman: *isn't it funny, isn't it funny, isn't it idiotic – a wall.* He approached the wall and leaned against it with both hands – it was wet and rough. There was a wall across the street too! He giggled like a madman, giggled like a madman – a dead end. *Wouldn't you know it. Everything is like that. Wouldn't you know it. Of course – it is dark, you could poke someone's eye out, not one light, not one lightbulb, of course it's a dead end.* Slowly he started to calm down. He sank down on to the cobblestones, crossed his legs, hung his head between his hands and sat. *Meditation. Introspection. Self-*

analysis. To hell with it! He felt how he started to shiver. Coincidentally, the cobblestones ended right there in that dead end. *Or maybe not – with the dead end the chain of conformity ends. Of course, now would probably be the best time to go off and wade into a sea of concepts and think, let's say, even about determinism. Aspirin. A plywood box full of useless objects. A river with no bottom. A dead end.*

He started to see tongues of light sliding across the wall. Jumping up, he pressed himself against the house. A car screamed through the narrow street. It stopped for a moment, drove into the yard, turned round and moved out on to the street again and stopped. A middle-aged man climbed out of the car, threw a raincoat over his head with one hand and in the other carried some large object wrapped in newspaper. The man ran, hunched over, to the closest building and disappeared into the stairwell without even closing the door behind him.

His head spun. The street, the apartment buildings, suddenly moved; it seemed as if the whole block had quivered and was melting in water, pulsating contours; only streams of rain continued to cut across his face. *Is it my feet? Or the echo of my footsteps? Or is it the beating of my heart – it was as if a train were passing by and there was nothing left, just the drops of rain coming down, just . . . just . . .* Again the houses of the Old City were dislocated by the rain – now they were even larger, even more threatening. Again they jumped up into the air. It seemed every second block had given a jolt and was slowly swaying down. Already pieces of brick were peeling off the walls, everything was shaking and smoking. *Got to get out of here, got to get out of here!* He didn't even realize how, but he was already inside, already leaning over the steering wheel, *think globally, calm down, don't worry, cool it, cool it, child, this is it*, and the car jumped forward and glided through the narrow street; through the rear view mirror he saw a man helplessly let his arms fall to his sides, then run a few steps forward and collapse face-first on to the cobblestones. Then for a third time everything jumped up into the air and started to fall: *coming down, smoking, a crazy whistling, noise, thundering, fear, faster, faster, let's get out of here.* The car wheels no longer touched the cobblestoned street, gliding the car through the narrow tangled streets – a turn in the road, another turn, a third turn, this time to the other side, finally screaming, the car jumped out into the main street of the Old City. The brakes squealed, the steering wheel lunged; he pulled the steering wheel back and again, howling, flew onwards. Twinkling lights merged together into one ball of fire: faster, faster, traffic lights, a yellow light, yellow, an old woman jumped aside like a frightened cat, she even dropped her bag, a curve. The world turned into a crazy spinning chaos of sidestreets, streets, prospects, trolleybuses, store windows, faces, lights and shadows all falling together – everything just glided, spun, fell apart, screamed as if the property of gravity had suddenly ceased to exist. Finally he reached the suburbs. On a road straight as an arrow he pressed the gas pedal even harder. The windscreen wipers beat back and forth, rhythmically pushing off streams of water; the car's headlights reflected off the bushes, trees, road signs. A curve! The car went out of control, steering wheel, steering wheel! It slid along the very edge of the road and glided onwards. *Irena, Monika, the baby's screaming, a half-empty tube of toothpaste, leave or stay, it fell, it broke, I'm going out, to buy a lightbulb, we are fishing in a well of darkness, we are searching there where there is nothing, waking up in the morning we ask one another where we were? where we came from? here? here? where? We are so lonely, so foreign to one another, we are looking for that thing, which can change everything, let's say, the lightbulb, let's say . . . everything is, by the way. Then you grow tired. That's how everything ends. A dilapidated couch. A plywood box of useless objects. A car flying into the night.* He saw a railway crossing and shuddered when he saw how the guardrail was coming down, when he saw how he wouldn't be able to stop in time, when he saw how a shiny train made a beautiful arc around the bend in the tracks. In one blink of an eye, one sigh, he pressed the accelerator to the floor and the train was right there – puffing, howling, snorting. With a sudden jolt the train tracks, the screeching of tyres, the grating of metal, the hissing of past and future time, the beating of the heart – a noise capable of breaking one's eardrums – a body tearing itself apart on all sides, grinding everything into one – clanging, howling, the screeching of brakes and a car – skidding across the asphalt, a car, finally stopped alongside the road. Collapsed on to the steering wheel, he heard the train wheels thunder off into the distance.

Slowly he opened the door, climbed carefully out of the car, touched the ground with his feet. He staggered over to the edge of the road, jumped over the ditch, threw his head back. The rain was stopping. Large wreaths of trees, it seemed, had jumped and separated themselves from their trunks and swung, rising high up towards the sky, floating like clouds. You could hear how their thick branches made a noise, how their leaves snorted, how drops of water slid down their leaves, how the leaves came crashing down, meeting with other drops, you could hear a stream of water babbling under your feet; how the ground drank the streams up and how it rejuvenated the earth's wilted grass. He hugged the old tree trunk, looked up at the sky, listened to the water, tried to feel what was beyond that trunk, beyond the sky, beyond the water, beyond eternal repetition, the combination of all things, beyond not being able to exist without one another. *What is it that we don't have, that we absolutely cannot live without? So the search for the end of the thread begins again. It's like fishing in a dark well, because, after all, the thing you call a lightbulb is not a lightbulb at all, not a lightbulb at all. And again everything starts all over again from the beginning, and so on and so forth, every day.*

Translated from the Lithuanian by Laima Sruoginis

Latvia

Andrei Levkin

The History of Yellow

Weighing heavily on our hands, their weight sinking into our hands, objects and things, the usual baggage on a journey interrupted by changes of transport: three stations, four stations; a landing stage and a harbour at the other end of the crossing; another sixteen stations, a hitched ride, a city bus, battered from taking everyone to the station; in torpid sleep legs jut into the aisle of a third-class sleeping wagon or an arm hangs from the side bunk into that same aisle; a journey with lamps in a window, lack of boiling water and hence of tea, vodka for fifty roubles from the conductor, at the price of the summer of 1991, lack of water in the carriages, washing one's head in the morning in the toilets using half a soapdish as a scoop; past log buildings, past concrete slabs made incomprehensible by the rapid jolting, and the plaited railway bedding dangles again in grey triangles from the top bunk onto the lower bunk.

Somewhere around Kineshma the cigarettes run out, so taking advantage of your femininity I send you to the end of the carriage to cadge some more off some fellow or other; a fellow – me – following you one and a half minutes later so that you wouldn't have time to smoke it all, I see a soldier in an unbuttoned jacket, a green shirt, unbuttoned, tie askew, epaulettes slipping off his shoulders, he rubs his back against the wall, gabbling full tilt as if that helped: at least relating his life story, which he does, finishing it around Vyshnaya Volochka, getting out at a local station where again there are oily lights among angular shadows, a heavy building, probably a warehouse, and the heavy humming of hidden, definitely military, machinery, as if this were the very spot where the weather is controlled for military purposes – given that he is a soldier – leaving us his left-over cigarettes of which, alas, none remained after his long confession, so that you had to be sent to the other end of the carriage to repeat the story, while the soldier who had got out moved away towards the epicentre of terrestrial noise that controls the weather, which usually has nothing to do with us, but where bunkers are stacked with fogs, cyclones, typhoons, sandstorms escaping vertically from the shafts and they may still catch up with us at Samara, at Nizhni-Novgorod, where we take the bus from the train to the landing stage for the voyage towards Kazan.

There, having shaken off the railway carriage detritus, we hang around the ship's stern, growing damp and cold on the river, not understanding why the wheels have grown softer so that the sound of their rotation has become liquid and jingles like tin and the soft jolts are nothing like those that made us feverish from Sankt-Armalyk to Novoskotoprigonevsk with the perpetually empty corridors between Krasnoselsk and Dneproderevensk; this is not a train, there's a bow-wave behind the stern and the jolts don't jolt each other, but are like spasms and force one to break off in mid-word, which is bad, but on the other hand it is damp and good and on the slopes of some hills totally overgrown with shadow one can make out rare, supercilious and, one might even say, useless lights and some strange-looking dark objects, as if it were night in the Lychakovsk cemetery in Lvov, where a dip in the landscape is filled with lamp-lights and I ask you: How did we get here? Where? – you ask, perhaps, and we lapse into thought.

Apparently we are between Nizhni-Novgorod and Kazan, my navigational system is incapable of a more detailed account; all in all it looks like we are in a bad way because we have been travelling a long time, so long that it is already hard for me to understand who you actually are, which no doubt works the other way round too.

Another thing is that because you are a woman you can permit yourself not to look round at the slightest pretext, since you are not travelling independently but with a man who should therefore be able to distinguish, at least by name, the town of Ekaterinburg from the towns of Ivano-Frankovsk, Stanislav and Opochka; we seem to be heading for Gatchina, although the route chosen is definitely roundabout.

When we get to Lvov, if we get there, things will go completely haywire: not to mention the Lychakovsk cemetery, which we will not reach even in summer, it's the sort of town where there won't even be water or tea or cigarettes; every visible thing around will again be yellow, although a nobler colour than other such colours of that colour, characteristic of journeys – including various types of national flag and the colour of the pillow-case and the rouble for bedding and the usual lights behind the heavy warehouse and even the colour of a little plant in the small front garden of the station masters' wooden houses – these are generally beautiful colours; and also the colour of passengers' faces asleep on lower bunks, that is, on the first or unevenly numbered ones, jolting, thundering across bridges: noticing, half asleep, that they are fast asleep below, I stretched out my hand between the bunks and touched you lightly, pushed you as if becoming part of the jolting – you said nothing but, pulling back your arm, turned from the window in which you had seen us crossing the river down which we were floating from Nizhni to Novy, you turned away, pressing yourself to the wall, simply pressed yourself into it, why I didn't know, and I got down, that is, climbed down or rather just crashed to the floor, and went off somewhere, to the end of the carriage, having discovered some drinkers who, around dawn, worked out that we were already in the Fastov region, heading towards Vinnitsa, from where a further journey would involve Odessa, which in no way entered my plans and hence one should have got out long ago at Grodno in order to turn back – since we needed Gatchina and in the morning, ending up on a seed-spattered platform in the early yellow of the railway sunlight, I asked you why you turned away from me and you answered that you didn't.

In this way both of us disliked Chelyabinsk. You neither wanted to know me nor see me nor touch me, nor even think of the same thing, not to speak of conversations – even about where we had to go and why. I went to the buffet, bought a strange and very sad fish on a piece of cardboard, we ate the fish and felt easier, then you fell asleep on a bench until the regular train came which would take us to Oranienbaum, strictly avoiding such disgusting places as Kakhovka, Cheboksary, Nezhin and Ust-Ilimsk – where there are perpetual blizzards and we are in our summer travelling clothes, that is, dressed any old how, which in general is unimportant, all the more so since I no longer understand who you are, what your name is, where you came from and why, although it is also unclear where I came from and what you need me for, apart from ending up in totally incomprehensible Pustoshka, in order to do what there? In the end it's not my fault at all if I get on your nerves, since for all that you don't take off somewhere, and now, having landed up with me at an empty local station between Volokolamsk and Kolymyiya, where there's not even a bench with arm-rests or a back, where it is deserted, a cock crows, a wicker fence creaks, dust rustles on the road, and you are left with nothing to do but lean against me while we wait for the regular mail train with its patriotically coloured carriages, and to fall asleep in the lowliest possible manner, fitting our bodies against each other in such a way that one might think a common, virtually combined mind were babbling the same thing, so that in half an hour you no longer even hated me and smiled faintly in your sleep.

Then it will be quiet because our ears will have grown tired of listening to the railway, various stories, bottles rolling across the floor; swollen lips will no longer be able to carry on either about love or offence: everything finished long ago, only for some reason it continues travelling, if only in search of one decent place on earth, some sort of Irkutsk, Yaroslavl, Kostroma, which, should they appear en route, would turn out not to be them but Peremyshl, Voskresensk, Sergiev Posad, Pavlovsk, Ustyug, Krasnodar, Tagan-rog, Oryol, Smolensk, Avtozavodsk, Industrialsk, Krasnoufimsk, Ust-Labaz, Bishkek, Amu-Darinsk, Volobuevsk and many other names, where we get so lost that there's nothing left for you to do but have a smoke with me at the end of the carriage as usual, leaning on your elbows, resting against me; although I now have no idea who you are, because I have seen you so many times that again it is hard to understand where you have come from, travelling past the usual warehouses, station masters, gasometers, uncoupled rolling stock, and so we'll stand for some time together in warm, crumpled clothes and stand rocking, stand sleeping among short words, either our own or addressed to us here, where again it is night outside and there is a total lack of Pechora, Oranienbaum, Blagoveshchensk, to which, to be honest, I have no desire to go.

Upper bunks, you, we, electricity trembles and we fall asleep, not having understood anything apart from the nature of the colour yellow which creeps into every hole and gap, giving the impression that it embodies something very important, although it is too untidy, but on the other hand, at least useful, moreover warm, smelling of an over-heated iron, and it likes us a little too much and continues spouting smoke even when we fall asleep and burns when we wake up – not, however, because we have finally arrived somewhere in the morning and the clear air, in a deserted, enclosed space, which is tranquil and unjolted, but somehow or other, in the night, because of the conductor's mistake, let's say, he having misread what he wrote on our tickets – what could we have understood, half asleep?

Once again we are somewhere in the area between Vologda and Orsha, again there is some sort of ginger-painted waiting-room with its already subdued, flat yellow colour and its bent plywood chairs for waiting, also yellow, its aluminium painted stove in the corner of the waiting-room; everything is set up in such a way that each separate space for separate waiting travellers is separated from the next by a pipe, metal, also bent, and we cannot even fall asleep in the heat until the next mail train which would take us out of this room with its ceiling that's too high, where – because of the echo – we cannot talk and once again everything seems, if not bad, then not good, and you go off to the side of the stove, spread your arms and begin to cry, and what can I do? I go out onto the street – not onto the platform but onto the street – walking almost past you because the stove stands next to the exit, lean against some peeling stucco column and have a smoke, looking out into the small night of a town in summer, a regional or even a provincial centre like Pskov, knowing that behind my back you are crying against the stove, and I can't even approach you – because firstly I don't have the strength; secondly I haven't finished smoking; and thirdly the waiting-room is a public place, yes and what would I do once I'd approached you?

Anyway, why did you turn away from me then, somewhere in the Slavyanogorsk area? Why did we stand dully on the stern of the little steamer for eight hours until we arrived in Astrakhan? as if

Astrakhan were something that . . . and why, once again, did they turn us out now at night? Finally, what can we do at night in this still unsleeping town of Saratov, if it really is Saratov, with the night heading towards morning, and you are actually standing by a cold stove and crying? Why does it smell of burnt bones here as in Vinnitsa? Where does this dark water in front of us come from as if this were still St Petersburg? Why is this fellow in search of handouts grinding out 'Ramona' in such a mechanical Muscovite fashion on the accordion? And where, in the end, do all these town wires stretch away to, and when is the next train, and is it really you, left behind in the waiting-room, are you still crying, going from the stove to the window-pane, and what can you see through it?

That is, of this alone I am convinced – because, turning round, I see you at the window-pane, pressed against it for some reason, in the, of course, yellow, square yellow window that seems to be pestering you, behind your back, that is – it, yellow, behind us, that is – already behind us, that means, we've escaped from it all the same, it means nothing to us now – although this has come to mind now if only in these words.

Translated from the Russian by Michael Molnar

Andra Neiburga

Mousy Death

You (or perhaps me? – what's the difference, we feel and live together, but if that isn't so, then you'd better not read my story) – you're waiting for a trolleybus, but there hasn't been one for ages, and once again you remember that poor mouse, the mouse in the mousetrap. Trivial but nasty – the mouse got caught in the trap during the night or early in the morning; thus ended the mouse's misfortunes, but yours had only just begun. You noticed it while you were getting breakfast, well, let's say – you opened a tin of sprats in tomato sauce, the fifth in the last two days, you're a busy woman and are unable (or unwilling) to keep queuing up for anything else. You had just washed, perhaps, even had a shower, which is unlikely, because you haven't got a bathroom, or you have one but it's shared with the neighbours, whose whole family is already queuing up outside the door, if they happen to be spotless folk, and if they don't, then they made such a mess of the bath last night that you haven't the slightest wish to go in there. To simplify things, let's say that you haven't got a bath, because it's easier for me to imagine a person living without a bath; a person with a bath is probably already inhabiting a somewhat different world from mine, and I have difficulty understanding them, for I assume that their thought has evolved somewhat differently (especially if they've had a bath since childhood) and possibly they have more inner freedom and are outwardly more easy-going and, perhaps, even feel themselves to be a little bit of a European, insofar as they can carelessly remark at any time: Oh, it was SO HOT yesterday that I had to take THREE SHOWERS!

So you've washed at the wash-basin and now you are opening the tin of sprats in tomato sauce and then you see the mouse. The sight afflicts you a little since you have a kind nature, you are even

311

sorry for the cockroaches and mosquitoes you struggle against, with variable degrees of success, but you are sufficiently educated to understand that a mouse cannot be allowed to run across the table (your children's allergic infections last year, the medicine it was impossible to obtain, black caviar of which they needed a teaspoonful a day, but you, of course, belong to the class of people for whom that is a PROBLEM), and therefore it is necessary for mice to die, there can be no plea for clemency, life is pitiless and fate inexorable. You remember that someone said something like life is not pitiless, it is indifferent, and you're prepared to agree with that, you suppress your pity and tell your husband of the mouse's death. (I assume you have a husband, and a good one too, it's enough that you have no bathroom, car, dacha, central heating and illusions.) Your husband promises to throw the mouse out after breakfast, you aren't able to do it yourself – its soft grey coat still seems to retain the warmth of its blood, the wire of the trap has clamped its poor rounded little body exactly in the middle, like a cushion, the insides of its ears are pink, the black beady eyes are still gleaming but the tail is already rigid. Sorry, sorry.

You and your husband sit together at the kitchen table with its worn oilcloth whose design can just about be made out as a bunch of grapes, a slice of watermelon and the remains of some sort of entirely unknown exotic fruit – oh, what a day, how nicely it's beginning! You two at the table, you still love one another a little after eleven years of living together (and only a pale, distant premonition, indistinct like the bunch of grapes beneath your cup, murmurs – yet it could have been better . . .). The whole flat, both rooms and the kitchen are yours today because the other family members have already gone off to the seaside where they have rented a little inhabitable shack; instead of six, there are two; unfamiliar and solemn peace and quiet, sunlight sifts into the kitchen through the dusty grey foliage of a lime tree, there is no hint of the dreadful heat that has been roasting the pavement and melting the asphalt and people outside since early morning; at home there is peace and semi-darkness, the muted radio quietly speaks of some sort of poison gas leak at Dubluti, and you relish this moment, relish the consciousness that you have sprats in tomato sauce and soft white bread, even coffee, dark as a black man's belly, real coffee beans, not chicory – I gladly present you with this moment of happiness, I'm not making you think about the laundry and the price of strawberries, or your husband about the girl he saw yesterday on the street. Perhaps it's just at the moment you are pouring coffee that out of the corner of your eye you notice a movement in the darkest corner of the kitchen, by the cooker, where the mousetrap is. You rapidly turn – a mouse. Three times (again) the mouse desperately jerks the upper part of its body, strangely contorted at the point clamped by wire, and you even seem to hear the low blows, muted by its soft grey coat, of the tiny body against the board of the trap. A scrap of dried fat vibrates above the mouse's nose.

– IT'S MOVING! you shout (or whisper in a strangled voice) and pour the coffee into the tin of sprats.

In his eleven years of life with you your husband has grown used to your shouts and your strangled whisper.

– What? he asks dreamily, perhaps he is thinking about the girl he saw on the street yesterday.

– THE MOUSE!

– Come off it – your husband bends over the table to see better and the mouse, in his honour, repeats its awful performance.

– So it is – your spouse turns pale. Probably that is why you run into the room crying, you cry a long while because your working day is unregulated, you're crying firstly over the mouse, then over your husband, over yourself, and then you cry over everything; you don't touch the sprats in tomato sauce again, as if you could! You haven't even got it in you to find out whether your husband killed the mouse, it would only be humane – but no. He's not capable of it, you think, though if there was a gun . . . And it's not clear whether this thought gladdens or grieves you.

After the tears your belly begins to ache, a blunt and monotonous pain; lately this has been happening more and more frequently.

That's what sort of a morning it was.

And now you are standing in the sun's glare waiting for a trolleybus, but it's taking ages. You've somehow masked the traces of tears on your face with the remains of your French powder, three little yellow pills have duped the pain in your belly, you've stuck new plasters on your feet where you chafed them yesterday, you have only just started to forget the matter of the mouse and come to the conclusion that, all the same, life is amazingly stupid and meaningless when you come to think about it, that the end of the world is at hand and that your husband is, all the same (all the same!), not one of the best, and at that point a piercing cry brings you back to reality:

– THIEVES!

A small dark man – only his striped shirt streaks past your eyes – knocks painfully into you and disappears into the swaying crowd of passers-by.

– A-a-a-ah!!! . . . as if at a signal, the people at the bus stop raise their arms, if they are free, and sigh in unison. You screw up your eyes in the hope of spotting him again, but it's too late, an enormous woman next to you swears in Russian, an inquisitive crowd forms a solid ring around you.

– Luk thair, that wumman was robbt?! – the giantess wails and dozens of eyes are turned upon you. You, of course, blush, because you are embarrassed to say that you're not the one who was robbed, and the hefty cow continues her inspired wail about the event, your face is red and wet, the awesome bulk of her breasts rocks with each of her gesticulations, a column of steam rises from her, an odour of sweat and garlic. You smile guiltily and listen to the words of sympathy and only some time later do you hear a timid whisper behind your back – that's the woman who was robbed. She is quiet and hunched, lean and yellow, with a sharp sunburned nose, she huskily mumbles something, from time to time flicking back a lock of greasy grey hair, and looking in perplexity at her empty hands, bending back one finger after another:

– Keys! . . . pension book! . . . tram tickets, sugar coupons! Oh, Lord, for the whole family . . . money! . . . keys! . . . coupons! . . . – the unhappy voice falls silent and nearby – u-u-u – a siren howls:

– Wot annimalls, eh? Fashists!

– Migod, that's what they are! – friendly, glad voices chime in again from the crowd and suddenly it scatters – a trolleybus is coming.

314

– A trolleybus! a trolleybus! – everyone is trying to stand nearer to the edge of the pavement, you screw up your eyes – is it yours? Yes, damn it, it is! Your sight is bad, my dear, just like mine, and this fills me with something like malicious glee, perhaps Olya from next door teases your daughter – 'Your mummy's a blind hen' – and you try to explain to your badly brought-up child that it has nothing to do with nationality if some woman on the street called you 'a blind sheep' in Russian – but the child doesn't want to understand, the child cries. Silly little girl.

Anyway, it's your trolleybus, you're one of the last to squeeze inside and wedge yourself between hot packages bound with coloured silk and dotted cotton. The lean woman with the pointed nose is left on the pavement. What weather . . . Silly child, you think, as long as Granny doesn't let her walk around without a blouse and bareheaded, the solar radiation is awful this year, they even spoke about it on the radio, there are rumours of fatalities, you don't believe the rumours, but even so . . . Even so.

The trolleybus jerked hysterically and jumped forward, you've found yourself an almost reasonable situation, you are standing on both feet, arms at your sides, and trying to drive away thoughts of radiation, these are unpleasant thoughts, radiate-radiate-radiation . . . ation . . . nation . . . And you remember the June demonstration. This thought doesn't calm you either, you feel terror in the pit of your stomach – God knows how it'll all end, how it'll end? – and there's a nasty ache in your belly (you haven't any of the yellow tablets with you). I really don't know how you feel now, we only coincided this day, but not in the past. Were your parents repressed in 1941 or 1949, or were they perhaps among those who carried out the repressions? Did your father serve in the Legion? Or was he perhaps a partisan? Don't tremble, my dear – did he shoot Jews? Or chase children destined for exile to Siberia across meadows of dandelions? And your grandmother – was she in the underground already at the time of the Czar (Jesus, how old is she?), did she survive 1937 by some miracle and in 1943 did she hide the very Jews that your father was, perhaps, shooting? Was she sent into exile again after the war? I don't know, I don't know, history presents so many possibilities, variations – hundreds – I'd better assume that all this had nothing to do with your family, your parents weren't exiled, and you yourself were too small to have killed anyone. And you yourself don't want to get involved in anything. When you see THAT flag at a demonstration, your knees tremble and it seems to you they'll start shooting straight away. You want peace, only peace and quiet. You're pinning some hopes on Gorbachev, and fundamentally on Peters. You are terrified of violence. You don't want to be hit in the face. That is the worst thing you can imagine.

Your belly aches more and more. Oh, God, how much can a person endure? As much as a mouse? More?

– Listen, woman, don't lean on me!

– Ouch!

Yes, you're really nothing but a woman. You're suffering from thoughts that have been tormenting you lately, reducing you to insomnia. They've reduced you to something worse – even with your husband you no longer experience everything you should. You have begun taking green tablets that calm you down when you want to sleep. And red ones that buck you up. When that's necessary.

– Move your bag!

– *Ne ponimaju!*

An enormous militiaman forces his way into the trolleybus and frees a place next to you. You perceive men in uniform as being excluded from the category of human, but the militiaman's breath is humanly disgusting. Why don't they open the roof hatch? Why is the trolleybus standing for so long? What? Another accident? Some air, comrades, let in some air! If there were some victims out there, we could get out for a breather. While they take the corpses away. Ugh, why corpses, perhaps everything's OK. Although there are corpses every day in the city. You crane your neck and stare through the dusty window. You see nothing of interest, only ascertain that the trolleybus is standing outside 'International Friendship'. Indestructible. You first noticed this slogan eight years ago, but your husband asserts that he remembers it from the first days of your marriage. Unlikely! They change it from time to time, don't they? The red light has changed to browny-pink, like cranberry mousse with apple. The trolleybus starts up, and possibly you pass the slogan completely indifferently. Or perhaps this is the moment that another alarming thought occurs to you – strange, you say to yourself, strange. Have I really become an internationalist? And you are troubled by unfamiliar words that are filled with horror – Alma-Ata, the Crimean Tartars, Nagornyi Karabakh . . . One small nationality is threatened with being swept from the face of the earth by the construction of the Tungus Hydro-Electric project. What is this nationality called? You can't remember and this annoys you. You admit with dissatisfaction that you'd be hard put to list fifteen of the nationalities inhabiting the Soviet Union. Inhabiting the boundless expanses of your Motherland. The 'Motherland' that you are taught at school to write with a capital letter. You remember the Estonian you met by chance at a friend's, a handsome fellow, fairly intelligent and polite. Over there in Estonia this fellow founded something informal – the Union of Independent Estonian Youth. What sort of youth was this? What was it independent of? 'Now is se time for us to act. Fe fill act, fe fill liff different' – that is what the Estonian said. Estonchik. (You liked him, it's true – he was young.) Estonians, brothers – that has a ring to it. And Tartar brothers? Russian brothers? Strange . . .

– *Probeike, pozhalusta!*

– You're welcome.

The coloured packet was preparing to get out and you occupied the marvellous position between two seats, the best position in the trolleybus if you don't count the seats themselves.

– He's driving like a madman!

In front of you, under the ticket punch, sits a soldier – officer, colonel, general? That's it, you understand nothing of these little stars and chevrons; worse still – in the cinema you can't tell the difference between Russian and German uniforms . . . You look mournfully at the officer (colonel? general?), at his khaki jacket, studded shoulders; onion, fennel and lettuce protrude from the briefcase clenched in his grasp. Oh, nitrates, nitrites – you think. What should one give a child, and what should one not? All your fellow-workers' children suffer from allergies – hospital, home, hospital. I cannot advise any diet, the doctor told you, and you yourself understand why. Strange, but the doctor's words consoled you. Although your finger-joints continue growing deformed, and it seems to me your neck vertebrae aren't in the best condition either. And your stomach as well . . . m-m-m, it aches, the pest – and you involuntarily frown. Your lungs are done in too (don't object, you know it yourself) from smoking. You, my dear, suffer panic fear of death but take no care of yourself at all. It's the times, you say in justification.

As long as the little girl doesn't start smoking!

One could not say that your train of thought is logical, but I won't reproach you for that. You're feeling bad. And your head is heavy. Perhaps your blood pressure. Perhaps magnetic storms are creating a disturbance. Or the curve of your biorhythms has touched its lowest point. Don't think of yourself any more. Think of something else. Of cosmonauts. How can they manage to be so healthy. Lately one flew in from Riga. What was his name? Sobolev? Samoilov? Again you can't remember, really it's a bad sign. There are some tablets, brown ones, that stimulate memory. I wholeheartedly recommend them.

– Oh, sorry, *atvoinoiet*!

– It doesn't matter.

You like it when people apologize, but this time your 'it doesn't matter' sounds angry because you remembered – next week you have to go on a business trip to Ventspils. For six days. You don't want to spend an entire six days breathing that poisonous red dust that is carried over the entire town from Ventspils harbour. For an instant what you heard this morning flashes through your mind, about Olaine and Dubulty, the Lipaiski atomic power station. Horrible. 'Fe must act.' But you know that you are not in a state to do anything. Except – fulfil your obligations at work, and not even that all the time. When they sent you to comrade N. on archive business, you only put it off for a day because of your family circumstances, and in that time comrade N. managed to die. That offended you. Really, life is indifferent.

– Next stop – Revolution Square!

– Can't this trolleybus go any faster? When there's a metro it'll be quicker. You imagine your house at the edge of a huge pit. Ha-ha . . . The house on the cliff. *Maja uz kraujas*.

'*Das Haus auf dem* . . .' No, you can't remember what the German is. '*Eine verrückte, verrückte Geschichte*,' said Günter Grass when Krupnikov related a short history of Latvia to him. And the graceful lady in glasses from the university history faculty coldly replied: 'HERE we have another point of view on that question.' 'I don't express POINTS OF VIEW, I'm setting out FACTS,' G. G. said bluntly. 'WE see these facts differently . . .' The alimentary canal as iron. Awful what's happening to us. And what else is going to happen? . . .

– Cow! – that was meant for you. That really vexes you.

You notice that it's grown darker in the trolleybus. Is it going to rain? You are afraid of rain – after Chernobyl. It seems that is called radiophobia. You very much hope that Granny won't let the child run out in the rain, bathe in the sea, won't let her eat cucumbers with their skin, pick berries from the roadside and stroke strange cats.

– Let me pass, I've a child!

– Please do, please do!

You have been pressed against the window itself, the infant looks at you with unexpressive eyes. Is he normal? What percentage is born sick? Perhaps it's just as well I'm not going to get caught out again, it's risky giving birth to a child nowadays. The dog next door carried two monsters and couldn't even give birth herself, they had to do a Caesarian. And one of her puppies from a previous litter has already died of chest cancer. The hardiest are the rats. Interesting, what about mice?

You shake yourself. The pain is increasing.

(But you can get used to pain.)

You can get used to everything – you think.

You look out of the window again and freeze in horror. What a queue! And it's still two hours till the shop opens. What a nightmare. Damn it all, where are you going to get hold of a bottle by the seventeenth? Your husband hasn't the time to stand in such queues, you haven't the strength. Moreover you have a clear-cut, I would say unfeminine, aversion to queues. And you've been trailing round the shops for three days already, worn out, looking for shoes. And a raincoat for the child. Or a jacket for your husband. Because he, your husband, has to go abroad, and he can't go without a decent jacket – what if there's some sort of reception? Or – he goes to the opera? By chance.

You'll have to take a second Cognac, you decide, and count the days till payday.

It's hot, unbearably, impossibly hot. You can feel the sweat running down your temples and you can't wipe it off, your hands are at your sides. Again you imagine the cattle trucks, an endless string of them hurtling eastwards (too much is written about that, too much!) There wasn't such a crush then . . . There were other problems. Starvation and dysentery. And fear.

You are afraid too. You fear bad people. Militiamen. Wars and everyday radiation. And in addition you have an utterly ordinary fear of trains, cars, motors and electricity. Of everything you don't understand. You still don't feel at home in this age of technical marvels. To tell the truth you are afraid of nature too. In the darkness your flesh creeps, the silence seems menacing, you don't like walking in a dark wood at midday – you, my dear, don't understand woods either. It's hardest of all at night when the fear of darkness blends with fear of the future. Thank God, it is only for a couple of days before your periods that these feelings are not subdued by the green tablets. Your husband doesn't understand you.

– Don't push!

– Sorry . . . – you moved too sharply and trod on your neighbour's foot, you are sharply and suddenly elbowed in the pit of your stomach.

And you're hungry. Because of that mouse . . . ugh.

Allergies, hepatitis. Cancer. All we need is the plague. AIDS?

Well, he shouldn't brake so suddenly! Perhaps someone was in the road?

The fiancé of one of your former classmates, a Finn, on whose account you envied her, was run over in Moscow. They drive like madmen there – it's the capital! They rushed him off to Helsinki by private plane and just as well they managed to in time. Our doctors failed to notice that his lungs were crushed and that he was haemorrhaging, a bit later and he'd have been a goner.

A goner. A goner.

The pain is getting worse. What is it? An ulcer? Oh, don't crush me, mates, don't crush me so hard, I'm human too! It's like a hoop round my body at the level of my stomach. Burning wire. Just don't get sick, you think. As long as they let you out. Give me a drink – water, give me some water – that's what wounded Soviet soldiers usually groan in films. There's no one for you to ask. Moreover, you're ashamed.

There, it's like a knife now. I can imagine red circles in front of my eyes, ears as if blocked up, unable to move a leg . . . God, why just now, today, damn it . . . No, you can't go on.

– Are you getting out? Let me past!

The red circles vanish and you come to yourself on the street, the back end of the overloaded trolleybus gracefully floats away round the corner of a grey building, perhaps you shouldn't have got out, it's even hotter here than in the trolleybus, the pain that had calmed down for a moment seizes you again with renewed force, the cold bluish hand of pain with long, powerful, yellow nails – it suffocates you, you can't straighten up, you mustn't straighten up, you must not allow the disgusting hand to grab deeper into your insides; hold out, hold out, control yourself, there, you can lean against that pillar.

That's it.

You look round in perplexity – where have you ended up?

Probably you got on the wrong trolleybus, you blind hen. A character in a tracksuit goes past with a loaf of bread under his arm. You daren't ask him where you are. You never learned how to tell the new suburbs apart. And what's that, what's that fuss over there? With difficulty you turn your head – three little boys are beating up another, the smallest of them all. Little wretches. The character with the bread walks past them on the grass. It's not getting any better . . . The biggest one trips the infant over and kneels on his chest, the others hold his arms and legs. The infant has grey hair, his dusty face is grey too. Only his tears have left bright tracks on his cheeks. And his dark eyes are glistening. Black beady eyes. There, the big one is deftly beating him about the face. First of all. Next – even harder. A young woman pushes a pram with a baby past you. You tear yourself away from the pillar. Bent over, you walk a few steps towards the boys. Each step has an effect on your belly and head. The big one beats him a third time, your eyes darken from the pain, the infant is lying on the asphalt, grey and helpless, not even trying to defend himself. God, how grey he is. You press your hands tighter to your belly (not to allow the bony blue hand with yellow nails any deeper!) and go up to them. The big one is beating him again. Idiot, why are you silent? you whisper.

– Why are you silent . . . idiot! – you yell as loud as you can – go on, shout, why aren't you shouting?!

You are soaked with sweat from the pain and tension, the blue hand has torn something out and reached your spine, the boys have taken flight like a flock of sparrows, slowest of all – the infant, he got to his feet with difficulty, and, running after the older ones, stuck his tongue out at you.

It hurts. But you can get used to pain.

You squat down. The asphalt smells so nice. A fat-legged woman in cork sandals walks past, she looks down at you in alarm. Her big, high-cheekboned face melts across the entire horizon. The pain grows even worse, if that is possible, but you hope that it will pass. The asphalt smells of home.

Translated from the Latvian by Michael Molnar

Estonia

Viivi Luik

The Beauty of History

The smoke from the factory chimneys rises vertically, iron gives a ringing sound, bare bulbs light up corridors and stairwells. You cannot trust the other. It is better not to tell anything of yourself. Fear is lit up by the white light of naked 40-watt bulbs like an egg, like butter or cream, like the forms of questionnaires. Clouds hover like circulars over the Baltic Sea with its long, lonely sandy beaches, over soldiers' boots and the tracks of bloodhounds. Woods groan in Bohemia and Moravia, the wind bends Lithuanian crops double, strikes Latvian bean harvests to the ground. More faith! More hope! More love! It does not do to forget that under the cushion lies the phone which cannot be used until secret language has been learned. He who has once understood can no longer escape, he is involved in everything that happens. Remember that on the phone you should not use the words 'book', 'papers', 'document', 'briefcase', 'letter' or 'men'. A book can be forbidden, in its entirety, or can be printed abroad, papers are the same as documents but a document could always be a forgery. A briefcase gives away the fact that things are being moved from one place to another. But what things? And from what place? A letter could always be brought in over the border by courier. Men could think *differently* for there are grounds for believing so. Men are always more suspicious than women. For safety's sake men's names should be changed to women's and Paris should be changed to Kiev, New York to Moscow. 'At auntie's', on the other hand, means in Kiev and 'at uncle's' means Moscow. The names Tallinn and Riga should also not cross one's lips unnecessarily. You can always speak about butter and eggs. It is even desirable to do so. You can speak about dogs but not about muzzles as muzzles attract unnecessary attention, and is that really a good thing? You can speak as much as you like about Aunt Olga, Mum, the polyclinic, cabbages and beets. Times mentioned should be during the day, as evenings are suspicious *per se*. It is better to say nothing at all about night, may God preserve you from the night.

If you wish to say: 'I'm coming next Wednesday evening at eight,' then say: 'Aunt Olga will send Mum those eight black coat buttons she asked for, next Wednesday.' Or eight and a half kilos of blackcurrants. Or seven tins of olives, black ones, not green ones. Or black slippers costing six roubles. At any event evening is black. You have to learn to talk about Aunt Olga's life. You shouldn't say 'telegram', but 'pack of butter'. You'll soon get the hang of it. Bears can be taught to dance. There's no point in wondering about every detail. When you worry about the fact that: 'Kuzminitshna's son-in-law hasn't been heard of lately, I wonder whether he's still working as an artist,' this means that the exit papers are still held up and the officer who is supposed to regulate this matter is on holiday, on a business trip or has been transferred to another department. All the organizers who do things *through contacts* are *Kuzminitshna's sons-in-law*, that has to be remembered and you shouldn't fuss about whether men or women are meant. They are always *sons-in-law*. Kuzminitshna herself exists: to her you take Latvian honey and cotton yarn, which Mother manages to get at the market.

She knows very little about Mother and Aunt Olga. In the future she will understand quite ordinary words wrongly for quite a time to come and for that reason she will have wild and secret imaginings about this family, which she has not yet seen, imaginings that she will not reveal to anyone. She has an obstinate impression that Aunt Olga catches *perch* in the evening, for she hears that Aunt Olga's *elbows* ache of an evening; the similarity of these two words in a foreign language trips her up. Secret language mixes everything up. She never understands whether they are really talking about buying butter or cream or whether there is secret news about the OVIR.

The parquet creaks all by itself. It is too dark already. Nothing can be seen. Perhaps whole decades flit back and forth in this darkened room, or perhaps a draught is moving the curtain. If it were not so dark, you would see every vertebra separately now. But you cannot see them, you read them together as if making a statement or swearing an oath, with the naked fist and quite alone. Both his names, both the secret Lion, and the public Levi, her own tomorrow and even her grandfather's grave in New York give her laugh a wavering faith and his look an arbitrary power which she herself cannot see in the darkness.

The other could not imagine that those selfsame fingers, whose bones during the course of today she has grown to feel as her own five fingers, are made of clay and even remade twice over, that those same fingers are now writing the Russian charm in Estonian directly on to the shoulder blade: 'What the pike commands is my wish,' and that the mouth whose corners she knows with her own senses has likewise been remoulded twice so that the same mouth laughs into the darkness in such a way as if human fate and the sadness of the land were merely mockery and jest.

The Angel of the Lord creases his brow and draws nigh. In the silence of the grave the night moves lands and peoples from West to East, so that not even a dog barks.

Translated from the Estonian by Eric Dickens

Rein Tootmaa

We Gaze Up into the Tops of the Spruce Trees

A thought walks along a woodland path, turns exhausted into a clearing, reaches a lake, stops, disappears for a moment, chases itself wearily away, catches hold of itself, swells large and hazy in the sun, disappears into the blue yonder.

There you are waiting with me, or is it the other way round? As you wish, it is of no importance. You speak to me, then I to you, or is it the other way round, that I speak first, then you?

You spoke and your expression was reflected somewhere in the distance; you were somewhere else entirely, not at my side. And I spoke and also gazed over to the other side, to quite another place from where you were standing; not at you.

Our thoughts had already started off on different routes; we ourselves were together, the two of us on the banks of the woodland lake.

That summer's day, the sun shone bright and warm, the woods breathed, the river carried its waters onwards in powerful waves. Onwards, simply onwards, to the sea. The lake water ran as a river into the sea.

You said that this river did not flow into the sea, that it flowed into another lake on the other side of the woods, that the waters of this lake were never allowed to reach the sea.

I do not believe you; at some point or other the water will reach the sea, no matter when.

*

Every day this water falls in love with new stretches of bank along the river, with new trees, bushes and meadows which the river meets on its course downstream. It falls in love and forgets, loves and leaves, loves and forgets, on and on. It will never become disappointed in its love. It need not yearn or suffer, it takes and leaves. Such is its nature. And when, one day, it reaches the sea, its love is still young and fiery.

You get up and go, and I follow. I do not know why I do so, it is no longer necessary. I follow you and see you home. We kiss on the doorstep, as if everything were fine; I promise to return the next day. I do not wish to shatter the illusion that we are still in love, nor do you wish to shatter it.

The next day we are again at the river bank and we have the feeling we are happy. In actuality it is already today and we laugh, walk and pick flowers. It is all so pleasant that you could think that what occurred yesterday had never taken place, perhaps it never did. But somewhere an inkling of loss peeps through.

I don't want to, don't want to; I stroke your hair, take your hands in mine, put a wreath of forget-me-nots on your brow, kiss your neck, embrace you, your body snuggles up to mine, my mouth seeks yours, seeks your eyes.

    Your eyes are wet, I carry on kissing them, kiss them dry, look into your eyes. They are gazing into the distance at the tops of the spruce trees. I ask what's wrong. You do not answer; I unbutton your blouse, your brightly coloured summer blouse, toss it into the grass, into the tall grass. The grass has not been mown although it is high summer. You wriggle out of the rest of your clothes. I kiss your breasts, the grass is too high, reaches up to your waist. I help you to lie down, I am in you, then I see your eyes again, they are looking through me, somewhere into the distance, towards the tops of the spruce in the heavenly woods. Then I too begin to gaze up at the treetops; we hold the treetops in the mirrors of our eyes. We look up at the tops of the spruce from the trampled grass, the grass and the soil sighing under our weight, but we do not leave, we are afraid of shattering the illusion that we are in love.

We stay there for a night and a day, we stay while summer and the warm autumn last; until the snow drives us back into warm rooms. Where there are no longer any treetops.

Translated from the Estonian by Eric Dickens

Belarus

Yurii Petkevich

Variations on the Seasons

Suplistov went through the first year of school for seven years in succession. Each year there were fewer and fewer children in the first class and Suplistov thought with dread that some day he would be left alone in the first class. But in his seventh year at school a little girl with a light face and light hair, a fat girl, entered the school. School became less sad for Suplistov and he began attending lessons with joy, even early in the morning, although the little girl was always late.

The teacher and his family lived behind the wall and in the mornings before lessons he berated his family, bellowing like a bull; the class filled with schoolchildren; the bell rang; the teacher entered and drank, hidden behind the blackboard, to cure his hangover. Finally the fat little girl knocked and came in sadly, head hanging, and the teacher questioned her and she remained silent.

Every spring an inspector came to the school to check on the teacher and sat in the last desk, next to Suplistov, smiling at him, liking only him because he was the best behaved of all. The inspector soon fell asleep. As always the pupils fired peashooters. The teacher collected up the peas himself and then went out into the corridor as if to throw them away, but didn't, putting them in his pocket instead. After a little while Suplistov raised his legs and exclaimed out loud, not standing up or raising his hand, interrupting the teacher: 'Already!'

The teacher then wiped up the pool under the inspector so that he shouldn't be embarrassed when he woke up and Suplistov lowered his legs. Those were the sort of inspectors they had.

In Suplistov's seventh year of schooling the inspector spent the night at his parents'. In the morning his mother fried up a full frying pan of eggs. The inspector only ate the yolks. When he left, Suplistov's mother said after him: 'I hope you burst.'

That day Suplistov stole a hundred roubles from home, so that they should suspect the inspector – he brought them to school and showed them to the boys in the first class. The next day they started bringing him whatever things they could find. One cheeky boy brought his granny's dentures and demanded forty roubles for them. The teeth delighted Suplistov, none of the other treasures had such an effect on him.

The fat girl liked walking by the stream with a bucket over her head and listening to the sounds. After school Suplistov went to the meadow, hid behind some bushes and stuffed the teeth into his mouth. The little girl wandered across the meadow with the bucket on her head, seeing nothing, and the breeze occasionally carried to Suplistov her puffing in the bucket. He laughed silently and crept like an animal up to the fat girl to frighten her. But it was not so much that the little beauty liked walking with a bucket on her head as that she liked being seen doing it. So when, amid the noise in the bucket and the various spring songs, she sensed rather than heard footsteps, she seized the bucket with her hands so that it should not knock against her head and ran to a hillock by the river, watching the grass and flowers under her feet. Suplistov ran after her at her heels and when the girl sat down on the hill and, from the heat of the chase and her delight, breathed passionately into the bucket, a fish leaped in the river and in his agitation Suplistov swooned, but soon came to himself and rose to his knees.

Fat flowers on slender stalks were wedged between his bare toes. The fat girl was sitting upright in her former pose with the bucket on her head, not understanding the noise of Suplistov's attack and afraid to look. Unusually tall, he kneeled before her, forgetting that he had wanted to scare the girl, and felt only the absurdity of his position, and saw that a horse and cart was coming along the track across the meadow. The fat girl did not breathe under the bucket. Spellbound, Suplistov watched the person in the cart. The frightened horse turned its head away from Suplistov with his double set of teeth. The cart slowly approached. Suplistov saw in it the teacher, looking at him in horror. Gradually the teacher went off his head, the cart carried on, and the already mad man did not even look round.

Then Suplistov remembered the false teeth sticking out of his mouth and seized the little girl by the arm so as to pull the bucket off from her eyes. She resisted desperately. Suddenly he felt his breath becoming tremulous and the tendons in his arms ached like the soul in his breast. He was horribly frightened, dropped his weakened arms from the fat girl and felt that she too was frightened, for the same internal reason. Nevertheless he managed to lift the sunwarmed bucket from her head and saw the girl's face with tears glistening on her cheeks, and she herself wanted to take the bucket off, but its handle had got stuck round her chubby chin and looked like a cowl. Suplistov was glad and smiled, showing his teeth to all the world.

At home they found the false teeth in his pocket and all sorts of treasures in his satchel, and in the morning his mother took him to school; the teacher was no longer there and for the first time it was quiet behind the wall, except that his unhappy wife wept and cried out from time to time. The pupils of the first class also cried and gave the money back, and his mother gave them back the treasures. Next day Suplistov did not go to school, but was sent as a shepherd to a strange official establishment not far from Yablonovka, where idiots, invalids and madmen lived.

In time Suplistov turned into a mature person of unimaginable height and, living among cows, became handsome. His eyelashes were so long that they curled. And his eyes stared like a cow's, though, it is true, they were blue and like a cow's they were sad. He no longer feared death as he had when younger, but persistently thought of his genius among the cows and remembered how he had wandered through Yablonovka as a child, to the white church among the sycamores, and how he had philosophized.

The director of the strange house was extraordinarily fat, they drove him around on the back of a lorry because he couldn't get into the cab, and winter and summer he always wore a padded jacket, boots and a peaked cap, and had a strawberries and cream complexion, and at one sitting would eat a great potful of potatoes and a frying pan of hog fat. They said that each of the managerial staff in this house had his own secret aide. The storekeeper distributed firewood to them and the lunatics stole the firewood from one another to heat up their favourites' stoves. If one of them caught a thief, they would fight to the death.

Once Suplistov ventured to approach the strange whitewashed house with its park and its lanterns. The lunatics strolled freely and did not run off into the woods because several of them had already run away, but had not had the brains to return. As soon as Suplistov approached these folk, one of them smiled and said, pointing a finger in admiration: 'You're wearing a red coat and a blue scarf.'

'Be quiet, please,' Suplistov begged.

'Don't embarrass him, Styopa,' another idiot said to the first. 'He's a genius too.'

One lunatic, tall and handsome like Suplistov, was singing and a small one was dancing round him; everyone was grouped round them, men and women, watching. Suddenly Suplistov saw his teacher: he was crouched down, thinking intensely, and did not even notice his pupil, but another lunatic was throwing pebbles onto the teacher's bald patch. Then, smiling, a lunatic came up to Suplistov and asked: 'What? Do you need land?' looking into the shepherd's cow eyes. 'I'll give you some straight away,' and he measured out three paces in length and two wide. 'There's land for you!'

Suplistov hurried to the cows, appalled by the thought that he, a genius and a handsome fellow, was the reason for the teacher being sunk in thought. It was damp and close from the rain. The rain had stopped for Suplistov. Suplistov felt that the last drop had fallen onto the edge of his lips. His handsome face grew red as fire from the moisture. He walked across the meadow, not knowing how to proceed, because he couldn't stand still. He wanted to throw himself onto the grass, but it was wet. But finally he took heart and gladly dived into it and rolled around like a beast, and then gazed upwards out of the grassy dusk: in places the grass was red from the light, and he loved fat women and fat flowers.

Soon Suplistov's relatives began dying, one after the other, and he understood that the merry lunatic was giving him land for a grave. The day that Suplistov left for a funeral at Yablonovka, they fixed up an electric fence at the strange house's pastures and the electric fence killed several horses, because they turned out to be more sensitive than cows. At Yablonovka Suplistov met the fat girl and now there was nothing out of the ordinary between them, only a pink arrow pierced Suplistov's organism, but the fat girl did not notice Suplistov, they had bought her pretty shoes, or perhaps she had forgotten him.

After funerals he would stroll at night in the garden of the strange house. Once, hearing a noise, Suplistov sensed something unawares, stopped and carefully took the bucket off his head. He spied something incomprehensible, inarticulate in the darkness and only guessed that there was a woman below. A terrible agitation shook Suplistov's soul, he started to go away, silently as a beast. But then he returned involuntarily and ran back, across the garden, and apples knocked against his head. The woman cried out and it seemed to him that it was the voice of the fat girl. Suplistov stood with the bucket in his hands and saw that the enormous director of the strange house had crept out on all fours and was looking at the woman, and she had begun riding round the lawn like a beast.

Suplistov never again saw the fat girl at Yablonovka, she disappeared somewhere, and Suplistov thought that she had died or gone on a journey. Life with its continual funerals terrified Suplistov – and he decided to change his life. He went to the city, but rich relations found him a job in a funeral band because, apart from playing music, Suplistov did not know how to do anything, and so the cows had to live alone.

When he first arrived in the city, Suplistov laughed at the unexpected quantity of cars and people. The town was large but wooden, like an enormous village. People died every day and every day Suplistov had one or more funerals. A mass of the blind, the lame and the hunchbacked inhabited the city – and they always took part in funeral processions. Aeroplanes in the sky, crowing of cockerels, shuffling of feet, the rumble of traffic held up behind the procession so that sometimes the end was not visible – all of this and other such noises annoyed Suplistov and made the skin of his palms and fingers tingle. Suplistov did not know whether to act pleased or offended and was therefore always amazed by the dead. Constantly finding himself in the presence of the very essence of humanity, which had hitherto suffered greatly, gradually, rising above everyone else in the processions because of his height, he felt an overwhelming anguish and became aware of his own mediocrity, and began to remember. Memories of childhood, when he chose the sphere of activity for his genius and wandered among the sycamores in the green grass he had trampled, around the white church – these would not lie down and die in the awful processions, to the beating of his drum. Once Suplistov almost burst into tears in front of the deceased, and then almost burst out laughing, but however long he worked in the band, he carried on repeating to himself, as they had taught him, in order not to go wrong or lapse into thought: 'Born . . . lived . . . died – damn him!' and irritated against the whole world by the noise, he beat his drum to the rhythm of these words, and once even wanted to beat the deceased over the head with his drumstick, but stopped in the middle of the procession that was already heading towards the dead man and forgot the music; the hair on his head ached at the thought of what he had wanted to perpetrate . . . and he began looking round at the trees, at the yellow leaves and the grey sky. A hunchback happened to be next to him in the procession. The hunchback said something to him.

'What?' Suplistov asked. 'You said, "Chrysanthemums".'

'It'll mess up the road,' the hunchback repeated.

'Oh, that's nice!' Suplistov exclaimed. 'You said, "It'll mess up the road,' and I heard, "Chrysanthemums".'

'I don't know,' the hunchback stated.

A stubborn cow stood as if nailed to the spot in the middle of the road and watched as fish were being sold in the open air. The cow was important like a general because it was in the city. Its owner and cowherd, dressed in a black suit (and the cow was black), tugged a string tied round its horns, but the cow was watching fish being sold. The funeral cortège stopped, then went round the cow, closing ranks. The silver and gold scales of the fish glittered in the autumn dusk. Finally the unhappy man in black dragged the cow off somewhere and the procession returned to the middle of the road. Someone stepped in the cowpat and groaned all the way to the cemetery. Suplistov forgot what the hunchback said instead of 'chrysanthemums' but felt it was beautiful.

The cemetery was enormous, grave upon grave, damp and shady from the rusty trees, fitted with stone and iron, and they said that there was a cave dug under the ground and at night criminals gathered there. The coffin splashed into water in the grave and when everyone began dispersing Suplistov went up to the hunchback, anticipating the beauty of the words spoken when he heard 'chrysanthemums'. But the hunchback had totally forgotten them and said: 'I was very depressed.'

. . . Once Suplistov spent the night in a city park high above the ground in the bowl of a fountain on a column. The fountain was not yet working after the winter. Suplistov was awoken by an unbearable glow, but in his bliss could not open his eyes and through the lids saw something beautiful. In the orange light something flashed and then Suplistov tore open his eyes and saw an enormous fat woman bending over him. When he opened his cow's eyes, the woman gasped with delight. He thought: How did she get into the bowl? – and saw that the sun was already high. A feather stuck out of the woman's hat, there was hardly any wind but it swayed back and forth on a ribbon, ready to fly off. Suplistov's skin felt the flitting of shadows across his face. Spring was rampant: apple trees blossomed, birds sang, fluff flew, specks of light trembled on leaves. Suddenly he became aware that he was not lying in the bowl of the fountain but on the grass, and leaped up: shrubs and trees were growing all around. The woman's head was completely and ideally beautiful, but at first sight her figure was hideous. Suplistov thought: how had he ended up here? He was so frightened that all his muscles went slack. The woman lightly brushed his arm with her hand which was very hot and his mind clouded over painfully. She sat down next to him. Suplistov felt that the ground rose slightly beneath him because it sank beneath her. He leapt up and ran off, first in the wrong direction, but heard noise and ran towards the noise. Suplistov broke out of the shrubbery and found himself on the square in the park, and the fountain was working . . .

Suplistov again tried to remember the hunchback's words, in place of which he had heard 'chrysanthemums' and saw something glittering, plainly not chrysanthemums, until he understood that it was a fish.

Translated from the Russian by Michael Molnar

Ukraine

Igor Klekh

Hog's Fat, Pancake, and the Sausage

For M. Epshtein: 'Ukrainianness, Sovietness, Russianness.'

Hog's Fat

1. Is there any connection between cooking and the destiny of a nation, its mental life and its philosophy?

Only a hopelessly blinkered mind could answer this question negatively. Yet we generally presuppose such a link without comprehending it. Why is this so?

Is it because of the 'myopia' of the senses of touch, smell and taste, overpowered by the wider-ranging senses of vision and hearing? Undoubtedly there is something in that. The human larva pulls everything into its mouth and this stage forms a deep sediment somewhere at the core of the adult, whose senses are shaped by the primacy of vision and hearing, and by the repression of cannibalism.

How many words in our culture signify taste? Sour, sweet, salty, bitter, astringent – and tasty; that seems to be all. Truly a vocabulary of bare essentials.

Yet one of the most primeval mysteries of a refined intuitive culture is named transsubstantiation and the Eucharist.

Evidently the sense of taste, though repressed by rationalistic culture, possesses something fundamental which penetrates all levels of humanity in the human being and projects beyond . . . into nothing.

One can eat one's fill and belch, one can 'stuff one's belly with kasha like a pipkin', one can abandon oneself to feasting and gourmandizing – but let us exclude gluttony, we will only concern ourselves with the satisfaction of hunger, the restoration of one's strength. Why should it be that in ethnic Ukrainian culture FAT should have now come to represent the anecdotic (this aspect merits especial attention) and mythic quintessence of strength? What is this foodstuff and what is in it?

2. For the Ukrainians, fat is what manna is for the Jews (and the golden apples of the Hesperides for the Ancient Greeks), – i.e. a transcendent and fatidic dish to differentiate them from their neighbouring southern races (or, so to speak, 'whack their gob'), from the Judeo-Mussulmanic, for whom it is undoubtedly non-kosher.

A dish at once societal and sacred, charged with polemical power. Eating it is like gliding on skis. In a world of foodstuffs that quickly spoil in the south – it is imperishable and in some way equivalent to gold. It is a manifestation of the cult of excess that goes back to the fat pagan gods of happiness – the biblical fat of the land – and to the dry, beggarly emergency rations thickly powdered with the salt of Ukranian cart tracks.

Its taste is strongly redolent of the road, either one takes it along on one's travels or it summons one to a long journey along the deeply rutted cart tracks of the Ukraine, drowning in soft, white dust.

The far-ranging wisdom of the first social mechanics stems from such carts with their axles and leather grease bags – 'You can't start if you don't grease the cart.' Thence also that specific Ukrainian 'melancholy', the sorrow of the traveller sitting by the roadside (for 'sad' is an early form of 'saturated', as in fat – it is what is deposited, what settles on meat – and thence both 'session' and 'sitting' . . .), yes, of the traveller lost in the steppe, sitting beneath an endless sky, beneath clouds – that fat of the heavens.

As a rule, he reaches for an onion and cuts it into four pieces, which eases the flow of tears in the eyes of the sad votary far from home.

A universal product – giving light when burned in an oil-lamp or in the form of the tallow candle. Wildly calorific when cut with a knife into fine 'rounds'. Its assimilability can be traced even in the phonetic form of its name – the slippery 's' and the damp glottal 'l' – *ao*. Salted fat, a bitter-sweet onion, poteen, fresh bread, slightly soured by saliva – in the open air – this is the fundamental repast of the steppe Slav. At this scene pride waxes in the heart as fat upon a pig.

3. (résumé) Ye canna deny it, 'Fat is the light of our warl'.'

Pancake

'A pancake will put a lining on your stomach.'

If you project a cross-section of the world tree onto Russian cookery . . . the result is a pancake.

One of the most unique cosmogonic myths is incorporated in the Russian folk tale of the old woman cooking pancakes on her old man's bald head. Using solar energy, of course. In general, echoes of the solar origin of the pancake are evident even to us, who no longer believe in anything. For the circular form is in no way simpler than, let's say, a triangle, and this is not a matter of economy alone.

The kitchen is one of the most ancient scenes of representation, especially as regards the basic dishes prepared with the minimum of means: flour, water, fire. A little oil.

The most Russian thing about cooking pancakes is that it is a gamble and when it is in full swing one is not put out by variants or by the notorious proverbial 'first pancake is a flop'. In this way it generated the constellation of griddle cakes, chthonic chapatis, barley cakes, wheat, oat and buckwheat pancakes, from fresh or sour dough, with all possible ingredients or without – butter pancakes, fluffy pancakes, blintzes. All in all, tea with pancakes and a samovar is nothing less than a model of the universe, the Russian national planetarium where cups and saucers circle in the orbits of Saturn or Pluto, and the boiling tea is analogous to the life-giving rays of the sun which, by the way, the crafty Russians learned to capture and tame in yellow butter and honey.

Thus the planets of pancakes, hitherto uninhabited, with their pitted surface like wet photographs of the moon, are settled by Russians, incorporated in the human cosmos and devoured. But the most highly charged form of pancakes occurs at wakes, where they are served first: pancakes with caviar.

Hot pancakes with cold caviar – this is a disavowal like a shroud concealing the hyperbole of fruitfulness. Death imbued with life. In the light of what has been said, the state monopoly on the title and merchandising of caviar can be seen as nothing less than a symbolical usurpation of the right of the fittest to perpetuate the species.

Though this thought did not penetrate the consciousness or self-image of the populace, it culminated, at the end of the years of stagnation, in the communal folly of the UFO – when emaciated, badly and insufficiently fed folk lifted up their heads and suddenly saw above them hot flying pancakes. Their scandalous characteristic lay in the fact that it was extremely difficult to enter into contact with them. But this very fact inspired people with the belief that they might sooner or later get through to them.

Thus it was that the prerequisites of *perestroika* appeared. It is significant that almost simultaneously with information about UFOs a new sonorous Russian swear word appeared: '*Blinn!*' ('Sugar!') – like a noisy slap in the face with a custard pie. At that point the Party understood that it was impossible to postpone *perestroika* any longer.

The Sausage as a Political Value

It turns out that negative or even imaginary values also exist in the material world.

One such value is the sausage.

Those who think that this value is self-sufficient and serves the digestion are mistaken – far from it. It has not been called upon to satisfy hunger (for there has long been no hunger in the USSR), but the libido. In evidence one can adduce its fundamental property – that it is always either lacking or in short supply. Metaphysics glints and sparkles through its physical nature and its enveloping psychic form.

One must assume that the sausage is a manifestation of that phosphorescing, deceptively substantial phallus by means of which the Party realizes its proclaimed unity with the people.

Perestroika graphically revealed this hidden nature of the sausage. When some of the Party's visible members atrophied and it temporarily ceased having it off with the people in all its nine orifices, and, busying itself with intensive massage of the head of its own clitoris, left itself only five of them, the people suddenly stood erect and, noticing that the Party no longer loved it as before, suddenly came to and angrily demanded sausages, threatening divorce should they be denied. But however much the Party strained all its fallopian tubes during the following five years, nothing emerged from them, apart from *glasnost*.

To the sceptics we will simply point out that what the people demand is precisely sausages – not meat, not content! – but the form. This has been proved by the successful attempts at substituting cellulose for meat in sausage filling, in consequence of which the queues for sausage – that political expression of love – merely grow. The insufficiently loved people acts like a child asking to be punished – lapsing into total licence in its quest for retribution – and despite all its tears, experiencing relief at the mother's symbolical slap or the father's belt, which finally deliver it from itself.

The ontological roots of the sausage stretch back deep into the structure of humankind, into both its intestines: the cerebral one and the one situated in its belly, both ideally adapted; one for the perception of the idea of the sausage, the other for the ingestion of its body. Is it necessary to specify that this very ingestion constitutes an act of politico-sexual cannibalism? In general it should be noted that the erotic nature of the sausage is overarching and complex in character. One can distinguish certain of its aspects, such as: the voyeuristic, the manual-oral, ending up with the fecal – eating the contents of the intestines (which, by the way, has long been etymologically comprehended by the people through the conceptual and phonic proximity of the words 'shit' and 'sausage').

It is understood that the mental life of any people that has occasional dealings with the sausage is deepened, the wealth and variety of its experiences immeasurably extended; such a people stands at the threshold of the sixth sense opened up by socialism – where the people and socialism, having once met, can never again be parted.

Worthy of note is the fact that even before the sunrise of our century – the century of the victorious advance of the idea of the Great October Socialist Revolution – the sausage, precisely in its Russian pronunciation as '*kol-ba-sa*', entered the international language of Esperanto.

And already the future is near, the time when the bright hallucinations of humanity will be incarnated – when the well-ordered SAUSAGE as such, free of any misnaming or miscategorization, will be wound on a telephone cable reel and delivered to grocers in lorries like fire engines, unrolled like a hosepipe, like a coiled and pulsing fire hose – to the entire queue in one go, until its full and final satisfaction.

Translated from the Russian by Michael Molnar

Russia

Svetlana Vasilieva

The Time of Peonies

A NOVEL

Part One

More than anything else in the world young Khudaiberdyev loved
reading books about capital punishment. He was particularly fascinated by episodes from foreign history. The inexorable claw of the
Inquisition, its refined gamut of tortures and the finale, a picturesque
auto-da-fé: whether on the scaffold or, better still, burning at the
stake. The fierce tongues of flame . . . The farewell peal of bells . . .

Khudaiberdyev even remembered by heart the song from
Hugo's *Notre Dame de Paris*:

> We'll hang the villains
> From the gibbets!
> We'll roast the heretics
> In the faggots!

Khudaiberdyev worked as a policeman. He was young and not
bad-looking. Sigmund Freud had nothing to do with his preoccu-
pation. As far as complexes were concerned, everything was fine in
young Khudaiberdyev's family. His mother had abandoned him
when he was still an infant, and he never knew his father. Consequently young Khudaiberdyev's character was well balanced, whoever it was he took after. He tried to love his enemies like those
closest to him, and those closest like his enemies. At the present
moment he had neither the former nor the latter. There were
women, but he didn't love them.

Young Khudaiberdyev wanted to live his life fast and vividly, like flame running along a fuse. He always had a whole pack of Alsatians at his command. Recently they had acquired new quarters, moving from separate wooden huts into a shared concrete block behind a concrete barrier. But he was increasingly having to concern himself with trivialities: house thefts without any breaking and entering, punch-ups without a lethal outcome, thimble-rigging without a hope of an honest person winning.

Nevertheless the young Khudaiberdyev nurtured some sort of sixth sense. Or seventh. Or not so much a sense as a feeling. Dim, unclear. Because the times around were like that – unclear. On the one hand the radio constantly repeated: 'Don't steal!', 'Don't kill!', 'Don't covet!' And on the other hand, there was practically nothing left to steal, covet or kill. On the one hand, witch trials no longer posed a threat to progressive humanity. And on the other – witches definitely continued to be found, especially among women. Although woman was still, as previously, the future mother.

That's how it was. Young Khudaiberdyev very much wanted to diminish the amount of evil in the world. Or of villains, which came to the same thing.

And then one day bells rang out in his life!

Part Two

It happened in a room under the eaves, on the premises of a former nunnery.

Once nuns had found sanctuary there, taking walks along the high walls and looking straight down from the top into the depths of the nunnery's deep moat where bright water gently lapped. Then the nunnery was transformed into a children's home. Then into a cooler. Then into a hostel. In winter children sledged in the moat, and in summer old men fished for carp. Then the carp vanished. The children grew up, went to serve in the army, and some were sent to prison.

Now, seven beautiful women, each more beautiful than the

next, have moved into the former nunnery – a small female collective of restorers of ancient monuments.

And then strange things began happening in the room under the eaves, large and small objects, all of some use, began disappearing: rouble notes, hats, hankies, stockings, tights, sugar, salt – everything that their beautiful owners had stocked up. Recently a Congress of People's Deputies had met and promised the people everything, and so they resolved that to be on the safe side they had better stock up on everything. And how they gazed into the water – the very same water that used to lap in the nunnery moat . . .

June arrived – the time of peonies, luxuriant flowers like the curly little heads of children. People tried to buy up the maximum possible quantity at the market and bore whole armfuls of them home, where for a short time they graced glass vases. And then, in a second, they scattered and entirely ceased looking like flowers, reminding one rather of little skeletons.

One day one such bouquet floated into the room under the eaves, carried there by its happy owner. She had deliberately bought flowers that were still unopened buds so that the next day she could lay them on the grave of her ancestors and at the same time on the boss's table, since it happened to be her birthday.

Everyone was full of admiration for the bouquet, they placed it in boiled sugar-water so it would last longer and sat down to drink tea without sugar.

That same night the flowers disappeared!

Without doubt they had been stolen by some evil hand.

Part Three

According to the rules one had to catch this hand and sever it from its arm at the elbow. But in the first instant the women were somehow confused. When their confusion passed, some bright person suggested bringing tracker dogs into the nunnery. Best of all, Alsatians. However, the Alsatians had gone on strike because the ceiling of their new quarters leaked. And early one June morning young Khudaiberdyev appeared at the nunnery walls, disguised as a telephone engineer.

It was with caution, even disgust, that he entered this former hotbed of clerical power and mysticism. But there was nothing to be done – the call of duty ... Even before the working day had begun, Khudaiberdyev had penetrated the room under the eaves and, instead of fixing the telephone, he inconspicuously scattered a mysterious odourless and colourless powder into the far corners of the table drawers.

Half an hour later the room was filled with carefree women's laughter. The women stuffed all the articles in short supply that they had bought into the table drawers: washing powder, children's soap, milk products, shampoo, macaroni, baby food and so on. They all joked together and sang songs from Alla Pagucheva's repertoire, gladdened by their boss's forthcoming birthday.

Finally she arrived and everyone immediately headed for the free co-operative canteen, named after the True Image of the Saviour. And when they finally returned, that was when everything happened.

Part Four

One of the girls had the unfamiliar name of Esmeralda. She was no longer a girl, but had neither husband nor children. However, she was in no hurry and never lost hope, after all she had loads and loads of time ahead of her.

And so Esmeralda, together with her colleagues, entered the room under the eaves, with no presentiment of the disaster that faced her.

Within a second she was crying out as if stabbed and pulling on her newly bought leather gloves, although the temperature in the room was entirely normal.

The girl's arms, above the elbow, still untouched by the summer sunlight, and also her neck, her face and even part of her clothing –

everything was rapidly covered by a red stain. And so she sat there: red all over and wearing leather gloves.

The women, of course, immediately understood everything and formed a close circle around her. And she merely whispered through her tears:

– Believe me, I'm innocent! I wanted to take someone's matches to light a cigarette. Believe me, believe me . . .

But matches had nothing to do with it, now that Esmeralda's face had been struck by the policeman's powder and was burning brighter and brighter. And within a second she had burst into flames as if doused in petrol. Burst into flames and burned away. Part of the fire immediately flashed across onto the ancient nunnery walls, crept up the eaves and reached the blackened gold domes. Within five minutes the flames were raging high and low and within ten minutes everything had been burned to a cinder.

When young Khudaiberdyev returned, to his amazement he found instead of seven beautiful women nothing at all. Not even a pile of ashes remained of the girl with the evil hand and her colleagues. Everything had blended together and been transformed into common ashes, to be borne away by the wind, to beat against the windows of strange houses . . .

Khudaiberdyev understood that the result of his actions had exceeded his wildest expectations. It is well known that even a hat worn by a thief will burn, but here an entire women's collective, together with their boss, had burned away!

From now on nothing would disappear without a trace or appear out of nowhere. The amount of evil diminished significantly.

Young Khudaiberdyev was content with his work. He went home, where an unfinished cup of tea awaited him, along with Hugo's novel open at the usual page.

Part Five

That same night people heard bells suddenly pealing out on the site of the one-time nunnery and a chorus of women sang out from the depths of the earth. Women's voices, unpleasantly but fairly clearly, wailed, howled and called out. Where and to whom – that was unclear. But one voice, people affirm, distinctly called out to someone of the name of Khudaiberdyev. The voice resounded, high and plaintively:

Give, give, give! Give me, evil as I am, my good hand! Give me my heart, my lungs, my eyes, my ears! Khudaiberdyev . . . I need you! Come to me . . . Whatever happens you won't find yourself a wife either on earth or in heaven . . .

And the following morning the moat was densely overgrown with purple peonies, like clotted blood. They stretched upwards, like the little heads of infants, towards the last of the June sunlight. July was approaching, August, September.

Epilogue

Khudaiberdyev lived a long time. His deeds were many, he rendered numerous villains harmless, reduced the amount of evil and was elected as a People's Delegate. He had neither wife nor children. One fine day he died. They buried him ceremoniously – with music and salvoes. And the following day someone came and laid a bouquet of newly cut peonies upon his grave.

Translated from the Russian by Michael Molnar

Zufar Gareev

Stereoscopic Slavs

How did it all happen? This is how. Mikhailov shouted, held the walls with his hands, running from one to the other, but the magnetic storm kept rocking the building, rocking everything: plaster started dropping from the ceiling and the cracks down the walls spread further and further. This storm took place on Earth in the four thousandth year of the flight of the pine tree on the high and distant sunny shore – in the unknown year of the flight of an ancient grey bird above the pine tree, above the shore, above the Earth. It screwed up its narrow predatory eye, listened to the air whistling beneath its wing. Girls wept in the crumbling building, sucked the cold air through their teeth, thronged the doors. The building collapsed. They managed to leap out the very second that grey concrete blocks tumbled behind their supple backs, sparking against their hair. Their hair instantly flared, blue light that illuminated the Earth from one end to another. The bird screwed up its eyes. It could see, far below, the transparent magnetic storm raging furiously, multicoloured lights flickering among its electric fields, through it a pale blue ball leaping madly.

Viktoriya Chepurnaya dozed in the government office, a red pencil in her hand. 'A pale blue ball . . . how about that!' she suddenly murmured, as if hearing of the storm, and sleepily raised the pencil to set down a resolution. An orthodox character shuffled up and stood next to her desk, gazing at her with his sightless pupils under the pink membrane of their lids. Chepurnaya sleepily stroked his head.

Meanwhile the driver Izvekov and security guard Sysoev were coming to blows in the courtyard. As if drowning in the viscous mire of slumber, Izvekov raised his left hand to his head. The intention was to scratch his head in bewilderment. At first sight his arm seemed immobile, yet it bore all the marks of displacement in time and space. From shoulder to elbow it was lit by today's midday. The remaining portion was touched by the shadow of approaching night. And the very tips of his fingers were illuminated by tomorrow's cloudless dawn, glistening dimly on the driver's chipped fingernails. Meanwhile part of the guard's round, attentive head – his bald spot, actually – was already silvered by the first frosts of September. It was as if it projected slightly into autumn. Another part – from crown to nape – smoked in last February's ground wind. Water dripped in glinting and tinkling streams from Sysoev's snowy shoulders – this year's July affectionately breathing down his back. It smelt of rotting leaves. 'Leaves . . .' Sysoev thought, consoled in his sleep, 'that's what it is.' Suddenly he distinctly heard a murmur in his ear: 'Fucking took a nap, eh? Listen to me, Sysoev, I said you're taking a nap . . .' 'That's right,' Sysoev was flustered. He opened his eyes wide and penetrated a state of clarity and wakefulness that gave him access to his thoughts. Mikhailov sat high up in his narrow window, tilted crookedly heavenwards, touched a sprig in a blue jar with his hand and froze over this lilac. His long head fell across the windowsill and the swooning lilac tenderly bunched over it. The neighbours, first-generation intelligentsia, had guests. People were already shouting drunkenly in their rooms, beating their spoons on the dishes, the blood and verdure of June was already rising – already hoarse, they attacked each other from all angles – and the centre was Chepurnaya:

'That is our Russo-Jewish-Calpathian question! This is our Soviet-human intellectual task!'

Mikhailov was also spared. When the dust scattered, when the crash of concrete, the squeal of window-panes and the grinding of steel frameworks was stilled, a vacuous pink evening fell. Sparkling like slime, the multicoloured wings of the tortured storm dangled from trees, piled up on roofs, lay on the asphalt. He walked gingerly round the edge of the evening as if afraid of breaking through it. Girls had fled to the city: they melted in the streets, into trees in the parks. And they froze among them like dreams carved from blue air. Naked, airborne, they cried for help, but only refined thought could have noticed them, only the sensitive heart could have responded –

for the rest of the world they were invisible. But Mikhailov lacked the vital speed to run with them, to freeze with them – mournfully he thought of his age. His grieving body always forestalled his eye, gazing out from among gathering wrinkles . . . so that if he now consoled himself with the thought of going after the girls, taking them by the arm, pressing his cheek against theirs or solicitously breathing upon their young fingers, silvering them with his breath – they would have snatched their fingers from his palm and spoken to him as he at times spoke to himself. Only the pupils of your eyes are young, only the pupils show devilry, but around them the aged lids, the wrinkled lids are entangled in the labyrinth of years. Even deeper entangled in wrinkles is the sickly body, and the fire of the pupils can no longer reach its outskirts. Soon the body will dry up, be transformed into a tiny bundle and in that bundle the devilry of your pupils will be extinguished.

When it was completely dark, rain came lashing down. It caught Mikhailov in some obscure back street. The rain rustled deep in the foliage: it neither began nor ended anywhere. The earth fell asleep, rocked by its rustling. Sparse, faint electric lights and the outlines of buildings swung in his mind, illusory and vacillating. One could rest one's cheeks against the branches and the rain to cool one's skin down to a dispassionate temperature, to cold purity: the rain and the branches: the branches and the rain. And idle tears – he whispered in reply – and idle tears . . .

'Now now, Beanpole, calm down . . .' Sysoev muttered. 'Why are you trembling wildly like that? Do you hear me: abandon your dark passions . . . You will be a night watchman in your life: while you work the blue moon will sway above our Soviet buildings . . . Or a caretaker: shovelling up paddlefuls of our snow . . . figure rowing, get it?'

Sysoev opened his eyes and thought: 'Vanya, you're right, we fucking dozed off, how did that situation occur?' Car horns blared behind the gates, the drivers cursed and Sysoev went out to raise the barrier. Izvekov leaped out of the first car and approached Sysoev, boots creaking in the snow, briskly stamping his feet. Silently he seized his neck and gradually began bending it to the ground. Sysoev listened to the creaking of his old neck with satisfaction, reasoning to himself: 'Listen to it creak . . . Like some pestilent old poplar.' Izvekov himself, hearing the rustle of Sysoev's twisted neck bending nearer and nearer to the ground, thought: 'Tough neck still . . . sixty years old and you can't just throttle it . . . it's creaking, crying, for God's sake. And you have to admit: I grabbed him hard, I've got a strong arm . . . had a country childhood, understand, that means hungry and hard-working . . . lots of books been written about that, we grew up strong folk, understand.'

Sysoev, as if listening to a storm outside, thought: 'He grabbed me hard, damn him . . . could crack a tendon! That's it . . . no point squealing like a stuck pig . . . It's like a cold wind over my shoulders . . . listen, it's like February gone wild.' In accordance with his observation, this year's snow scattered from Izvekov's lids, and he began plucking last year's leaves from his hair with his frost-covered free hand. Heartened by the frost, Sysoev kept exclaiming, drawing his finger across the paper, quietly dozing from time to time: 'I see: point one – delivery of a load. Point two – bugger's fixed to the tailboard. Point three – Not Valid . . . I can see the damn load, and the tailboard too, but where's your Not Valid, for fuck's sake?'

Locked together, struggling, they crawled into the cab – swearing, spitting pine-needles and leaves. Snow tumbled from their backs, the snowstorm began scattering flakes over Sysoev's lids. But flying away into a distant, childish dream under its roar, Sysoev sensed that Izvekov's tenacious claw was not relaxing its hold on his neck. Sysoev rocked in distant half-slumber, and memory, as if cradling him, kept whispering: He'll start crying like a child, he'll start crying like a child . . . At that point the winter's day completed its short round above their heads. The storm had grown still. Diamond stars swarmed out across the black sky. Beyond Izvekov's temples, beyond his shoulders powdered with snow, Sysoev could clearly make out endless spiky snowdrifts. The terrifying expanses of the Russian night opened like an abyss. Decorating it, little gold sleighs glided into the distance, like graceful old-fashioned mono-grams. An immortal, curly-headed Moor sped by in them, his hand tick-tocking as if alternately designating Izvekov and Sysoev, one as a beast, the other as a child. Observing these marvellous sleighs,

Sysoev thought with delight: 'Suddenly my head is clear for great, endless thoughts! In truth we have no power over its dawning . . .' In actual fact endless distances had come into view, as far as summer itself, as far as a miraculous July full of silver falling stars. In the depths of the days transparently revealed, one after another, in the depths of the summer, at the arbitrary point from which it stretches out equidistantly in all directions with the precision of a geometrical plan, stood Mikhailov. Tall, flat-arsed, he turned towards Sysoev and his eye, moist and brown, strove miserably to free itself from the captivity of his equine face.

'Is it winter already?' he asked sadly.

His phrase dropped rhythmically into space, he listened attentively to its rustling. Mikhailov's glance fell upon part of the refrigerator factory that stood below the railway embankment along which he was wandering, swaying gently, whether from hunger or from the fact of being a profound illusion, Sysoev could not make out. Mikhailov smelt fluoro-chlorides. They were what caused the ozone hole. A cosmic, vacuum tunnel of cold stretched out from the factory. Birds that accidentally transected it fell to the ground dead. A locomotive crossed the bridge. A clear-eyed driver sat in the high cabin, an expression of frozen merriment upon his face. He was dead. His hair, eyebrows and face were silvered with the cosmic cold of absolute zero. The track of the tunnel was designated on the ground: a wide yellow strip stretched across the faded grass, clambered over fences and buildings, left the city, crossed the ring road, stretched beyond – across days and nights lit by the morning sun or the light of the moon, lost in rain or mist, or glistening with midday snow. It crawled further, towards the Antarctic . . .

He awoke at dawn when the rain ceased. He awoke under trees, fatigued, his equine face towards the dawn. It bent over him, it touched his forehead with its cold fingers and sat next to him for a long time, lost in thought. Around midday it became hot in the small sunny park. He turned on his stomach, his fingers groped tree roots under last year's foliage and stayed there. Soon overfed children with little melting eyes arrived in the park. At first they uttered piercing cries above him, then they began jumping across him, treading on his head, his back, his arms. Each of them tried to pinch him, he distinguished something bird-like in their voices: it seemed to him that these were birds circling above him and pecking his skull. He pressed himself closer to the roots, his large equine face ached. They picked a hole in his skull, squealed when blood spurted, fled in all directions. Mikhailov leaped up – a current of hot steam surged above his head.

'Is it winter already?' Mikhailov asked quietly.

The white wind tore the whisper from his lips, bore it over the empty white city, shredded it in back streets: it was winter. And then he belatedly wound his hot arms around the trees, imploring, his eyes climbing higher and higher, hastening in pursuit of the golden pine borne away on its trunk into the millennial eternity of summer: it was winter. And then he belatedly huddled up, and his wet clothes, embracing his body, exuded steam, and the wind began tossing this steam above his poor head, it whistled in the hole, his white whisper flew over the speechless city:

'It's winter.'

There are no leaves, buildings are scarlet like fire. If you stretch out your hands to warm them, the fingers are immediately covered with hoarfrost. And your lips as well.

He spent that night in a half-ruined building. He was woken at midnight by the rustle of the orthodox in motion. First he became aware of their odour; the smell was caustic, miasmic. He began to feel sick. He went to the crippled window. A grey mass – perhaps it was the body of a gigantic snake? – was rhythmically flowing along the street in the pale luminescent glow. The face of each of the orthodox was alive with its own petty rat-like life. It seemed as if they were gnawing something as they walked, their jaws working rapidly. Their eye-sockets, veiled with a pink membrane, blind, were fixed upon the back of each other's heads. The frame of gold glasses glinted faintly. An invisible woman cried out feebly and plaintively from the flow. The voice approached, the woman was shouting something, clasping her children to her – to her sickly, undeveloped breasts. The children were also shouting something, turning their faces towards Mikhailov.

The cold of mystery pierced his heart: they were his children, it was his wife. She fell upon one knee, then on both knees, but the current covered her and swept her away. Brought to his senses by the shock, he rushed into the street. The orthodox were already far away, in other streets. Only their track remained: slimy, whitish, as if a gigantic snail had crept through the city. The air was filthy and saturated with the heavy moisture of this track – it did not diffuse but seemed to stick to the rough walls. Mikhailov ran along the track, slipping and falling, his face and hands slapping against pavement and walls, summoned by the persistent voice of his wife and the voices of his children. He felt they were still nearby – there, in a nearby street, round the corner, behind a kiosk, beyond a bus stop. He ran, driven wild by pain and tenderness, covered with clods of grey gelatinous slime.

'I won't quarrel with that, it's winter . . .' Sysoev mumbled, dropping deeper into the cradling crackle of Izvekov's palm on his neck, no longer able to make out his face, buried in melancholy snowdrifts of meditation. Once again the graceful gold monogram of the genial Moor flashed before him in the ineluctable darkness of Russian nights – and so distinctly that Sysoev felt that in a moment he would see his face peering over the gleaming beaver collar, would see his narrow hand which, in a sheer feminine manner, he was swinging tick-tock back and forwards, as if humouring Sysoev and his perpetual openness to great thoughts.

'Are you going to open your eyes or not?' Sysoev heard Viktoriya's voice above him. The warmth of the office rapidly enveloped his body, he raised his head from Viktoriya's shoulder. This occurred at the very moment that Viktoriya took the red pencil in her hand, clasped the official file so as to set down a regular resolution on regulation paper. 'Sorry, love,' Sysoev thought. The door opened, Mikhailov entered. An orthodox character shuffled in, stood next to Viktoriya, turned his face upwards, drew in air between his small, bared teeth.

'What's your business?' Viktoriya asked.

'The paper about my pecked head,' Mikhailov replied.

'The paper about his pecked head,' the orthodox character repeated.

He froze, like an upright icicle. His sightless eyes dodged like rapid tumours beneath the pink membrane of the lids. Sysoev gave a forced smile denoting his absolute joint disposition to resolve the question in accordance with the spirit of the times.

'Leave the document.' Chepurnaya raised her finger to the hole, caught the flow of steam, stuck it to the report, laid it on top of the pile, scrawling boldly: 'For in-depth analytical study of guard Sysoev's case, which coincides with that of Izvekov. To be carried out instantly, the matter must not be postponed.'

'Wait for an answer.' She nodded.

'Wait for an answer, flat-arsed beanpole,' Sysoev repeated.

The orthodox character kissed her lips. She laid a hand on his head, on his thin covering of hair, closed her eyes and her heavy body lapsed into a sensuous frenzy. Mikhailov tarried, an unwilling witness of another's love. Viktoriya Chepurnaya tore herself away from the orthodox character and stared at Mikhailov, majestically throwing back her head, framed in flaming bronze hair. Her earrings trembled ponderously, shook as if gears had at that moment been shifted and she was setting off. Mikhailov's imagination could easily extrapolate her trajectory in space and time. By adding the basic terrestrial velocity of her mind's and body's motion (in physics designated as delta v zero) to the headlong velocity of the earth's flight through the colossal chambers of the raging magnetic storm (that is, cosmic V), one might represent the velocity of her flight. In essence, that velocity was monstrous and terrifying, although they found themselves, within the space of the room, at total rest relative to one another, and only her heavy gold earrings trembled, filling Mikhailov with dread. In this trembling he distinguished hidden and horrifying forces, whose vectors projected outwards from the centre of gravity of his mind and body and threatened to disrupt them. Perhaps only the ancient grey bird flying above the earth, scattering the ashes and dust of long-burned cities, libraries and museums from its wings – only the bird could tranquilly screw up its narrow eye that contained neither thought nor feeling. It gave a tired flap of its wings, which were already lit by the light of the next day. It could see what Mikhailov could not yet see. In the sunny early morning of the next day, deep below on the floor of a swimming pool of air, a small woman walked the convex Earth – hardly touching it with her feet, covering her thin undeveloped breasts with her hand. Her eyes were wide open in horror, the first hoarfrost lay on her hair, as also on the trees, a gigantic file – already weightless – stretching away in the same direction. The bird kept flying. When the light of midday fell on its grey wings, a sharp tug at her hair threw the woman on her back, drew her deeper into the current of trees, crushed together trunks, branches and roots from which clumps of earth dropped slowly – and dragged them there, to the Antarctic, to the hole that had already turned completely white, glistening with hoarfrost. Only Sysoev paid any attention to this glint – it struck his eyes. Sysoev raised his snow-powdered lids, freeing himself a little from Izvekov's seasoned claw. At that very instant the bird cast an indifferent glance at the two folk in canvas boots, frozen in a wrestler's hold amid the endless snowy plains – and at that moment Sysoev's ear turned to stone, grey and ancient like the bird itself . . .

Translated from the Russian by Michael Molnar

Viktor Lapitskii

Ants

I remember very well how it all began. I always took great care of my fingernails and kept them long, clean and manicured, but suddenly I noticed something black, some sort of little black lump under the nail of my right index finger. I immediately picked it out with a sharpened match; it turned out to be an ant. At first it floundered about a little on my palm, then fled away, with me after it, and I crushed it. I had not yet guessed that my insides were rearing ants. It was hard to work out where it came from. I knew that ants infested certain apartments, obviously a particular domestic species, and lived no worse a life there than any other domesticated insect: fleas, lice, bedbugs, cockroaches, clothes moths, flies, ticks, worms. However, every time I went out for dinner or a night out, I left powerful insecticides behind in my room: fluorophosphate emulsion and a sprig of mistletoe, consequently I never noticed a single insect at home. So I was left totally amazed and ignorant as to its provenance, that is, about the history of this tiny insect. I understood everything much later, after ants began persistently finding their way out of me into the open. Even now I have never seen the actual moment when they emerge from my flesh, I have my own ideas on that score but will speak of them later. At first the ants appeared primarily from under my fingernails, though they may simply have been more noticeable there. Then they began crawling out of my nose, out of my nostrils, crawling out of the right and left ones with more or less equal frequency. They only crawled out of my mouth in my sleep. That was in the beginning, then they gradually took over almost the entire surface of my body. They especially loved, and still love, appearing in my hirsute parts, I first noticed that combing my plaits over a virgin sheet of laid paper. A dozen or so black dots rapidly began sketching incomprehensible trajectories. At that time I was trying to crush them, annihilate them as quickly as possible, at the same time I wanted to grind them to powder, to dust, so that nothing at all should remain of them, I was ashamed of them, I aimed at annihilating their traces and not a single one of them on the paper, on that sheet of laid paper, the Laid Virgin, out of that first convocation, as I afterwards dubbed it, not one escaped me. Then I first began to think, should I not go to the doctor, but I was deeply ashamed and took refuge in the usual home cures: hot baths of slightly poisoned syrup, vodka and honey taken internally and kohl applied to the acupuncture points. Then I took nosedrops and tried to breed ladybirds in the garden, in a chamber pot with kerosene and spirits – my first attempt at a bio-defence system, but it failed because there weren't any of the pests. All this was as effective against the ants as whistling in the dark. And the ants were crawling full speed out of my sleeves and cuffs, out of my tee-shirt and pants, out of my hankies and gloves, not to speak of my caps, ear-flaps and hats. It was much later that I noticed how often they crawled back under my clothes and disappeared without a trace. True, it now seems to me that they simply hadn't learned straight away how to crawl back into me, since they also hadn't learned straight away, as I said, to crawl out, creep over my face, and if required I could produce a chronicle of their successes in invading more and more uncultivated regions of my body. By the way, they appeared especially frequently on my face, almost constantly, when nobody was looking at me and I myself was not looking in a mirror. Nowadays they all creep back into me during the night, but what they used to do in the evenings, and how they learned, I still don't know, after all not a single one of the ants I then saw remained alive. They wake up and begin their activity, very busily, it must be said, as a rule at cock-crow and, apparently, long before me, inclined as I am, I must confess, to get up late and, if possible, go late to bed. But to return to my, to our, evolution. Thus I could not persuade myself to consult a doctor. I was ashamed ... Yes, and would it help? Furthermore there were always such queues for the veterinary parasitologist. I tried making an appointment with a specialist entomologist. But my specimen ant aroused active antipathy in him, he abused its appearance, said it lacked breeding and announced that he would not speak to me until I could produce its genealogy. Well, I wasn't going to pull my own passport out of my trouser pockets for him. By that time my irrational anger and hatred towards the ants had already passed, I was thinking more and more about what and who they were. These minute tiny little devils, were they not my flesh, flesh of my flesh? Here I remembered a couple of historical precedents, perhaps my predecessors: Plutarch's meticulous description of the unfortunate Sulla, whose flesh suddenly turned into worms, and Hadrian, from whose nose, according to his own words, there frequently crawled out little yellowish pupae like tiny chicks, nevertheless maggots – but these are not ants and not even ant larvae, especially since larvae practically never crawled out of me. Apart from that, in the first instance flesh was simply transformed into worms, and in the second worms (apparently yellow cerebral vermiculi) only crawled out of the nose. Well, the case described by the crafty surgeon in no way resembles my own. As for larvae, mature ants began evacuating them from me when, as an experiment, I took a heavy internal dose of DDT. It must be said that even under these extreme circumstances I still did not manage even once to glimpse the moment when the ants appeared from under my skin. I think that either one's gaze occasions some unknown kind of pressure on the skin, or, possibly, causes it in some respect – whether physical, chemical, biological or mathematical – to become impenetrable. Or perhaps the skin is a semiconductor, diode or triode, it only allows movement in one direction, either the gaze from outside or the ants from inside . . . Sometimes when I suddenly doze in broad daylight I dream that an enormous white ant is crawling out of my mouth. Once when I had a sudden temperature and a battle took place under my armpit between a dozen red ants and a bevy of black, I dreamed that my tongue was a penis. It slowly grew erect, struggled with my jaws, I did not want to let it out, I clenched my teeth, but that only encouraged it and it balked, it thrust its head out of my mouth, I felt it looking round, straining, straightening its swelling limbs, stretching up to full height, its thighs atremble in agitation, its body shuddering and with a lunge and a spurt and a plunge, it was off, swift and impetuous like a white foam-comb on a mountain stream, imperceptibly shifting from trot to amble – a large, beautiful, terrible white ant. After this pollution I had frequent and regular flows, almost each lunar month. But I was never able to find out whether they were accompanied by ants. In theory I think that the entire sphere of the organs of excretion, whether or not they coincide with the organs of generation, is not the ants' domain, not the termites' province; although I find them from time to time under the foreskin, but this only happens when the head has been washed spotless and there is not the slightest trace of any sort of liquid, and then only because they didn't circumcise me in infancy. It is probable that scarabs and associates of the eagle-owl are responsible for the excretory organs, and now they no longer want anything to do with man, hence the continual regression, the pollution of man's internal world for millennia, beginning with the defeat of Ancient Egypt in the Seven Day War with Israel. And I, in the form of a sphere, more precisely the sphere of my ego, floating, seeping through the darkness of internal crossings, passages, exits, entrances of the ant heap, thus remained in ignorance as regards the mechanics of excretion of substances processed by the ants, while I float, seep through the darkness of my ego. The darkness within is full of colours, it glitters vainly and vacuously, bright variegated spots can be discerned, the light tastes bitter, completely bitter, everything is black within blackness, beyond darkness. A multitude of approaching ants, crepitation, noises or faces. I never bump into them which is surprising. They cannot notice me. It interests me to watch them conversing, touching antennae, deciding to communicate, perhaps about me, I am alone and there are many of them, in the lower circle of my extremities they are smaller, probably these are simply worker types, sexless, that can be sensed. Strange that I am setting this down, for my sphere has no memory. There is nothing comparable to memory. All one can say about it is that it is black, that it is absolutely impenetrable and that it is endless, boundless and isotropic inside. That its interior is endless, boundless and isotropic. And it has no centre, no navel. And it seems that not only has it no memory but that that is *a priori* excluded. Although possibly it somehow uses my memory. This is difficult to understand and believe. It still seems to me that the repulsive, fat, greasy worms are somehow connected with memory – the white larvae that live in compost, at the very bottom, under the ant heap, below, in the region of the brain, senseless, mindless allies of my ant heap. But in nightmares they appear to me not as allies but enemies, dreadful monsters whose appearance makes my flesh creep, toothed and fanged, craving flesh and blood, with a serrated beak like a pelican, they nest in the depths of sand dunes, patient and assiduous, lugworms, larvae of the lion-ant, incarnating the battle of the Hittites with the Myrmidons for the right bank of the Acheron. It is not known whether the lion threatens the sphere. Probably not. For the sphere is completely impenetrable, just like my skin, to the gaze. Sometimes I had the impression that in both cases the reason was the same – the gaze, its poison. It is very likely that someone, furthermore very possibly I myself, watches the sphere all the time – from within or outside, it doesn't matter – ensuring its impenetrability, like that of the skin. I set up a series of experiments with the gaze. I looked at myself in the mirror, my face was impenetrable. Then I looked through a mirror at the mirror reflecting me and the result was the same. Then I looked through a mirror at a mirror reflecting the mirror that reflected me, and all the time it was the same as if I was looking directly at myself, into my own eyes. On the basis of these findings I began constructing a theory of reflections. But could I be a basilisk? And no sooner did I close my eyes, lie down to sleep, than twice-born creatures ran forth across my cheeks as from the head of Zeus. At times I was overcome by weakness, and despair was also at hand, within my grasp, something within me demanded that I change something in myself. At such moments and minutes I usually took new, decisive measures. Once I armed myself with the largest encyclopaedia, which is called Soviet, for its scope, and studied everything I could in it, all the articles on insects and articles on the internal world of humans and their soul. This greatly extended my rather narrow range, jogged my imagination, helped me to a new conception of many, if not all, phenomena in the real environment. In particular it forced me to have recourse to Freud's theories, and I now decided that the sexual problem was closely linked to the formic aspects of reality and my psychic life. I felt that, for a start, I should normalize my sexual life. I took to frequenting the local brothel. But failure awaited me there. All my partners, all as one woman, immediately began giggling as soon as I touched their bodies, and when I got as far as the loins they simply guffawed, howled out that their skin was crawling, that it tickled, tickled intensely and that I should desist. I took fright and desisted. Having endured a fiasco, for a time I left my penis in perfect peace, I decided to change my circumstances, to travel, perhaps the ants were an attribute of my house, my apartment, my room, my corner. But here too failure awaited me. The first night I rented a chic furnished room in a fashionable hotel. Numerous bedbugs inhabited this chamber, but in the night my ants drove them out and the next morning there was a row and I was forced to leave, and lucky for me they didn't fine me as well. I returned home terribly depressed, life was merciless. After a couple of days' torment, I decided to settle my accounts. I set off for the market and acquired a couple of bunches of white toadstools. I then cooked myself the most exquisite dish to be found in Escoffier: *filet* of boiled salmon stuffed with mushrooms in a cyanide sauce and laid my final banquet. Afterwards I was not even ill, not even slightly unwell, on the other hand the ants died in their thousands, their corpses and carcasses, deformed by their final convulsions, horribly swollen, already decaying, rained from my skin. Extruded intestines, piles of filth fallen from burst abdomens, convulsed tumours, feebly quivering palpae, snapped extremities, blue tongues, a heavy sweetish odour of corpses . . . The result was something like bloodletting and it must be said that it greatly invigorated me, and at the same time bleached my thoughts. I had a bath and began a new phase of measured existence. My habits changed. I distanced myself ever more frequently from the noise and vanity of the city, I spent ever more time in woods, gardens and parks, amidst brooks and breezes, observing the local ant heaps, sometimes casting a disapproving glance at passing dragonflies, my gaze caressing the swarms of dear little insects. The ants scurried among the knot-grass like birds in buckwheat, here and there they erected hills of their habitations, homes for their own kind, followed their occupations, and in the branches above squirrels leaped, gnawed pine nuts and occasionally the shadow of a solitary soaring snow goose floated past. I wanted to blend in and become part of nature and for hours lay deep among the ants, I wanted there to be an exchange of substances between myself and the grass around, an exchange of ants, although I never once found ants similar to mine in nature, let alone identical! In the evenings I wandered homewards through the incessant chirping of the cicadas, lazily flapping away swarms of importunate green woodpeckers, I listened to music, I came to myself: my musical tastes gradually changed; whereas previously my favourite singer was Tito Gobbi, now I decisively awarded the date palm of precedence to the hymns of Formico Ruffo. I fell asleep to the strains of his enchanting soprano, and there was no ant heap, no black sphere in my dreams. The head of a needle perhaps. More precisely some sort of point, a point in space smaller than an ant's eye and imbued with my vision, my consciousness, my memory, my desires, my name. And it turned out that it was no longer my consciousness, it was something larger . . . Again I do not know what to call it. This point appeared in a closed garden . . . On a hill, in the midst of emerald grass, in the trilling of birds, in the shadow of cascading trees, among the aroma of flowers, to sweet sounds, perhaps of a harp and the bourdon of bees . . . And next to it a beautiful lady, or girl . . . Always the same one . . . No, each time a different one . . . Oh, not a beggarly one, no . . . In luxurious bright garments like a beautiful great butterfly, a swallowtail. Awaking, I refined my vision-dreams against the whetstone of my consciousness, put my reason in charge of them. And at these times I very much wanted to marry and have a quiet family life, preferably a happy one. I dreamed of a quiet tender spouse, a young girl with long flaxen hair, with as many lice as possible, and not only there, and not only them. But all these tender, heavenly dreams were rudely shattered, trampled upon by brazen reality. I do not even want to speak of what followed . . . I put a small ad in the lonely hearts column, my main requirement was the presence of a great quantity of insects upon my spouse, basically my heart was set on blondes and lice. However, first of all, I met a flea-ridden brunette at a cocktail party, but alas – her fleas did not survive our first encounter and we parted. I already understood that the same thing would happen with the lousy Nibelungen blonde. And naturally I was not wrong. In this manner my matrimonial mania was cured. Thus I lived, nothing formic was strange to me, but nevertheless the sexual sphere remained a blatantly vacant ecological niche in my universe. True, I learned how to sense my womb, my testicles, from within, their orgasm covered me with gooseflesh, but that was all. But everything fell into place when I bought an anteater from the zoo. It was a highly unmarketable item and they sold it to me with gladness and a collar, and cheaply too. To tell you the truth I did not myself know why I was buying it, intuition, pure intuition. Naturally the feeding of the anteater posed no problems, but at first I fed it mainly from my hands. Then I expanded his menu and only much later did we work out what and how it should be done, there were actually two completely different methods. Have you ever seen an anteater, its snout, its mouth, from close up? Probably not. Well then, its snout ends in a long vaginal horn with soft but muscular walls – cheeks much more pleasant to the touch than a standard palate – and at the same time this horn is very narrow and presses firmly, tremulously, on all sides, especially when it makes a swallowing motion, which is how it reacts to any liquid in its mouth. But its tongue! It has an exceedingly long, soft tongue and its mastery of it knows no rival, neither do I. It could twist it into a spiral, form a spoon or a Moebius strip, can sting with the tip, could lick stickily, silently suck, could even administer a gentle beating, a scourging, as with twine, well, what couldn't he do with it! We did not live long together, but I had become attached to him heart and soul, to my little bear, my pussycat. It all ended sadly. I left for two days, on an outing of young naturalists to exterminate all those singing birds that exterminate ants, and when I returned, he misjudged his own capacities, gorged, choked, suffocated and expired. I bitterly mourned him. At the zoo they told me that the production of anteaters had been suspended on account of total lack of demand from the general public. The loss was irreplaceable. Those were difficult days for me, days of torment, days of purgatory. But then I suddenly noticed that my unnatural deselection of ants had worked to the benefit of the ant heap as a whole. It had restructured itself, significantly simplified its fundamental group, reduced it to about two-tenths of those who had formed it, of whom only one-tenth were free, the ants had become stronger, more vigorous, united, now one was indistinguishable from another, wherever they emerged they were identical; in a word, the entire system had taken an extraordinary and great leap forward. Having survived this catharsis, cleansed of filth, I understood that the anteater had been a great test imposed upon me, I suppose, by the highest ant heap, by the black-eyed spirit, that I had undergone an initiation, that now I know and believe that my ant heap has now achieved its purpose, formed a mystic union with the highest ant heap. Now I also discovered my own sexual destiny. I set out for the city park, found the largest ant heap under a juniper shrub and performed upon it a solemn and sexual act. Thus was accomplished my second birth, a birth from chaotic darkness, from a lost life swarming with errors, into the eternal gleaming truth of the heavenly ant heap to come, washed in unseen heavenly light, which I, begrimed with vice and sin, considered blackness. I believe that my soul, having cast aside the black sphere of a central point, will freely and joyfully soar towards that inexpressible aphanistic ant heap, inhabited and dwelt in by ants that are themselves ant heaps incommensurably excelling my own . . .

Therefore, now, as I sense the approach of death with its lion's wings, I, at the threshold of transubstantiation, implore you:

Construct an ant heap upon my grave! Pile pine-needles upon it!

Translated from the Russian by Michael Molnar

Olga Novikova

Philemon and Baucis

After Phil and Ba had seen their only daughter married to a tall, tow-haired student, come to Moscow to 'make better his Russian' – the son of one of Phil's old English colleagues (so long-standing that one could even call him a friend, if that word, applied to a foreigner, had not been so hopelessly ruined by such official turns of phrase as 'my African friend'), after the beloved, bright voice, more clearly audible from distant London than nearby Lianozov, and detailed letters, like alms thrown down by the post – sometimes generous, sometimes meagre – had helped to heal the separation, Phil invented another treatment – strolls around isolated landmarks of courtly and literary Moscow, of Yusupov and Aksakov, those that had been transformed into poor museums or luxuriant ruins, not because this served anyone's purposes, not to punish the past, but because the only houses that were of any use were those that could be used as dachas by a superior brand of citizen.

But they did not talk of politics, although each step – from the bus stop with the smashed glass canopy and the small litter bin that had gorged and choked itself on rubbish, to the stately home, repainted the wrong colour (the original was depicted in paintings by numerous artists, thanks to which a cottage and artist's studio was built before the revolution, and afterwards – a two-storey sanatorium and dormitory with absurd white columns and impractical corridor-rooms) – each glance furnished material for far-reaching generalizations.

It was already long ago that Phil and Ba had discovered the fault in the historical development of their strange country, and new evidence of their correctness brought no joy, but simply grieved them more deeply.

They imagined the fresh red and yellow fretted leaves rustling in the tranquil empty park of the past, long before that fork where life took a wrong turn.

– How close together those two trees have grown! As if from a single root, but so different!

Ba craned her neck to see better which of the two giants was nearer the sun, but a gust of wind snatched away her green, wide-brimmed hat and carried it off into the air, and her hair escaped from the hairgrip and fell onto her shoulders and into her eyes.

First of all Phil sprang to Ba, but rapidly realized that nothing had happened to her, that she wouldn't disappear, and he ran after the hat which was already tiring of its flight and slowly, as if unwillingly, gliding to earth.

– That's an oak. And that's a lime. As defenceless as you.

Phil embraced Ba, and they wandered down an asphalt path with a drainage channel alongside, scattered with faded twigs and leaves.

Sudden darkness gave warning of bad weather, but left no time to prepare for it, and they reached for their umbrellas only after the rain had begun, washing away the entire space between the low sky and the earth.

On the avenue Phil immediately raised his hand, but car after car sped past without braking, and one insolent lorry driver drove through a puddle brimming with black scum and spattered Ba with brown sludge. The umbrella turned inside out and became a vessel for collecting water.

Then a miracle happened – a dark-green car stopped; a broad-shouldered stalwart bent back and, without saying anything, opened the back door, quietly waited while they fixed the umbrellas and, each giving way for the other, slid onto the back seat.

– You don't mind me turning my back to you? I see that their excellencies are returning from their country house? Do they wish to be taken to their town residence?

What was it created this comfort?

The warmth, the humming of the fan demisting the sweating windows?

A freedom and ease of conversation known only to those who

had been abroad or those whom one can imagine as heroes of Aksyonov's or Gladilin's books?

The teasing about the awkwardness of Phil and Hera (as they called their rescuer), about the stains that appeared on their Levi's jackets with their identical warm chequered lining, after fussing around a punctured back tyre?

The trustfulness with which Ba expounded the principal features of their life?

The consideration of and attention to the story about Hera's friend at whose dacha he had spent several days?

Sympathy arose and seized the reins of their life like a charioteer: they took to meeting, or, in the words of Hera's new idiom which did not encumber the spirit, they intersected no less than once a week; they would be together at rehearsals of someone acknowledged in their circles as a genius, at the film club, and when they spent the evening in front of the television (they tried not to miss *Fifth Wheel* and *Viewpoint*) a bed was made for Hera on the divan.

It was easy being together.

But in its passage from one age to another the word 'sympathy' has grown tattered, run to seed and divested itself of such romantic semantic luxuries as that of an unmotivated attraction.

Not for everyone, it is true.

Ba lived semantically in the nineteenth century.

If one did not consider, as a reason or caprice, the satisfaction of seeing that Phil, having at last found an adequate interlocutor, impatiently waited for a slowing down or hesitation in order to insert his opinion (customary or spontaneously generated) into the conversation, to convert it into his monologue; for it was not an interlocutor he had found but a listener sufficiently cultured to grasp the essence of multi-layered economico-ecological theory and to appreciate the relevance of a comparison of our reality to a field intended to produce wheat, but methodically sown with weeds.

If one did not consider the baking of various pies, cakes and tarts by deciphering foreign recipes to be a whim or caprice.

If one considers that apart from our daily bread everything is a whim.

At the end of the winter Zina appeared, with a cropped, geometrical haircut, in a long quilted coat, with two nimble infants, a dark red Zhiguli and a bearded husband-chauffeur, such a free and easy . . . person, girl – both words clumsily resist, but what other ones should one choose if 'young girl' is inexact, 'lady, woman' too adult, she should have decided herself, and for the sake of objectivity one must confess that these words aged Zina; one would have had to decorate and adorn them with the epithets 'young, youthful', reliably to differentiate the generations.

While the adults smiled, became acquainted, drank coffee, while Zina, sweetly and defencelessly kept bending to the right and at identical intervals remembering her irreproachable carriage, enthusiastically confessing that her academician father had praised Phil's doctoral dissertation, that for a whole year she had tried to entice him to their dacha, meanwhile flashing her shining grey eyes and occasionally throwing in a conjunctive 'Remember?!', correctly reckoning that nobody would interpret her enthusiasm as such, but only for what it was – a caprice, a majestic whim; during this short time the little children had taken over the nursery, wrecking its comfort and order, scattering the little wooden, plastic and rubber figures from which the daughter had enjoyed forming various fairy-tale or real-life compositions, and, before leaving, had set up Tom Thumb, Jemima Puddleduck, Peter Rabbit and variously dressed tiny folk in front of the toy train which took her to England.

The road to the dacha seemed unreal, toy-like: black, and not the usual muddy grey with dark bald patches, a ribbon neatly drawn in fresh whiteness, occasionally turning along the edges into a dotted line beyond which . . . what that was, one could only guess, imagine; probably something picked up from life in the West – from films or personal impressions: how it is 'over there' – only that was the way people chose to live whose profession was patriotism.

And so that travellers should not deviate to the right nor the left, that is, not drive there – there was nothing to cross, the forest on both sides was hidden behind a curtain, iron, behind a net that scrawled oblique lines across pillars, although there's not even a whiff of abroad here 'No Entry' signs stood, true enough, not the ones that hit you in the face, but round, white signs were scattered around, one with painted brown reindeer, another with militiamen, alive, in brand new uniforms like in films.

Suddenly it became bumpy, the car dodged potholes, puddles, hummocks, wailed in plangent vexation as it mounted sandy hillocks and skidded in the slushy slew, all in all the fairy-tale was cut short and true life approached, without any transition, without the little bridge that usually completes fairy-tales: 'and they lived happily and died the same day', and she grinned impudently, baring her teeth as if she were not a kind, sly old lady telling it but a wicked witch or a dragon.

Already there were wide fields, thick woods casually powdered with snow and looking like a decorative tableau, a maquette of 'the central Russian belt'.

All in all confusion, sarcasm and irony defaced the beauty of nature and there remained . . . but nothing remained, not even a gurgle, vacuity and sadness remained.

Could everything good be a sequence of words in lines or a set phrase: 'there is a hidden limit to human intimacy', a violet-purple border and coat-tails of amazing peacock's eyes or veiled emerald eyes that made the whole body prickle as if with needles, as if tiny champagne bubbles were bursting – could all this be only in order to extinguish bitterness, annoyance, to put out grief?

Could only the idea of those in a worse condition be of comfort – which the thoughtful intellectual, the free beggar and the sacked bureaucrat can also find?

Does reason offer comfort and do only sympathy and compassion quell pain?

But who will alleviate the suffering of an old woman sent to the almshouse by her own daughter – for those infants who were deprived of God at birth are now seventy-five years old?

*

– What a rich life we lead! It's never happened to me before, to meet so often! But let us not subordinate reason to the passions! We get bored – we become enamoured of separation . . . Do you remember our first journey? I wore a worse coat on that occasion. So as not to embarrass your wife, Phil ('by my youth and splendour' Zina did not add, as something that went without saying). – She turned out to be totally unlike a grey mouse – Zina purred, openly, in front of Ba.

All that was left was to smile knowingly. Ba did not sense any danger or threat.

She was not a mouse.

But it is not only the inoffensive representatives of the cat family that purr.

It is not clear whether it was habit that was deceptive, the need to share with someone near and dear; whether it did not deceive one as to the limit where one must choose, as if it were impossible to love or befriend two people simultaneously – thus Zina grew alert on learning of Hera's existence.

But he rapidly won her over – without direct words or explanations, simply by jokes, mockery, exaggerated praise, which to witnesses seems like lighthearted, inoffensive clowning, but the object is at first amazed by its insight, then subdued, subordinated, charmed, captivated – he has proved that she might count him among her splendid, select retinue, her admirers, that she has no rivals here and 'there could not be any!' – in a whisper, breath tickling her ear, but aloud: 'I doff my hat!' – with an ornate wave that combined the intimate confession – to Zina, and the official – to Phil (well, it would be a shame to waste such a fine gesture on one person).

– Phil was inimitable, was Phil – he savoured the doggerel. – First the heavy artillery of scientific argument, then the buckshot of literary comparisons – and the enemy scatters – in particular talk of Philemon and Baucis rang out – though people don't know the classics they have great respect for them. The flood was the revenge of the gods. You're not a god, mister, it's a mean trick to score off people – in Lenin's tones, placing his left index on an imagined waistcoat and throwing out his right arm, now Hera was no longer parodying Phil but it looked very much as if he were basely and perfidiously baiting him.

Ba and Phil smiled identically, then became confused, attempted to conceal, to hide their satisfaction at the praise – Ba took to admonishing the little children whose parents were paying no attention to the racket they were kicking up, and Phil firmly switched the conversation to Hera.

He clammed up, insisted on joking, did not want to speak about his affairs.

But then – who would have thought that it was a dirty business?

Instead of sleep, night brought all sorts of noises enveloped in ringing silence: coarse scraps of talk (familiar to those who, if only once, have positioned themselves on the dragon's tail, known as a queue – that is, familiar to every Soviet citizen), a timid knocking, then a thumping, a crashing, a crack, a crunch (the aluminium and glass entrance door has no key), a rumbling in the pipes, the sharp clap of car doors – unmysterious, comprehensible noises, the last belch of a bitter, unhappy day.

Phil abruptly turned on his back, threw his arms behind his head, closed his eyes, but then Ba, half asleep, released her hair that he was lying on, he felt the warmth of the body trustingly clinging to him, the gentle weight of a drawn-up leg, the cool cheek on his shoulder, and dim forebodings, unhappy thoughts, alarm and tenderness took refuge in dark corners.

Such a familiar unease and each time an unexpected desire bumped into a tight strip of fabric – another four long nights, three bitter mornings, three working days and three wearisome evenings remained for him to lie still and wait.

In the morning he had to drink a bitter, acrid liquid – the coffee grinder emitted a smell of burned rubber and shuddered to a halt.

A bad sign?

That's not the point.

In order to fix this lack, one would have to search out and visit, either on foot or by bus, all the repairers, which, evidently for the inconvenience of citizens, were situated in the regions around the outermost underground stations, and to plan buying a new one could only be done by taking into account the state, Soviet sense of that verb – whether you'll succeed tomorrow or in a year's time, the devil only knows.

A splinter it is so difficult to extract.

The familiar feeling of discomfort, of having been done.

Anyone can understand, well, if not about a coffee grinder, then about a television set if you can't live without one, or about a peacock butterfly if your collection lacks that particular specimen.

You can say – it's a whim, superfluous, it's easy to do without all of that.

That is also how they speak at the highest governmental level. And to whom? – to American senators. They probably think that the subject is private swimming pools – which is a luxury for them too, it's hard even to guess. And the ones who are speaking are those who possess that luxury, both in the American and Soviet sense of the word.

In the afternoon of a dull day in early summer, when tears are about to pour from the scowling clouds, when misfortunes curdle, when clumsy words and meaningless actions pile up – there is little hope that the morning will wash away all the garbage; Zina, who called Phil such names to herself, searched for a manual coffee grinder, completely useless for her household and so essential to his.

Looking for a telephone box, he walked all the way round the internal and external circumference of a gigantic block, some kind of letter or a hieroglyph sticking up in the centre of Moscow.

Dust everywhere, the enormous, rusty iron word 'Communism' lay in the shed, at the head of the swelling queue a woman in a raincoat and ragged sandals (clothes from various seasons) calls out numbers from a ledger in a voice that will always be prepared for a slanging match.

Poverty has become legal – a mumbling old man with a blue-white litre carton of milk.

Scratched in English, in capital letters on the silvery telephone box, is the obscenity familiar to every Soviet citizen: GO FUCK YOURSELF (we have, after all, taken something from Western civilization), and in the receiver there is not even silence but the final crackle of a device expiring that very moment.

Everything's going to the dogs, not only old estates, palaces, churches, not only mind, honour and conscience?

The apartment code came back of its own accord. In the lift – a battered cage with mirror eyes – Phil prepared his first phrase: 'I'm sorry, I didn't bring any flowers, I've only dropped in for a moment', but didn't have time to utter it: Zina, in tight short trousers, a knitted, décolleté tee-shirt, with a hair-dryer held to her temples like a pistol, commanded: 'Look after the coffee,' and vanished into the bathroom.

To run full speed into loneliness!

A disciplined train of thought went askew, turned through the very doorway into which, only a few days previously, Phil had forbidden himself to glance.

Fragments of rumours, hints and unstated thoughts arose and took shape. Hera, he was the only one well enough acquainted with the cuisine that, following Phil's recipes, concocted decisions about the fate of a patch of ground dear to many, to find one of the many and become the chief and well-rewarded advisor to that person.

And since there should be no clear evidence of that treachery, nothing will collapse – neither the world, nor a career, nor personal life, nothing will change – one could get up in the morning in exactly the same way, go to work, return home to a solicitous and understanding Ba – this made it even more bitter, even harder.

Phil shuddered and recoiled from a tender touch. – You don't have to be so desperate, love – it was as if Zina had read his thoughts. – You're not to blame for anything at all. You're simply too noble, too trusting for these vicious times.

And her clothes – her soft, comforting intonations, and her naked essence, hard to recognize in the disorder, could have helped to overcome the tension, to step out of a dumb auditorium where those sitting in the wrong seats are told off, onto a stage where one would have to act something familiar from memories of one's unmarried youth, from books, from frank male conversations; it wouldn't matter if one made a mistake – the director, who had picked the leading role for himself, was there at hand.

And the décor was suitable: a rectangular brown bottle, crystal tumblers, a spacious empty apartment, the room alert, a solid oak door, not a glass one, heavy shutters, a parquet floor squeaking honestly underfoot; glass-faceted eyes sparkle.

Embraces on the sofa where you cannot evade a smouldering glance, the touch of a thigh, the stab of breasts.

His back prickled from the woollen plaid, his self-love from the question – 'That's it?' and the business-like warning: 'Careful not to stain it,' offered together with a roll of toilet paper.

So she knew what would happen all along?

And complaints unexpectedly torn from her about the taxi-driver's praise: 'I wouldn't mind sleeping with somebody like you'; about her philoprogenitive boss, father of two minors (of his children – such a word!) with whom she fed a foreign scientist in the Sofia restaurant and afterwards drank vodka straight from the bottle in the square in front of his home; about her large breasts too frequently attracting men's gaze; could this all have been artillery practice, artistic, one had to admit, and, as it turned out, well calculated?

Ba never found anything out.

She naturally understood that some misfortune had struck Phil.

Phil and not herself.

He is silent, not wanting to hurt her.

But why the evasive glances, the guilty smile?

'Don't touch!' – says the mind, but the tongue is attracted to the tooth, the ragged edge of thought, to confirm that the pain is in place.

The body is already waiting for the pain to obstruct, to fence off the stark horror that has come striding through a door trustfully flung wide.

The air wrinkled above the wet road, the car sputtered in agitation, lividly spattering dark filth across its face.

They sped as if waiting somewhere at hand were sun, clear skies, dry level asphalt.

A guest of the capital swathed in her rags ('you don't know anyone in Moscow, dress in your worst possible clothes'), in her wallets and her life, flashed across the path of the lorry towards a queue that was growing in front of her very eyes.

The young soldier at the wheel unexpectedly, mistakenly, veered and encountered an experienced taxi-driver, exchanging Phil and Ba's impending future (Sheremetevo, flowers, their happy daughter) for a far distant one, a fairy-tale finale: they lived happily and died the same hour, the same instant.

Translated from the Russian by Michael Molnar

Biographical Notes

SERBIA, CROATIA, SLOVENIA

BORA ĆOSIĆ, born in 1932, is a prolific Serbian writer of fiction and essays. His books include: *The Thieves' House* (1954), *All the Mortals* (1958), *Visible and Invisible Man: A Subjective History of Film* (1962), *Sodom and Gomorrah* (1963), *Stories About Trades* (1966), *My Family's Role in the World Revolution* (1969), *Why Did We Fight* (1972), *The Tutors* (1978), *Bel Tempo* (1982), *An Interview at Lake Zürich* (1989), *Musil's Notebook* (1989), *The Disintegration* (1991), *The Zagreb Analysis* (1991), and *Look of the Feebleminded* (1991).

DRAGO JANČAR, born in 1948, is an eminent Slovene prose writer, essayist, playwright, editor and translator. His prose works include: *Pilgrimage of Mr Houžvička* (1971), *Galjot* (1978), *The Pale Sinner* (1978), *Northern Gleam* (1984), *Death at Mary of the Snows* (1985). His articles and essays have been collected in *Along with Time* and *Terra Incognita* (1989).

SLAVENKA DRAKULIĆ, born in 1949, is a Croatian journalist and cultural commentator, and was the co-founder of the first feminist group in Yugoslavia in 1979. The author of two novels, *Holograms of Fear* (1992) and *Marble Skin* (1993), she has also written several non-fiction books, including *How We Survived Communism and Even Laughed* (1992) and *The Balkan Express* (1993).

DAVID ALBAHARI, born in 1948, is a Serbian writer primarily known for his short stories and literary anthologies. His books of short fiction include: *Family Time* (1973), *Judge Dimitrijević* (1978), *Ordinary Stories* (1978), *Description of Death* (1982), *A Shock in the Shed* (1984), *Simplicity* (1988), and *Zinc* (1989).

POLAND

PIOTR SZEWC was born in Zamość in 1961. He is a poet and critic. *Annihilation* (1993) is his first work of prose. Set in a small Galician town, some time before the Second World War, the novella records an apparently uneventful day and night in the life of the town and several of its inhabitants. It is a book about time and a world that moves quietly towards its inevitable end.

HANNA KRALL, born in Warsaw in 1937, is renowned in Poland for her incisive interviews and reportages. Krall worked as a reporter in the Soviet Union, travelled in Western Europe, America and provincial Poland. Her books of reportage include *East of Arbat*, *To Outwit God* (a book-length interview with Marek Edelman, one of the leaders of the Warsaw ghetto uprising), *Six Shades of White*, *Hard to Get Up in the Morning*, *Hypnosis* (1989) and *Legoland* (1991). Krall is the author of two novels: *The Subtenant* (Solidarity Cultural Award, 1986) and *Windows* (1987). She presently contributes to *Gazeta Wyborcza*.

JERZY PILCH was born in Wiśle in 1952. He moved to Kraków where he taught at Jagiellonian University. During martial law he co-founded *Na Głos*, the influential 'talking magazine'. His first novel, *The Admissions of a Clandestine Author of Erotic Prose* (1988), received the Koscielski Foundation Prize in Switzerland. *The Register of Adulteresses: Travel Writing*, has recently been published in Poland. Pilch contributes to the literary journal *Puls* and the Catholic weekly *Tygodnik Powszechny*.

PAWEŁ HUELLE was born in Gdańsk in 1957. He worked in Solidarity's press information office before the onset of martial law. From 1988 to 1989, he guided one of Poland's 'talking journals', which featured semi-clandestine readings of writers and journalists who were unable or unwilling to publish their work in the Communist-controlled press. His first novel, *Who Was David Weiser?* (1991), gathered many awards and was acclaimed as one of the most innovative works of fiction in post-war Polish literature. Huelle works as a literary critic and reviewer. 'Mina' comes from his new book of short stories *Moving House* (1994).

HUNGARY

PÉTER NÁDAS was born in Budapest in 1942. Throughout the 1960s he worked as a reporter and photo-journalist, publishing his first volume of short stories in 1967. His highly successful first novel, *The End of a Family Novel* (1977), has been translated into several languages. Nádas's second novel, *A Book of Memoirs* (1986), which tackles themes of memory, personal identity and historical continuity, is regarded by many as the masterpiece of post-war Hungarian fiction. Since *A Book of Memoirs*, Nádas has concentrated primarily on a form of essay-writing which fuses discursive and imaginative prose.

LÁSZLÓ MÁRTON was born in Budapest in 1959. He graduated from Budapest University in 1983 with a degree in German and sociology, then went to work for a major Hungarian publisher. He is widely recognized as the most talented of a younger generation of Hungarian prose writers. His works include *The Great Budapest Ghost-Hunt* (1984) and *Refuge* (1985). 'The Sunken Apple Tree' was published in 1991.

PÉTER ESTERHÁZY was born in Budapest in 1950. He graduated in mathematics from the University of Budapest in 1974 and published his first volume of short stories in 1976. His first novel, *A Novel of Production* (1979), immediately established his reputation as the most challenging and experimental writer of his generation. Over the following seven years Esterházy published a series of novels and short stories under the umbrella title, *An Introduction to Literature*, collected in one volume in 1986. *Helping Verbs of the Heart* (1992) and *The Book of Hrabal* (1993) have been translated into English. 'Down the Danube' is from Esterházy's latest novel, *The Glance of Countess Hahn-Hahn* (1994), a 'fiction' about the meaning and significance of the river.

LAJOS GRENDEL was born in 1948 into the Hungarian minority in Slovakia. He studied English and Hungarian at the University of Bratislava, graduating in 1973. He published his first novel in 1979, but it was his three subsequent novels, *Live Ammunition* (1981), *Gang* (1981) and *Transpositions* (1985), which established his reputation as one of the most important Hungarian novelists living and writing outside Hungary. His most recent novel is *Einstein's Bells* (1992). Grendel played a significant political role in the Hungarian-Slovak community in the transition of 1989. His fiction explores the plight, psychology and everyday life of a national minority struggling to come to terms with its own past and identity.

CZECH REPUBLIC

BOHUMIL HRABAL was born in 1914, studied law, and has been a railway worker, a travelling salesman, steel-worker, wastepaper packer and scene shifter, author of short stories, fiction and essays. English versions of his works include: *Closely Observed Trains, The Death of Mr Baltisberger* (short stories), *I Served the King of England, Too Loud a Solitude,* and recently, *The Little Town Where Time Stood Still* (1993). 'The Pink Scarf' is one of a series of letters, to a young American woman, depicting events in Czechoslovakia leading up to, and beyond, the 'Velvet Revolution' of November 1989; a number of earlier letters are translated in *Letters to Dubenka* (1994).

EDA KRISEOVÁ was born in 1940. During the 1960s she worked as a journalist and travelled widely in Europe, Turkey, Algeria, Israel, India, Cambodia and Japan. Her fiction of the 1970s and 1980s was published abroad; she has worked with Václav Havel and is author of *Václav Havel, a Biography* (1991). 'The Unborn' is taken from her collection *Arboretum* (1987).

ALEXANDRA BERKOVÁ was born in 1949, studied glass-making and Czech, and writes for television (recently, a series on marital problems); 'He Wakes Up' is taken from her début volume *Book with a Red Jacket* (1986). This was followed by her satirical-allegorical novella *Magoria* (1991).

ONDŘEJ NEFF was born in 1945, and has worked in publishing, photography and journalism; writes science fiction as well as studies of science fiction. 'Brownian Motion' is taken from his story collection *Fourth Day to Eternity* (1987).

SLOVAKIA

PAVEL VILIKOVSKÝ was born in 1941. He is the translator of Virginia Woolf, William Faulkner, Malcolm Lowry, Ian McEwan, William Burroughs, Kurt Vonnegut and others, co-editor of *Romboid*, the most independent-minded Slovak (and Czechoslovak!) literary journal of the 1970s and 1980s, author of short stories and other fiction, much of it printed many years after it was written. 'Escalation of Feeling', from his short-story volume *Escalation of Feeling* (1989), dates from the 1970s.

JÁN JOHANIDES was born in 1934, studied art history, and has been a freelance writer since 1969, and author of novels, novellas, short stories and plays; he was unable to publish for some years in the 1970s. Several books have been translated into Hungarian and German. 'Memorial to Don Giovanni' is taken from his recent book *Cry of Thrushes Before Sleep* (1992).

DUŠAN MITANA: born 1946, studied film and television, worked for the literary magazine *Romboid*, from 1975 a freelance writer, author of fiction, as well as TV and film scripts. 'On the Threshold' is the title story from his collection *On the Threshold* (1987).

RUDOLF SLOBODA was born in 1938, studied briefly, worked as a miner, builder's labourer, and foundry worker, later as an editor and in films. His books include novels and short stories. 'The White Dog' is taken from his short-story collection *Men's Night Out* (1986).

BULGARIA

IVAILO DICHEV was born in 1955. 'To those of us born in the mid fifties, when thermonuclear testing was at its height, mutation is not something out of the ordinary. On average five inches taller than our parents, we were introduced to television and tape recorders quite early in our childhood, which makes sense since television and tape recorders entered Bulgaria at about the same time at which we entered the world. The important thing was to live better than our parents, although the world we ended up living in turned out to be rather plastic at times. Eventually, we reached our collective orgasm in 1989, and the unfolding events have since given us the opportunity to renounce everything and to start anew. A new birth, a new childhood amongst the ruins: the cherished West stretching before us from horizon to horizon. And there is my humble self sitting in front of the computer, disturbed by the first symptoms of claustrophobia, trying very hard to interpret everything, to rearrange things, to mutate . . .' Publications include: *Identification* (1987), *The End of the World* (1989) and *Literalisms* (1991).

VICTOR PASKOV, who was born 1949, is very guarded and reclusive when it comes to volunteering information about himself. He has published three novels – one of which, *Ballad for Georg Henig* (1990), exists in French and English translations. He took a degree as a musician at the Conservatoire in

Leipzig, but decided to pursue a literary career. He is now regarded as the foremost contemporary novelist in Bulgaria.

IVAN KULEKOV: 'I was born in 1951 in the village of Hirevo. This village is not shown on most maps of Bulgaria for the same reason that Bulgaria itself does not appear on some maps of the world – an inferiority complex. Understandably, perhaps, I have spent most of my adult life trying to overcome this complex: I went to university in Sofia, spent nearly sixteen years with Bulgarian National Radio, spent a further three years making regular appearances on Bulgarian television, published three books, and even put myself forward as a candidate in Bulgaria's first presidential elections although some people took me seriously . . . As a result of all these activities, I have now developed an even bigger inferiority complex. Consequently, if you try to look me up – be it in literature or in Bulgaria – I won't be there.' See *My Past, My Future* (1991).

STANISLAV STRATIEV: 'I was born in Sofia in 1941. With a degree in Bulgarian literature from Sofia University, I embarked on a ten-year journalistic career and then for the past twenty years I have been writing plays – mainly comedies and absurdist dramas. I happen to be the resident playwright at the Theatre of Satire, perhaps Bulgaria's most popular theatre. But I also write prose, short stories, novellas and so on. Some of my books have been translated and published in more than twenty languages. Six of my screenplays have been made into feature films. So looking back over my career, I cannot see anything out of the ordinary – just a great man getting on with great things. Nothing special to note really.' His Bulgarian tourist comes from *The Bulgarian Experience* (1991).

ROMANIA

MIRCEA CĂRTĂRESCU, born in 1957, is Romania's leading postmodernist writer. The cornerstone of the 'Eighties Generation', Cărtărescu first became established as a poet, then broke new ground with his breathtaking novel *The Dream* (1989), picturing man's subconscious attempt at reappropriating the planet's natural history, rather than the political history of a country. Cărtărescu has recently emerged as a noteworthy literary critic, and is currently teaching at Bucharest University.

ANA BLANDIANA, born in Timişoara in 1942, has moved through the past decade escorted by a substantial retinue of Ceauşescu's secret police, whom she managed to antagonize with her poetry. Banned from publication for varying lengths of time, Blandiana has remained true to her belief in literature. Her novel, *A Drawerful of Clapping*, could only be published after the demise of the dictator. 'The Open Window' was published early in 1990, in her weekly column for *România Literară*.

GEORGE CUȘNARENCU, born in 1956, is biding his time as a journalist. 'The War' comes from his début collection of short stories *Treaties of Permanent Defence* (1983). Recent publications include: *Tango of Memory* (1988) and *Dodecahedron* (1991). In his late thirties, he still has time on his side, considering that before 1989 he had to keep a low profile.

ȘTEFAN AGOPIAN, born in 1947, is a traveller in time. Had he lived a few centuries ago, he would probably have laid the foundation for science fiction. But as it is, the stories in *The Textbook of Occurrences* (1984), though placed in a safely distant past, are unnervingly contemporary. His works include *Days of Fury*, *Tobit*, *Sarah*, and a collection of short stories, *Notes from Sodom*.

ALBANIA

ISMAIL KADARE, born in 1936 in the southern museum-city of Gjirokastër, he is Albania's foremost poet and novelist. His first major prose work, the novel *The General of the Dead Army* (1963), laid the foundations for his career as a writer of international reputation. Works in English translation include: *Chronicle of Stone* (1987), *Doruntine* (1988), *Broken April* (1990), *The Palace of Dreams* (1993), *Albanian Spring: the Anatomy of Tyranny* (1994), *The Three-Arched Bridge* (1994) and *The Concert* (1994).

MIMOZA AHMETI was born in 1963 in the mountain city of Krujë, north of Tirana. She finished her studies in Tirana in 1986 and has since taught literature. Ahmeti began her literary career with the verse collections *Be Beautiful* (1986), and *Especially Tomorrow* (1989), which proved her to be a virtuoso of poetic technique. Her short stories have evinced a remarkable freshness and individuality. Mimoza Ahmeti is also a painter and graphic artist of note.

TEODOR LAÇO, born in 1936 in the Korçë region of southeastern Albania, first made a reputation for himself as a prose writer in the 1970s. Former head of the Albanian film studios, Laço is the author of nine collections of short stories, and of numerous novels and plays. Together with Ismail

Kadare, Dritëro Agolli, Nasi Lera, Sabri Godo and Dhimitër Xhuvani, Teodor Laço was among the most widely read Albanian prose writers of the 1980s. In recent years, since the fall of the Communist dictatorship, he has been active in politics and is presently leader of the Albanian Social-Democratic Party.

LITHUANIA

JURGA IVANAUSKAITĖ, born in Vilnius in 1961, was the first Lithuanian writer openly to explore taboo subjects in an extremely repressed Soviet-occupied Lithuania. Her characters led bohemian lifestyles, immersing themselves in the 'counterculture' and usually were hippies or punks or members of some other 'unofficial' social group. Her first collection of short stories, *Year of the Lilies of the Valley* (1985), created great controversy. '"Two Stories about Suicides" were the first stories I ever wrote. At the time, social realism, Marxism and Communist doctrine were crammed down our throats. The atmosphere was entirely militaristic. At that time, young people, especially intellectuals, lived fatalistically. The only enlightened person you could hope to meet would most likely be an inmate in an insane asylum; almost all artists passed through that "spiritual school".' Her works include: *The Moon's Children* (1988), *How to Raise Fear* (1989), *The Gardens of Hell* (1992) and *The Witch and the Rain* (1993).

VALDAS PAPIEVIS was born in 1962, in the village of Anyksciai. He studied Lithuanian literature at the University of Vilnius and later returned there to teach. He has also worked in the Lithuanian Ministry of Culture and Education. Presently, he is unemployed. Papievis started writing and publishing short stories when he was a student. He has published a novel, *Autumn in the Countryside* (1989), and a collection of short stories. He was one of the original editors of the formerly underground literary journal *Sietynas*, and is currently a member of the Lithuanian Writers' Union and PEN Club. 'I haven't published anything recently. In general, I think I'm an idealist. I believe in the magic that words can create: dramatic upheavals; but that which is most important occurs first of all in one's soul – quietly and unnoticeably.'

LATVIA

ANDREI LEVKIN, born in 1954, works at the intersections of cultures and conceptual fields. Mathematician turned writer, bilingual in Russian and Latvian, he lives in Riga. He has edited the journal *Rodnik* and worked for television. Two collections of short stories have been published: *Ancient Arithmetic* (1986) and *Quiet Events* (1991). His 'History of Yellow' charts both the history of the Soviet Union and a couple's relationship. In Levkin's fictions geography, history or the sciences are forms of creative imagination.

ANDRA NEIBURGA, born in 1957, worked as an editor for various literary publications and published her first short story in 1986. Pollution pervades Andra Neiburga's 'Mousy Death'. For its heroine/victim in the last days of Soviet Latvia, ecological and political dysfunctions blend: socio-industrial disorder and the emblems of power alike denote infection, the presence of foreign bodies in the environment. With the minimum of means (a mouse in a trap, a trolleybus ride), the author presents another descent into one of our many contemporary infernos.

ESTONIA

VIIVI LUIK was born in 1946 in southern Estonia where she grew up in the countryside. At the age of sixteen, she published her first poems and by the age of twenty was something of a celebrity in the world of Estonian poetry. Her first novel, *The Seventh Springtime of Peace* (1985), became a bestseller in Estonia. It deals with the Stalinist period of the early 1950s seen through the eyes of a girl of six. As Viivi Luik once said in an interview, she and her generation 'loved Stalin'. Children readily believed the ideological folk tales served up to pacify a country with a million inhabitants. Her second novel, *The Beauty of History* (1991), deals, some-what impressionistically, with the relationship of a rather narcissistic young Estonian woman and a Latvian Jewish artist. It is a semi-autobiographical work and has caused much debate in Estonia.

REIN TOOTMAA, born in Torva in 1957, belongs to a generation of younger writers who matured during the Brezhnev era, and thus had no direct experience of Stalinist times. His writing style, while less directly poetic than that of Viivi Luik, reflects European modernism. 'We Gaze Up into the Tops of the Spruce Trees' from his first collection of stories, *Piano*

Playing Holiday (1987), exhibits a laconic romanticism with echoes of the island of Saaremaa where Tootmaa has lived since 1982. His second novel, *There, Beyond the Open Field* (1991), experiments with narrative techniques, introducing satire and ironic humour.

BELARUS

YURII PETKEVICH, born in 1962, grew up in White Russia and graduated in cinematography in Moscow. He now lives in the Minsk region of Belarus. He works in film and art, as well as literature. In the wake of the Great Russian Childhoods bequeathed by Aksakov, Tolstoy (Lev and Aleksei) and Nabokov (and, in cinema, Tarkovsky), *Variations on the Seasons* offers us a hallucinatory and anti-idyllic version of growing up in the provinces of the Soviet Union. The fragment published here forms part of a longer Soviet 'éducation sentimentale'.

UKRAINE

IGOR KLEKH: Propp and Lévi-Strauss are only two of the ingredients in Igor Klekh's three-course critical supper. 'Hog's Fat, Pancake, and the Sausage'. Like lard in the hands of Joseph Beuys, the materials in his essays reveal properties beyond their culinary function. A misunderstanding about bread or brioche was a prelude to the storming of the Bastille; in Poland meat riots brought down a government. Klekh understands that the stomach is the heart of a nation and that folklore of food may provide the best diagnosis of its condition.

RUSSIA

SVETLANA VASILIEVA was born in Moscow and had an extraterritorial childhood in Buenos Aires. Her husband is the writer Evgenii Popov. She has published as a theatre critic, written plays and short stories, and co-edited *Bearing No Ill-Will* (1990), a collection of women's writing. Victor Hugo, fairy tales and the clash of (male) law and (female) desire frame 'The Time of Peonies: A Novel'.

ZUFAR GAREEV has worked for the newspaper *Komsomolskaya Pravda* and as a janitor. As a Bashkir, he is able to look down, from a high vantage point, on Russian society and on Moscow where he now lives with his family like the dispassionate bird that flaps across 'Stereoscopic Slavs'. Here, aeons and galaxies interfere in everyday reality; in the nightmarish dimensions of infinite time and space his characters battle with the laws of physics, as well as with each other. Like Chagall's version of Vitebsk, Gareev's Moscow lies in the eye of a cyclone.

VIKTOR LAPITSKII, born in 1951, is a mathematician and a translator from French (he has translated Artaud, Barthes, Derrida, Lacan and Blanchot). His work has appeared mainly in samizdat journals such as *Chasy*. 'Ants' was published in *Mitin Zhurnal*. Etymology couples with entomology: 'Ants' might have emerged from the French verb *fourmiller* (from *fourmi*, ant) – to swarm, teem. In this story the image engenders metaphysical speculation, a gnostic cosmogony – and memories of the worker ants that burrowed in the foundations of Soviet ideology.

OLGA NOVIKOVA, born in 1950, has worked for the eminent publishing house Khudozhestvennaya literatura and as a critic. She is the author of *V. Kaverin* and *The Woman's Novel* and places herself in the tradition of such European women's writing as Jane Austen and the Brontë sisters. Her 'Philemon and Baucis' refracts the life of the Moscow intelligentsia through convoluted syntax riddled with doubts and hesitations, and through the Greek myth of the title. But in Novikova's 'Philemon and Baucis', Zeus is displaced by his consort, Hera, goddess of marriage.

Acknowledgements

SERBIA, CROATIA, SLOVENIA

'Russians By Trade' by Bora Ćosić translated by Ann Bigelow. First published in *Price O Zanatima*, Belgrade, 1980. Reprinted with the permission of the author and translator.

'Repetition' by Drago Jančar translated by Lili Potpara. First published in *Contemporary Slovene Short Stories*, Ljubljana, 1991. Reprinted with the permission of the author and translator.

'The Balkan Express' by Slavenka Drakulić translated by Maja Šoljan. Reprinted from *The Balkan Express: Fragments from the Other Side of War* by Slavenka Drakulić, with the permission of W. W. Norton & Company, Inc. and Hutchinson, a division of Random Century Group. Copyright © 1993 by Slavenka Drakulić. Copyright for this translation © 1993 by Maja Soljan.

'The Pope' by David Albahari translated by Ellen Elias-Bursać. First published in *Jednostavnost*, Belgrade, 1989. Reprinted with the permission of the author and translator.

POLAND

An extract from *Annihilation* by Piotr Szewc translated by Jarosław Anders (first published in Poland in 1987). Reprinted by permission of Jarosław Anders. The complete novel is available in a different translation by Ewa Hryniewicz-Yarbrough, published by Dalkey Archives.

'Retina' by Hanna Krall translated by Jarosław Anders. First published in *Gazeta Wyborcza*, April 1990. Reprinted with the permission of the author and translator.

'The Register of Adulteresses' by Jerzy Pilch translated by Jarosław Anders. First published by Puls Publications Ltd, 1993 © Jerzy Pilch 1993. Reprinted with permission.

'Mina' by Paweł Huelle from *Moving House and Other Stories* translated by Antonia Lloyd-Jones. First published by Bloomsbury Publishers Ltd, 1994. Translation copyright © Antonia Lloyd-Jones 1994. Reprinted with permission.

HUNGARY

'Vivisection' by Péter Nádas translated by Judith Barnes Kerrigan. First published in the collection *Leiras* by Szepirodalmi Konyvkiado, Budapest, 1979. Reprinted with the permission of the author and translator.

'The Sunken Apple Tree' by László Márton translated by Barbara Egerváry. First published in Hungary, 1990. Reprinted with the permission of the author and translator.

An extract from *The Glance of Countess Hahn-Hahn* by Péter Esterházy translated by Richard Aczel. Reprinted by permission of Weidenfeld Publishers.

'The Contents of Suitcases' by Lajos Grendel translated by Richard Aczel. From the collection *The Contents of Suitcases*, published by Madách, 1987. Reprinted with the permission of the author and translator.

CZECH REPUBLIC

'The Pink Scarf' by Bohumil Hrabal translated by James Naughton. First published in Bohumil Hrabal's *Růžový kavalír* by Pražská imaginace, 1991. Copyright © Bohumil Hrabal 1991. Reprinted with the permission of the author and translator.

'The Unborn' by Eda Kriseová translated by James Naughton. First published in Eda Kriseová's *Arboretum* by Index Publishers, Cologne, 1987. Copyright © Eda Kriseová 1987. Reprinted with the permission of the author and translator.

'He Wakes Up' by Alexandra Berková translated by James Naughton. First published in Alexandra Berková's *Knížka s červeným obalem* by Práce, Prague,

1986. Copyright © Alexandra Berková 1986. Reprinted with the permission of the author and translator.

'Brownian Motion' by Ondřej Neff translated by James Naughton. First published in Ondřej Neff's *Ctvrty den az na veky* by Ceskoslovensky spisovatel, Prague, 1987. Copyright © Ondřej Neff 1987. Reprinted with the permission of the author and translator.

SLOVAKIA

'Escalation of Feeling' by Pavel Vilikovský translated by James Naughton. First published in Pavel Vilikovský's *Eskalácia citu*, by Tatran, Bratislava, 1989. Copyright © Pavel Vilikovský 1989. Reprinted with the permission of the author and translator.

'Memorial to Don Giovanni' by Ján Johanides translated by James Naughton. First published in Ján Johanides's *Krik drozdov pred spanim*, Hevi, Bratislava, 1992. Copyright © Ján Johanides 1992. Reprinted with the permission of the author and translator.

'On the Threshold' by Dušan Mitana translated by James Naughton. First published in the volume of the same title by Tatran, Bratislava, 1987. Copyright © Dušan Mitana 1987. Reprinted with the permission of the author and the translator.

'The White Dog' by Rudolf Sloboda translated by James Naughton. First published in Rudolf Sloboda's *Pánsky Flám*, Slovenský spisovatel Bratislava, 1986. Copyright © Rudolf Sloboda 1986. Reprinted with the permission of the author and translator.

BULGARIA

'Desires: The Erotica of Communism' by Ivailo Dichev translated by Robert Sturm. First published in Sofia, in 1991. Reprinted with the permission of the author and translator.

'Big Business' by Victor Paskov translated by Lyubomir Nikolov and Roland Flint. First published in Sofia, in 1992. Reprinted with the permission of the author and translators.

An extract from *My Past, My Future* by Ivan Kulekov translated by Robert

Sturm. First published in Sofia, in 1991. Reprinted with the permission of the author and translator.

'A Bulgarian Tourist Chats to an English Pigeon in Trafalgar Square' by Stanislav Stratiev translated by Galina Holman. First published in Sofia 1992. Reprinted with the permission of the author and translator.

ROMANIA

An extract from *The Dream* by Mircea Cărtărescu translated by Florin Bican. First published in *Editura Cartea Românească*, Bucharest, 1989. Reprinted with the permission of the author and translator.

'The Open Window' by Ana Blandiana translated by Florin Bican. First published in *România Literară*, Bucharest, 1990. Reprinted with the permission of the author and translator.

'The War' by George Cuşnarencu translated by Florin Bican. First published by *Editura Cartea Românească*, Bucharest, 1983. Reprinted with the permission of the author and translator.

'The Art of War' by Ştefan Agopian translated by Florin Bican. First published in *Editura Cartea Românească*, Bucharest, 1984. Reprinted with the permission of the author and translator.

ALBANIA

An extract from *The Concert* by Ismail Kadare, a novel written in Albanian and translated into English from the French of Jusuf Vrioni by Barbara Bray. First published by Harvill, 1994. Reprinted with the permission of William Morrow.

'The Secret of my Youth' by Mimoza Ahmeti translated by Robert Elsie. First published in the periodical *Nentori*, Tirana, 1990. Reprinted with the permission of the author and translator.

'The Pain of a Distant Winter' by Teodor Laço translated by Robert Elsie. First published by Naim Frasheri Publishers, Tirana. Reprinted with the permission of the author and translator.

LITHUANIA

'Two Stories about Suicides' by Jurga Ivanauskaitê translated by Laima Sruoginis. First published in a collection of stories entitled *Pakalnuciu Metai* by VAGA Publishers, Vilnius, 1985. Reprinted with the permission of the author and translator.

'I'm Going Out, to Buy a Lightbulb' by Valdas Papievis translated by Laima Sruoginis. First published in *Literatura ir Menas* in 1986. Reprinted with the permission of the author and translator.

LATVIA

'The History of Yellow' by Andrei Levkin translated by Michael Molnar. First published in *Index on Censorship* vol. 21 no. 10, November 1992. Reprinted with the permission of the author and translator.

'Mousy Death' by Andra Neiburga translated by Michael Molnar. First published in *Rodnik*, Riga, December 1988. Reprinted with the permission of the author and translator.

ESTONIA

An extract from *The Beauty of History* by Viivi Luik translated by Eric Dickens. First published by Eesti Raamat, Tallinn, 1991. Reprinted with the permission of the author and translator.

'We Gaze Up Into the Tops of the Spruce Trees' by Rein Tootmaa translated by Eric Dickens. First published by Eesti Raamat, Tallinn, 1987. Reprinted with the permission of the author and translator.

BELARUS

An extract from *Variations on the Seasons* by Yurii Petkevich translated by Michael Molnar. Reprinted with the permission of the author and translator.

UKRAINE

'Hog's Fat, Pancake, and the Sausage' by Igor Klekh translated by Michael Molnar. First published by *Rodnik*, Riga, October 1990. Reprinted with the permission of the author and translator.

RUSSIA

'The Time of Peonies: A Novel' by Svetlana Vasilieva translated by Michael Molnar. Reprinted with the permission of the author and translator.

'Stereoscopic Slavs' by Zufar Gareev translated by Michael Molnar. First published in *Solo 4*, Moscow, 1991. Reprinted with the permission of the author and translator.

'Ants' by Viktor Lapitskii translated by Michael Molnar. First published in *Mitin Zhurnal* 47–48, St Petersburg, September/December 1992. Reprinted with the permission of the author and translator.

'Philemon and Baucis' by Olga Novikova translated by Michael Molnar. Reprinted with the permission of the author and translator.

MICHAEL MARCH was born in 1946 in New York. After graduating in history from Columbia College, he left for Europe. He is the author of *Goya* and *Disappearance*, the co-translator of Zbigniew Herbert's *Barbarian in the Garden* and Gojko Djogo's *Ovid in Tomis*, for which he received a Translators Fellowship from the National Endowment for the Arts. He is the creator of the East European Forum, opened by President Václav Havel, in London. He is now director of the Prague International Book Fair & Writers' Festival.

IVAN KLÍMA was born in 1931 in Prague, where he lives today. He was the editor of the journal of the Czech Writers' Union during the Prague Spring. He is the author of plays, stories, and novels, all of which were first published outside his own country, where his work was banned until a few years ago. In America, his most recent novel is *Judge on Trial*.

BALKAN GHOSTS
A Journey Through History
by Robert D. Kaplan

"Combines up-to-the-minute political reporting and literary travel writing." —*The New Yorker*

As Kaplan travels through the breakaway states of Yugoslavia to Romania, Bulgaria, and Greece, he reconstructs the Balkans' history as a time warp in which ancient passions and hatreds are continually resurrected.

History/Travel/0-679-74981-0

THE CAPTIVE MIND
by Czeslaw Milosz

"A faultlessly perceptive analysis of the moral and historical dilemma we all face." —Jerzy Kosinski

This classic work by Nobel Prize winning–novelist Czeslaw Milosz reveals in fascinating detail the often beguiling allure of totalitarian rule to people of all political beliefs and its frightening effects on the minds of those who embrace it.

Fiction/Literature/0-679-72856-2

DICTIONARY OF THE KHAZARS
A Lexicon Novel
by Milorad Pavić

"An ebullient and generous celebration of the reading experience." —*The New York Times Book Review*

Dictionary of the Khazars, written in two versions, male and female, which are identical save for one crucial variation, is the imaginary book of the Khazars, a people who flourished somewhere beyond Transylvania between the seventh and ninth centuries.

Fiction/Literature/0-679-72461-3 (Male)
0-679-72754-X (Female)

DISTURBING THE PEACE
by Václav Havel

"A textbook for defiance."   —*Chicago Tribune*

This collection of interviews with Václav Havel is at once political autobiography, a history of Czechoslovakia under communism, a meditation on the social and political role of art, and a guide for all people of conscience facing conscienceless regimes.

Autobiography/Current Affairs/0-679-73402-3

A HISTORY OF RUSSIAN LITERATURE
From Its Beginnings to 1900
by D. S. Mirsky

With a keen and penetrating sense of values, fortified by a style sharp enough to carry every nuance of his meaning, D. S. Mirsky explores one of the most complex and fascinating literatures of the world.

Literature/History/Criticism/0-394-70720-6

JUDGE ON TRIAL
by Ivan Klíma

"Impassioned and wrenching."   —*Washington Post Book World*

Ivan Klíma's epically scaled novel is an inquest into the enduring mystery of the totalitarian era in Eastern Europe. Part thriller, part domestic tragedy, *Judge on Trial* is a novel in the grand traditions of Kafka and Dostoevsky.

Fiction/Literature/0-679-73756-1

LENIN'S TOMB
The Last Days of the Soviet Empire
by David Remnick

"Totally remarkable."   —*Washington Post Book World*

Winner of the Pulitzer Prize, this monumental account of the collapse of the Soviet Union combines the vision of the best historical scholarship with the immediacy of eyewitness journalism.

History/Current Affairs/0-679-75125-4

LOVE AND GARBAGE
by Ivan Klíma

"[Ivan Klíma] demonstrates why he must be regarded as Czechoslovakia's greatest living writer of fiction."
—*Philadelphia Inquirer*

Set in Prague in the years before the Velvet Revolution, *Love and Garbage* explores themes of conscience and betrayal within a world in which everything may be reduced to garbage and only love has the power to grant permanence.

Fiction/Literature/0-679-73755-3

THE MAGIC LANTERN
The Revolution of '89 Witnessed in Warsaw,
Budapest, Berlin and Prague
by Timothy Garton Ash

"A wonderful combination of first-class reporting, brilliant political analysis and reflection." —*The New York Times Book Review*

Garton Ash creates a stunningly evocative portrait of the revolutions that swept Communism from Eastern Europe in 1989 and whose after-effects will continue to shape events for years to come.

Current Affairs/History/0-679-74048-1

MEMOIRS
by Andrei Sakharov

"Destined to take its place as one of the great testaments to human freedom in this or any age." —*San Francisco Chronicle*

Memoirs, written over twelve years and completed in spite of repeated confiscations by the KGB, provides a deeply personal portrait of Sakharov—Nobel Peace Prize winner, father of the Soviet atomic bomb, and champion of human rights.

Autobiography/0-679-73595-X

Available at your local bookstore, or call toll-free to order:
1-800-793-2665 (credit cards only).